THE
RUNAWAY
TRAIN

HENRY H. KURTZ

To Judy; Thank you for YOUR
INTEREST in history.

Henry H. Kurtz

JANUARY 6, 2020

Outskirts Press, Inc.
Denver, Colorado

Outskirts Press
http://www.outskirtspress.com

ISBN-13: 978-1-4327-0845-0

ACKNOWLEDGEMENTS

I am especially indebted to William Pittenger's authored book, "In Pursuit of the General", that fueled the inspiration and the creation of crafted scenes, original dialogue, physical and psychological character descriptions, and analytical narrative to produce this historical fiction novel.

I have also heavily drawn upon the Wilbur G. Kurtz papers based upon my grandfather's carefully conducted rese⸺⸺ interviews of surviving pursuers an⸺ ⸺s. Additional research reference⸺ ⸺e bibliography of "Hijac⸺ ⸺ Andrews Raid Re⸺ ⸺ber, 1990, the

⸺formation
Public
⸺ the
⸺d

enthusiastic. My heartfelt thanks to her. I would also like to thank Mrs. Percella House for her production of the first draft, thus shortening the time to complete the manuscript.

The Fleming County, Flemingsburg, Kentucky Public Library provided gracious assistance in answering several questions about key Flemingsburg citizens. I am especially grateful to Atlanta Railroad Historian, Colonel James G. Bogle, U.S. Army Retired, for his invaluable guidance, while writing a college research paper about the Andrews Raid, entitled "An Attempt to Capture a Locomotive". Records Custodian, J. Harmon Smith, of the Georgia Department of Archives, discovered a Civil War letter written by John Sharpe Rowland to Georgia Governor Joseph E. Brown about the hijack of the "General". I cannot thank him enough for this nugget of serendipity.

Moreover, the late Franklin Miller Garrett's 1955 anecdotal three-volume work, <u>Atlanta and Environs</u>, provided useful information regarding the military situation in early 1862 as well as pertinent, interesting data about the early 1900's in Atlanta, when Wilbur G. Kurtz, Sr. arrived to interview Captain William A. Fuller in search of accura complete details of the Andrews Raid.

Joy Branum provided a copy Jr.'s letter to his father abou circumstances, and I Collins, R.N., courtroom mill collective contributions that shaped this finished literary product.

Last but not least, I owe my wife, Nancy, and son, Jared, for their prayers, patience, and understanding during the countless weeks of writing and researching, which took away much family time.

TABLE OF CONTENTS

CHAPTER 1
ANDREW'S BACKGROUND

The Andrews family had endured a very hard year in 1859, in that the constant planting of the same crops led to the depletion of the soil, and consequently, much discouragement pervaded the Andrews family household. Three family members were conversing at the kitchen table in their rural home, in or near, what is today known as Weirton, West Virginia, in Hancock County.

"James, there's no longer any money in farming. You see how the late freeze killed all our vegetables, and the corn isn't worth a plug nickel. Your mother and I are thinking very seriously about moving to Southwestern Missouri next year. You don't have to go with us. You've got your own life to live," said John Andrews, a six-foot, bearded man.

"That sounds like a good idea. The bank could foreclose on our farm. We can't go on like this," said James J. Andrews.

"I'm glad you see reason, James," said his

mother, Glory Bea. "You've got a whole life ahead of you. Paw and I are willing to start over at his brother's farm in Missouri."

Taking a spoonful of deer meat stew, John said, "The newspaper says there's a flour mill for sale – only five thousand dollars. We could make a lot of money."

"Where is it?" asked James.

"Maysville, Kentucky. Let's you and me go take a look at it. I'll get the horse and wagon ready," said John.

"Good idea," said James, whose face transformed into a broad smile.

The father and the son parked and left their horse-drawn carriage near the dock, and down the Ohio River the speculative pair traveled until they reached Maysville, Kentucky.

"Maysville! Stand by for docking," shouted the short, flamboyant steamboat's captain. The shore looked bigger and bigger until the river vessel slightly bumped the dock.

As the men were walking off the steamboat, the townspeople eyed them with suspicion. A young man whittling a piece of wood to make a whistle, looked up momentarily at the two strangers in town.

"Gentlemen, can I help you?" asked the young, long-haired, blue-overalled, slightly-tanned man.

"We're looking for a flour mill for sale. Do you know where we can locate the owner?" asked John.

"Yes suh, I believe I can help you. The flour

mill owner lives in that white house, the only one with a picket fence – down at the end of First Street. Watch out for his mean dog."

As expected, a mean, ornery, mangy dog alerted the entire neighborhood of the coming of the duo. The dog owner cracked his front door to see what the barking was all about.

"Good afternoon, gentlemen. You don't look like you're from around here. Is there something I can do for you?" asked the tall, slender, knock-kneed man with blue eyes and a crew cut.

"We saw an ad in the Hancock County Journal about a flour mill for sale. Some young man said you are the owner," said John.

"That's right," said the flour mill owner.

"And you want five thousand," said John.

"Five thousand is my price," replied the mill owner, Robert Lilly White.

John asked, "Would you show it to us?"

"Come with me. It's downstream about a mile. I'll drive you over there," said Robert Lilly White, obviously anxious to close the sale.

As the men pulled up in front of the flour mill, they were immediately impressed with the freshly painted wood.

The owner said, "I kept this mill up for twenty years. I'm selling 'cause I ain't been feeling good this year."

"How much were you making?" asked John.

"Very good. We couldn't produce enough flour to meet the demand. The Union Army has been

3

buying up eighty percent of our flour. If you buy this mill, I will help you get started on the next U.S. Government contract that begins in two weeks. I hear tell the slavery issue is upsetting a lot of people, and one of the Union officers said he wouldn't be surprised if the North has to fight the South," said the owner.

"That could mean a lot of business," said John Andrews.

"Well, what do you say, Mister?" asked the owner.

"We'll buy it," said John, as he removed a wad of currency from his pocket.

"Let's ride back to the house, and I'll write you up a Bill of Sale. The terms are 'as is.' The present flour mill owner dipped a sharp quill into a small inkwell, quickly drawing up a neat, legible legal document.

"My son, James, will be the new owner. This is my gift to him. James will assume all responsibility for the upkeep and running of the mill," said John.

"Thanks, Father, I'll do you proud."

"James, you are now the new proud owner of the Maysville Flour Mill, and the back door is right by the river. All you do is load the ships as they come in to buy the flour."

"I'm excited already," said James.

"Good luck. The next boat will leave out of here in the morning at 6 o'clock. Where is your home?" asked White.

"We're living in Hancock County, Virginia," said James.

"Oh, yes, beautiful country. I suppose you'll be moving here," said White.

"Yes, I'll be back in five days to get started", said James.

"Good. That'll give us enough time to meet the first Government order," said Robert Lilly White, the flour mill seller.

Bidding farewell, the Virginia men walked toward the Maysville Hotel, to spend the night before returning by steamboat to Hancock County, later becoming a part of West Virginia, on Sunday, June 20, 1863.

After returning home, James J. Andrews built a raft to guide the makeshift watercraft down the Ohio River. Fortunately, his father had given him one hundred dollars to survive all living expenses during the first year of the business. Starved, he arrived at the boat dock where he abandoned the raft. He would not ever see his parents again, as they will have relocated to Missouri the following year.

James went to the previous owner's house and knocked on his door at 11:30 a.m., only three days away from home. "Hello, Mr. Andrews. Are you ready to go to work?" asked the former mill owner.

"Yes, I am. Please show me the ropes," said Andrews.

"With pleasure. Let's have some lunch first. I've already arranged to put you up in the Maysville Hotel for five dollars per month," said White.

"That will be satisfactory," said Andrews.

The men talked business over lunch, outlining their hiring needs, business expenses, and accounting procedures. Having thoroughly interviewed Andrews, Robert Lilly White mentioned he would have to conduct a week of on-the-job training in all phases of managing a business, since Andrews had no previous business experience.

Two years later, James J. Andrews was still running a flourishing flour mill business, and to top it all off, he was dating Dixie Goldbricker, a sister of one of his mill workers.

Everything seemed to be going well for the new mill owner, until a fly appeared in the ointment – a tall, sinister figure smashed a front window of the flour mill with a kerosene-soaked torch, and set fire to the wool-carded wooden structure. Unknown to Andrews, the perpetrator was a young Southern sympathizer who had opposed the sale of flour to the U. S. Army. He had previously worked for Andrews as a loader in the flour mill.

The woolen insulation rapidly ignited, causing flames to shoot up over the flour mill as panic-stricken citizens screamed for help.

"Fire! Fire! Get Help!" shouted a bearded, black-haired, blue-eyed, 25-year-old pudgy man. Citizens rushed out in their pajamas to the street, bewildered by the unexpected fire.

"Fill the buckets! Form a human chain," said the young man. "Start digging a firebreak around the mill."

Despite the speedy response, all of the water

buckets and all of the energetic mass human effort could not put out the blaze accelerated by a flammable insulation material, wool carding. Within a half-hour, the old flour mill had burned to the ground. Unfortunately, Andrews had failed to purchase fire insurance.

This former flour mill owner and operator had been courting pretty little Miss Dixie Goldbricker of Hancock County, West Virginia for the last two years. Although harmony characterized their relationship, the courtship also went up in smoke, upon the receipt of a "Dear John" letter from Dixie Goldbricker. Sitting on his bed in the Maysville Hotel, Andrews felt as though a ton of bricks had fallen upon his head. The unfairness of life had dealt a severe blow to his self esteem.

Suddenly, he heard a knock at his room door. Removing his head from his hands, he asked, "Who is it?"

"Mr. Andrews, we've taken up a collection on your behalf – seeing as how you've lost the mill and all..." said Archie B. Smith, the hotel proprietor.

The bewildered ex-business owner ran his fingers across his neatly, well-trimmed black beard. "This is incredible – so-o-o unexpected," said Andrews in his high, melodious voice.

"I have more good news for you: before, during, and after the mill caught fire, a Union scout mounted on horseback, had been observing a young man with a torch, running very quickly toward the mill. Even though it was too late to prevent the burning, the scout hid behind a dense thicket and lassoed the man. The Military have the man in custody," said Archie.

"Are they going to bring him to trial?" asked James.

Archie replied, "The soldiers will escort him in chains, in a horse-driven carriage this afternoon. We're planning to throw a party to celebrate."

"Well, I didn't think anyone would have set the fire on purpose. My sister got wind of the bad news and blamed me for the fire, and my fiancée dropped me like a hot potato."

"Mr. Andrews, things will get better. Nothing ever stays the same – just a run of bad luck – that's all."

"Yes, I know, Archie, but my future is very cloudy right now. That fire destroyed my livelihood. I'll never be able to recover the financial loss," said Andrews.

"Something else will come along. Just you wait and see, Mr. Andrews. Don't sit around, mope, and wallow in the blues. Come downstairs. Dinner is on the house. We've got piano music, dancing girls – and oh – I want to introduce you to a really nice gal. Time's a wasting," said Archie, winking his left eye.

"Let me get cleaned up first," said Andrews.

"We haven't got all day, now," said Archie.

"I'll be down directly. Save a place at the table for me, Archie," said Andrews.

"Yes sir," Archie said, while descending the

wooden hotel stairs.

The Maysville Hotel had a large dining room, which had been wallpapered ten years ago. A repetitive pattern of steamships docking at a small town was plainly visible on an oakwood wall extending twelve feet from the ceiling.

Each hickory table had dimensions of five feet by three feet, and four hickory chairs were placed at each table. Glass salt and pepper shakers and a glass-lid-covered sugar dish graced each table. A sprinkling of white rice grains served to retain the freshness of the sugar and salt containers. A large silver cuspidor stood to the left of the front entrance of the dining room of the hotel, which heavily relied upon tourism as the backbone of its economy, since steamboats often docked at Maysville, a transfer point to other Ohio Valley destinations. The Maysville Stagelines Company provided the ground transportation.

In the dining room near the pianist, who was happily tickling the ivories, were six young, energetic, ravishing women cloggers bearing bright smiles. A standing-room–only crowd was clapping their hands to the inspirational beat of "Yankee Doodle". A large United States Flag draped the top of the piano. Townspeople had brought in covered-dish dinners, unquestionably welcomed amenities to the 5 p.m. music-and-dance attraction, that an itinerant entertainment company, Dancealot Enterprises, was providing to the people of Maysville. The entertainers had performed the previous night at a Union Army campfire, tucked away in the woods five miles from town.

Dancer Maggie Swiftsure riveted her dancing brown eyes on James J. Andrews, dressed in a white shirt with round gold cufflinks, a solid blue tie, and a large pair of boots and black socks. She sensed the commanding confidence and suave demeanor about this man. She was twenty-six years old, single, available, and always in search of a candidate for a husband. She was an eye-popping brunette with a nice, well-proportioned broad face with tastefully applied lipstick and rouge. Her hands were small and dainty, and her skirt was two inches below the knees – just enough to keep all the men guessing. This delightful, pleasant woman wore a corset and a bra; she was not the type of woman who threw herself at men. Prudence was central to her daily conduct in all matters.

The music stopped and Archie Smith directed everyone to be seated. As Andrews took his seat at one of the hickory tables, Archie escorted a young woman to the table and said, "Mr. Andrews, I would like to introduce you to Maggie Swiftsure from Flemingsburg, Kentucky. She's a traveling dancer and I told her about the mill fire."

"I'm James Andrews. How do you do?"

"Fine, thank you. I'm Maggie Swiftsure."

"It's a pleasure to make your acquaintance, Miss Swiftsure."

"Enjoy yourselves and the fine food. If you'll excuse me, folks, I have to attend to some guest registrations," said Archie Smith.

"James, please call me Maggie. I'm sorry to hear about the flour mill fire."

"Yes, my five-thousand-dollar investment went up in flames."

"Oh, but don't let that kind of thing ruin your life. No problem is too big for God to solve," she said.

"Hmm, that's true. My sister blamed me for the fire and let her emotions get the better of herself."

"You and I know what really happened. It was arson," she said.

"Maybe so," said Andrews.

"James, are you free tomorrow?" she asked.

"I suppose so," Andrews replied.

"I hear tell you have a very nice singing voice," said Maggie.

"How did you know?" asked Andrews.

"Archie said he heard you singing yourself to sleep one night last week. James, please sing with us tomorrow night in Flemingsburg," said Maggie.

"Yes, if your boss approves," said Andrews.

"It's all right. You can ride with us on the stage at 7 a.m.," said Maggie.

"I accept your boss's offer," said James.

"Then it's settled. We'll ride with the other members on the stage coach to Flemingsburg," she said.

"Sounds great," said Andrews.

The two-hour ride to Flemingsburg was a hard seventeen-mile trek, during which the stage driver kept a shotgun near his feet, though the stage was not carrying any valuables. The passengers were seated so close to one another that there was a lack of elbow room.

Andrews was happy to earn some extra money as a singer working in Flemingsburg. The land trip was uneventful while traveling over rickety, bumpy dirt roads, bereft of the modern conveniences of available public restroom facilities and indoor plumbing. However, it soon became apparent to all the other employees that he and Maggie were getting sweet on each other. Jilted by his former fiancée, Andrews readily basked in the newly found female acquaintance, who served as a healing balm, his own way of handling rejection from his sister and Dixie Goldbricker.

"James, when we get to Flemingsburg, you'll see a much different world and perhaps more job opportunities. Believe me, there's a lot happening there, and I heard the Union Army plans to change Kentucky from a border state to a free state. That means we'll be a Northern State and all the slaves in Kentucky will become free!" declared Maggie.

"I never believed in slavery. It's cruel, inhumane, and splits up black families. Right now they can't vote, and nobody will allow them to get a formal education," said James.

"This is America. Everyone should have the right to better himself in the Land of the Free. Even the Irish in New York experienced job discrimination. I heard people telling me about signs that read, "Irish need not apply," said Maggie, gradually falling asleep in her seat.

The stagecoach driver reined in the tired horses upon arrival at a livery stable, for the exchange of horses in a small town located halfway to the intended destination. Dancealot Enterprises paid for all travel expenses including food and lodging, to the delight of Andrews.

On the following day, the entertainment company rendered three scheduled musical performances at 10 a.m., 2 p.m., and 4 p.m. Tickets sold for one dollar apiece. Andrews sang the first line of a song: "Peas, peas, peas, peas, eating goober peas. Goodness how delicious, eating goober peas..." His next song included the following words: "Tenting tonight, tenting tonight, tenting on the old camp ground. Many of our hearts are weary tonight, waiting for the war to cease." Andrews sang a third song entitled "The Battle Hymn of the Republic," which especially drew a sustained applause.

One high school principal in the audience was impressed with Andrews's clear-dictioned, melodious, well-controlled voice. The principal's wife was especially moved by the eloquent rendition of the third song. At the close of the evening performance, the principal, Bobby Seekemout, the self-appointed talent scout, saw some potential in 32-year-old James J. Andrews.

"Young man, come here. I want to talk to you," said the smiling high school principal. "My name is

Bobby Seekemout, principal of Flemingsburg High School. You have an excellent singing voice."

"Thank you, sir," said Andrews.

"Are you from around here?" asked the principal.

"No sir, I hail from (West) Virginia," said Andrews.

"What is your name?" asked Seekemout.

"James Andrews, sir."

"I can use you as a music teacher at Flemingsburg High School. Would you be interested?" asked Seekemout.

"Yes sir, I would be glad to talk to you about it," said Andrews.

"Very well, Mr. Andrews. See me Monday morning in my office," said the principal.

"When should I arrive?" asked Andrews.

"Anytime during the morning is fine," said Bobby Seekemout.

"I will see you then," said James.

Maggie was ten feet away, easily overhearing the conversation. "James, did I hear what I think I heard?"

"Maggie, he offered me a music teacher position at the local high school. He wants to discuss it with me on Monday," said Andrews.

"Well, I can't blame you for choosing steady employment. By the way, in case you didn't know it, I'm the one who hired you. Dancealot Enterprises is actually my own business," said Maggie.

"So, you hired me," said Andrews.

"Yes," she said.

"Well, I'll be darned," said Andrews.

"It'll be a month before I'm back in Flemingsburg. It is very likely you will get this job, and I will not stand in the way of anyone who wishes to better himself."

"You're a doll, Maggie. Let's keep in touch. I always enjoy being with and talking to you," said Andrews.

"I feel the same way," she said, as they embraced lightly upon going their separate ways. Love was definitely in bloom on the dance floor of the Maysville Hotel, at the end of the entertainment show.

The next month slipped away, and a familiar person was observing a music class under professional instruction, before quietly stepping forward to speak to James Andrews.

"James, how is the job working out?"

"Maggie, long time no see. I'm enjoying the job, but I need to supplement my income. The war has driven up the prices of everything so much. If you know of anyone who wants his house painted, please let me know."

"Sure, James. I'll help you any way I can," she said.

"Are you still working on the road?" asked Andrews.

"No, it was too much for me," she replied. "I'm looking for a job near my home," said Maggie.

"I tell you what. The principal, Bobby Seekemout, is looking for a teacher's aide in my class. If you're interested, see the principal."

"Oh James, I can do that job."

"Sure you can. I have thirty students. Lord knows I can use some good help," said Andrews.

"I'll let you know how the interview turns out," she said.

"See you later Maggie,"

Walking back to his hotel room, Andrews noticed the letter carrier departing on horseback.

Andrews smiled and waved at the tall, bespectacled letter carrier dressed in a light-blue shirt, dark-blue trousers and high leather boots. Joel "Stringbean" Mullinax stood at six-feet-two-inches, weighed 175 pounds, and had long sideburns on a long, thin face that had broad ears from which three-inch long hairs protruded. He was a 55-year-old Mexican War veteran walking with a limp, as a result of an ankle bullet wound.

"Mr. Andrews, come sign for an official business letter," said the postal carrier.

Feeling a lump in his throat, the former mill owner and operator had an inkling of the contents of the letter.

"Thank you," said Andrews, upon receipt of the letter.

Andrews walked away, tucked the letter in his pocket, entered the hotel, and glided past the clerk's desk. Slowly he climbed the stairway so as not to attract any attention. Slitting the envelope with a metal letter opener, his pupils widened at the print. It was a summons to testify at the trial of the young flour mill burner. The Union Army would be trying him in a military court on Monday, June 17, 1861, in Flemingsburg, Kentucky, the county seat of Fleming County.

Maggie's interview with the principal was in progress, while Andrews was perusing the written summons.

The principal cleared his throat and addressed Maggie, seated, dressed in a cute homespun yellow dress.

"Maggie, I'm impressed with your singing background. How long were you traveling?"

"Five years, sir."

"From what high school were you graduated?" asked the principal.

"Maysville High School," said Maggie.

"Mr. Andrews has vouched for your integrity. I'm hiring you to be a teacher's aide for him, and whenever he's absent, you will substitute for him. Can you start work on Monday?"

"Yes sir."

Warmly shaking Maggie's hand, the principal said, "Welcome aboard, Maggie."

"Thank you, sir," she said.

Only a short block away, wheels were turning in Andrews's mind: he would have to arrange for a substitute during his time in the courtroom. Fortunately, the Maysville Judge had granted a change of venue due to the strong pro-Union sentiment and mass hostility against the flour mill burner.

Meanwhile, in Maysville, some townspeople were restive. The burning of the flour mill had produced a devastating multiplier effect on the town's economy. People in flour-industry related employment were having to leave Maysville to look for other work.

Presently, Union officers were preparing to transfer the prisoner to a neutral town, Flemingsburg. Surrounding the prisoner, whom they had chained, the officers escorted the suspect to a horse-drawn wagon, and then mounted their horses for the seventeen-mile ride to Flemingsburg. A moderate cloud of dust resulted from the noisy hoofbeats of the six military horses; three of them were traveling on each side of the wagon. Curious onlookers stared as the entourage faded into the horizon.

Back in Flemingsburg, Andrews informed the principal about the written court order to appear at the trial, which had to be moved away from Maysville to Flemingsburg.

"Mr. Seekemout, here is a subpoena directing me to be in court on the fifteenth," said James.

"I'll have Maggie sub for you. Let me know if you have to go to court more than one day," said Seekemout.

"I will, sir," said Andrews.

"By the way, Mr. Andrews, I hope you're not in any trouble," said Seekemout.

"On the contrary. A Union scout caught a young scoundrel torching my flour mill in Maysville. I lost five thousand dollars – money that my father had given me. My sister refuses to speak to me because of it – and to make matters worse, my girl broke up with me," said Andrews.

"It seems she showed her true colors," said Seekemout.

"What you mean is that she would have married me for my money and not for love."

"Precisely, Mr. Andrews."

"Perhaps God was protecting me from a nasty divorce settlement," said Andrews.

"Only you and God can answer that question."

"I value your wisdom, Mr. Seekemout," said Andrews.

"'Tis nothing," said the principal.

The school bell rang and classes convened at 8:30 a.m. Andrews stepped into his classroom in the small school house that held 200 school children and six teachers.

"We're going to spend a few minutes on a voice lesson. Do, Re, Mi, Fa, Sol, La, Ti, Do! Children, repeat after me...."

"After school, at 4:30 p.m., a horse-drawn vehicle carrying a handcuffed prisoner chained around the legs and the undercarriage of the wagon, was quite a spectacle to behold in a small town, where a humdrum, day-to-day, routine existence was the norm.

Dolly Dunn, the owner of Retail Detail General Store, gasped at the visual anomaly of a transported felon.

"Harry, look out the window."

"What's so important?" asked Harry Dunn, her husband and co-owner of Retail Detail General Store.

"Come quickly. The Union Army is bringing in a prisoner." said Harry, wearing a clean boiled white apron, he had been restocking the grocery shelves: the bullets, clothing, and school supplies.

"I also see photographers and reporters homing in like vultures," he said.

A Union officer halted the wagon in front of the jail and ordered the prisoner to sit still without moving a muscle, while photographers were taking pictures with their portable dark rooms. One of the photographers was the famed Civil War shutterbug, Matthew Brady, who said, "Face the camera. Be perfectly still! That officer will shoot you if you move."

A Union officer smartly unsheathed from his scabbard, a sharp, shiny saber, which he raised to warn an unruly crowd forming near a wooden plank sidewalk located in front of the jail. The crowd cringed in fear of being cut to pieces. Instinctively, they knew that Lt. Harry Yearwood meant business, as indicated by the horse's front legs taking forward and backward steps to serve as a threat to hack the curious, excited throng on a hot, muggy late afternoon in Flemingsburg. Other observers were shielding their eyes from the reflection of the sun, while standing on the balcony of the local hotel.

The officer fired a shot in the air with his Colt .45 revolver, before addressing the crowd.

"Citizens of Flemingsburg, lend me your itching ears. This captive has committed a serious war crime disrupting military operations against the rebel states, who have chosen to secede from the Union. Since an Army travels on its stomach, we are trying this man in a military court for intentional burning of a flour mill in Maysville. Disperse and resume your normal daily activities", said the pompous officer.

All six officers dismounted, disconnected two chains from the waist of the sitting suspect whom they led to a solitary cell inside the jail. Sheriff Guy W. Flintlock, a 30-year successful sheriff's department veteran, locked the heavy cell door.

"Sheriff, I strongly suggest you limit the visiting hours by posting a written notice," said the Union officer.

"I couldn't agree with you more, Lieutenant. I don't want to see a line of women bearing cooked foods and pies."

"I need papers for this prisoner," said the Lieutenant.

"Certainly, Lieutenant," said the complaint sheriff.

"Good day, sheriff," said the officer unsmilingly, as he and the five other officers left the office to return to their unit with the Government-issued horse-drawn carriage that bore the distinct letters: "U.S. Government" etched on a rear wooden license tag. As the townspeople gawked at the military vehicle, a gust of wind suddenly blew dust in their faces.

One half-mile beyond Flemingsburg, Lt. Yearwood said, "Gentlemen, those girls look gorgeous and very healthy."

"A second lieutenant smilingly said, "Yeah, I saw those women standing on the balcony and smiling at us. I can't wait to get a pass. Eat, drink, make love; for tomorrow we may die."

"Amen to that," said Lt. Yearwood, still making tracks halfway back to the military camp.

Suddenly, charging out of a thicket was a huge, mean Kentucky wildcat snarling at the men in blue. "Look out men, it's a bad cat. Wait until he gets close enough to us...Fire!"

Bullets riddled the hostile feline, mostly in the legs; one round pierced the wildcat's skull, exiting from the back of its head.

Lt. Yearwood quipped, "Even the wild animals seem to be full of anti-Union sentiment. O.K., put it in a bag. We'll get the cook to skin, prepare, and cook the creature. As I previously stated publicly, an army travels on its stomach. This fine catch of animal protein will fill a lot of hungry bellies. Place the animal on its back in the carriage in a 100-lb. potato sack." Fortunately, the officer driving the carriage managed to whip the frightened horses to a halt near a stand of tall pine trees. It was a close call. The wagon and the horse could have gotten away."

Meanwhile, five miles to the soldiers' north, in Flemingsburg, Maggie and Andrews were pleased to be working together in the music classroom.

"I'm glad to be working with you, James."

"Maggie, as soon as we get off work, I want to

take you to the restaurant and buy us some dinner."

"Oh, James, you're such a sweetie."

"It's our chance to relax. I meant to tell you about a summons I received in the mail several days ago," said Andrews.

"Huh?" she asked.

"The local military court is scheduled to try the prisoner on June seventeenth. That's on a Monday," said Andrews.

"You mean the one they just put in our jail?" she asked.

"Precisely. They summoned me to testify in court. I suppose the Union scout will also take the witness stand," said Andrews.

"We could use some excitement around here," said Maggie.

"I could do without it," admitted Andrews.

On Friday morning, June 14, 1861, Bobby Seekemout was conducting a staff meeting before the beginning of the school day. It was 7:30 a.m.

Seekemout said, "Hattie just heated some coffee in the kitchen. She will serve it to us by the cup. She runs a great kitchen. Any questions or concerns?"

"Yes, what's the story on those phony advanced college degrees?" asked Ida Teachwell, a 49-year-old snaggle-toothed spinster woman who wore her hair shoulder length, her blue dress extending down to the ankles. She had blue eyes, small ears, small feet, and stood at five-feet-five-inches.

"Good question. Mirage University has been selling false degrees that required no course work.

Teachers simply bought Masters and Doctorate degrees for one thousand and two thousand dollars, respectively."

Andrews asked, "How did those teachers find out about this business?"

"Another good question. Evidently, Mirage University has been advertising through the medium of the telegraph system. The telegraph operator posts all the junk telegrams on the outside of the telegraph office. Then gullible, naïve, or perhaps, greedy teachers follow up with the ads and present a mailed certificate of a falsely obtained degree."

"What will happen to these teachers?" asked Andrews.

"They have the choice of receiving one hundred lashes or one year's suspension without salary," said Bobby Seekemout, with a stern expression.

"Has anyone from this school bought one of those degrees?" asked Andrews.

"Paul Ergle purchased a regular four-year degree for five hundred dollars. The County School Board will reach a decision next month about the disposition of six wayward teachers in Fleming County. This problem could have serious statewide repercussions. Thank God only one of them is from our school," said the principal.

The conversation abruptly halted when Hattie arrived with individual cups of coffee, to cheerfully serve the teachers in conference.

"Thank you, Hattie," said Seekemout.

"You is welcome, suh," said Hattie, a smiling,

five-foot-three-inch, African-American woman with ivory-white teeth, brown eyes, long eyelashes, and an oval face partially encircled by kinky hair. Her cheeks were healthy-looking for a 39-year-old female, who had been awarded her freedom for nursing her master back to health from an accidental axe wound to the left leg, that eventually healed by applying an herbal poultice.

Without missing a beat, she rhythmically shuffled her feet toward the kitchen while carrying an empty wooden tray in her care-worn hands, which showed obvious markings from years of picking cotton in the fields. The principal had hired Hattie for the position of school kitchen manager, due to her background as a successful cotton field hand since the age of two. After thirty years of picking cotton, she suddenly won her freedom. The Jones Plantation had matched and withheld a portion of her salary in a bank savings account, as an additional reward for her continual, faithful service to J. O. Jones, the compassionate founder of the plantation.

Andrews sipped his coffee thoughtfully and said, "Mr. Seekemout, the trial begins tomorrow at 8:30 a.m."

"You're excused from duty for the duration of the trial, but send a message by courier if the judge sequesters the jury. You will be paid full salary," said Seekemout.

"I'll keep you informed," said Andrews.

The prisoner breakfasted at 7:30 a.m. at the

Flemingsburg jail, and just as he was devouring his last morsel of grits, the remaining food on the plate, Lt. Yearwood and his five fellow officers rudely interrupted his tranquility and virtual solitude.

"Time to go, traitor," declared Lt. Yearwood. "Get up out of that chair. On your feet. Stretch out your hands." Click went the handcuffs and the officers chained the man's legs and padlocked the chains. Another padlocked chain severely restrained the armpits.

"Take him outside and dunk his head in the horse water trough. We can't have the judge citing him for smelly armpits," said the officer.

"Lieutenant, sign the release papers," said the sheriff. "He won't be coming back here again."

Feeling a lump in his throat, the prisoner started to get an uneasy feeling about his future disposition.

"What did he mean by that?" asked the prisoner.

"Shut up," said the Lieutenant. "No talking."

Passing through the front door of the sheriff's office, the clanking of the chains reverberated all the way down the dry, dusty street, marginalized by two sidewalks of oak planks. All eyes were focused upon this wretched suspect, accused of setting fire to a flourishing flour mill in its faithful performance of United States Government contracts to feed many soldiers stationed in a defense perimeter encircling the city of Flemingsburg, as well as in other locations of Union occupation forces in Kentucky.

The tall male public defender accompanied the accused man across the street to the old Fleming

County Courthouse, already surrounded by musket-bearing soldiers spaced ten feet apart. Newspaper photographers made photos while the officers pointed their muskets at the subject to ensure high-quality "still" photographs. The mayor, attired in a white shirt and blue cotton trousers, had received the minutes of the City Council meeting from the previous evening about a newly passed ordinance, which required housing upgrades to maintain the beautification of the community and the preservation of sound property values, for the purpose of guaranteed revenues.

"My fellow citizens of Flemingsburg, lend me your ears. Our City Council enacted a new ordinance last night. Every house and building must maintain painted surfaces, free of chipping, cracking, and peeling. This ordinance is effective immediately." The mayor stepped down from the elevated wooden sidewalk, and into the crowd the puffed-up, baby-kissing politician disappeared, with a lighted cigar hanging out of his mouth.

James J. Andrews was standing across the street and taking in every mayoral word, as wheels were turning in his mind. Now he was mulling over the opportunity to embark upon a part-time job of self-employment as a house painter. But first, he would have to rearrange his work schedule. Would the principal approve of any schedule changes? Although the summer solstice would occur on Friday, June 21, 1861, a full day would still be necessary to perform house painting and carpentry work.

The crowd began to synchronize the rhythm of its movement with the advancing Union detail of officers, escorting the accused man to the doorsteps of the courthouse.

Lt. Yearwood shouted, "No guns are allowed in the courthouse. Hand over your firearms to the sergeant at arms."

One of the young local male slaves was ordered to stand with a ready pail of cold water to wipe the brow of every perspiring Union sentinel and officer, excluding the prisoner. Some of the onlookers were taking bets about the outcome of the trial, and one rag-tag, shirtless, barefoot ten-year-old boy was industriously peddling lemonade in the street, but was quickly running out of product. Unquestionably an astute entrepreneur, the boy had bought five dozen strong, leak-proof, hand-made paper cups from some paper originally manufactured at William S. Whiteman's paper factory in Nashville, Tennessee. Whiteman, the leading paper manufacturer in Tennessee, was always looking for a reliable delivery man, since most of the male labor supply had been drafted to serve in the Civil War.

The courthouse steel double doors slammed with a resounding finality. The sky gave way to an advancing dark cloud cover, slowly blanketing the sky as though the God of the universe were laying out a long piece of dark carpet on its celestial floor. Court was about to be in session, amid white plumes of cigar smoke, almost causing poor visibility inside the courtroom, where an armed bailiff stood at the entrance.

The bailiff shouted, "All rise. Judge-Advocate William Holt presiding. Hear ye, hear ye, the Northern Kentucky Military District Court is now in session. Be seated."

The Judge said, "The defendant is charged with treason and arson. The defense will begin oral arguments at this time. I remind the audience that any verbal outburst or other disruptions will result in contempt of court."

"Your honor, my client is a victim of hearsay. Only one witness allegedly saw the flour mill burn. Secondly, it was too dark for anyone to even attempt to make a positive identification. There was no moon that night," said the defense attorney.

Facing the twelve-member all-male jury, the defense attorney continued:

My client's opposition to the Union reflects an exercise of freedom of expression. The defense argues that the prosecution has arbitrarily and prejudicially arrested my client on account of his anti-Union political views. And I wish to remind the jury that my client is innocent until proven guilty. Simply because my client openly supports the Confederacy should in no way suggest a natural inclination to destroy property used in the Union war effort. I must also state it is common knowledge that both the North and South have divided opinions on this war. In the North, the Copperheads have spearheaded an organized opposition to the war and likewise, the South has its own dissident groups, but most of them have not come out of the closet. Nevertheless, we have written documentation that many people have borne convincing reports of an indisputable existing groundswell of Union sympathizers living in the South. Ladies and gentlemen of the jury, the burden of proof rests upon the prosecution. You, the jury, must decide whether or not my client has been mistakenly identified to be used as a scapegoat, to punish someone for the loss of an army's food source – namely, a flour mill.

"Mr. Defense Lawyer, have you anything else to present?"

"No, your Honor."

"The Prosecution will now present its oral arguments."

"Ladies and gentlemen of the jury, the Prosecution will set out to establish beyond a reasonable doubt, that the seated defendant did, in fact, set fire to and totally destroy said flour mill."

"Get to the point, Mr. Prosecutor."

"If it pleases the Court, I call to the witness stand, Mr. James J. Andrews."

Taking his seat, Andrews placed his hand on a thick copy of the Holy Bible.

"State your name."

"James J. Andrews."

"Do you swear to tell the whole truth and

nothing but the truth, so help you God?"

"I do."

"Mr. Andrews, is it true you owned the flour mill in question?"

"Yes, my father gave me five thousand dollars to purchase the mill."

"How long had you owned the mill before the fire occurred?"

"Two years."

"Is it true there was a disgruntled former employee who espoused anti-Union sentiment?"

"Yes, he was an unhappy, argumentative worker. He wanted to do everything his own way, and refused to follow the manufacturing procedures to the letter."

"Be specific."

"He would often stack the flour sacks in a haphazard manner. The bags would tumble down and cause loading delays. He was often tardy."

"Did he ever engage you in any political discussions about the war?" asked the Prosecutor.

"Yes, he always said he was for slavery and regarded the Union Army as a threat to his nice, neat life."

"Did he ever threaten bodily harm to you?"

"No."

"Did you see any suspicious people hanging around the mill before the fire broke out?"

"No."

"Were you present when the fire started?"

"No, I was asleep."

"So, there is no way you could have identified the person who set the fire."

"That is correct."

"Last question: Can you identify the former employee of the mill?"

"Yes, he is the man in handcuffs, sitting at the table."

"Your honor, let the record show the witness has testified that the former mill employee is none other than the defendant, B. J. Moaner. Thank you, Mr. Andrews. You may leave the witness stand."

The Judge interjected, "Mr. Andrews, you must remain inside the courtroom in the event you are called again to testify."

Andrews nodded and seated himself in the audience. The bailiff raised the two windows to the left of the audience to allow sufficient ventilation and cooler air, that foreshadowed a probable thunderstorm.

"Your turn, Mr. Defense Lawyer."

"Your Honor, the Defense wishes to show on this hand-drawn map of the flour mill surroundings, that a creek is located exactly 200 feet from the flour mill. At that distance it is highly unlikely that anyone could have been close enough to discern the identity of the alleged mill burner. Furthermore, I must emphatically submit to you, ladies and gentlemen of the jury, it would have been impossible for anyone, including the Union scout, to positively identify the person who allegedly burned the mill, coupled with the absence of the moon in the sky that night."

'Is that all, Mr. Defense Attorney?"

"Yes, your Honor."

"Mr. Prosecutor?"

"Your Honor, I wish to submit exhibit 'A' as evidence. I hold in my hand a fragment of a torn shirt that the Maysville sheriff found attached to an overhanging tree branch."

The Judge said, "The defendant will rise and approach the witness stand."

"State your name."

"B. J. Moaner."

"Mr. Moaner, in my hand is a torn piece of a red shirt. I want you to remove your shirt and place it on this table."

"You're going to have to make me take it off. I ain't doing it."

The Judge demanded, "Mr. Moaner, do as the attorney directed, or I will hold you in contempt of court."

"All right, Judge," said Moaner.

The defendant removed his red shirt and placed it on the long wooden table, located in front of the first row of seats.

"Let the record show that the torn piece of shirt completely fills the gaping hole in the clothing, like the final missing piece of a jigsaw puzzle," said the Prosecutor.

The audience gasped in amazement.

The Prosecutor said, "Your Honor, at this time I would like to call a witness to the stand."

"You may proceed."

From the back of the audience in the courtroom, a young Maysville deputy sheriff approached the witness stand, while every eye focused on the wiry, five-foot-nine-inch, blond-haired, blue-eyed, sinewy, long-time resident of his community.

Standing and facing the court clerk, he listened and responded to the boiler plate questions.

"State your name."

"Deputy Knight Owler."

"Deputy Owler, did you see or hear anything unusual during your night patrol, on the night of June 10, 1861?" asked the Prosecutor.

"I was patrolling around the east end of the flour mill and noticed a man with a torch in his hand. Before I knew it, he had set fire to the flour mill. All the town's men and all the sheriff's firemen couldn't put out the fire."

The Judge asked, "Is the man you're speaking of in the courtroom?"

"No, your Honor."

"Where is he?"

"Your Honor, the man who torched the mill jumped on a brown horse tied to a tree. Then a terrible thing happened: The horse was so scared of the fire that he bucked and threw the man to the ground."

"So what happened next?" asked the puzzled Judge.

"He broke his neck when he fell. His head struck a big rock."

"How can you convincingly prove he burned the mill?" asked the Judge.

"His last words were: 'This is what I get for burning the mill. Oh, God, forgive me'."

The Prosecutor said, "Your Honor, I object to this line of questioning. This is inadmissible evidence."

"Objection overruled. I must question the witness," the Judge said. "Did the witness write the dead man's words on a piece of paper?"

"Yes, your Honor," said the Deputy.

"When did you record the man's words?" asked the Judge.

"Immediately, on a piece of blank paper that I always keep in my wallet," said the Deputy..

"The Court must now explain to the jury the meaning of a legal concept known as a Dying Declaration. When reduced to a writing, it is considered admissible court evidence. With this legal explanation in mind, I now charge the jury to determine the guilt or innocence of the defendant. The jury is to retire to its room for deliberation. This Court is in recess until the jury reaches a decision." The Judge slammed down the gavel on his desk.

One hour later, the jury returned.

"Mr. Foreman of the jury, do you have a verdict?"

"Yes, your Honor. We the jury find the defendant not guilty."

Andrews's heart sank, as he had hoped to

receive restitution for his charred flour mill.

"This Court is dismissed," said the Military Court Judge-Advocate William Holt. Andrews walked out of the courthouse with disappointment written all over his bearded face. Maggie ran up to him and they briefly embraced. She had truly felt sympathetic toward him for the untimely financial loss of the flour mill, an asset to the war. The couple wended their way through the vocal throng of people making a mass exodus from the courtroom.

Andrews turned to Maggie and said, "Let's go to the restaurant and have some conversation and food."

"After a long school day, I'm tired. James, I can appreciate your job. It'll be so good to have you back tomorrow. I'll just be a teacher's aide. Mr. Seekemout will also be glad to see you back tomorrow," said Maggie.

"Maggie, there's something I must tell you: I asked Mr. Seekemout to shift me to the Adult Education evening music class," said Andrews, looking straight into Maggie's eyes.

"Why?" she asked.

"The war has inflated the cost of living. Horse feed has gone up fifty cents a pound, and shoe leather costs five dollars more. I'm glad I only have to walk to the school," said Andrews.

"Are you looking for a second job?" she asked.

"Yes, Maggie, a man asked me to paint his house. One of my students recommended me to her father," said Andrews.

"Sounds like she put in a good word for you," said Maggie smilingly.

"I told him if I could rearrange my teaching schedule, I would accommodate his wish. He doesn't want to get fined for an unpainted house due to the recent city ordinance to keep up good home appearances. So, Mr. Seekemout said I could teach night music classes starting next week," said Andrews.

Oh, yes, I heard about that law. More power to you," she said.

"Be as it may, nothing ventured, nothing gained. It might generate much more income."

"James, I admire you for being a hard worker. Nobody can accuse you of laziness."

"Thank you for the compliment, Maggie."

"You're welcome, James."

"Maggie, I had another reason for having coffee with you today, not just because the trial's over. Yes, I lost five thousand, but at least it's settled. Now get this: The fire spooked the horse. Then the horse threw the man to the ground, but he hit a rock and broke his neck. So, the man who burned my flour mill is dead. Case dismissed."

"I know you're glad the trial is over," she said. "James...why did you bring me here?"

"Maggie, will you marry me?" asked Andrews while still sitting upright in his oak chair.

Tears of joy streamed down her face, transforming itself into a broad smile. "Yes," she responded.

The two-headed couple locked themselves in a solid, romantic embrace, kissing lightly.

"Oh, I thought you'd never ask me, James."

"Isn't it odd how God works things out?" asked James Andrews.

"How do you mean?" asked Maggie.

"Mr. Seekemout has given me his blessing to teach night music classes, so I can paint houses during the day. The school system won't allow husbands and wives or other close kin to work together in the same classroom."

"Oh, I see," she said, while suddenly wheezing.

"Maggie, are you getting sick?"

"I'm o.k. It's just a cough," she replied.

Unknown to Andrews, Maggie had been visiting a neighbor confined in the local hospital isolation room. She did not wish to alarm him, for she felt he did not have a need to know. Since there was a virtual lack of knowledge of diseases, universal precautions of the use of gloves, masks, and protective clothing were not even in the works.

"You ought to go home and rest," said Andrews.

"I'll be all right. I'm just tired. I feel like a horse and buggy just ran over me," said Maggie.

"That does it, Maggie. I'm walking you home to make sure you rest," said Andrews.

"My, oh my, my fiancé does indeed love me," she said.

"You bet your sweet engagement ring," said Andrews, as he slipped the pretty jewelry item on her little, dainty ring finger.

"You are really serious, aren't you," said Maggie.

"Oh yes, more than you'll ever know. You are the gal for me. When shall we set the wedding date?"

"What about August the first?" she asked. "That's on a Thursday."

"That's fine," said Andrews.

The engaged couple parted with a kiss, drank up their refilled cups of coffee and went to their separate dwellings.

As the sun rose brilliantly on the next day, Andrews saddled his horse at the Flemingsburg livery stable, intent upon locating an out-of-town, large, gabled, white two-story frame house.

Suddenly, two men appeared from behind a large oak tree near the right side of a level stretch of unimproved road. At the sight of a thick hangman's rope, Andrews had the presence of mind to duck his head against the neck of the horse, as the noose end of the rope missed his head.

Miraculously, Andrews escaped possible death by hanging, while riding in the saddle, and fortunately rushed away from the potential horsejackers, who practically choked on a cloud of dust.

Horace Roach, a scraggly, bearded rustic man, stood at five-feet-five-inches with a broad, friendly face that had a mouth half full of teeth, along with blue eyes, long black sideburns, and untrimmed hairs extending like antennae out of his ears. He was bulging in the belly, drank brandy twice a day, and stared at women while driving his horse-drawn carriage into Flemingsburg every Friday afternoon. His mouth continually reeked of the smell of chewing tobacco. He had won a recent watermelon seed spitting contest – seventy feet. He was a widower since his wife had died the previous four years, of a staphylococcus infection on her neck.

From the road, the house was set back via an s-shaped dirt driveway. Hearing the approaching hoofbeats, Horace Roach looked out the front door in anticipation of the hired part-time housepainter. Andrews tied his horse to a tree in the front yard and addressed the resident.

"Mr. Roach, I'm James Andrews. At your service, sir."

"Mr. Andrews, I have a big house. How much do you charge?"

"Twenty five dollars for the whole job," said Andrews.

"Splendid. You may begin work, and finish at 4 o'clock each day," said Horace.

"I agree to your terms. Just furnish the paint, brushes, scraper, and drop cloths," said Andrews.

"I have already arranged for your supplies. If you have any questions, you'll find me in the backyard garden. I hope you like watermelon and tomatoes. That's a bonus, of course," said Horace.

"Yes sir. That's good eating," said Andrews.

Later, at 3:30 p.m., a tall, thin letter carrier, Charlie Bilbo, galloped up to the Roach home with several letters for the householder. Upon hearing of Bilbo's failed physical exam at the Union Army Induction Center in Cincinnati, Ohio, a Union Army captain later used his influence to secure a postal job for Mr. Bilbo, on account of his charismatic, affable, winsome personality, and people skills. In 1860, he was voted letter carrier of the year in Flemingsburg, Fleming County, Kentucky.

Hour after hour, with a wire brush, Andrews scraped wooden surfaces, the trim, and the two front gables of the house, as the sun continued to sink lower in the sky. At four o'clock, day one ended as Andrews literally was scratching the surface of a lengthy odd job. It was time to ride to the school to teach an evening singing class.

Stirring up a small dust cloud, the hooves of Andrews's horse dug into the dirt, while a Union Army convoy of ten horses and ten horse-drawn wagons were advancing at 25 miles per hour, a relatively high rate of speed, leaving even a much larger dust cloud, reflecting the dry weather conditions of the previous six months.

Sharp-eyed Andrews noticed a strange object ahead of him in the middle of the road. As he drew much closer, he reacted with fear and trembling. Immediately, he halted his horse and hurriedly dismounted to the road.

Motioning to the soldiers, he said, "It's going to blow – stay back. Picking up three sticks of dynamite tied together, he tossed the explosives into the woods – coincidentally at the same two men who had earlier attempted to horsejack Andrews. The dynamite backfired on the two potential roadside bombers, and their barely recognizable bodies lay in pieces at the other end of the fuse line, that the malicious men had ignited with a wooden match. The loud explosion shook up all the soldiers and frightened the horses so much, that the four-legged creatures almost bolted and ran away, were it not for the composure and presence of mind of their riders.

"Advance and be recognized," said Major Robert Streetsmart.

"I'm James J. Andrews. Look over there in those bushes at two dead men and a long fuse."

"Why didn't we see that?" asked Major Streetsmart.

"Sir, a thick coat of dirt covered the fuse line. I knew something was wrong, when I saw a pile of dirt in the middle of the road," declared Andrews.

"Mr. Andrews, we owe our lives to you. Those are probably the same men who have been responsible for three roadside bombings during the last three months. Ten of our men were killed. Mr. Andrews, we consider you to be loyal to our Federal Union. What is your occupation?" asked Major Streetsmart.

"I'm a night school music teacher and a part-time housepainter, sir," said Andrews.

"Where are you going?" asked the distinguished officer.

"I'm returning to Flemingsburg to teach tonight

at school," said Andrews.

"How would you like to spy for the Union? Are you interested?"

"Yes sir, Major Streetsmart," said the young civilian entrepreneur.

"Very well. We'll contact you," said Major Streetsmart, before uttering the command, "Forward....m-a-a-r-ch." In a matter of minutes, the mass of blue uniforms disappeared over a ridge toward an undisclosed location, perhaps to engage pockets of resistance in nearby towns. As a border state, Kentucky was politically divided and was not yet under complete Federal control. With regard to the business at hand, the soldiers left the corpses to decay in the woods.

Andrews quickened the pace toward Flemingsburg, while warily observing the road in front of him. The beautiful June scenery seemed to move rapidly past him as though he was standing still, but it was, of course, merely an optical illusion.

Arriving in town, he pulled up to tie his horse to the school hitching post, noticing that the principal, Bob Seekemout, appeared downcast while standing in front of the school building.

"Mr. Andrews, classes have been canceled due to a consumption epidemic. The hospital is full. We are closed until further notice. Oh, by the way, one of our employees is ill."

"Who?" asked Andrews.

"Maggie. She's not doing well," said Bob Seekemout.

"Thanks for telling me," said Andrews.

Worried, Andrews proceeded to Flemingsburg Hospital and inquired about Maggie's condition.

"I'm asking about Maggie Swiftsure," he said, with a slight hesitation.

"Her condition is fair. She's resting right now but cannot be disturbed," said the head floor nurse of the 50-bed hospital, having doubled its capacity. "We can't allow visitors. We're under a quarantine order. Avoid sick people and go home."

"I'll do that, ma'am," said Andrews, turning around from the hospital nurses' station to exit the under-staffed, overcrowded, one-story, white wood-frame hospital. Andrews was in a serious, pensive mood regarding the probability that his life was about to undergo cataclysmic changes, the kind that he would rather not even think about. Also on his mind was the cryptic reference implying a Federal job offer from Major Robert Streetsmart and its future impact. Essentially, he realized he had little control over the course of his own life; consequently, he was forced to acknowledge the supremacy of the Supreme Being in charge of his life.

Five days later, James J. Andrews had finished painting Horace Roach's house and rode back to Flemingsburg with an extra twenty-five dollars cash. Since he was a civilian, he was not required to bear arms, and by nature, he was a peaceable man who shunned firearms. Willingly, he accepted the risks of wartime travel.

A few minutes later, he approached the scene of

the roadside bombing attempt; the smell of dead human flesh was rank. Hundreds of flies freely swarmed about the human remains, the buzzards having obviously taken their share of the dismembered corpses. But that unpleasant incident had not changed his aversion to using firearms. Andrews tended to be fatalistic in his attitude toward life, reasoning that his Maker would recall him at the divinely appointed time.

Entering the city limits of Flemingsburg, Andrews noticed several horse-drawn wagons being driven toward the town funeral home.

"What's going on?" asked Andrews to a short, blue-eyed pedestrian crossing the main street.

"Haven't you heard? Consumption is killing people. Those people didn't make it," said the stranger.

Andrews said, "Sounds like it's getting worse."

"Yes, that's true," said the pedestrian stranger.

Andrews suddenly thought of Maggie again.

Dismounting and tying his horse to the wooden hitching post, he proceeded inside the hospital to the nurses' station.

"Excuse me, ma'am. I'm here to see about Maggie Swiftsure," said Andrews.

"Sir, she is very ill. We will allow you to visit her," said the Head Floor Nurse.

"Thank you," said Andrews.

Walking down the corridor, he entered Maggie's room and found her coughing, and struggling for breath. She looked emaciated due to a substantial weight loss.

"James, I'm so glad you came. The doctor does not expect me to live. I'm getting worse each day. Maybe one day they will find a cure for consumption, but it'll be much too late for me and others," she said.

"Oh, don't say that Maggie. We have plans to get married. So, nobody knows the cause of your illness, and there's no medicine to treat it," said Andrews.

"Unfortunately, no," she replied as her voice weakened to a barely audible level. Her eyelids closed as she drew her last breath. An observant doctor came into the room and said, "I'm sorry. The patient is not responding." Soon the doctor pronounced her dead.

Tears welled up in Andrews's eyes. He was counting so much on having a happy married life to a woman with whom he was so much in love. The nurse walked into the room to cover the deceased woman with a white sheet. His sweetheart's death had come so quickly. The grim reaper had cut down a lovely, charming woman in the prime of her life. Grief-stricken, Andrews silently and tearfully withdrew from the expired patient's room and left the hospital. The town's atmosphere was filled with doom and gloom – nothing but bad news in the form of killed-in-action lists posted on gas lamp posts along certain streets near the town square.

As if the battlefield statistics were not bad enough, tuberculosis was aggravating the death toll, which now stood at fifty tuberculosis (consumption) deaths on a miserable Saturday evening in this small Kentucky town.

At eleven o'clock on Sunday morning, after the farmers had milked the cows and had dutifully driven their wagons into town to attend the church service at Rev. Alfred Lowe's Church of the Campbellites. A 30-year-old female singer, five-feet-three-inches tall, stood near the pulpit and performed a moving rendition of "Swing Low, Sweet Chariot Coming Fo' to Carry Me Home. A Band of Angels Coming After Me...." At the end of the ethnic spiritual, the pastor commented, "Anytime you want to sing, you name the day." The congregation responded by clapping their hands in agreement, as the young African-American woman stepped down from the stage.

At the conclusion of the service, Horace Roach approached Andrews.

"Mr. Andrews, I'm sorry to hear about your fiancée. Have you met Mr. and Mrs. Lindsey?"

"No, I haven't," replied Andrews.

"Mr. and Mrs. Lindsey, this is James Andrews, an excellent housepainter," said Horace Roach.

"I'm glad to make your acquaintance, Mr. Andrews," said Mr. Lindsey, an aging stoop-shouldered man, who had suffered a severe back injury at age 25.

"My pleasure, sir," said Andrews.

"Look, Mr. Roach tells me you did a very nice job of painting his house, and I want to hire you to paint my small house here in town. What do you say?" asked Mr. Lindsey.

"Yes, I'll do it. My days are free until I teach night singing classes. I can work up to four o'clock," said Andrews.

"That will be satisfactory. I'll furnish all the paint and anything else you'll need. I will expect you tomorrow at nine o'clock," said Mr. Lindsey.

"I'll be there," said Andrews.

"I'll see you in the morning," said Mr. Lindsey.

Maggie's funeral would be scheduled for Monday afternoon, July 1, 1861, at five o'clock, at the grave site in the local cemetery. In the meantime, life had to go on.

Leaving the church property in their brand new horse-drawn wagon, the Lindseys were deep in thought.

"Sweetie, Mr. Andrews just lost his fiancée, and I think we know of a young woman who would be good company for him," said Mr. Lindsey.

"Yes, dear, I've been taking in a lot of sewing jobs lately. She could help me catch up the customer orders. I will invite her to spend a few days with us," said Mrs. Lindsey.

"Then it's settled. While Mr. Andrews paints, you will introduce them to each other. Everything will dovetail so nicely – if you get my meaning," said Mr. Lindsey.

"Yes, dear," she replied laughingly. "You know I'm a natural schemer."

"Of course," said her husband.

"Now, when it comes time for lunch, we'll all sit down on the back porch and have her eat with us. That young man needs a woman," said Mrs. Lindsey.

"The Good Book says it's not good for a man to live alone. The Lord knew what he was talking about," said Mr. Lindsey.

The carriage continued to roll the short distance from the old, quaint green country church to their small, white one-story, wood-framed home that had a wide brick chimney, a necessity for every house roof where the winters are very cold.

On Monday morning, July 1, 1861, Andrews arrived at the Lindsey home.

"Mr. Andrews, start scraping the front of the house and work your way to the back porch."

"Yes, Mr. Lindsey."

Soon, it was after eleven o'clock, when a tall, graceful woman with an appealing figure, showed up at the Lindsey front doorstep. Her father had dropped her off after a thirty-minute wagon ride from the country. She was a "plain Jane" in the face, yet she was pleasant to look at, not necessarily placing last in a beauty contest. More importantly, she was reserved, straight-laced, and was definitely a no-nonsense person, certainly not a humorous, witty, charming, outgoing person. She was one or two years Andrews's senior, but what mattered the most was that the couple were attracted to each other via positive chemistry, and by mutual religious views, as she was a Campbellite Christian sect member also espousing pro-Northern views.

"Mr. Andrews, you can eat lunch with us on the back porch. First, let me introduce you to Miss. Elizabeth Layton. She lives just two miles outside the city limits," said Mrs. Lindsey.

"I am pleased to make your acquaintance, Miss Layton," said Andrews.

Shyly, she replied, "I'm pleased to meet you," as she shook Andrews's hand in a friendly manner.

She was withdrawn, due to a sheltered home life, without ever having traveled beyond Flemingsburg; whereas, Andrews was a well-traveled man of the world. Basically, the couple would be a viable match, even though Andrews was more of a social mixer than Elizabeth.

"Are you from around here, Mr. Andrews?" asked Elizabeth Layton.

"No, I was born in Hancock County, (West) Virginia on a farm. I ran a flour mill, until it burned down."

"What caused the fire?" she asked.

"A Confederate sympathizer. He didn't want me to make flour for the Union Army."

"Did they jail him?" asked Elizabeth.

"His horse threw him and his head hit a rock. He confessed his guilt as he was dying. So that was the end of that," said Andrews.

"That is truly a shame," said Miss Layton.

"Well, what are you going to do? That's life," remarked Andrews.

"So, what do you do now, besides painting houses?" she asked.

"I teach singing lessons at night," said Andrews.

"Oh, you are a very well-rounded person," she said.

"The Lord has gifted me with a good voice and the ability to teach," stated Andrews.

"My, you're such an humble person," Elizabeth said, before eating a piece of cornbread and drinking a glass of lemonade, under the roof of the back porch facing north toward a wooded area.

"Well, time to get back to work. I've enjoyed the food and pleasant conversation, Elizabeth," said Andrews.

"So have I, James," she said.

Andrews worked from Monday until completing the job on Friday, and during that time, he and Elizabeth had brief talks, discovering their shared common interests in the Holy Scriptures. She was the least interested in current events, in that she was an ostrich in terms of dealing with the unpleasant reality of the Civil War, otherwise known as the War Between the States, or the War of the Rebellion.

On Friday, Andrews asked Elizabeth a question. "Elizabeth, I have enjoyed your company so much this week. Would you like to join me for dinner at five-thirty? I teach class at six-thirty."

"Yes, I would love to do that," she said.

"I will rent a carriage and pick you up at your house at five," said Andrews.

With the latest infusion of cash, Andrews was more than making ends meet, but the escalation of the Civil War would depress the house painting market. He learned, to his chagrin, that Union naval ships had imposed a blockade around the seacoasts of the Confederacy, thus creating a logistics problem not only for civilians, but also for the Confederate Army. The thought occurred to him: why not beat the system by becoming a blockade runner?

CHAPTER 2
BETTER OPPORTUNITY

While entertaining this thought, a courier came running toward the Flemingsburg Hotel and knocked on Andrews's door at five o'clock on Tuesday, August 5, 1861.

"Mr. Andrews, please sign for this telegram," said the young, black-haired, five-foot-six-inch, thin 21-year-old man, who had not yet been drafted for military service.

Date: 5 August 1861
To : James J. Andrews
From: First Kentucky Army, Louisville, Kentucky
Employment Interview scheduled for 10 August 1861

Andrews scanned the telegram with raised eyebrows. Major Robert Streetsmart must have put in a good word about the attempted roadside bombing. Without delay, the former housepainter scrawled a reply on a sheet of paper.

"Send this message right away," said Andrews. The terse reply read, "Will come. Andrews."

The telegrapher nodded his head affirmatively, and began transmitting the message in Morse code. Andrews had obviously found favor with the distinguished Union officer.

Next, Andrews had to "gas up" his horse with enough horse feed to put in the saddlebags for the ride to Louisville, only five days away.

While walking toward the hotel, Mr. J. B. ("Brack") Jackson, the proprietor, stepped out on the sidewalk, a cigar hanging out of his mouth.

"Brack" Jackson removed a sharpened pencil from its resting place atop his right ear, and poked the eraser end of the pencil on Andrews's right arm.

"I can use you as a temporary hotel clerk. Business has been picking up. What do you say, Mr. Andrews?" asked Jackson.

Withholding the news of the upcoming interview with the United States Secret Service, Andrews replied, "Yes, I'll take the job. What are the work hours?"

"It's flexible. You can have weekends off if you wish. It won't conflict with your evening school job," said Jackson.

"I'll take the job, since house painting is down," said Andrews.

"It pays two dollars an hour. You can keep any gratuities earned. Remember, don't ask any couple if they are married or not," warned Jackson.

THE RUNAWAY TRAIN

"Yes sir," said Andrews.

"All we want is their money – no questions asked. Their private life is their own business. However, we are not a house of ill repute, so use your own judgment. Don't let things get out of hand."

"Yes, Mr. Jackson," said Andrews.

During the following three months, in October, 1861, Andrews often worked not only during the day, but he would work for Jackson from 7:00 p.m. until midnight, when the hotel owner routinely relieved Andrews. This temporary part-time job ended up with an approximate $25-a-week salary – a rather tidy sum of money in those days.

As the sun rose brilliantly on a clear, cloudless morning, Andrews was seated at the Flemingsburg Hotel desk, looking out the lobby window at the unpaved main street. In rushed a telegram courier with a dispatch hot off the telegraph wires.

The telegram, addressed to James J. Andrews, read the following:

To:J. J. Andrews
From:First Kentucky Army
Re:Appointment
Wait until further notice

Andrews was puzzled at the cryptic message. Had the Army changed its mind about holding the interview? Perhaps the telegram writer deliberately encrypted the message so as not to tip his hand in case the telegram was to fall into the wrong hands. Andrews folded the message and shoved it into his back pocket, away from prying eyes, amid a politically charged border state and a small town where divided loyalties also existed. Two days later, at one o'clock, a man disguised with a beard, spectacles, and a wig, stepped off a stagecoach and brought one suitcase into the hotel. The man spoke in a low tone, as he was signing an assumed name instead of his real name. He laid ten dollars on the desk for a one night stay, and thrust his brown cowhide wallet back into his left front pocket.

"Mr. Andrews, when do you eat dinner?" asked the disguised man.

"Five o'clock," said Andrews, puzzled that an unrecognized person knew this clerk's name.

The secret visitor glanced at his pocket watch, attached to a long gold chain connected by a hook to his inside right coat pocket.

"Is there a relief clerk?" asked the stranger.

"Yes, Mr. Jackson will stand in for me," said Andrews.

"Good, not another word. I'll see you in the dining room," said Major Robert Streetsmart, clad in a dark-brown suit with a tie, tie clip, and an expensive brand of cufflinks. His shoes were black and well shined. He also wore a white shirt. His face was slightly covered with dirt from wind-blown road dust and much perspiration. Needless to say, he was especially tired, cranky, and starved, without beneficial roadside facilities.

"Sir, here is the key to room ten," said Andrews.

The man grabbed the key and went directly to his room to freshen up after a long, arduous 70-mile-trip from Louisville to Flemingsburg. Soon, "Brack" Jackson relieved Andrews at the hotel registration desk, allowing Andrews to converse with Major Streetsmart in a quiet corner of the adjoining hotel restaurant.

"Andrews, the state of our nation is very critical. We are fighting to preserve the Union. I need patriots like you to obtain vital intelligence information. If you decide to accept the mission, I will hire you to be in the U. S. Secret Service. Events are happening at a very fast pace. Now is the time to join us. The pay is a thousand dollars a month," said Major Streetsmart.

"Major, I want the job. Tell me what I have to do," said Andrews.

"You will be responsible for penetrating enemy lines. Observe and note their troop strength and movements. Find out everything you can," said Streetsmart.

"It's a deal, Major," said Andrews smilingly.

"You probably want to know why I traveled in this disguise. Ever since an attempted roadside bombing, I've had to be more alert. I can only say that an undetermined number of Confederates have infiltrated our ranks. That is why we must fight fire with fire by using counter-intelligence. I have to protect myself," said the officer.

"I don't blame you a bit," said Andrews.

"In a hundred years from now, the history books will be inadequate to do us justice. This war is far too complex. There are still a lot of things we don't know about the American Revolution, because time fogs up recorded history. A lot gets lost in the translation through distortions, opinions, errors, and you name it. The historians will never know the full picture of this War of the Rebellion no matter how many volumes are written," said Major Streetsmart, stiff-lipped.

"I appreciate stimulating conversation, Major."

"Don't mention it. Look, Andrews, give your employers two weeks' notice and join me at my headquarters in Louisville. I'll be expecting you. Do you have any questions?" asked Major Streetsmart.

"How much are my meals?" asked Andrews.

"Andrews, you will eat free as long as you can keep up with us," said Streetsmart.

"Thank you, sir," said Andrews.

"Otherwise, you will have to forage for yourself," said the officer frankly.

"Very well, Major. I'll make it work," said Andrews smilingly.

"I'm sure you will. We did a background check on you and your ownership of a flour mill. You were a great asset to the war effort, not to mention your saving our lives," said the seasoned fighter.

""I'm glad I passed muster, sir," said Andrews.

"I'm leaving early in the morning. I saw your boss sizing me up. Be sure to tell him you're leaving. Are you single?" asked Streetsmart.

"I'm in love with a sweet girl," said Andrews.

"Oh, God, help her. Women become widows far too easily in protracted wars like this one, but that is your decision. I have a wife and two teenage daughters at home, and I'm sure they're worried to death about me. We live in a dangerous world," said Major Streetsmart.

"See you in two weeks," said Andrews.

"Take care of yourself, Andrews," said Major Streetsmart, as he walked circumspectly toward his hotel room.

Andrews was sensing a turning point in his life, prompting him to contribute meaningfully to the cause of the preservation of the Federal Union.

"Brack" Jackson voiced his irritation at Andrews. "It's about time you came back to relieve me. I have to eat, too, you know."

"I'm sorry, Mr. Jackson. I was taking care of business."

"So I noticed. Who is that strange man?"

"I will only say that he offered me a Provost Marshal position, but actually it is a cover for Secret Service activities," said Andrews.

"What?! You're leaving me to become a spy? You're crazy. I'd advise you to forget it. Your head will end up on the wrong end of a rope," said Jackson.

"Mr. Jackson, I'm giving you two weeks' notice. I'm resigning. I'm at a point in my life where I need to do something or get off the outhouse seat," said Andrews.

"Since you have made up your mind, I can't talk you out of it. It's your funeral, Andrews....Well, I hate to lose you. You're the best hotel clerk I ever had," said Jackson.

"Thank you. I will be moving to Mrs. Eckles's Boarding House, since business and politics don't mix. I think it would be for the good of your business that I move away," said Andrews.

"Suit yourself, Mr. Andrews. I can see your point. You don't want any trouble with local Confederate sympathizers," said Jackson.

"You're correct, sir. Here's my last week's rent," said Andrews, as he cordially shook Jackson's hand to signify a harmonious parting of the ways, agreeing to disagree. "I hope there are no hard feelings."

Jackson stated, "I just don't like the idea of reading your name on the obituary page. Lord knows I've read more than enough of them already."

Like a coach penciling on a piece of paper the plays of an upcoming football game, Major Streetsmart was formulating an espionage plan, while bouncing up and down in the Government-contract rental stagecoach, without modern factory shock absorbers. His hand shook with each written stroke of the pen. If only laptop computers had been invented in his lifetime, everything would have been so much easier for him; whereas, he had to settle for a wooden clipboard on top of his lap, while seated inside the stagecoach.

THE RUNAWAY TRAIN

It was common knowledge in those days, that in some cases, people professing to be Confederate sympathizers were actually plunderers who robbed people, big-bucks banks – even cash-carrying stage coaches.

Out of the corner of Major Streetsmart's left eye, twenty-four young men of medium height wended their way down a heavily forested hillside. The hoofbeats not only quickened but were also becoming louder and louder, as the equestrian traffic abruptly entered the unpaved highway, five miles north of Flemingsburg.

This Government-leased stagecoach was carrying a strongbox full of United States currency, the payroll for the First Kentucky Army. Wells Fargo had shipped to Flemingsburg the strongbox, which had been stored in the First Flemingsburg Bank, and had been conveniently placed on top of the stagecoach, right between the driver and his guard riding shotgun.

Both the driver and the guard turned their heads to the left to notice the four horsemen, hell-bent in their pursuit of the coveted, unmerited money. Major Streetsmart shouted upward at the driver and guard, "Don't shoot until I give the order."

In front of Major Streetsmart were one shotgun and a secret weapon, hung up on the front wall of the conveyance. He carried two revolvers holstered at the hips, and two derringers, one in each coat pocket.

Streetsmart reached for the upper shotgun,

removing it from the wall brackets.

"Ready, aim, fire!" shouted Streetsmart.

The lead horseman returned fire; but his horse was wounded in the left hind leg. The three defenders fired additional rounds. Two of the riders fell from their horses.

Having mounted a Gatling gun on the left stagecoach door window, Major Streetsmart fired automatic rounds at the outlaws. One by one, they fell dead. The driver and the guard gasped in amazement as the stagecoach came to a halt.

"Major, what in blazes did you do to those masked men?" asked the driver.

"I eliminated them," said Major Streetsmart.

"You sure did some fancy shooting," said the driver.

"We'll just leave it at that − get going. Time is precious," said Major Streetsmart.

Mrs. Sarah W. Eckles, the vivacious, people-loving owner of a beautiful, white two-story, rectangular, wood-frame house, had bought the dwelling in 1851 for $2,000.00. She was a 200-lb., five-foot-two-inch, cheerful, round-faced, blue-eyed 65-year-old woman, a devout Protestant. She was well known for her sweet tooth, as she had a penchant for eating cakes, fried pies, and pancakes loaded with maple syrup. In a word, this genial lady was an undiagnosed diabetic, who had lost her left big toe to gangrene as a result of diabetes. A hospital emergency visit would probably be her first and last, since medical science was especially limited in 1861. Her condition automatically made her vulnerable to kidney problems, high blood pressure, cardiovascular disease, and strokes.

Tying his light-brown horse to the hitching post, Andrews entered Mrs. Sarah W. Eckles's Boarding Home, dressed casually in blue jeans and a long-sleeve cotton shirt, over which was a black leather jacket purchased before the naval blockade went into effect. His dark beard was trimmed neat and short, giving him a gentlemanly appearance. Andrews wore a top-of-the-line brand of black leather boots and white cotton socks. He was six-feet-four-inches tall, weighed 185 pounds, and his face bore a luxuriant black beard.

"Good morning, sir. How may I help you?" chirped Mrs. Eckles in her lighthearted voice.

"Ma'am, I'm James J. Andrews. I want to rent a room."

"I'm Mrs. Eckles, the owner. The rent is twenty-five dollars a month, due on the first of each month. No women are allowed in the same room, unless the couple is married. Are you single or married?"

"Single," replied Andrews.

"Curfew is at ten o'clock. Lights out at eleven o'clock. You are responsible for cleaning and keeping up your room, making the bed and exchanging the linen every Tuesday. All dirty clothing and linen must be at the washboard by 10 a.m. Meals are included with all the services I've mentioned. Meal times are posted inside your room door," said the Mrs. Eckles.

"I will agree to the rules. Please show me my room," said Andrews.

"Room thirteen, Mr. Andrews. I trust you are gainfully employed," said Mrs. Eckles.

"I'm newly employed as a U.S. Provost Marshal for the Eastern Kentucky District," he replied.

"Oh, my, that's highfalutin; unemployed boarders don't last long here," she said.

"I wonder why," said Andrews.

"You're funny, Mr. Andrews," she said with a laugh that shook the rest of her body as though it were gelatin. Andrews noticed she was well insulated. "I'll see you at lunch," she said, taking the first step toward her office.

After lunch, Andrews received a telegram from Major Streetsmart's Louisville office. For security reasons, the Major did not wish to divulge any information about the attempted highway robbery and its very bloody aftermath. So, the telegram simply read the following:

To:Andrews, J. J.
From:R. S.
Subject:Meeting in Louisville. Location to be announced. Come ASAP.

Walking over to speak to Mrs. Eckles in the kitchen of the boarding house, Andrews said, "Mrs. Eckles, I may be gone for a few days. You have my month's rent in advance. This job requires some traveling, so I'll see you later."

"Goodness gracious, Mr. Andrews. You hardly got here, and now you're fixing to light out of this place. May God protect you," said jolly Mrs. Eckles.

"He has been faithful, believe me," said Andrews.

"Good bye," said Mrs. Eckles.

"I'll be back."

Already packed like a Colonial Minuteman, within ten minutes, Andrews rode out of town toward Louisville, which was at least a hard three-hour horseback ride.

Meanwhile, in Louisville, Major Robert Streetsmart was closely reviewing the intelligence plan he had formulated during the previous, exciting stagecoach trip.

Pensively laying down his pen, Streetsmart said to another soldier, "Sgt. Lynn, did you set up that meeting with General Nelson?"

"Yes sir, Major," said Sgt. Casey Lynn.

Streetsmart stated, "I just hired James Andrews to spy for us. Both armies need food, clothing, and medical supplies. The blockade is a two-edged sword."

"Major, there's a gentleman to see you about a paper contract."

"Send him in, Sergeant."

A five-foot-nine-inch man wearing a gray suit stepped into the Major's tent. The paper merchant's eyes were brown and his hair was medium length. He wore a pair of black leather boots, and smoked cigars, perhaps as much as General Ulysses S. Grant.

"Major Streetsmart, my name is William S. Whiteman. I own and run a paper factory in Nashville. I'll get right to the point. I'm seeking a Government contract to supply the Union Army with writing paper. I'm looking for a deliveryman. Can you help me?"

"Yes, I can, Mr. Whiteman. I'm expecting someone else to arrive today. From what I know about him, he would be just right for the job," said Major Streetsmart.

"Very good, sir."

Suddenly, a rush of hoofbeats peppered the road. Andrews had arrived at the First Kentucky Union Army Camp.

Peering into the tent, the sergeant said. "Sir, Mr. Andrews is here to see you."

"Send him in, Sergeant," said Major Streetsmart. "Mr. Andrews, meet Mr. Whiteman."

Shaking hands, Andrews said, "How do you do, Mr. Whiteman?"

"I am pleased to make your acquaintance, Mr. Andrews. I'm William S. Whiteman."

Major Streetsmart said, "Mr. Andrews, Mr. Whiteman is a Nashville paper manufacturer seeking to expand his market outreach. If you accept this business proposition, he will bankroll you, and you will receive a percentage of the profits. Is this right, Mr. Whiteman?"

"Sir, you are essentially correct. I will need to

discuss the details with him," said Whiteman.

"That's fine. Before he meets with you, I need to see you, Mr. Andrews," said Streetsmart.

The afternoon sun had dipped so low in the sky that twilight would soon be upon the land. The Major spread out a map across his wooden table.

"Mr. Andrews, this is a map of Eastern Kentucky. Colonel John S. Williams is their area Rebel leader. According to previous reports, Williams has been recruiting Confederate troops near Prestonsburg, but we don't know where they're going. Your mission is to find out his battle plans."

"How can I help, Major?" asked Andrews.

"I was hoping you would ask," he said with a smile, exposing his tobacco-stained teeth.

"Here's the plan: you are to ride twenty miles eastward and meet with Colonel Williams. Pack your saddlebags with ten reams of paper. An anonymous medical supplies contractor, for security reasons, has selected Whiteman as a middleman. So, anything else besides paper will be included with the delivery items."

"Very interesting, Major."

"There will never be a dull moment, but let me emphasize that I don't care how much money you make as a blockade runner. Your primary mission is to learn everything you can about the enemy. Your neck could be on the line. Spies make people mad. However, you will be paid for every scrap of intelligence information." Major Streetsmart added, "Feel free to ask the supply sergeant for additional items as needed."

"Thank you, sir," said Andrews.

Leaving Major Streetsmart's tent in high spirits, Andrews saw Whiteman standing patiently under a shade tree and chomping on a cigar. Crooking his right index finger, he motioned to Andrews.

"Mr. Andrews, snow will be coming on soon. I'm looking for a traveling salesman. You seem to have the gift of gab and a love for people. I've been observing you," said Whiteman.

"What do you have in mind, Mr. Whiteman?"

"I want you to know I'm expanding my business operations to the battlefield. I need you. That's where the action is. The war has not been conducive to conducting business. However, both armies have one thing in common. They can't run to the neighborhood general store and buy all the things they need for day-to-day living. You can be their traveling general store. As the Union Army advances south, you'll need to follow your target market. It is my gut feeling the North will win, but it makes no difference to me whether money passes from Northern or Southern hands into ours," said Whiteman.

"I'll work for you," said Andrews.

"Good. As you have a need to know, I will tell you where to pick up the merchandise. Suffice it to say, I use rail connections for shipment to secret branch warehouses that could be located even in a barn, in the countryside, or in a brick building in a small town. You will check every telegraph office for telegrams from me. We have a good system. You and I can work together and make good," said Whiteman.

"I'm game, sir," said Andrews.

"Follow me to my carriage so I can give you some merchandise," said Whiteman.

The sun hid behind a cloud, the temperature quickly falling into the 40's. It was Tuesday, October 15, 1861.

"Do I make all deliveries by horseback?" asked Andrews.

"Yes, carriages can suffer wheel or axle problems. Horses are much more reliable. Both the governors of Tennessee and Kentucky have asked me to supply both armies, especially with canned foods, so neither army will plunder as many farms. They know we can't stop all of the foraging for food, because that is the nature of war – but politics being what they are – no farmer is going to re-elect a governor who allows his troops to steal crops."

"When do I leave to meet Colonel Williams?" asked Andrews.

Thirty minutes later, Andrews saddled up his horse with loaded merchandise consisting of six reams of blank white paper, pens, ink bottles, cornmeal and salted ham.

"Mr. Andrews," said Major Streetsmart, poking his head out of the headquarters tent, "the enemy will have scouts posted."

With bulging saddlebags, the courageous, adventurous Andrews disappeared over the first hill toward Eastern Kentucky. He had eaten a substantial campfire-cooked breakfast of salted pork, hardtack, and a bowl of grits.

Fortunately, Whiteman had provided the horse feed. Andrews wisely "gassed up" his horse for very rough, hilly, rocky terrain over uneven, sometimes treacherous dirt roads caused by rainfall washouts in the most unexpected places. Such road conditions would affect his "gas mileage," and so it behooved Andrews to carry along sufficient horse feed. Watering the horse would be in order while passing through each town. In case of an emergency re-shoeing due to a broken horseshoe, Andrews was hoping that a blacksmith would be on duty. He tried to repress the thought of a broken horse's leg or the remote chance of a snakebite to one of the animal's legs.

Riding over a rise during the halfway point in the journey, Andrews noticed a long train of horses and horse-drawn wagons stirring up enough dust to cause one to gag. As they were quickly approaching the itinerant distributor, he squinted his eyes, due to the position of the sun, which was now behind his back and sinking lower into the western sky. Astonished at the sight of covered wagons, he thought he had been transported back in time to the migration of Daniel Boone and other settlers, going through the Appalachian Mountains via the Cumberland Gap.

Both parties met on the crest of the hill, and a tall, burly, six-foot, blond-haired, blue-eyed, thin wagon master had halted the wagons for a rest, just before Andrews's arrival.

"Hey, mister, where do you think you're going?" asked the wagon master.

"Prestonsburg," said Andrews.

"I wouldn't go there if I were you. The Confederate Army is shooting it out, and we had to evacuate our homes."

"Thanks for the warning. I'm a risk-taker."

"I will keep you in my prayers. I'm Odell Fambrough. What's your name?"

"I'm James Andrews."

"What are you doing here?" asked the curious wagon master, a leader of political refugees.

"I'm on official U. S. Government business," said Andrews.

"Well, Mr. Andrews, you sure are going to need a lot of prayer," said Fambrough.

"Please pray for me, Mr. Fambrough," said Andrews.

"I shall indeed. May God always be with you. If I don't see you again, one day we'll meet again in Heaven," said the wagon master, Odell Fambrough.

"I'll be looking for you," said Andrews.

"So long, brother," Fambrough said, as he motioned the wagon drivers and horsemen toward Flemingsburg. Like a column of ants as viewed from above, the evacuees pushed onward at a slower pace.

Three hours later, a Confederate Army scout suddenly appeared from a roadside thicket at 4:30

p.m., almost one hour before twilight.

"Halt! Dismount. Advance and be recognized," said the Confederate scout. "Identify yourself."

"I'm James J. Andrews. I am a traveling merchant. I'm delivering medical supplies, canned foods, and other items."

How much stuff do you have? It sure doesn't look like very much," said the scout, having raised his musket at port arms.

"This horseback shipment is just enough for right now. My boss will send more supplies as soon as I telegraph him," said Andrews.

"Follow me," said the scout.

The Confederate camp was only one mile away along a dirt road, wide enough to facilitate the transport of troops, cannons, mules, and horses.

Approaching Colonel Williams's camp, Andrews noticed two long, evenly-spaced rows of canvas tents camouflaged to blend in with the foliage. Within a few minutes, the scout led Andrews to the front entrance of Colonel Williams's tent.

"Mr. Andrews, wait until I come back."

Sgt. James Jones, a five-foot-five-inch, 180-pound, sharply-dressed, blue-eyed, seasoned soldier, smartly saluted Colonel Williams. "Sir, I wish to introduce Mr. James Andrews. He is selling some things we can use – morphine, bandages, belt buckles, and other supplies."

"Send him in, Sgt. Jones," said Colonel Williams.

"Yes sir," replied Sgt. Jones, with a well-executed salute and a subsequent "about-face".

"That will be all, Sergeant," said Colonel Williams. Shifting his eyes, the seated officer then said, "Mr. Andrews, I'm Colonel Williams."

Lt. Orville Hightower entered the tent and saluted. "Sir, dinner is served. Roast deer is the main course."

"Thank you, Lieutenant. Nothing beats deer meat, especially when you're very hungry. Have the road guards relieved every two hours –including perimeter pickets."

"Yes sir," said Lt. Hightower.

"Tonight, we will enjoy our dinner," said Col. Williams.

"Where shall I sleep?" asked Andrews.

"You will share a tent with two other men. When the bugler blows reveille, we'll eat breakfast and then ride up to Prestonsburg to check for Yankee pickets," said Colonel Williams. "Five sharpshooters will serve as bodyguards."

"Will we have enough men, sir?"

"Mr. Andrews, rest assured. Too many men will attract too much attention. This is a scouting unit. A nice way to spy," said Colonel Williams.

"What effect has the blockade had on the South?" asked Andrews.

"We're short of muskets, bullets, cannon, food, and clothing. We're really kind of broke to wage war," said Colonel Williams. Andrews was storing this bit of intelligence in his memory bank. "As time goes on, we're going to have to make do with what we've got."

"This deer meat was so delicious. Thank you, sir," said Andrews.

"My pleasure, Mr. Andrews. Let's turn in and get a good night's sleep. Tomorrow will be a long day," said Colonel Williams.

At daybreak, the sun was hidden behind the clouds over mountainous Eastern Kentucky in November, 1861. A 40-degree chill was in the air, as the scouting detail left camp and blended in with the woods.

Meanwhile, in the rear of the column, was a squad leader named Sgt. Joe Miff, a 21-year-old, tall, slender, brown-eyed, bearded partaker of snuff and hand-rolled cigarettes. Bereft of significant gray matter, this five-foot-nine-inch man had been scrutinizing Andrews, riding at the head of the scouting detail with Colonel Williams.

"I don't like the looks of that civilian. He don't belong here. He may be up to no good," said Sgt. Miff to one of his fellow soldiers. And another thing, I've never seen an officer go out on a high-risk mission," said Sgt. Miff.

Sgt. G. W. Hatley, a 200-pound, blue-eyed, five-foot-six-inch, blond man perked up at Miff's comments, and said, "Miff, you've been in the field too long. You need a furlough. Everything seems to be bothering you."

"Hatley, you just don't understand. I'm suspicious of the civilian's motives for being on this spying mission."

"Miff, only time will tell. We'll wait and see what happens," said Hatley.

Three hours later, Colonel Williams and Andrews struck up a conversation, while still riding through the woods.

"Mr. Andrews, where do you live?" asked Colonel Williams.

"I'm staying at Mrs. Eckles's Boarding House in Flemingsburg, Kentucky."

"Do you have plans to settle down someday and marry?"

"Well, Colonel, I've been going with a nice gal in Flemingsburg. I'm in love with her, and she also loves me."

"If you love her, marry her. You want children to carry on your name in case you become a war casualty," said Colonel Williams.

"It's been in the back of my mind to ask for her hand. I'm working up the courage to ask her very soon," said Andrews.

"Mr. Andrews, I'm going to write a letter to Mr. Whiteman to give you two weeks' time off. You might want to use the time to propose marriage," said Colonel Williams.

"Perhaps," said Andrews.

"Do it before it's too late," said Colonel Williams.

"Amen, sir," said Andrews.

Meanwhile, back in Flemingsburg, cheerful, bubbly Mrs. Sarah W. Eckles was engrossed in reading the front page headline which read: "Kentucky Falls to Union Forces".

"Oh, dear God. Ellie May, get me some spirits of ammonia. I'm feeling a might puny," said Mrs. Eckles.

Ellie May was a homely-looking 28-year-old, blue-eyed brunette woman, who was only five feet two inches tall, enviably slender, and her housekeeping duties included mopping, dusting the living room, and cleaning the windows.

"Relax, Mrs. Eckles. If the Yankees take over Kentucky, we're completely helpless, but I just know we're in God's hands," said Ellie May, a single woman serving as a live-in housekeeper subject to Mrs. Eckles's beck and call, 24/7.

Meanwhile, in Eastern Kentucky, Sgt. B. W. Beasley rushed into Colonel Williams's tent, shortly after Andrews departed the Confederate camp, and said: "We've been tricked. I saw Boston horseshoes on Andrews's horse. He must be a Yankee spy. He's been looking very closely at everything."

"Sergeant, capture that man. Shoot only if necessary. I want him alive," said Colonel Williams.

"Yes sir," said Sgt. Beasley.

Shooting out like a bullet, Sgt. Beasley hurriedly reached a full gallop in hot pursuit of James J. Andrews, spy and contraband merchant.

Upon hearing the pursuing hoofbeats, Andrews dug his spurs into the horse, riding like the wind, such that he flew past a visibly surprised road guard.

"Stop that man. He's a spy!" said the pursuer. Instantly, a minieball whizzed through Andrews's right sleeve, slightly below the shoulder.

"Damn it. We almost got him," said Sgt. Beasley. Both he and the road guard were cursing, practically gnashing their teeth between each spoken word.

The road guard said, "I though
get away from our outhouse smel'

"No, you fool. I saw the v.
over our camp," said Sgt. Beasley, ⌐
pursuer.

Nervously chewing a plug of tobacco, the roa⌐
guard said, "He sure tricked us."

"Soon, the Yanks will know where we are, and they're going to know we're planning to attack them at Prestonsburg," said Sgt. Beasley.

"He looked good, smelled good, and he said all the right things," said the disappointed road guard.

"We let a big fish get away, and the Colonel won't like it," said Sgt. Beasley.

It readily came to Andrews's attention that the blockade runner job, coupled with spying, entailed greater risks than he had ever imagined. Foiling a dynamite explosion set up by two roadside bombers was unsettling enough, but a very close shot narrowly missing the flesh, was altogether a much more personal matter to James J. Andrews. Despite hotelier J. B. Jackson's admonition, Andrews was still determined to make it work, come hell or high water.

The sun was sinking lower in the Western sky, a few days before Christmas, 1861. Now, Andrews could ride without fear of being captured, as he had greatly outdistanced the sentinel's outhouse post; but yet gnawing hunger suddenly became an immediate concern.

While hurrying to reach Mrs. Eckles's Boarding

ouse in time for dinner, sleet was suddenly falling and pelting Andrews's head and coat, amid a bitter cold afternoon in wintry Kentucky. Flemingsburg was only three more miles, according to a standing wooden sign with black lettering. Returning to the boarding house would indeed be a sharp contrast to the alternative of possible capture, flogging, and imprisonment in a filthy, rat-infested Confederate prison, providing only meager rations and virtually a hopeless future. Not only was a table full of cooked and prepared food awaiting his cold, starved, tired body, but a surprise visitor would be present among others inside a warm house, close to a huge fireplace providing maximum indoor comfort, away from a harsh, inhospitable fifteen-degree temperature.

Parked in front of Eckles's Boarding Home were three horse-drawn wagons, belonging to the Flemingsburg Campbellite Church. The twelve passengers had left the wagons to enter the boarding house, with the singing of Thanksgiving songs beginning with "Come Ye Thankful People Come".

This particular scenario sparked Andrews's curiosity, as he pulled up to secure his weary horse to the wooden hitching post. Cautiously ascending the slippery steps, he entered the boarding house smiling at the welcomed sight of Elizabeth Layton, who was leading the caroling session in the living room.

As soon as she noticed him, her eyes lit up like a Christmas tree; she could hardly contain herself.

Her rosy cheeks stood out so much among the other female carolers. Obviously, she was imbued with the joy of Christmas from the spiritual standpoint, for no commercialization of Christmas occurred in those days.

Andrews positioned himself by her side and joined in with the singing. Immediately he recognized the faces of former music class students to whom he had taught singing lessons. He construed this gathering to be very much like a reunion. After the carolers had sung their last song, the residents clapped appreciatively, shedding genuine tears of joy.

Elizabeth smiled shyly and said, "James, where have you been? Do you still paint houses? I checked with the school, and the principal said you had resigned."

"Elizabeth, let's get some fresh air. Let's talk outside."

"Certainly," she replied as they discreetly walked out to the wrap-around porch.

Standing directly in front of Elizabeth, Andrews said, "My new job might make some enemies. I'm a blockade runner. I find out where enemy soldiers are going, what they're up to, and what they're going to do."

"Are you a spy?" she asked.

"I'm determined to serve my country. This is the only way I can do it. I don't believe in killing people or using guns," said Andrews.

"Whose side are you on?" she asked.

"I work both armies so I can make enough money to support myself and my wife-to-be."

Elizabeth looked surprised and taken aback at this startling revelation.

"My dear Elizabeth, I love you. I want you to be my wife. Will you marry me?" asked Andrews.

"Yes, I will marry you, James. I've been waiting all of my life to hear those words from the right man." She reached in her purse and pulled out a cloth handkerchief, to wipe away the tears coursing down her cheeks.

During this tender love scene, miles away at Louisville, profound political events had been rapidly developing, such that the state of Kentucky was like a tempest in a teapot. Forty-six-year-old Kentucky Governor Beriah Magoffin, a Confederate sympathizer, had been stripped of his authority to recruit Confederate troops, upon the establishment of a five-man military board composed of all Unionists, whom the Legislature authorized to organize and arm the Home Guards. Since the June 20, 1861 Congressional election, by a majority of 54,000 votes, State Unionists, Congressmen, and Senators attained a three-fourths majority in both the Kentucky House and Senate. The formation of the Union Club in Louisville grew within six weeks to a six-thousand member unidentified secret society, held together by a loyalty oath to the United States Flag and to the Federal Government.

Since Andrews's narrow escape, on November 8, 1861, he reported without delay the intelligence information to Major General Nelson's secret camp. Shortly after the intelligence briefing, Andrews rode with General William Nelson into the Eastern Kentucky mountains a few miles west of Prestonsburg. Nelson was pleased with Andrews's stealthily obtained information that Confederates had been busily gathering their forces east of Prestonsburg, deeply committed to invade Central Kentucky.

Major General Nelson had been charged to recruit and arm Union recruits in Eastern Kentucky and, in due course, he had assembled detachments of several Kentucky regiments along with two Ohio regiments, which forced Colonel John S. Williams's troops to retreat to Pound Gap, through which they sought a safe haven in nearby Virginia. For now, the Union troops had repulsed the Confederate threat to the security of Central Kentucky.

But, alas, young women in love were not generally interested in current events, especially a sheltered person like Elizabeth Layton, whose comfort zone was closely knit fellowship of the local Campbellite religious sect, separated from the harsh realities of a cruel, wicked world. To avoid unnecessarily upsetting Elizabeth Layton, Andrews wisely refrained from discussing the apparently dangerous nature of his job. Even though both sensed its dangers, neither person wished to spoil the joy of being in love. Elizabeth would later realize the nature of his work, especially as the months passed without receiving either a handwritten letter or a telegram.

The probable final contact was at or about Friday, February 1, 1862. The couple agreed to set the planned wedding date for Saturday, June 7, 1862, but fate would intervene to alter their wedding plans. However, Andrews spent time seeing Elizabeth each day during the Thanksgiving and Christmas holidays of 1861, but duty would soon be calling for the espionage services of James J. Andrews.

CHAPTER 3
PENETRATING THE SOUTH

E arly in February, 1862, Andrews parted company with his friends in Flemingsburg, Kentucky, and said what would be ultimately his last "goodbye" to his fiancée, Elizabeth Layton. According to various written accounts, Andrews continued his secret activities as a double espionage agent and traveling merchant to sell contraband items, in spite of logistical constraints imposed by the Federal Naval Blockade. As events later unfolded, Andrews moved to Nashville, Tennessee, where he encountered Judge M. A. Moore, a former Flemingsburg, Fleming County Judge, who had also left Kentucky for political reasons.

Anxiously knocking on Andrews's room door in Nashville's largest hotel, the exiled Judge said, "This is Judge Moore. Open the door! We have to talk."

"You look familiar – can't place you," said Andrews, astonished, after opening the door.

"Don't you remember me? I'm Judge M. A.

Moore. Look, I have some things to talk about over a delicious, hot breakfast."

"Judge, if you're buying, I'm eating."

"You are my guest, Mr. Andrews," said the judge, as he walked with his fellow defector to the hotel dining room.

Taking their seats, Andrews spoke first.

"Your Honor, I thought you were the number one Yankee in Fleming County. How come you're also here?" asked Andrews.

"I saw how things were falling apart in Flemingsburg, and I got plenty of telegrams thoroughly documenting how the politics was getting out of control, so I jumped ship," said Judge Moore.

"They certainly lost a good judge," said Andrews.

"You don't need to butter me up, Mr. Andrews. If nothing else, I can always pass a bar exam and practice law. I saved plenty of money for a rainy day," said Judge Moore.

"You obeyed your own wise counsel," said Andrews.

"Mr. Andrews, let's be realistic. It's only a matter of time until the Yankees take over Nashville. In the meantime, I want to offer you a business proposition," said Judge Moore.

"I'm all ears," said Andrews.

"Listen. I'm going to introduce you to several Confederate officers and talk over a contract, to deliver medical supplies and other items to troops in the field. Do you remember Mr. Whiteman?" asked Judge Moore.

"William S. Whiteman?" asked Andrews.

"Precisely," said Judge Moore.

"What's this all about?" asked Andrews.

"Right now he's preparing to move his paper manufacturing business to Chattanooga in the very near future. I'm a silent partner in charge of managing the blockade running business. You have been well recommended, due to your excellent performance as an intelligence observer and covert merchant in Eastern Kentucky," said Judge Moore.

"Thank you, Judge Moore," said Andrews.

"Together, Whiteman and I will bankroll this underground business of delivering medical supplies, bandages, morphine, quinine, crutches – to name only a few of the sorely needed items," said Judge Moore.

"I accept the challenge," said Andrews.

"I had no doubt about your acceptance, Mr. Andrews. Now that we have finished our conversation.....You know......business before pleasure. Let's enjoy this delicious breakfast the waitress is bringing us," said Judge Moore.

"Judge, my fiancée is a well-formed woman and I sorely miss her. I wish she could have come to see me, but that would have put her in danger during travel," said Andrews.

"There is a time for everything, according to Ecclesiastes 3:1-6: a time to marry, a time to die.....you get my meaning?" asked Judge Moore.

"Yes, that's a familiar scripture verse," said Andrews.

The five-foot-two-inch, rosy-cheeked blonde, blue-eyed, slim waitress smiled through her pearly-white teeth, surrounded by a fair-complexioned oval face, with a light shade of lipstick as the only applied makeup. She wore flat, brown leather shoes. Her below-the-knees skirt was cheerfully light-blue, and her fingernails were slightly ragged, due to her devoted day-to-day kitchen labor.

"Gentlemen, your breakfast is served. My name is Ann. Is there anything else I can get you?"

"This is fine, young lady. Thank you," said Judge Moore, his mouth watering at the sight of scrambled eggs, bacon, grits and red-eye gravy.

"Mr. Andrews, these Southerners really can cook, and they know what's good to eat."

"I'll take your word for it, Judge," said Andrews.

"Eat it and you'll see for yourself," said Judge Moore.

A short while later, both men left the hotel, observing a bearded elderly man displaying a huge lettered sign that read the following: "Repent now. The end is near".

Walking past the sign bearer, Judge Moore said, "There's always a religious fanatic somewhere." Andrews merely listened without commenting.

Confederate headquarters was only a five-minute walk from Nashville's largest hotel. A musket-bearing sentry stood guard outside the front door of the general headquarters brick building. The streets were teeming with people – the troubled, the sick, the elderly, anxiety-ridden wives, daughters, and girlfriends. People were queuing up to read the list of war casualties. Some readers were weeping uncontrollably upon the discovery of unpleasant news from the battlefields. The town hospital was grossly understaffed and abysmally under-supplied. Andrews observed the miserable plight of the masses and privately, he was having mixed emotions about plying his illegal commercial activity; but he so much wanted to make a difference in serving his country and expressing his humanitarian concern for people, whether they were Northern or Southern troops. Perhaps he was compensating for the loss of his flour mill in Maysville, Kentucky.

"We're lucky to cross this busy street without being run over," commented the Judge wryly. "Oh, look at that fancy cigar store."

"Looks like Nashville is the place to be," said Andrews.

"Don't get too comfortable. The Yankees will win the war. The South doesn't have a pot to collect urine. Our treasury is running dry. Troops are marching without soles on their shoes – no shoes at all, and we're short of blankets, rations, weapons, ammunition, horses, boots, weapons, and medical supplies; not to mention the fact the troops are dying like flies on the battlefield, mostly of diseases."

"Judge, that's where I come in," said Andrews.

"Precisely, and that's why we're going to see the top generals at their headquarters. Between Whiteman's money, mine, and your willingness to risk life and limb, we can make big profits from both armies," said Judge Moore.

"How is Whiteman getting the merchandise?" asked Andrews.

"He and I have friends working for the railroad. Suffice it to say, it's a North-to-South smuggling operation," said Judge Moore.

"Very interesting, sir," said Andrews.

"Just do your job. Don't ask questions. We'll tell you as the need to know arises."

"Fair enough, Judge."

Inside the Confederate headquarters building, 44-year-old General Pierre Gustave Toutant Beauregard and 47-year-old General William Joseph Hardee were talking about the state of the war.

"I'm glad the sensation-seeking newspapers are kept from sending too many reporters to the battlefield. The civilians don't understand why we treat prisoners as rough as we do," said General G. T. Beauregard, a seasoned commander, displaying a very rugged countenance with a jawline set in concrete.

"Can you imagine the hue and cry if people had access to an instant means of listening to a news reporter tell about the successes, disappointments, and the atrocities of war?" asked General Hardee.

General Beauregard said, "I could see the stir it

would create, if people had such advanced communication. Surely the press would be much more influential in American politics, and that would give Congress more ammunition to undermine our war efforts."

"What if people could see and hear everything on the battlefield, as things are happening?" asked General Hardee.

If this ever happens while I'm in the army, I'll put in my retirement papers. We have nothing to hide. Such a news medium would certainly stifle our military operations by hindering our ability to prosecute the war. God forbid such a terrible invention from ever happening," said General Beauregard, puffing his cigar while in deep thought. "Such outlandish inventions don't concern me in the least. I suggest we turn our attention to our logistics problems. The further we drive a wedge into the South, the more we extend our supply lines."

General Hardee said, "The best things we have going for us are the railroads. If we lose control of them, we might as well turn in our swords to the enemy."

"You're absolutely correct," said General Beauregard. "The railroads are the key to moving our troops and supply shipments much more rapidly than simply marching an army hundreds of miles. Napoleon Bonaparte did that scenario. Oh, how he would envy our railroads if he were alive today." General Beauregard sat down in his chair and struck a wooden match against his left boot heel and said, "In due course, we will be receiving two civilians assisting us with our supply distribution. One of them is a blockade runner and a spy." Suddenly, the room turned silent.

There was a knock at the door. A guard ushered in two men, Andrews and Judge M. A. Moore.

"You must be Judge Moore and James Andrews," said General G. T. Beauregard.

"Yes sir," replied Judge Moore. "This is Mr. Andrews."

"I'm General Beauregard. Meet General Hardee."

"It's a pleasure, gentlemen," said Judge Moore, shaking hands with both generals.

Andrews followed suit.

"We've been expecting you both," said General Beauregard.

The room was musty and reeked of cigar smoke. A cuspidor had been provided for the convenience of tobacco chewers, and several wooden chairs had been arranged within speaking distance of the two generals' desks.

Clearing his throat, General Beauregard said, "I am told that you gentlemen can smuggle medical supplies and other items to our troops in the field. Is this true?"

"Yes sir, I'm managing the blockading operations, and Mr. Andrews takes all the risks," said Judge Moore, smiling proudly. Andrews refrained from commenting.

"I'm giving both of you some passes to go to our camps. This will make it easy for you to distribute the items," said General Beauregard.

"What is my first assignment, sir?" asked Andrews.

"Mr. Andrews, you are going to Fort Donelson. Here's the first pass. When you return, I will issue you the second pass."

"I'm ready to ride," said Andrews.

"Here's a paper voucher to pay the blacksmith for a bag of horsefeed. I'll also give several other vouchers for later horsefeed fill-ups. Be sure to get the maximum calories per pound per mile," said General Beauregard.

"You might be interested to know we had to shake Jefferson Davis's piggy bank for the horsefeed funds," said Beauregard jokingly, while pressing his tongue into his left cheek. General Hardee started laughing along with Andrews.

"You now have your horse-riding orders, Mr. Andrews. May God be with you. Take care of yourself. As for you, Judge Moore, I would like to appoint you as a Judge-Advocate of Nashville. You will try cases pertaining to civil and military law. We abolished jury trials due to the exigencies of war," said the short general, an average-looking person.

"Yes, General Beauregard, I will accept the position," said the judge.

"The salary is five grand a year," said General Beauregard.

"That is reasonable," said Judge Moore.

At the end of the meeting, Andrews left the Nashville Military Headquarters Building to locate a Government-issued, well-fed, pre-saddled horse waiting for the adventurous spy. As he was walking at a quickening pace, a familiar face caught his eye while crossing the busy main street.

"G-D-it! What in hell are you doing here, Andrews?" cried Judge Dewey Berry, dressed in a sharp gray suit with a polka-dotted tie, black shoes, and white socks. This former Fleming County, Kentucky judge was wearing a gold-plated Swiss wristwatch.

"Hello, Judge Berry. I was planning to look you up after just settling in."

"I've got to hand it to you. You saw the light much sooner than I. Come join me for a drink," said Judge Berry.

"Nice of you to offer. I have business to take care of....... I'll take a rain check," said Andrews.

"I'm willing to bury the hatchet. I was quite mistaken about you, and I harbor no ill feelings against you. I had thought you were going to turn me in to the Union Army," said Judge Berry.

"I'm not like that. See you later," said Andrews, deliberately losing himself in the street crowd.

Dark clouds loomed on the horizon. Business was booming at Women For Hire Saloon, as men returned to the street with empty wallets and big smiles on their faces. One religious enthusiast was twisting and turning a paper sign that read the following: "The Torah – The Book – The Bible", and one man was preaching from a wooden sidewalk and urging the people to get right with God.

"Believe on the Lord Jesus Christ and you shall be saved. Everyone will spend eternity somewhere. Repent of your sins or live in the flames of Hell forever without escape. Remember, today is the day of Salvation. If you die without Christ, there will not be a second chance," said the zealous rag-tag street preacher, shouting and waving his arms as though his sleeves were on fire.

A few persons were visibly moved by the impassioned plea for Salvation, but the majority of the townspeople acted as though the sermon was meaningless and irrelevant to their day-to-day existence.

"Now I want to talk to the people who belong to the Lord: according to Second Chronicles 7:14, 'If my people who are called by my name shall turn from their wicked ways, I will heal thy land.' Ladies and gentlemen, even the good Christian people have turned their backs on God," said the street preacher.

As the street preacher continued his harangue, sixty miles away at Fort Donelson, on Monday, February 4, 1862, at 6:00 p.m., three Confederate Brigade commanders were informally talking military strategy. General Joseph E. Johnston had made a controversial decision to divide his forces: only fourteen thousand troops would be sent to defend Fort Donelson on the Cumberland River, a distance of twelve miles eastward from the other defending fortification known as Fort Henry, a smaller and much more vulnerable military wilderness outpost; whereas, sixteen thousand soldiers would be assigned to protect Nashville.

In attendance at their war room were Generals Simon Bolivar Buckner, Gideon J. Pillow, and John B. Floyd. Of the three Generals, the most ethical, qualified, levelheaded officer was General Simon B. Buckner. The least suitable leader was General Gideon J. Pillow, who was under indictment for embezzlement of a large amount of United States Government funds, as Secretary of State under the administration of President Buchanan. Pillow was said to be jealous of General Buckner. Several years previously, these two officers had words, and a cloud of enmity lingered over their stormy, acrimonious association. In essence, Pillow was an angry man fueling the flames of unresolved bad blood between him and Buckner.

General Simon Buckner said, "General Johnston seems to be more interested in protecting Nashville, because it is much bigger and is a principal commercial center of the South. That's why he is sending fewer men to Donelson. Money talks and bull stink walks."

"That says a lot. I think Johnston knows the Yankees are going to use their gunboats against us and beat us to a pulp," said General Floyd.

General Pillow said, "We're sitting ducks in the wilderness. As you all know, I used to work as

Secretary of State under Buchanan. Johnston thinks like the establishment. So......I was a part of it and I know the Union Army is going to whip us with their vast store of resources. Johnston deliberately chose Fort Donelson to catch the bullets, while he marched his sixteen thousand troops in relative safety."

"Yes, Gideon, everybody knows what you did in Washington. You made your bed and you must take the consequences. I concur with your statement," said Buckner. "Nevertheless, we will defend this Fort to the best of our abilities, even though it may be a sacrificial lamb," said Buckner.

"General Floyd said, "I don't expect Fort Henry to last long. They're practically defenseless and worse off than we are, to be honest. Only one gunboat is needed to take out Fort Henry."

As the Confederate officers ended their conversation before going to dinner, Andrews was making good time on his Jefferson Davis-issued horse. Fortunately, Andrews had not encountered any wild animals unsafely crossing the dirt roadway; he had an aversion to the concept of road-kill, being a tenderhearted nature lover. Periodically, he would necessarily stop for a short snack break of nuts and several square slices of Southern cornbread. As nightfall approached, Andrews started looking for a place in the woods to sleep overnight and a tree to which he would secure the horse.

Waking up to sixty-five degrees of relatively

temperate weather, the man on a secret mission remounted his horse after eating a meager breakfast of dried fruits, nuts, and more cornbread, hardly enough calories for such an arduous journey. It was 5:00 a.m. on Wednesday, February 6, 1862. Within five hours he would reach Fort Donelson on the Cumberland River in Tennessee.

Twelve miles up the river, ominous things were happening at a rapid clip. As a fulfillment of prophecy, Fort Henry surrendered to the persistent Union gunboats that delivered the expected military outcome along with superior Union troop numbers. Among the 2,500 fleeing Confederate defenders, was Union Major Robert Streetsmart, dressed in the butternut Confederate uniform, a clever act of infiltration, not at all an uncommon wartime occurrence. Moreover, during the twelve-mile retreat, Major Streetsmart had turned his ankle, while traversing a gorge in very rocky terrain. It required the supreme efforts of two Confederate soldiers to transport this unknown spy by a stretcher hewn from a felled tree.

At noon, Andrews had pulled up to the entrance of Fort Donelson, in utter exhaustion and extreme hunger.

"Advance and be recognized," shouted the front gate sentry.

"I'm James Andrews. I'm a civilian with medical supplies for sale. Here is a pass from General Beauregard."

"I'll be right back," said the astonished sentry.

Suddenly, Andrews heard the sounds of Union cannons in the distance, not too far from Rebel-held Fort Henry. Seizing the moment, Andrews carefully observed the height, strength, and the location of rifle pits, which were staggered one above each other and positioned on the landward side of the fort. The rifle pits would be formidable obstacles to the charging enemy troops. Yellow clay overlaid an irregular line of logs extending without any breaks from Hickman's Creek to the outside of the southern city limits of the town itself. Andrews would later see the positions of nine thirty-two-pounder guns and one ten-inch Columbiad in the northern lower water battery, and an additional Columbiad, also bored and rifled as a thirty-two-pounder, was placed on the northern side of the bluff, located thirty feet above the Cumberland River. These guns were nestled in strong traverse-supported bunkers consisting of dirt-filled coffee sacks.

Felled tree branches surrounded the fort. On the surface, Fort Donelson was impregnable, but was it?

The sentry opened the entrance gate to admit Andrews. A dozen soldiers rushed forward to inquire about his merchandise. Major Robert Streetsmart instantly recognized Andrews. Both had the immediate presence of mind to keep silent, so as not to blow their cover.

Opening both saddle bags, Andrews proudly displayed the quinine, morphine, foot powder, headache powder, bandages, splints – enough items to tide the troops over for awhile. Confederate eyeballs bulged in amazement at the array of immediately accessible necessities. As a bonus item, Whiteman included three rolls of thin paper for outdoor restroom visits.

"Where did you get all this stuff?" asked a Second Lieutenant infantry officer named A. J. Cunningham.

"Sir, I'm a blockade runner. My sources are privileged information. For one hundred dollars, all of these things are for your troops. This is a package deal, and we're passing the savings on to you. Our costs were dirt cheap. I'm not here to take advantage of your dire needs, just to make a fair profit."

"I really do believe you, Mr. Andrews," said Lt. Cunningham. Twelve onlookers stared in awe at the coveted merchandise for several minutes, and then dispersed to carry on their fortress duties.

Boom! The sound of more cannon was sending Andrews a message, and Major Robert Streetsmart also sensed the urgency to address the matter.

"Mr. Andrews, long time no see," said Major Streetsmart.

"Major---oh, yes. Fancy seeing you here," said Andrews.

"I want you to get word to my unit sixty miles from here. They're just above Nashville by now."

"Look at you," said Andrews.

"Never mind that," said Major Streetsmart, a

Union officer disguised as a Confederate soldier in the typical butternut uniform.

"Move out now. My unit will send reinforcements. You tell them General Grant is on his way to this fort – and it will only be a few days. Ride hard, Mr. Andrews. Godspeed," said Streetsmart, casually walking away to follow through with his official duties as procurer of supplies. A supply sergeant was under his direct supervision.

Without delay, Andrews mounted his horse and hightailed it out of the fort.

Somewhere north of Nashville, General Don Carlos Buell's Union army was advancing southward with the intention of occupying Nashville. Andrews would have only a very short time to report to General Buell, the upcoming Union invasion of Fort Donelson. As it turned out, Andrews finished a hard sixty-mile ride to Buell's camp located about twenty miles north of Nashville.

As the morning sun rose, the tired rider approached sixty white tents arranged in a grid pattern; enlisted Union soldiers were walking and saluting occasionally visible officers.

"Halt! Who goes there?" cried the camp sentry, Sgt. Joel A. Swafford, a tanned, brown-eyed, 250-pound, muscular, six-foot, 23-year-old man.

"I'm James Andrews. Major Streetsmart sent me as a messenger. He turned his ankle when the Rebs evacuated Fort Henry."

The sentry read the note and realized Andrews

was telling the truth. Scratching his beard, the sentry said, "All right, mister, let's go down to General Buell's tent."

Among rows of white tents, soldiers were talking and standing outside, curiously observing the civilian visitor in street clothing, and undoubtedly most of the recruits and battle-hardened men secretly envied the freedom Andrews possessed – to go almost anywhere without restriction.

The sentry called out, "Sir, Sergeant Swafford reporting with a visitor. Request permission to enter the tent."

"Come in Sergeant," said General Buell, who had led his troops from Bowling Green, Kentucky away from the prying eyes of General Joseph E. Johnston's forces. Skillfully, Buell managed to march his troops around Johnston's camp, without alerting the Confederate pickets.

"Sir, this is James Andrews with a message from Fort Donelson."

"Very good, Sergeant. You're dismissed," said General Buell, returning Swafford's well-executed salute. Said the foxy commander, "State your name and business."

"I'm James Andrews, sir. I'm a blockade runner and an employee of the U. S. Secret Service."

"I see. Sit down. Now, tell me more," said 36-year-old General Buell, with a slight indication of curiosity. Seemingly, Buell was low-key, not easily riled.

"I've just ridden sixty miles all night to tell you

the news that Grant has taken Fort Henry, and Major Robert Streetsmart also said Grant is moving on Fort Donelson," said Andrews.

"Why isn't Major Streetsmart here?" asked General Buell.

"Sir, he said he turned his ankle during the evacuation of Fort Henry," replied Andrews.

"How many escaped?" asked General Buell.

"Twenty-five hundred," said Andrews.

"How many were left behind?" asked General Buell.

"Less than a thousand," said Andrews.

"Less than a thousand?!" asked General Buell in disbelief.

"By the way, we heard the cannon sounding at Fort Henry on February sixth," said Andrews.

"Hmm.... That's proof of an attack on Fort Henry. You made very good time, Mr. Andrews," said General Buell.

"General Buell, here are some sketches I made of the fortifications," said Andrews.

General Buell took the map and started poring over the well-drawn depiction of the fort's defenses.

"I can use you and I will pay you according to the value, timeliness, and usefulness of the intelligence information," said General Buell.

"I accept," said Andrews.

"I want to know how many troops General Johnston has stationed in Nashville. Find out where their weak defenses are located and where the enemy stores its ammunition. Anything else that you come up with will be considered gravy on hardtack," said General Buell.

"I understand, sir," said Andrews.

"Get some rest. Leave at 0500 hours. When you leave Nashville, meet my outfit at Stone River near Murfreesboro, Tennessee," said General Buell.

"Yes sir, I'll be there," said Andrews.

To sleep inside a tent under a woolen army blanket was almost like lodging in an expensive Northern hotel of the 1860's, except for the lack of four solid walls. All through the night Andrews slept comfortably, in contrast to sleeping unprotected and unsheltered in the woods.

As the bugler sounded reveille, its characteristic wake-up call, Andrews arose quickly from his supine position and joined the Union troops for breakfast.

Sgt. Swafford said, "Mr. Andrews, we have a few eggs left from a henhouse raid. As our honored guest and Union loyalist, we are giving you the last four eggs as a delicious cooked omelet seasoned with salt and pepper. I daresay we are better nourished than the Johnny Rebs."

"I know that is true, Sarge," said Andrews.

"I admire your courage, Mr. Andrews. I know your life is probably more at risk than that of the average combat soldier."

"That could be. At any rate, I enjoy what I'm doing. I love America and the Union must be preserved at all costs – even if it means my life. If I have to bust a gut, I'll leave my skeleton in the

South," said Andrews, as he shoveled in a forkful of omelet, the most substantial meal he had eaten in several days.

"Would you care for anything else to eat?" asked the cook, Sgt. Stu Cook.

"I'm full, Sarge. Thank you. I had best be on my way," said Andrews.

As Andrews's horse disappeared in the woods, General Buell called in his staff for a meeting in his tent.

"Gentlemen, I have studied the sketches of the fortifications at Fort Donelson. I'm going to tell it like it is. General Grant can easily knock out Fort Donelson with his gunboats. He has more than enough troops to take the Fort.

"General Buell, what about the heavy guns?" asked Lt. Boney Jaw.

"Not a problem. Grant is a tactician mastermind. He performed well in Kentucky and now it's ours."

"Does that mean we won't send reinforcements?" asked Lt. Boney Jaw, a short, blue-eyed, 180-pound, five-foot-eight-inch man.

"No reinforcements are necessary, Lieutenant," said General Buell.

"Where do we go next?" asked Colonel Guy Hopalong, a six-foot-three-inch, 180-pound cavalry officer, who was secretly a civilian at heart, regarded the war as an unwarranted, grievous interruption of his young life, in his comfortable, cozy, big-city lifestyle in Cincinnati.

"Gentlemen, our next objective is Corinth,

Mississippi; but first, Andrews will provide needed information on the Confederate defenses of Nashville. I'm going to send General Mitchel to Shelbyville, Tennessee, and then I'm going to assign him the duty of knocking out Huntsville, Alabama, and taking Chattanooga."

"Sounds like a brilliant plan, General Buell," said Lt. Boney Jaw.

"Lieutenant, I want you to keep an eye on Andrews. I sense he is more concerned with making a fast buck than providing us with useful, timely intelligence. What I'm telling you may be a self-fulfilling prophecy," said General Buell.

"Sir, I'm kind of leery of him myself. He's obviously a vulture of a war profiteer. I can see the gleam of greed in his eyes," declared Lt. Boney Jaw.

At this very same moment, Andrews was observing the activities in downtown Nashville, including the outward signs of establishing a permanent foothold in the city, with the hope of securing the city from Union Army attacks. While taking in everything he saw and heard in his travels, the thought of earning more money led him indirectly to meet William S. Whiteman, at the businessman's corporate headquarters in an impressive, well-run paper factory.

Andrews soon walked into the lobby of the paper factory and spoke to a five-foot-two-inch, homely, long-haired, 22-year-old receptionist, who was processing some local merchants' orders for

THE RUNAWAY TRAIN

various quantities of paper.

"How can I help you, sir?" she asked, while sipping a glass of water at her medium-sized oakwood desk.

"Ma'am, I'm James Andrews, and I'm here to see Mr. Whiteman."

"Is he expecting you?" asked the receptionist.

"Yes ma'am," said Andrews.

"Wait right here, please. I'll tell him you're here," said the receptionist.

Within two minutes, a lively-stepping, pot-bellied man entered the lobby, as though he were racing against the clock.

"Time is money, Mr. Andrews. Come to my office," said the entrepreneur to the contraband merchant.

He led Andrews into a large office suite, where Andrews sat down on a comfortable large sofa facing Whiteman's mahogany executive's desk, on which a cardboard soldier graced.

Picking up a previously lit cigar that had been resting on a glass ashtray, he flicked the cigar ashes into the receptacle and took a lusty puff.

Looking directly into Andrews's eyes, Whiteman said, "Here's ten grand for the purchase of medical supplies and other necessary items for both armies. I know you're a contraband merchant, and I'm asking you to help me expand my business into the blood-soaked battlefields of this Confederacy. You can make a lot of money, Mr. Andrews. You are the man for this job," said Whiteman.

"What is my sales route, Mr. Whiteman?" asked Andrews.

"It's as big as you want it to be, but practically speaking, your marketing area will basically cover the territory where current fighting is taking place in Alabama, Tennessee, and Georgia. Even during the lull between battles, you can still make a lot of sales," said Whiteman, taking a quick puff on his cigar.

"Where shall I start?" asked Andrews.

"Good question. General Buell will be moving some troops to Murfreesboro, Tennessee. I suggest you call on the Union army – Buell's camp – as you work your way down south," said Whiteman.

"Well, I'd best be going, Mr. Whiteman," said Andrews.

"Send me a wire often, Mr. Andrews. The telegraph is the quickest means of communication – especially in business, when time is money," said Whiteman.

"Yes, sir. That is so true," said Andrews as he left Whiteman's office, with a white envelope full of cash hidden inside his coat pocket. Whiteman waved at Andrews, while taking a puff from a cigar. An hour later, Andrews observed the military situation in Nashville's Confederate military establishment and perceived no threat to the southward advancement of General Buell's Army.

Two weeks later, Andrews was leisurely riding his horse toward Murfreesboro, located on the Duck River, as General Buell was steamrolling his army to set up housekeeping in the form of neatly arranged rows of white tents, only a short distance from Murfreesboro.

During a morning military conference, General Buell spoke to his staff officers. "Here we are in April, 1862, and I'm itching to engage the enemy."

Lt. Boney Jaw said, "Sir, if it means anything to you, the troops are acting like chickens with their heads cut off."

"As long as we behead chickens – not people – we will remain civilized. Only barbaric countries practice such repugnant atrocities," said General Buell.

"Just to think about that makes me so sick at my stomach," declared Lt. Boney Jaw.

One of the listeners was General Ormsby Macknight Mitchel, a very distinguished, well-educated man whose hobby was astronomy. He had earned an engineering degree at the University of Cincinnati prior to the Civil War. Higher headquarters selected Mitchel to bear the responsibility of building bridges. His physical appearance seemed to enhance his innate leadership abilities, as his subordinates readily took note of Mitchel's dark eyebrows and discriminating eyes – hallmarks of an impressive countenance.

General Buell glanced at General Mitchel and said, "Ormsby, you're too quiet."

"Sir, I have had a lot of things on my mind lately, and I wish to discuss something in private with you," said General Mitchel.

"Very well. The staff meeting is concluded, gentlemen. The next military decision rests on the strength of Andrews's information about Nashville," said General Buell.

As everyone else quietly left Buell's tent, the occupant asked General Mitchel, "Is something troubling you, Ormsby?"

"General, if we're going to end this war soon, we must destroy the railroad link between Atlanta and the rest of the South," said General Mitchel.

"How do you propose we do that?" asked General Buell.

"If we send twenty or more men to capture a locomotive in Georgia, they could destroy the tracks and keep troops and supplies from reaching Corinth. If successful, we could paralyze the South for good," said General Mitchel.

"Your idea is very interesting, Ormsby. When you arrive at your next duty station near Murfreesboro, I will give you permission to plan, recruit, and organize your special project. You have my blessing," said General Buell.

Wheels were already turning in Mitchel's very active mind. Of course, he knew whom to select to spearhead this very hazardous mission.

Two hours later, Andrews rode into the camp, tired and hungry. It was Tuesday, April 8, 1862. While Andrews was dining with the Union troops, General Mitchel approached him.

"Mr. Andrews, I must talk to you alone," said Mitchel.

"Certainly, General,"

"I already told General Buell about your findings at Nashville, but that's not what I'm here to discuss with you," said General Mitchel, his jawline taut.

"It isn't?" asked Andrews, somewhat taken aback.

"I need your help to win this war soon. I found out you work for the Secret Service. I have a job for you. If it is successful, you could go down in history," said General Mitchel.

"Please continue, General," said Andrews, inclining his left ear toward Mitchel, within several feet of the woods at the end of a clearing.

"Let me put it to you straight: I am in the process of recruiting volunteers to steal a locomotive in Georgia to wreck the railroad and telegraph lines between Atlanta and Chattanooga. That action will enable us to shut down the South forever," said General Mitchel.

"Sounds like a brilliant idea. I'll do it for the Union," said Andrews.

"Good. You will wait for the men outside of Shelbyville on the Wartrace Road, at 0600 hours on Tuesday, April eighth," said General Mitchel.

"I'll be waiting for them, General," said Andrews.

Shaking hands in mutual agreement, the men parted to partake of the delicious barbecued pork from a stolen pig, procured at gunpoint at a nearby farm. The camp menu also included some baked beans and corn. All in all, the Yanks were eating better than the Confederates.

CHAPTER 4
A DARING PLAN

P reviously, in March, 1862, under the auspices of 44-year-old General Don Carlos Buell, U.S.A., Andrews had taken eight civilian-clad Union soldiers to Atlanta to steal a locomotive, but the engineer did not show up at the rendezvous point. Of course, Andrews was chafing over the first attempt to capture a locomotive in Georgia, but since Buell had taken the rest of his troops to fight the Battle of Shiloh, General Mitchel, conveniently present, responded positively at Andrews's proposal to try again this time with more men, including two chosen engineers ready, willing, and able to effect the capture of a locomotive at Big Shanty, Georgia (now Kennesaw, Georgia).

A soon-to-be-selected Andrews raider was a Corporal William Pittenger of Joshua Woodrow Sill's Brigade of the Second Ohio Infantry in General Mitchel's Division, Company G. The mysterious disappearance of his cousin, B. F. Mills, a former messmate at First Bull Run, was a matter of such concern that curiosity drove him to ask Captain James F. Sarratt about the whereabouts of Mills, during March, 1862.

"Captain Sarratt, what happened to B. F. Mills, my cousin. I know that he and some other men have been gone for days. Did they desert or go north as spies to hunt deserters?" asked Pittenger.

"Pittenger, stay out of this. I can't say anything," said Captain Sarratt.

"Am I still being considered for promotion to sergeant?" asked Pittenger.

"Yes," replied Captain Sarratt.

Pittenger saluted and walked away, ill at ease about his cousin's safety, which overshadowed his interest in making the next rank. This Union corporal probably suspected that his cousin had been sent to spy on the Confederates.

From March to April, all Pittenger could think about was the possibility of being selected to go on a thrilling spy mission, the nature of which he would later be told. General Mitchel probably interviewed Andrews either on the evening of Sunday, April 6, 1862, or sometime before sunrise on Monday, April 7, 1862, the same time frame of the crucial battle of Shiloh in the Corinth, Mississippi area.

General Mitchel was especially receptive to Andrews's plan, since Mitchel could not tolerate the horrendous timidity and indecisive leadership of General Buell, who did not send reinforcements to Fort Donelson and to Shiloh, a battle that General

U. S. Grant almost lost, according to William Pittenger's book entitled "*IN PURSUIT OF THE GENERAL*". However, despite the lack of reinforcements, General Grant was still able to take the 15,000 square miles of targeted Shiloh real estate, with superior numbers of troops to do the job. In addition to the Confederate losses of Fort Henry and Fort Donelson, the Federals seized Island Number Ten on Tuesday, April 8, 1862. Obviously, the Union army was on a roll while in the process of driving a wedge deep into the South.

On Monday, April 7, 1862, General Mitchel selected the volunteers to participate in the famed Andrews Raid of Saturday, April 12, 1862.

Interestingly enough, the entire crew of the aborted first raid declined to volunteer for the Andrews Raid, but that fact did not deter Pittenger from walking to General Mitchel's tent to receive orders for the secret mission.

As Pittenger was walking hurriedly past rows of white tents on both sides of the grassy walkway, one soldier called out to him.

"Hey, Pittenger, how about playing a card game with us?"

"Can't do it now, guys. I'm on my way to town," said Pittenger.

"Aw, come on. You can't be that busy," said a disappointed private holding a hand of cards. "You lucky dog. We could sure use a pass, too."

Within a few minutes, Pittenger saw Sgt. Marion Ross walking toward the fringe of the camp.

"Ross, did they also give you a pass to town?" asked Pittenger.

"Yes," replied Ross.

"Are you going shopping in town?" asked Pittenger.

"Yes," replied Ross.

"What are you going to buy?" asked Pittenger.

"Clothing," replied Ross.

"Let's go together. Sounds like we'll be gone for awhile," said Pittenger.

"You too, Pittenger?" asked Ross.

"Yes, me too," said Pittenger.

Having been satisfied with Ross's answers, the two men walked away from camp toward Murfreesboro, where they saw Andrews coming out of a clothing store.

James J. Andrews was six-feet-four-inches, 33-years-old, weighed between 180 and 190 pounds. His features were distinguished: dark, gray, uncommonly attentive eyes, a healthy complexion, and a pleasantly soft, musical, even firm tone of voice, which he never raised.

Pittenger stated to Andrews, "We were told to report to you, Mr. Andrews."

"What are you talking about?" asked Andrews.

"A special assignment," said Pittenger.

"State your names, ranks, companies, regiments," said Andrews.

Pittenger said, "I'm from Second Ohio, Company G."

"I'm from Second Ohio, Company A," said Ross.

"Can't talk here. Meet me about twilight on the Wartrace Road, a mile or two away from Shelbyville. We can talk better there," said Andrews as he mounted his horse to ride out of town.

After Andrews disappeared, Pittenger buttonholed Ross. "What do you think of Andrews?"

"He appears to know what he's doing, but the secret nature of this mission really concerns me. Quite frankly, I'm scared to death," said Marion Ross.

"He's definitely a cut above the average man – he has courage. I think we can trust him," said Pittenger.

"Whatever you say, Pittenger," said Ross.

"I would stake my life on him," said Pittenger.

The men returned to their camp, wearing civilian clothing purchased in town. Curiosity swept over the men who had observed the civilian-clothing-clad men.

"Pittenger, are you being discharged?" asked one soldier.

Another soldier asked, "Are you going to spy on the enemy?"

Pittenger remained tightlipped as though he were deaf. Several minutes later, Pittenger snuck into B. F. Mill's tent.

"I don't believe this. Andrews sweet-talked you into his mission," said Mills.

"Not really. I must borrow your revolver," said Pittenger.

"You'll be sorry for doing this. It's better to be bored in camp than to volunteer for risky assignments," said Mills, frowning.

"Good-bye, B. F.," said Pittenger, upon

receiving Mills's revolver and shells before leaving cousin Mills's tent. Ambling down the street between two rows of white tents, Pittenger shook the hands of various soldiers; Captain Sarratt was especially grim-faced, unable to summon any words, believing Pittenger had already signed a death-warrant. The general consensus in camp was that the troops would not ever see him or any other volunteer again.

These soldiers had developed a common bond through memorable experiences, such as pulling guard duty in freezing temperatures, suffering facial frost while sleeping outdoors, and navigating rivers and streams on makeshift wooden conveyances.

Pittenger and Ross traveled together from the camp to a village named Wartrace on the road to Shelbyville, and suddenly a snarling dog attacked them. Ross sustained a minor leg bite and the canine also tore Pittenger's coat. Ross aimed and fired his revolver but missed the dog.

These men were the first Andrews Raiders to arrive south of Shelbyville, where the dog lived in a house located a short distance from the roadway. At twilight they doubled back, assuming they had overshot the rendezvous point, but their anxiety was relieved when they encountered from their outfit two other civilian-clad Union soldiers, who provided more accurate directions to Andrews's meeting site.

In due course, Andrews appeared and called every man present to assemble on level ground below a hilltop. In attendance were twenty-two men speaking low enough to avoid arousing suspicion in the neighborhood.

From an adjacent valley, a barking dog sounded.

"Let's move off the road, boys," said Andrews, getting up from a kneeling position. "I don't think anyone else will be coming."

A strong wind whipped through the trees surrounding the group, and a loud thunderclap with sheet lightning revealed their faces, only for a few seconds. Then all ears were attuned to Andrews.

Boys, listen up. Here's the game plan. I want you to divide up into small squads of two, three or four. Go east to the Cumberland Mountains, south to the Tennessee River. Then cross the river and board a train at Shellmound. That's the Memphis and Charleston Railroad. You must be in Chattanooga by Thursday afternoon and arrive in Marietta, Georgia Thursday evening. Be all set to go north on Friday morning. It's a very hard trip, only three days to make the southbound train from Chattanooga. You must be in Chattanooga on time or it will be too wet to plow. I can't stress that enough. Everybody will get enough travel and food money.

"Will you be traveling with us?" asked Pittenger.

"I will be using the same road as you boys, but I may be ahead or behind you, so people don't get suspicious. Remember, we will be in enemy territory," said Andrews.

"What if someone stops to question us?" asked Ross.

"I might have enough influence to spring you from jail, since I'm widely known in these parts, but do your best to keep out of trouble," said Andrews.

"What do we say if they catch us?" asked William Campbell, a renegade civilian who decided to join this risky venture with his close friend, Marion Ross.

"Tell them you didn't want to be put in a Yankee jail. You are from Fleming County, Kentucky, and you plan to join the Southern army – but only as a last resort. I need every one of you in Marietta."

"What are we supposed to do?" asked Pittenger.

This is a very dangerous mission. If anyone has any misgivings, now is the time to drop out. You won't hurt my feelings. I want totally committed men. If we succeed, the war will be over much more quickly. Remember, our mission is to isolate Chattanooga, and the only way to do that is to tear up the tracks of two different railroad lines that meet at a certain junction near Chattanooga – the Western & Atlantic Railroad and the Memphis & Charleston

Railroad. The first one runs north and south; the second runs east and west. We must also burn the bridges in North Georgia. If we succeed, we will steal the train and meet Mitchel in Chattanooga. Once Mitchel takes Chattanooga, we'll shut down the South. It will then be possible to capture East Tennessee. So, be in Chattanooga right on time to meet the five o'clock train. If you get left behind, you may find yourself on the end of a rope. We all could lose our lives.

Intermittently, Andrews tapped each squad leader on the shoulder, stating the number of men to take, so that each squad would be sufficiently spaced away from each other, during the long trek through some very rough, inhospitable terrain in Southern Tennessee.

A sudden lightning flash illuminated the faces of the last three men in the covert group, and they, like the others, kept walking on the railroad ties, which led to Wartrace, located slightly beyond the Federal perimeter guard range. Thick fog contributed to poor visibility, and the raiders lacked matches, water-proof blankets, and their most urgent need – shelter from the constant rain.

Wilson, Shadrach, and Campbell, three of the four members in Pittenger's squad, had particularly noteworthy personality traits and behaviors that perhaps influenced their roles in the Andrews Raid.

George Wilson was a 32-year-old journeyman

shoemaker, who was well-educated, well-traveled, and was a sharp-tongued, outspoken person. As a shrewd, very skillful debater, he was fearlessly quick to match words with any challenger. He was tall and slim with high cheekbones, overhanging hackles, alert gray eyes, and long, thin whiskers.

Perry G. Shadrach was a 22-year-old, heavy-set, happy-go-lucky man, with a boundless, cheerful nature; moreover, another positive attribute was his willingness to quickly forgive persons who had wronged him. He was a life-of-the-party type of person, willing to give the shirt off his back to help someone in need. He came from Pennsylvania to live in Knoxville, Ohio, to join the Second Ohio Regiment.

Third in Pittenger's squad of four men, William Campbell was a burly, 250-pound social drinker, who had the agility of a circus carney, and was a daredevil when confronting danger of any kind. He had very little fear of death. He was a civilian visiting Shadrach at the military camp, and out of curiosity and the desire for a thrill, Campbell enlisted as a volunteer in the Second Ohio Regiment. Lacking the modern effective means to conduct criminal background investigations, the Union army could not have known about Campbell's criminal record.

According to William Kerr, a very ill Ohio pension attorney, from a letter to the late Atlanta Historian, Wilbur G. Kurtz (Atlanta History Center, MSS 132, Box 1, Folder 10, dated January 3, 1904), "ill fame" described William Campbell's background. The lawyer, a resident of Irondale, Jefferson County, Ohio, wrote that Campbell had been an owner and operator of a house of "ill fame" in Louisville, Kentucky, corroborated by reports from a number of soldiers of the Second Ohio Regiment, Companies G and K, commanded by Captain David Mitchell, when the regiment was stationed there.

Moreover, Campbell allegedly knifed to death a male customer at the bad house. In essence, Campbell used the Union army as a means of refuge to avoid prosecution for homicide. Since childhood Campbell had rebelled against his mother's attempts to instill within him a strong religious training in the United Presbyterian Church. His father's anti-religious views unfavorably influenced William Campbell's life, through the neglectful, irresponsible child rearing of two wayward boys, John and William, notorious troublemakers involved in assault and battery of other children and for shooting a neighbor's dog. Perry G. Shadrach had met Campbell who managed the house, and was as evil as Campbell.

Squad after squad, the Andrews Raiders walked through incredibly thick mud and swollen creeks during virtually incessant rainfall. Suddenly, a cloudburst at Wartrace slowed their progress, and a Union sentry detained Pittenger's party under a sheltered porch, until it could be determined these men were actually Union soldiers.

THE RUNAWAY TRAIN

The messenger rode into the Second Ohio Volunteers' camp to ask Captain James F. Sarratt about the identities of the men.

"Yes, these men on your list were sent on a secret mission. That is why they are wearing civilian clothes," said Capt. Sarratt.

"Very well sir," said the messenger with a departing salute, which Captain Sarratt smartly returned.

Later, the messenger rode his horse to the porch and stated, "All right, here is a written order allowing you to leave and be on your way. Good luck, men."

"Goodbye," said Pittenger, as he led his squad away from the porch. A little while later, a cooperative horseman agreed to ferry the men separately across the river, for an unknown fee. The Duck River had crested on Tuesday night, April 8, 1862.

Later that evening, Pittenger and his squad roomed at a slave hunter's house, which was simply a rustic log cabin of notched logs held together by plenty of clay.

"Good evening, gentlemen. What can I do for you?" asked the cabin owner.

"We're from Kentucky and want to join the Southern army. We had to get away from all those Yanks," said Pittenger.

"I'm John Chase. I've been looking for some company. It sure gets mighty lonely in these parts. My wife is going to cook you men something to fill your bellies."

"That's very nice of you," said Pittenger, serving as the squad leader and spokesman.

Sitting down at the dinner table, John Chase and his wife Emma struck up a conversation. John said, "My main living is hunting runaway slaves. They ain't got no business running away from their jobs. They need to learn to be responsible people."

"The Southern people need the slaves to work the fields. If all of them leave, who will harvest the crops?" asked John Chase, making a fist with his right hand.

"Those are my exact sentiments, sir," said Pittenger. This lie about the practice of slavery gnawed at his conscience.

"My name is Emma. You men sure look real tired. Will you spend the night with us?"

"Ma'am, we would appreciate it," replied Pittenger. Ross, Wilson, and Campbell shook their heads in approval.

"I've got two extra comfortable beds, but I'm afraid somebody will have to sleep on the floor," said Emma apologetically.

"We'll be fine," said Campbell. "I'm tough enough. I can sleep anywhere."

"If you men ever see a slave running loose, let me know and I'll cut you in on some of the reward money," he said proudly.

"Thanks for the offer, Mr. Chase, but we'll be leaving for Atlanta in the morning to join up with the army. We couldn't do it half as well as you can, because we don't have any bloodhounds," said Pittenger.

"My dogs do a great job."

"I'm sure they do," said Pittenger.

After a good night's sleep, the Pittenger squad left the cabin on the morning of Wednesday, April 9, 1862. After the first hour of walking, a willing wagon driver gave them a ride for several miles – at an unknown price.

Two hours later, Pittenger's squad walked to the base of the Cumberland Mountains where a soft mist mingled with sunshine, while a large shadow came down from the mountain, ushering in some additional rain, increasing the difficulty of further vehicular travel.

At noon, the men ate lunch at a dilapidated shack. Strong pork and half-ground cornbread were the only menu items, reflecting the poverty of the occupants of the house, a family of three that included a bald, toothless, blue-eyed, 70-year-old, thin, five-foot-six-inch man; and his five-foot-two-inch, snaggle-toothed, white-haired, brown-eyed, 68-year-old woman.

"Boys, I'm sorry. This is all the food we've got. You're welcome to what we have," said the embarrassed man.

"Sir, we are grateful. There are no eating places in this neck of the woods, and so we appreciate your hospitality," said Pittenger.

"How come you're wandering around in these here hills?" inquired the householder.

"Sir, we're trying to join up with the Confederate army in Chattanooga. We left

Kentucky because the Yankees took it over," said Pittenger.

"Oh, they did, did they?" exclaimed the man of the house with surprise. Thank the Lord for brave men like y'all. We need all the men we can get, so we can lick them Yankees."

Pittenger said, "You're already making that possible – you're feeding a small part of the Southern army – by the way – the pork is very delicious and the cornbread tastes so good."

"I'm glad you boys like my food," said the woman beaming with pride.

Pittenger was the last lunch guest to finish eating. He said, "Ma'am, it's been downright nice of you to have us for lunch, and if we ever pass this way again, we'll bring you some food."

"That's right kind of you to say that," she said, revealing her missing teeth.

"We'll be going now. Thank you for everything," said Pittenger, in a folksy tone of voice.

"You're welcome," she said politely.

Down the road, as the squad was approaching the base of the Cumberland Mountains, Mark Wood, another raider, was staggering drunk, weaving from side to side, with a nearly empty bottle of apple brandy in his right hand.

"Mark, get a grip on yourself. Stay with us. We don't want you to get arrested for public drunkenness," said Pittenger.

"Ahhhh....... That ain't going to happen. I can

hold my liquor better than three Johnny Rebs," said Mark.

"I don't think so," said Pittenger, with disgust written across his bespectacled face. "You're drunk as a skunk."

At about 2 o'clock on Wednesday, April 9, 1862, the five-man squad ran into a Confederate soldier on a steep incline of the Cumberland Mountains.

"Hey, who are you guys?" asked the soldier.

"We're from Fleming County, Kentucky, and we're going to join up with the army in Chattanooga."

"Oh yeah? I'm home on leave. I fought at First Bull Run. You should have seen us beat the tar out of them Yanks. We had those Blue Bellies on the run," he said laughingly and boastfully.

Campbell said, "Too bad we couldn't have been there to lend you a helping hand. We hate Blue-Bellied Yankees, too." Annoyed, Ross elbowed Campbell to be discreet in his comments on political matters.

Stepping away from the Confederate soldier, the ill-clothed traveling Yankees noticed the tears welling up in his eyes.

"One of these days I hope and pray we'll be fighting together for the glory of the South. There is no higher cause than whipping them Yankees."

"You take care, boy. We're a-going up this slope," said Pittenger, deliberately imitating the mountain people's dialect, releasing himself from the soldier's two-handed grasp of the war correspondent's hands.

"Oh, by the way, where's a good place to sleep overnight?" asked Pittenger.

"Go to the next mountain house. A secessionist man lives there. He'll let you stay all night," said the Confederate soldier.

"Thanks," said Pittenger. Resting for two minutes, Pittenger and the four other squad members ascended the six-mile wide summit, full of young stands of pine trees.

As difficult as it was to climb the mountain, it was nonetheless a dangerous descent over steep rocks, deep gorges, and huge gullies. When the Union squad finally reached Battle Creek Valley, Pittenger met a local resident who related a story about the meaning of the valley's name.

Hill Williams, a five-foot-eight-inch, lanky, blue-eyed, blond 35-year-old farmer, saw Pittenger's squad at 300 feet.

"Howdy, men. I'm Hill Williams. What's your name?"

"Bill Pitt," said Pittenger, who was the first of the five men to introduce himself.

"What ya a-doing in these parts?"

"We're just a-passing through. We come from Kentucky to join the Southern army," said Pittenger.

"Oh, do tell. We've got to whip them Yankees. We can't let them take us over. They need to leave us alone. We weren't doing anything but minding our own business," said Williams, apparently indignant.

"What's the name of this place?" asked Pittenger.

"Battle Creek Valley," said Williams.

"Where did they get a name like that?" asked Pittenger.

"Got a few minutes?" asked Williams.

"Sure," said Pittenger.

"Two Indian tribes hated one another. One tribe attacked the other tribe's teepees and stole lots of their things. The women were not treated so good. For a while they couldn't find their clothes. Guess you know what I mean."

"Go on," said Pittenger.

"Well, the second tribe got back at the tribe that started the whole mess, but something went bad: It was foggy during the battle, and they split up their tribe and attacked each other from each side of the mountain. After the battle, they found out they had killed their own men, instead of the tribe they were mad at," said Williams, sad-faced.

"Oh, my. That is really such a very sad story," said Pittenger.

"Yeah, you could say that," said Williams.

"Hill, we had better get a-going. You take care," said Pittenger.

"Nice meeting you fellows. I look forward to seeing you again so we can talk some more. Y'all kind of take care of yourselves," said Williams, as he placed a rolled-up cigarette in his mouth and struck a wooden match to ignite the tobacco product, soon becoming a human chimney, as Pittenger looked back in disgust.

"That's one habit I don't have, thank God," said Pittenger, as the other men refrained from comment during the next three miles to stop at a secessionist's cabin, due to their extreme travel fatigue and hunger.

An hour later, knocking on the abolitionist's heavy mountain cabin door, a bearded 280-pound man curiously peered out at the approaching strangers.

"What do you want?" he said gruffly.

"We've left Kentucky. Things got crazy up there. The Yankees took over, and we had to get away. We're going to join the army in Chattanooga."

"Well, bust my buttons. You men must be tired and hungry. You've sure done a right smart lot of walking. Come in and make yourselves at home. It's not much, but we call it home."

"You are far more blessed than you realize," said Pittenger, scratching his sweaty, itchy face.

"Yes, I agree," said the male householder. My name is Abe O. Lish, and my wife is Harriet Beecher Lish."

Entering the only door to the abolitionists' cabin, the Union men were very pleased to experience once again, the touch of home and its familiar trappings: a comfortable bed and a bright, warm fire to relieve the mind of the rigors of foot travel through unfamiliar territory.

"Gentlemen, if my wife and I do nothing else, you can bet we will crusade against slavery until our dying breath," said Abe.

"And I was named after Harriet Beecher Stowe, the author of *"UNCLE TOM'S CABIN"*. In case you haven't figured it out already, my husband and I are abolitionists. We want no more slavery in this country. See that book on the shelf? That's what Harriet Beecher wrote; it sure makes good reading."

"That's very interesting, ma'am," said Pittenger. "We'll have to read a copy of it sometime."

"Mr. Pitt, you sit yourself down and just read the first chapter, so you'll get a good idea of what it's all about," she said.

"Yes ma'am, I'd like to read at least part of it. That must be your only copy," said Pittenger.

"Yes, Mr. Pitt, it took me two months to save enough butter-and-egg money to order this book, all the way from New York City," said Harriet.

That was Abe O. Lish's cue to crank up a long-winded conversation, mostly one way, about the inherent evils of slavery. His hands trembled as his emotions escalated, and sounded like a preacher fervently exhorting the elimination of slavery. The monologue lasted into the early morning hours near a very warm fireplace. Pittenger was also opposed to slavery on the grounds of its evil, immoral nature of dividing families and holding people back on account of their skin color, in denying them the right to pursue an education. Pittenger was keenly aware that a slave was counted as three-fifths of a human being.

Next morning, Pittenger led his squad to Jasper. But where was Andrews and what had he been doing?

Shortly after the roadside conference, as the last squad of raiders had walked down the Wartrace Road toward the vicinity of Manchester, Tennessee, Andrews waited fifteen minutes – long enough – so that the departing men could not determine the direction of the sound of his horse's hoofbeats. Andrews knew that the exceptionally rough terrain of the Cumberland Mountains would not be suitable for horseback travel; therefore, he would spend Monday night, April 7, 1862, in a hotel in Wartrace, take the train south to Alabama, and meet all the squads later in Jasper, Tennessee. As Andrews entered the Hotel Wartrace, he said, "Hello, Mr. Jones. I need a room for tonight only."

This was the most appropriate time to ply the contraband activity – during his absence from his fellow spies, to maintain a healthy cash flow. As things stood at this point of the mission, Andrews had distributed more than $400 in cash to the other traveling spies. However, he was almost out of cash. Hence, necessity demanded that Andrews must access his market by railroad travel, for what should be clearly logical reasons. Andrews could not tell his men that he would actually be by-passing them to earn more money to continue financing the Andrews raid, for fear of being perceived as a disorganized, weak leader.

"No problem, Mr. Andrews. Here's the key to room 13," said Mr. Jones.

"You would give me an unlucky number," said Andrews.

"Surely, it is meaningless, Mr. Andrews, but if you feel better about number 14, I will accommodate you," said Mr. Jones.

"Mr. Jones, I'd appreciate it," said Andrews, as he walked slowly down the hall to a 20-foot-square room that needed a fresh coat of paint, but due to the blockade, paint was one of many scarce items. At best, the hotel room was a short-stay arrangement.

Andrews slept soundly from 8:00 p.m. until 8:30 a.m., due to extreme fatigue from one visit to a nearby Confederate camp, where he had sold medical supplies, socks, boots, harness belt buckles, quinine, saddles, and letter-writing paper. Gradually, Andrews was re-establishing his cash flow to meet all unforeseen travel expenses, during the top-secret Georgia mission to steal a Confederate locomotive.

On Tuesday, April 8, 1862, the sun was still hidden behind the clouds, as rain continued to fall at Wartrace and throughout Tennessee and North Georgia. No respite appeared to be in sight. Eating a delicious omelet, grits, ham, and fried potatoes, Andrews was trying to determine the quantity of items to buy from the bootlegged shipment that had originated in Cincinnati, Ohio, in response to

Whiteman's telegraphed order for the goods that Andrews would be very soon picking up at the Wartrace train station, which was merely a small building thirty feet long by twenty feet wide. A small shipping-and-receiving area took up only a thirty by ten foot space in the rear of the building.

Dressed as sharply as the typical traveling businessman, Andrews was well known wherever he went to transact business in and out of Southern lines. He wore a white cotton shirt, a bow tie, wrist cufflinks, a neck scarf, a small hat, and well-shined black boots.

He warmly greeted the shipping-and-receiving clerk at the window, and paid for the freight charges. About thirty minutes later, the contraband goods were loaded into a boxcar, and Andrews's gray "company horse" was taken to a special boxcar for animals.

The train departed the Wartrace Station at 10:30 a.m., arriving later arrive in Stevenson, Alabama at 6:30 p.m. on Tuesday evening, April 8, 1862. When Andrews got off the train at Stevenson, he immediately claimed the shipped goods, rented for twenty dollars a horse-drawn wagon, and delivered the smuggled items to a Confederate camp located outside of and several miles from Stevenson.

An air of complacency seemed to permeate this sleepy railroad town, located on the Memphis and Charleston Railroad, the westerly link to Corinth, Mississippi; one of the bloodiest battles of the Civil War would be waged in the vicinity of Shiloh

Church, most commonly referred to as the Battle of Shiloh, occurring at the same time Andrews had met with his fellow spies, near the Wartrace Road at twilight on Monday, April 7, 1862.

A few miles outside Stevenson, Andrews stopped at a Confederate picket checkpoint and submitted to a routine search.

"Halt! Remain in your seat until I've checked your wagon," said a Confederate private on guard duty, closely scrutinizing the horse-drawn cargo.

"All I have are medical supplies, harness belt buckles, and personal items for sale to the troops," said Andrews.

"You are cleared to go into camp," said the guard. "You have until dark to finish your business."

"Thank you, private. I'll be through in plenty of time," said Andrews.

"See you later," he said to Andrews.

Later, at the two-story wooden hotel in Stevenson, Andrews ate a light dinner of four vegetables that included corn, peas, cabbage, fried okra, and well cooked, flavorful roast pork. He drank two cups of coffee with apple pie for dessert.

He kept to himself to avoid probing questions about his reason for traveling to this small Alabama town, as he had to be very careful to avoid detection of his true motives.

Andrews awoke Wednesday morning, April 9, 1862, at eight-thirty, promptly partaking of a breakfast consisting of three fried eggs, ham with red-eye gravy, and two plain biscuits. Naturally, he drank the finest blend of coffee for two dollars per cup at the currently inflated wartime prices, due primarily to the aggressively enforced Union Naval blockade of the Atlantic Ocean and Gulf of Mexico seacoasts. In contrast, the disguised traveling Union soldiers were struggling to complete a long journey from Wartrace to the railroad station in Chattanooga, without an inkling of the circuitous route of their leader. The main reason for his separation from the others was to quickly access his contraband market area by rail.

As the hotel restaurant waitress walked briskly toward Andrews's table to ask, "Can I get you more coffee or anything else?"

"No thank you, ma'am. I'm full," said Andrews, while glancing out of a front window at the Provost Marshal's Office of John Fults, wearing a metal badge centered on his left breast pocket. Over the years, Andrews had acquired a knack for reading lips.

John Fults was intently listening to the hotel manager, Ellis Youngblood, a 60-year-old, five-foot-eight-inch, pudgy, blue-eyed, blond man.

"Chief, I've never seen that bearded man before," said Ellis.

"Relax, Ellis, that's James Andrews. He sells bootlegged merchandise to our soldiers. He's well known throughout the South. We need him. He's all right," said the heavy-set, five-foot-eight-inch, brown-eyed, black-haired, 40-year-old law officer.

"Maybe so, but he gives me a bad feeling," said Ellis.

"Ellis, I have to have evidence to make an arrest. He has not broken any laws," said Fults.

"I can see I'm wasting my breath," said Ellis.

"Ellis, go back to work. You worry too much," said the white-haired, distinguished-looking Provost Marshal, turning around, walking toward his dusty, musty office located across the muddy street.

Suddenly, a train pulled in to stop at the Stevenson, Alabama railroad station. The passenger door flew open; an anxious, young, aggressive courier ran at breakneck speed to the newspaper office and shouted, "The Yankees are coming!"

Having just paid for a passenger ticket, Andrews was within earshot to hear the alarming news that would have a profound impact upon the Andrews Raid schedule. With perfect timing, he boarded the 8:30 a.m. eastbound train for Bridgeport, Alabama.

Quickly, he paid the livery stable attendant for all animal feed and rental fees, before riding his "company horse" to the animal transport car. Andrews was, of course, shocked at General Mitchel's quicker-than-expected eastward advancement, despite heavy, drenching torrential rains, and very muddy, almost impassable roads. Instead of asking the newspaper editor, wisdom dictated that Andrews pump the telegrapher for the needed information.

The first order of business was essentially to

keep himself alive. Even though Andrews was recognized, and for the most part, unchallenged as a traveling blockade runner, one small slip of the tongue could lead to the death penalty for spying.

Sauntering toward the telegraph office, Andrews then opened the old, heavy wooden door, whose hinges squeaked eerily like fingernails scraping an old slate chalkboard.

"Mr. Andrews, what can I do for you?" asked Joe Robinson, a five-foot-two-inch, stocky, freckled-faced husband of an expectant, five-foot-five-inch blonde, blue-eyed, 30-year-old wife of three years. His first wife had died at age twenty-two of tuberculosis, a common killer in those days, instead of heart disease and cancer.

"Joe, I need your help. I heard a courier hollering about Yankees coming. Is that true?"

"I have more than messages to prove it. General Mitchel has been spotted with an estimated 10,000 Yanks marching toward us from Huntsville," said Robinson.

"Any other news of troop movements?" asked Andrews.

"Yes, things are shaping up for a big battle near Corinth, Mississippi. General Beauregard is going to need a lot of gunpowder. I can't show you all my dispatches. I know you need to know this information because you make your living selling medical supplies and other items to the Confederate army," said Robinson.

"I appreciate the information, Joe," said Andrews.

"Anytime, Mr. Andrews. Have a good day," said Robinson.

"The same to you, Joe," said Andrews, as he walked out of the telegraph office to board the train to Bridgeport. It was Wednesday morning at nine-thirty on April 9, 1862. Anxiety was building up in Andrews's mind, as he recalled William Shakespeare's famous literary quote that "...time and tide wait for no man..." Now he realized he was swimming against the current of time, more than ever, and he did not like it at all.

Later, at twelve o'clock, the train stopped for lunch at Bridgeport, another small town on the Memphis and Charleston Railroad. Andrews ate a light lunch at a railroad café, nothing heavier than a pork sandwich. After lunch, he went to the livery stable and paid the blacksmith for re-shoeing the horses.

"Mr. Andrews, you sure do put a lot of mileage on this horse. The total comes to ten dollars – that includes horsefeed, parts and labor," said Paul Bellows, the blacksmith of Bridgeport.

"Paul, where's the nearest private ferry crossing on this side of Chattanooga?" asked Andrews.

"Take Highway Road northeast for twenty miles to Mike's Ferry. You can be there in two hours if you ride hard. I gave your horse some extra vitamins in his horsefeed. He will run like a steam engine," said Paul.

"You're all right, Paul. Just for that, I'm tipping you with five dollars."

"Thank you, Mr. Andrews. That will cover my business license renewal fee next week. You're a prince of a fellow," said Paul.

"God blesses and cares for us in mysterious and unexpected ways," said Andrews with a joyful smile.

Suddenly, a horseman ran wildly down the main street. The courier shouted, "Yankees are ten miles from Huntsville – closing in fast."

Andrews raised his eyebrows, obviously troubled.

"That don't sound good, does it Mr. Andrews?" asked Paul.

"You aren't going to feel like whistling 'Dixie' when those Yankees get here. By that time, I'll be long gone," said Andrews.

"Where are you going, Mr. Andrews?"

"Paul, I've got to make a small delivery in Jasper, Tennessee on Thursday, April tenth," said Andrews.

"Mike's Ferry is your best route to Jasper," said Paul.

"How long will it take to get to Jasper?" asked Andrews.

"Well, it's twelve-thirty now. You should be there by three-thirty. You'd better hurry. Mike may leave at four o'clock. He eats dinner early so he can go to his Wednesday night prayer meeting."

"So long, Paul. If we don't meet again, I look forward to seeing you on the other side of the Jordan," said Andrews.

THE RUNAWAY TRAIN

"May the Lord bless you, keep you, and make his face to shine upon you," said Paul.

"God bless," said Andrews, as he mounted his gray "company horse" to travel the last leg of the trip.

Arriving barely on time at three-thirty, making every movement count, the determined spy-contraband merchant struggled to meet the deadline at Mike's Ferry, where Mike Greer, the owner, was relaxing in a comfortable wooden chair on the porch of his conveniently located log cabin, while stroking his long-haired female cat named Fantasticat. Apparently frightened by Andrews's unexpected appearance, the cat sprung from Mike's lap, and jumped out the window, from the floor of the cabin.

"What can I do for you, sir?" asked the long, curly-haired, tanned, brown-eyed, bearded, 45-year-old, broad-shouldered, muscular man.

"You must be Mike," said Andrews.

"I am. I take it you want to cross the river," said Mike.

"Yes, I do. How much is the ferry ride?" asked Andrews.

"It will be five dollars for you and two dollars for your horse," said Mike.

"Here is seven dollars," said Andrews, pulling out the money from his left breast pocket.

"I've never seen you before. Where might you be going?" asked Mike.

"I'm crossing here to go to Jasper, Tennessee on business," said Andrews.

"What kind of business? If you don't mind my asking," asked Mike.

"I'm delivering medical supplies to the Confederate army," said Andrews.

"I see. You're in a good occupation...... O.K., let's cross the river," said Mike, who seemed satisfied with Andrews's answer.

After a ten-minute crossover, Andrews said goodbye and thanked Mike for the ferry ride. In two more hours, Andrews arrived in Jasper to greet the members of the lead squad, sitting inside Towns Grocery Store, talking about the current military events.

The storeowner, John Stocker, said, "Well, what have you delivered for me?"

"I have some soap, bandages, writing paper, belt buckles, and more....in my saddlebags," said Andrews.

"I don't see how you could stuff so much in those saddlebags, Mr. Andrews. You sure are amazing," said Stocker

"I learn to make do with what I have, John," said Andrews.

"What do I owe you?" asked Stocker.

"Fifty dollars," said Andrews.

"It's a deal," said Stocker, after viewing all the merchandise Andrews had quickly removed from the saddlebags. Daniel Dorsey, an ex-school teacher, looked on as Andrews completed the transaction with the storeowner. As the grocer turned his back while beginning to stock the purchased items on the shelves, Andrews motioned to Dorsey to follow the leader outside Towns Grocery Store, to converse out of earshot.

"Dorsey, I'm appointing you to pass the word around. There's a one-day delay due to bad weather. Where are the other squads?" asked Andrews.

"We're waiting for three more squads to meet us here in Jasper," said Dorsey.

"Good. Where are you guys spending the night?" asked Andrews.

"The grocer recommended the Widow Hall's Hotel. It's a place to lay your head down. Better than nothing," said Dorsey.

"Did anyone question anyone's identity?" asked Andrews.

Dorsey replied, "We all said we were from Fleming County, Kentucky, to join the Southern army."

"Sounds good. Now listen. We'll spend Wednesday night in Jasper. We will probably be in Chattanooga on Friday. In the meantime, this will give us plenty of travel time. It's the best we can do because our squads are scattered all over," said Andrews.

"Yes, Mr. Andrews, but everyone should be in Chattanooga by Thursday night," said Dorsey.

"Probably so," said Andrews.

"No matter what, we'll be staying two more nights on the road, before we can board the southbound train from Chattanooga to Marietta," said Dorsey.

"You're right," said Andrews, walking away from Dorsey to avoid answering additional questions.

It would take one day's travel from Jasper to reach Chattanooga on Thursday evening, April 10, 1862. During that very stressful time, each squad would relay the news of the travel delay to the next straggling squad, until all the raiders had received the disturbing news.

Early Thursday morning, Andrews awoke to discover that most of the squads had assembled at the Widow's Hall on Wednesday night, presenting an opportunity for their Thursday morning briefing, a critical point in the dangerous mission.

"I want one squad to stay in town until the last squad gets here. The rest of the squads will spread out – just like we started out near Wartrace (on a beautiful knoll on the Holland Farm, slightly less than two miles east of Shelbyville, near the Duck River, on present-day Tennessee Highway 64)."

No one spoke. Everyone was ready to continue the trip southward, having enjoyed the large guest room that had a very warm, desirable crackling fire providing warmth and much illumination. Located on the North side of the Tennessee River, the Widow's Hall had available two very comfortable beds located in opposite corners of the large room.

"Now there's one more item to mention: You have probably heard people in Towns Grocery talk about the Battle of Shiloh and the big Confederate victory and taking out 500 Union gunboats. Don't believe any of that nonsense. When you listen to the wrong voices, you start thinking bad thoughts." This partial gathering of risk takers shook their heads in agreement with Andrews's statement.

Pittenger said, "Mr. Andrews, we acted like we didn't know one another when we joined in singing with the old men. And get this: they thought we were just a group of country hicks who didn't know when to seek shelter from the rain."

Andrews laughed and said, "That is just as well."

Meanwhile, William Reddick and John Wollam were enroute to Jasper after spending Wednesday night at a large double house owned by a big-shot Confederate. Although this two-man squad was probably the last to reach Jasper, as soon as it made contact with the waiting squad in Jasper and learned of the delay, both squads remained a discreet distance apart, until they walked one-half mile south of the Jasper city limits, to avoid detection and apprehension.

The practice of staggering the squads was effective, but not an efficient means of movement, especially when time was of the essence.

Accompanied by a guide, Reddick and Wollam later approached a ferry crossing at the Tennessee River, where they persuaded the ferryman to direct his own sons to transport the Union men across the river, on a boat loaded with several tons of bacon for the Confederate army. It was Thursday, 2:00 p.m., April 10, 1862.

The ferryman, a husky 45-year-old, six-footer with blue eyes and a scowl on his face, agreed to allow Wollam and Reddick to cross the river.

"The law allows only ferrymen to ferry people across the river. You will have the advantage of reaching Chattanooga two days early, and it's only a half-mile walk to Shellmound. Catch the train there, and it's a short trip to Chattanooga," said the ferryman, J. B. Allums, who had a beautiful 30-year-old, five-foot-two-inch, fair-skinned, blue-eyed brunette wife who was expecting another child.

"Mr. Allums, that's great news. Thanks a lot," said Reddick.

"You tell my sons I said you can cross the river," said Allums.

In due course, Wollam and Reddick would catch up with the rest of the raiders, with the good fortune of taking the ferry and boarding a late passenger train at Shellmound. The train was actually scheduled to pick up and discharge passengers at twelve noon; but an irregularity occurred in the train schedule: Upon boarding the westbound train to the battle site at Corinth, Mississippi, Reddick and Wollam readily observed that most of the passengers were drunken Confederate regimental soldiers. Perhaps this fact accounted for the considerable delay.

Upon boarding the train at Shellmound, Tennessee, the troops courteously greeted the disguised Union men, and then a telegrapher left his booth to make an announcement.

THE RUNAWAY TRAIN

"Attention soldiers, your trip to Corinth, Mississippi has been canceled. You will report to General Danville Leadbetter for duty in Chattanooga."

"Dang, our orders have been changed," said a drunken five-foot-eight-inch, 19-year-old, brown-eyed, 180-pound private. "That don't sound too good. Something must have gone wrong at Corinth. I'll bet the Blue Bellies are going to attack Chattanooga. That must mean General Beauregard don't need us." The telegrapher had already turned his back to return to his telegraph booth, to avoid discussion of the telegraphed message from General Leadbetter's headquarters.

Murmuring soldiers were voicing their disappointment, as they had their adrenalin pumped up to engage their foes in a very challenging battle at Corinth. The new assignment probably called for protecting and defending Chattanooga from a possible attack by General Mitchel's eastwardly advancing troops. Mitchel had considered the conquest of Eastern Tennessee as the top regional military priority.

While the raiders caught separate trains at Shellmound, General Mitchel had rolled into Huntsville, Alabama with 5,000 troops. Each Union soldier carried forty rounds of ammunition with a haversack full of rations consisting of sugar, salt, and crackers. It was absolutely important to maintain a dry, loaded musket and ammunition throughout the march on extremely muddy roads, impeding the movement of cannons, horses and wagons. In two days, Mitchel's troops had covered twenty-seven miles from Shelbyville to Fayetteville in Tennessee, as skirmishers and cavalrymen rode some distance ahead to provide protection for the rest of the invaders.

Mitchel assigned one brigade to remain at Fayetteville to guard stored wagons and baggage. The two invading brigades slept until noon, while another brigade chose to march much longer – until nightfall, when they wisely slept on their muskets, without attracting attention with a campfire or pitching tents. The Federal seizure of Huntsville was at hand, as the weather turned dry and windy.

At the same time, in Chattanooga, all of the Andrews Raiders had finally assembled on Thursday night, April 10, 1862, when Andrews shook hands with the last of the stragglers.

All twenty-two raiders lodged with two very sick Confederate soldiers suffering from malnutrition, extreme fatigue, high fever, and extreme thirst. Even though a card attached to a bell on the doorknob specified that a twenty-five cent charge for each water request would be collected, the raiders willingly contributed generously on behalf of the seriously ill Confederate troops, out of a humanitarian gesture. Nevertheless, it was necessary to ring the bell a number of times to address the patients' insatiable needs for water. The two sick men were touched by the raiders' compassion and wanted so much to reciprocate the favor.

THE RUNAWAY TRAIN

The Union spies spent the morning sightseeing Chattanooga. Among the attractions were the commissary and ordnance departments of the Confederate Army. Later in the morning on Friday, April 11, 1862, all the men, a few at a time, visited a photograph gallery to see an artist use a pen knife to make a picture frame from a wooden cigar box.

"You are a resourceful person," commented William Pittenger, who observed with great interest, as the artist was carefully making a wooden picture frame.

"Heck, the dadburn enemy blockade keeps me from getting frames, so I have to be my own factory," said the picture frame maker.

"Even so, you're doing a very good job," said Pittenger. "Do you think you'd have time to make me a picture frame?"

"Sir, I'm making this frame for Mrs. Swims – you know – the jailer's wife down at the Swims Jail."

Pittenger shuddered on the inside. He did not relish the idea of doing time in a Confederate jail. As far as he was concerned, to be killed in battle would be much more honorable than to rot in a penal institution, such as the notorious Andersonville, Georgia Prison, where countless thousands died from disease, abuse, neglect, and starvation.

CHAPTER 5
TO HIJACK A TRAIN

All twenty-two Andrews Raiders boarded a southbound train for Marietta, Georgia on Friday, April 11, 1862, at 5:30 p.m., as the sun was sinking lower toward the horizon. Many of the passengers were Confederate soldiers who had been drinking too much brandy, as evidenced by the slurring of their words coupled with befuddled thinking.

Lost in thought while sitting on the uncomfortable engine's coal box, Pittenger reflected upon fond memories of having sat with old friends gathered around a bright, crackling campfire. Perhaps he would not ever again see his friends, in the light of the uncertain outcome of the top secret mission into Georgia.

Nestled among the majority of the train passengers, the Union spies concentrated their energies on listening to the drunken chatter, about individual war experiences and how badly the Southern troops had defeated the Union troops at

Shiloh. After a while, the "Foreigners" were tired of hearing the drivel, which was sharply interrupted by the booming voice of the conductor: "Dalton. Twenty minutes for supper."

Andrews noticed that no security personnel stood guard at the locomotive. He readily assumed this to be a uniform transportation practice throughout the South. However, he noticed a telegraph office at Dalton, where a locomotive theft would be unthinkable. Two additional characteristics of the Western & Atlantic Railroad strategically linking Atlanta to Chattanooga, were the slow traveling speed of 15 to 18 miles per hour and the one-way track, controlled by a switchman in each rail-connected town.

After all the passengers and crew had eaten their meals, the conductor checked all the new passenger tickets, mailbags, and carry-on baggage.

Standing erect at the entrance to the passenger cars, the conductor said good naturedly, "You people are causing my ticket puncher to work too hard."

One Confederate soldier quipped, "We thought you looked like you needed a job."

"If it wasn't for this war, they wouldn't have hired me," said the 25-year-old conductor with a hearty laugh. The conductor had blond hair, blue eyes, and stood at five-feet-eight inches. "All right...All aboard."

Among the returning Union spies was Robert Buffum, a small, agile man, who preëmpted a seat on the train by sneaking under a Confederate officer's arm.

"Now, if I didn't know any better, I'd say that was a Yankee trick," said the officer to the Massachusetts native.

Momentarily, across the aisle, William Pittenger decided to move from the top of the coal box to a comfortable passenger seat, while the misbehavior had diverted the attention of the other passengers. A concerned conductor then said, "Behave yourselves. We still have a long ride."

"Listen up fellows. I'm going to follow our conductor's advice. I have a letter I think you're going to like," said a bearded Confederate sergeant with a wide grin on his swarthy-complexioned, dirt-caked face. He was a portly 200-pounder with gray hair, about 40 years old, and was five-feet-eleven-inches tall.

"Everybody be quiet. It's a letter from his son on the battlefield," said the small, thin private seated to Sgt. Bailey's left.

Sgt. Bailey began talking about the letter. "My son sent me this letter. He writes that he hopes to stay in good health, so he gets to kill a Yankee or two at least." Laughter ensued in the passenger cars, but none of the disguised Union soldiers smiled.

Now, get this. He wants me to tell his brother John to send his old picture to keep the mosquitoes away from his tent. He writes: 'they pester me powerfully.' Also, my son had to march to join Stonewall Jackson's Army. 'Several men got wounded and two were killed.' My son was unhurt, but listen to the way he put it: 'But it looks like a miracle that I did not get killed, for the bullets come as thick as hail and out whistled anything I ever heard; Pa, we whipped the Yankees clear out and continually have whipped them every fight....for six days.....we charged a Yankee battery in this forest....our regiment fared very well....getting blankets to sleep on. The Yankees run off and left knapsacks, blankets, oil cloths and everything used about a campfire....'

An unidentified private crowed, "Your son got a big dose of fighting. Now he knows what it's like to be shot at."

"That's my boy," said Sgt. R. J. Bailey, Sr.

"They done a right smart job of running them Yankees off," said the unknown private.

"Yep, Johnny Rebs rule. Yankees drool," said Sgt. Bailey with a proud, triumphant look on his dirty, sweaty face, overgrown with facial hair and a smelly cigar hanging out of his mouth. The conductor was obviously pleased with the reading of a battlefield letter, which seemed to soothe the traveling beasts, riding on a train that would be stopping at several small towns along the way to Atlanta. However, the spies would keep their radar focused on every little jot and title while passing through each of the towns, including Marietta, their final southerly destination.

A few miles back in Dalton, a puzzled, young, blue-eyed, blond, 22-year-old, six-foot-two-inch, stout young man was meditatively sipping a cup of coffee in Susan's Café, attached to the train station. He was seated with the ticket agent, a bespectacled, bewhiskered, five-foot-two-inch, 150-pound, square-jawed, snaggle-toothed man, who had just reached his sixtieth birthday and fortieth wedding anniversary within the previous two months.

The telegrapher, Edward Henderson, said to John Squeakly, the ticket agent, "I can't put my finger on it, but there's something odd about those strange civilians on that southbound train."

"What do you mean, Edward?" asked Squeakly.

"In the first place, they don't look like or talk like anybody around here. Secondly, why weren't they in uniform?" asked Edward.

"Well, they just look like a bunch of country fellows out for a train ride," said John Squeakly.

"John, I have my doubts. Something tells me they are up to no good," said Henderson.

"Oh, you're letting your imagination run wild," said Squeakly.

Henderson said, "One of them was a big man and his coat was open – a revolver was behind his belt. It was no ordinary revolver. I know weapons very well. That looked like a northern-made revolver."

THE RUNAWAY TRAIN

"You know, come to think of it, that was the same heavy-set man wearing a pair of fancy boots. I know darn good and well those cottonpicking boots were not manufactured in the South," said Squeakly.

"Confound it! I'd be willing to bet my paycheck those were Yankee spies; and if they are, I believe we will see them again or hear something bad about them," said Henderson.

"Edward, have you been drinking? That's silly," said Squeakly.

"You can't change my mind. It's made up," said the young telegrapher.

"That's what your mama always said about you. When your mind is made up, that's it," said John Squeakly, in his high effeminate voice.

"You mark my words. Someday security will be tightened, but it'll happen only when we lock the barn after the horses are stolen," said Henderson, as he gulped down some more coffee in his northern-manufactured coffee mug. Lying on the table beside the cup was a silver spoon imprinted with the following information: "made in Chicago." Henderson dozed off for a brief nap, and the ticket agent wisely slipped out of his New England-made chair, to return to his upright wooden booth to count all the money.

Farther south, the locomotive and passenger train had discharged and picked up passengers at Tilton, Resaca, Calhoun, Adairsville, and was getting ready to pull in at the railroad station in

Kingston at 10:30 p.m., on Friday, April 11, 1862.

"Kingston," announced the conductor, while stepping forward to the train door. The train gradually coasted to a steam-escaping stop.

In a livery stable in Chattanooga, Andrews had left the "company horse" in the care of an attendant, until the spy leader and blockade runner would perhaps return to that Confederate-defended city, upon the anticipated successful completion of the Andrews Raid.

The ringleader had carried with himself saddlebags full of undisclosed items, not excluding the possibility of substantial cash from his employer, to buy contraband items for resale to both opposing armies. Perhaps $10,000.00 in Confederate money comprised the bulk of the saddlebag contents, but no hard evidence or testimony has surfaced to confirm or deny the theory. In any case, Andrews chose the saddlebags to be part of his carry-on baggage. Logic would also suggest that Andrews could have stored his costume inside the saddlebags until he wore it on Saturday morning, at the beginning of the hijack of the locomotive "General", and throughout the 87-mile chase in the mountains of North Georgia.

The Kingston, Georgia train depot was a stone-and-wood building, with dimensions of sixty feet long and twenty feet wide, and a wooden platform surrounded this building. The ticket agent's office was situated on the north end of the building, and the passenger waiting room made up the other half of the northern portion of the depot. A ticket window was accessible between the agent's office and the waiting area. On all four sides of the train station, was a roof that overhung the platform. Wooden steps extended there to four-and-one-half feet downward to the ground level from the northern side of the platform. As a matter of interest, the Kingston railroad yards were constructed to run in a different direction, from west to east, even though the general direction of the Western & Atlantic Railroad was a single-track line running directly north and south. State militiamen would regularly conduct close-order drill on a vacant lot located perhaps one-quarter mile to one-half of one mile northwest from the depot, and was in a slightly northeasterly position from the fork in the tracks, where the Rome Railroad initiated its westward direction toward Rome, Georgia. Most likely, Andrews did not see any signs of militia presence at this point in his trip south to Kennesaw, then known as Big Shanty. So far, so good; circumstances for train thievery seemed to be favorable.

Pittenger drifted off to sleep shortly after the southbound train pulled out of the Kingston railroad station. Confederate soldiers were noisily snoring to the rhythmic train wheel motion, as the darkened passenger cars slowly traveled through the hills of North Georgia, later crossing the Etowah River Bridge; and to its left, on the north side of the river, was a railroad spur track that led conveniently straight to the Cooper Iron Works, the manufacturer of Confederate cannons. Whether or not Andrews was aware of this factory is anyone's guess; but in any case, his planned destruction of the fifteen Chickamauga River bridges, located further north in Georgia, including the strategic severance of telegraph wires and the timely lifting of rails, preventing the railway shipment of cannons, cannon balls, powder, and other essential supplies for the Confederate defense of Chattanooga, an indisputably vital railway link to the Eastern and the Western fronts of the Confederacy.

Andrews looked at his expensive pocket watch attached by a chain to his belt. It was 11:20 p.m., on Friday, April 11, 1862. Most of the passengers, including all of the onboard Confederate soldiers were very much absorbed in dreamland. However, Andrews could not sleep much due to the anxiety of the uncertainty of the secret mission's outcome. While passing south at this time, he heard the conductor shout, "Big Shanty. Fifteen minutes." That was everyone's cue to go to the outhouse, as sanitary facilities did not exist on trains in those days. The outhouses at the Lacy Hotel in Big Shanty had no blinds. The following information about the Lacy Hotel was submitted by Mrs. J. B. Sewell of Atlanta as told to Atlanta Historian Wilbur G. Kurtz, Sr. (Notebook #2, MSS 730, Atlanta History Center). Her father, George M. Lacy, managed the hotel whose previous owner was Lem Kendrick and Miss Sallie Kilby, the previous manager, under a lease from 1859 to June, 1864.

The features of the hotel included wooden shutters for each window, a picket fence built around the side and front of the house, and a fence of horizontal boards at the rear lot. Located north of the hotel were freight cars full of commissary supplies. The Lacys kept some ducks in a low ground area of standing water between a short railroad spur line and a fence. Spanning each side of a picket fence was a long plank bench for train passengers or guests. Railroad employees and others washed their hands in pans supported by a wooden plank between porch columns. Cloth towels were placed on rollers, one on each side of the front door.

"All aboard!" shouted the conductor, as the wheels spun on the track for a few seconds, before taking off from Big Shanty Station. Presently, back in Dalton, 17-year-old Edward Henderson, the telegrapher, was still thinking about the civilian-clad young men. Were they actually soldiers on leave or deserters? Or could these men be a threat to the security of the South? He could not dismiss the strangers from his mind, nor could he provide proof of suspected wrongdoing.

Farther south, the train blew its final whistle signifying its approach to the Marietta train depot. Andrews and the other spies deboarded the train, while acting as though none of these men had ever met one another. It was 12:01 a.m., Saturday, April 12, 1862. Still very tired, the men walked toward the Fletcher House to register as one-night-only guests. The hotel clerk, a five-foot-six-inch, 50-year-old man, who walked with a slight limp, was puzzled that none of these guests had brought any suitcases, except for Andrews's saddlebags. Such irregularities aroused the clerk's curiosity, but he tried not to give himself away.

Looking condescendingly at the men, the clerk said, "I can rent you six single rooms. I trust this will be satisfactory. Oh, y'all are all together, right?"

Andrews replied, "We want to see what Atlanta is like. We never have been anywhere except our little hometown."

"I know you'll like the big room down the hall. Here is your key. Oh, I'll have to put two of you in the hotel down the street. Someone will take them to it."

"Thank you, sir," replied Andrews with a smile, as he led his men toward the hotel room.

As the last man closed the door to the room, Campbell remarked, "I'm glad we're staying only one night in this flea bag. We have real decent hotels where I come from."

"Shh! Don't talk too loud. Walls have ears," admonished Andrews. "Boys, I suggest we turn in right away. Tomorrow is going to be a long day. You'll need your rest," added Andrews.

John R. Porter, the second engineer, and Martin J. Hawkins, slept at 46-year-old Henry Greene Cole's Marietta Hotel, located south of the town square, where William Knight and Wilson Brown also spent the night. Cole assisted his civil engineer superior, Stephen H. Long, in laying out the track of the Western & Atlantic Railroad. Both the Marietta Hotel and the Fletcher House were Northern-owned.

The desk clerk crisply said, "For one night, each person pays five dollars. Wake up service is two dollars extra." No one responded since their cash flow had unfortunately run low. Perhaps Andrews was the only spy who was still well-heeled.

During the short night of sleep, Andrews could not sleep at all. In the back of his mind, the unexpected one-day delay made him uneasy, but it was too late to back out of his commitment to steal a Confederate locomotive. Andrews might have been secretly meeting with Cole for a few minutes while the other Andrews Raiders slept, since both were staunch Unionists. However, no documentary exists to corroborate the fact.

At 5:30 a.m., darkness still hung over the land, as Andrews and his fellow roommates were getting ready to check out of the Fletcher House (now the Kennesaw House, a museum) to board at the adjacent track, William A. Fuller's northbound passenger freight and mail train, originating at 4:00 a.m. in Atlanta, almost thirty miles south of Big Shanty. This train was the steam-powered locomotive known as the "General", manufactured in Patterson, New Jersey, by Rogers, Ketchum & Grosvenor, at a cost of $8,850.

The spies held a brief conference at Andrews's bed, which he would share with three others. At the same moment, Porter and Hawkins were still asleep in their separate hotel room. Within a few more minutes, they would be left behind in Marietta, while sleeping off their extreme travel fatigue, but their failure to wake up on time to meet the train would come back to haunt them.

Perhaps it was not in Andrews's nature to conduct head counts, for he had not rendered one at the secret rendezvous point near the Wartrace Road in Tennessee; nor did he ever physically account for his men at any other time, during the trip from Shelbyville to Chattanooga. Why was he like this? Andrews believed in voluntary participation – not coercion – in the commission of a high-risk plot to steal a locomotive behind enemy lines. As the train left Marietta, Georgia, the two left-behind men decreased the number to twenty participants. Even though Porter and Hawkins ran as fast as their legs could carry them, it was a bitter pill to swallow as they reluctantly watched the "General" fade away northward behind the first bend in the W&A single track.

Upon rising from the hotel bed, Andrews quickly opened his saddlebags, from the left side of the bed, from which he grabbed to don the costume. The costume included the following items: a hat with a wide bell crown and a distinct brim; a blue-black overcoat two inches below the knees; a cape extending below the elbow, perhaps as low as the waist; a top button near the collar; a frock coat located within four inches of his knees; a slightly low-cut vest that was cut square in the front; a watch; ordinary cut of lapels on the coat; the bottom of the coat cut square in the front.

At the time of the Andrews Raid, James J. Andrews had black hair and a mustache, in addition to the detailed preceding description of his costume.

"Boys, listen to me. You are to buy tickets to separate towns so people don't get suspicious. Pittenger, your ticket is to Ringgold. Ross, your ticket is to Dalton....." said Andrews, as he continued to assign various ticket destinations to his men. His face drawn taut, he added, "When we get to Big Shanty, wait until the train is empty. Then we'll disconnect the cars from the engine. Remember there is a military camp across from the eating place. Be quick when I give you the signal to go into the boxcars. The engineers will join me in the cab. Any questions?"

Ross commented, "I have a bad feeling. We're one day late. I don't believe we can do this. Those troops will get us."

"Boys, I messed up once. This time we will do it right – or else I'll leave my bones in the South," said Andrews.

Ross said, "Well, since you put it that way, we have no choice." One could have heard a pin drop in the hotel room, as Andrews kept a stern, uncompromising expression on his face.

Picking up his saddlebags, Andrews said,

"Boys, check your revolvers. This is our only shot for the Union. We must not fail." All the disguised Union troops followed Andrews to check out at the hotel desk. Within a few minutes, the men saw a freight and passenger train, the "General", arriving at the Marietta train depot at 6:00 a.m.

The locomotive "General" performed its first run on the railroad in January, 1856, as a freight hauler, and during the Civil War this iron horse hauled essential supplies upon which the lifeblood of the Confederacy very much relied. According to the Atlanta newspaper, the "Southern Confederacy", Saturday, April 12, 1862, a 138-mile train ride from Atlanta to Chattanooga cost five dollars. Andrews probably funded the train rides for an estimated $180.00, not including food, lodging and miscellaneous travel expenses, which could have been an additional 440 dollars that Andrews distributed in twenty-dollar increments, during the secret rendezvous on Wartrace Road in Tennessee at the outset of the daring mission.

Sometime around 3:30 a.m., William Allen Fuller, a five-year Western & Atlantic Railroad career employee, walked briskly from a rented room of the Washington Hotel, following gas light poles down Lloyd Street in downtown Atlanta, arriving at the Car Shed, a 400-foot long red brick railroad depot, where he conducted a pre-trip maintenance check of the "General", before embarking upon another of many previous runs to and from Chattanooga, Tennessee. Fuller had bettered himself through diligent work habits that advanced him from train hand up the rung of the corporate ladder to the position of brakeman, until he became a conductor, which involved a detailed job description of multiple demanding administrative functions such as, being responsible for keeping good accounting records of business transactions. This railroad job was a far cry from working on a cotton farm in Henry County, Georgia before moving to Atlanta, a city of nearly 10,000 people.

What was Fuller's personal appearance and dress? He was within three days of his twenty-sixth birthday, standing five-feet-ten and one-half inches, weighing 169 pounds, and had black hair cut long and down to the collar. He was attired in a blue cloth cutaway coat with metal buttons, and a dark plush vest that was double-breasted with a ruffled linen shirt bosom. The coat was blue-black, and the lower front of the coat was cut rounding – thus, the vest was cut low. He wore a necktie and a very colorful shirt full of light, pink-colored, one-quarter-inch checkered squares alternated with black squares.

Rain was sporadic in various towns along the road on Saturday morning, April 12, 1862. William A. Fuller grabbed hold of the chain attached to his large, heavy pocket watch hidden in his left vest pocket. Later he sold the watch to an African-American barber named Peter Perkins. Fuller also wore a soft hat, not a broad-brimmed hat, and his knee boots extended up slightly below the knee, always wearing trousers outside of the heavy thick-soled boots.

Engineer E. Jefferson ("Jeff") Cain and conductor William A. Fuller were the keepers of the engine "General". Cain was a Pennsylvania-born 35-year-old man, appearing to be in ill health. He had a thick mustache and very large ears. Also on board was 32-year-old Anthony Murphy, foreman of Machine and Motive Power of the Western & Atlantic Railroad, who had the responsibility to evaluate an engine, designed to furnish sufficient power to cut wood and pump water for the locomotives at Allatoona, a very small town located forty miles north of Atlanta. Murphy had made sure that the "General" had received a thorough servicing prior to this run.

According to the Atlanta Office of Roadmaster report of October 1, 1866, both the "General" and the "Texas" had four cylinders that were fifteen feet in diameter, and their cylinder strokes were twenty-two feet. Each cylinder displaced five quarts per inch, requiring an enormous amount of oil for lubrication to handle the tremendous friction of the wheels against the tracks. As for energy needs, a cord of wood would last about one hundred ten and one-half miles; thirty-four miles to one pound of waste.

In contrast to these engines, the "Yonah" had a smaller cylinder diameter of twelve feet and a smaller stroke of eighteen feet, simply because the "Yonah" was manufactured for use as a short-distance hauler of manufactured Confederate cannons from the Etowah Iron Works, along a spur track to the main railroad. The "Yonah" was put on the Road in April, 1849, while the "Texas" was slightly younger than the "General", with the initial run date of October, 1856.

After a short wait at the Marietta depot, all the raiders boarded the train as William A. Fuller punched each passenger's ticket. Curiosity must have shown on Fuller's face, as he had not ever seen so many civilian-clad young men of military age on one train at one time. He initially thought these were just country boys taking a train ride solely for the sake of enjoyment.

Fuller looked perhaps cautiously at the Andrews Raiders, but he did not question or challenge the men. Andrews was familiar to Fuller, who did not know Andrews by name, but only as a frequent passenger evidently dressed as a businessman engaging in seemingly lawful activities.

Soon, Fuller shouted, "Big Shanty. Twenty minutes for breakfast." At deboarding time, probably at 6:30 a.m., no rain was falling at Big Shanty, but some rain probably fell one-half hour afterwards and became a harder rainfall at Kingston, north of Big Shanty, where the ground was very wet and sticky, due to the intrinsically present limestone mud. Since daybreak, the weather had been damp and misty at Big Shanty.

The passengers leisurely filed into the restaurant inside the Lacy Hotel in Big Shanty, as Fuller seated himself to partake of a breakfast consisting of eggs, grits, butter and sorghum on pancakes, biscuits with gravy, and hot coffee. Joining the conductor at his table were Anthony Murphy, Fuller's immediate supervisor, and the engineer, E. Jefferson ("Jeff") Cain.

"Mr. Fuller, Mr. Cain, and Mr. Murphy, how are y'all?' asked the five-foot-two-inch, brown-eyed, brunette, named Cindy Lou Jones, a personable 18-year-old waitress.

"We're fine, Cindy Lou," said Fuller as his colleagues nodded their heads affirmatively.

"Enjoy your breakfast, gentlemen," she said, with a friendly smile and a well-executed curtsy, as she shifted her eyes toward Corporal Henry Whitley, who was walking his beat along the eastern edge of Camp McDonald, only fifty feet from the "General" and its passenger cars. Moreover, many white tents dotted the landscape along with 3,000 troops, three parade grounds, stables, a corn field, a garden, and a small military hospital.

Meanwhile, outside the restaurant, Andrews said to Knight, "Uncouple here and stand by." While disconnecting the three boxcars from the first passenger car, Knight adroitly removed the pin and carefully laid it on the draw bar. Andrews made sure the track was clear of southbound trains, since the W&A Railroad was single track – one way only.

Returning to the passenger car, Andrews said, "Now." Going directly in front of Andrews, Knight jumped into the engine, cut the bell rope, and grasped the throttle bar. His body stood rigidly in a forward-leaning position while concentrating his attention on Andrews, who grasped the upright railing with one hand as he watched his men run forward.

Brown, the second engineer, and fireman Alf Wilson, hurried to join Knight on the engine, and at the same time, the other men climbed up and into the breast-high rear boxcar.

"Get in-get in-move it," demanded Andrews in his high, melodious voice, as he ascended the steps into the engine cab. Steam rushed out as Knight opened the valve. The wheels slipped on the track, grabbed the rails, and instantly the "General" took off like a bullet toward a defined target – Chattanooga.

"No more playing Reb, boys. We are Yankees for real – now and forever," declared Dorsey.

"Not so fast, Dorsey. We're not home free yet," said George D. Wilson, with a stiff upper lip and a tight jawline.

Andrews remarked, "Can't this train go any faster?"

"We were in such a hurry to get started that I forgot to close the dampers," said Knight.

"Knight, do what it takes to speed it up. We have a long way to go," said Andrews.

Meanwhile, everyone at the Big Shanty depot was shocked beyond belief at the sight of a locomotive hijacking, a most unimaginable event that had not ever crossed the minds of the railroad officials. The young sentry shouldered a "Joe Brown" Pike while staring blankly at Andrews, who was only fifty feet away from the basic trainee.

Fuller raised his eyebrows, as his mouth flew open and said, "They're stealing my train." It is doubtful that the sentry could have stopped the train thieves, even with a loaded musket.

Suddenly, Fuller rose from his chair, leaving behind his warm twenty-five-cent breakfast. The determined conductor dashed on foot down the tracks, as Cain and Murphy followed Fuller to the trackside and helplessly saw the engine and the three attached boxcars vanish around a distant curve. After a brief discussion, Fuller initiated and sustained a two-and-one-half mile run, despite the very thick limestone mud. The surprise train theft had left disappointed, angry passengers standing, after having sat down to eat breakfast at the Lacy Hotel's restaurant, while other onlookers were laughing and jeering at the three railroad officials running after a speeding locomotive under seemingly insurmountable odds of recovery.

A 22-year-old woman named Peggy Sue Blinker stormed into the restaurant. She wore a cabriolet bonnet, which was a flared brim bonnet named after the carriage called Coal Scuttle Bonet. She had donned a bodice, a corset-like, fitted portion of a dress spanning the area from the waist to the upper chest. This clothing item was sometimes secured up and down the back with hooks and eyes and boned

THE RUNAWAY TRAIN

in front. A bertha, a frilled and ribboned border, covered the sleeves and fell over the top of her bodice. To round out her dressy appearance, under her short skirt, she wore frilled trousers gathered about the ankles, popularly known as bloomers in the 1860's fashions.

Swinging her caba (small handbag) in a circular manner, she said: "I have never seen such an awful thing like that happen in all my life, Miss Sallie Mae."

"What do you mean, Peggy Sue?" asked Sallie Mae Jones.

"Why, the train was stolen. What else could I be talking about?" said Peggy Sue, somewhat irritated.

"Calm down, sweetie. Our men in gray will catch them rascals just as sure as shootin'," said Sallie Mae.

"Did you see those railroad men run after that train?" asked Peggy Sue.

"I was standing right here with a pile of dirty dishes in my hands. I sure hate to see some of this food go to waste, but I know them train men ain't coming back today. That Mr. Fuller ran like a bull down that track. He'll see to it he gets his train back. Mark my words," said Sallie Mae.

"It makes me so darn mad. I'd shoot those thieves – if I only had a pistol," said Peggy Sue.

"Peggy Sue, I know what's eating you. You wanted to go visit your boyfriend in Chattanooga," said Sallie Mae.

"How'd you guess?" asked Peggy Sue.

"I was once as young as you. I was a Mexican War Bride in 1845. We had to wait to get married until my man got back from the war. Believe me, Peggy Sue, I've been there and done it," said Sallie Mae.

"I'm glad you understand….May I have a mint julep?" asked Peggy Sue.

"Yes you may, my dear. Today it's on the house," said Sallie Mae.

"Oh, how sweet of you, Sallie Mae," said Peggy Sue.

"Just enjoy your mint julep," said Sallie Mae.

While the running trio was forging ahead, inside the Lacy Hotel, the cashier was trying to regain her composure.

"Cindy Lou, I'm shaking so bad my nerves are on edge. Whoever stold [sic] our train must be Yankees. Nobody else would have dared to do a thing like that," said Sallie Mae, the attractive five-foot-five-inch, square-jawed, 29-year-old blonde, blue-eyed, 200-pound restaurant manager. "Please pour me another cup of coffee to settle me down."

"Yes ma'am. Coming up," replied Cindy Lou, the waitress.

Slogging through the limestone mud on the main dirt street of Big Shanty, was the Chief of Police, James Smith, a six-foot-tall, wiry, 170-pound, blue-eyed, long-faced man with a handlebar mustache.

"What's going on, Sallie Mae?"

"Chief Smith, some men done stold our train," said Sallie Mae.

"No, you've got to be kidding," he said.

"No sir. Mr. Fuller, Mr. Cain, and Mr. Murphy done took off running like wart hogs down the track after the train," said Sallie Mae.

"Where's Lem Kendrick?" asked Chief Smith.

"He's down at the feed store, I think," said Sallie Mae.

"Thanks. I'll find him," said Chief Smith.

Stepping out of the restaurant of the Lacy Hotel, Chief Smith spotted the young former owner of the eating and lodging establishment.

"Lem! Come here," said Chief Smith.

Lem Kendrick placed a large bag of horsefeed on his horse-drawn wagon and walked briskly toward Chief Smith.

"Yes sir. What can I do for you?" asked Lem.

"Lem, did you hear the train was stolen?" asked Chief Smith.

"Well, I heard a commotion and some yelling. How did it happen?" asked Lem.

"Some of our soldiers from Camp McDonald probably ran off with the train just to get away from military service," said Chief Smith.

"What do you want me to do, Chief?"

"Saddle up a horse at the livery stable. You're riding a City horse to Marietta. Find a telegraph operator and send this written message to Kingston. Whoever those train thieves are, we must catch them."

"Consider it done, Chief. See you later," said Lem.

"I'll be waiting to hear from you," said Chief Smith to Lem, who then spurred his fresh horse down the main street, leaving horseshoe imprints in the mud.

People were still milling around at the train depot in a state of shock and disbelief. The men wore stylish 1860's clothing as follows: boiled shirts, bowler hats (formal stiff felt hats with narrow brims and round crowns), brogans (heavy high-ankle work shoes), and frock coats, made to look very much like the military coats, extending downward to the knees.

"What is this world coming to?" asked Jimmy Watson, a frustrated barber taking an outdoor cigar-smoking break.

Alvin Formwalt had come into Big Shanty to get a haircut, then smoked a cigar with the barber, following the haircut.

"Mr. Watson, I think that train theft is an omen of more bad things to come to the South. I wouldn't be at all surprised if those men were Yankees. I don't think they were deserters. There's more to this thing than meets the eyes," said Formwalt.

"You could be right. Only time will tell," said Watson.

Meanwhile, seven miles south in Marietta, John R. Porter and Martin J. Hawkins had awakened from a deep night's sleep. They had overslept, missing the train ride to Big Shanty. It was 7:00 a.m.

What should they do?

Rubbing his eyes, Porter said, "We're going to get caught. Here we are in enemy country and we're stranded and almost broke. We're going to stick out like a sore thumb."

"I'm an experienced engineer. Andrews sorely needed me on that train. I can't figure out why one of the men didn't come wake us up. It doesn't make sense," said Hawkins.

"Let's go eat breakfast before we figure out how to get back to Tennessee," said Porter.

All of the raiders were registered guests under assumed names at the Fletcher House, a hotel situated about fifty feet from the Marietta train depot. The raiders could easily look out of a window, since the three-story brick hotel directly faced the railroad track, to enable them to watch for the incoming 5:15 a.m. train to pull in to the Marietta train depot.

"I think I know why we got left behind," said Hawkins, while walking side-by-side with Porter on the stairwell leading to the first floor.

"Why?" asked Porter.

"Nobody wanted to wake us up," said Hawkins, not thinking that the time spent in sending someone to awaken and get Porter and Hawkins, could have resulted in a missed train, leaving behind more men.

"Hawkins, you're probably right. But I have to be blunt. We failed to pay the clerk to wake us up," said Porter. "We must own up to our actions."

"I agree, but I guess I thought the train whistle would have waked us up," said Hawkins.

Porter said, "And that's why Andrews didn't bother to come check on us. He assumed we would hear the whistle blow," said Hawkins, noticeably wearing a hangdog look on his face.

"It doesn't matter now. We are definitely in a very bad situation," said Hawkins.

Fifty feet away from the Fletcher House, station manager Clarence Bilbo was tallying up the purchased tickets and noticed a shortage of two tickets, an unusual occurrence in a small town such as Marietta. Scratching his head, curiosity gnawed at him.

Clarence reviewed the passenger head count sheet made by conductor William A. Fuller. Clarence's pupils enlarged as he perceived the obvious disparity in the head count and the punched ticket count, which meant that two passengers had failed to board the train to Big Shanty. Clarence wanted to know why, and he was determined to carry out his investigation to the "nth" degree.

Meanwhile, Lem Kendrick's horse was struggling through the wet limestone mud amid a very light rainfall and an overcast sky. The church steeple was coming into full view as Kendrick drew closer to downtown Marietta. Axes were swinging at 7:30 a.m. to chop wood to provide for cooking and heating needs. Neighborhood women were boiling their family clothes in huge outdoor cauldrons, and were occasionally stirring homemade soap with long wooden paddles, some of which were scratched, pitted, or splintered due to years of constant use. People would burn hickory wood and place the ashes inside of a wooden box that had a hole in its bottom. Then they poured water over the hickory ashes to produce caustic soda, commonly known as lye, when mixed with hogfat to make soap.

Porter and Hawkins were in the middle of eating their breakfast at the Marietta Café, located 500 feet away from the train station, in a separate brick structure. In the northwest corner of the restaurant, Police Chief Jones was enjoying his after-meal cigar, along with a cup of coffee made from the last can of coffee, before the Lincoln Administration imposed the naval blockade of the Confederate coastline. Suddenly, the steely-eyed, blond six-footer zeroed in on the two strangers; instantly, an invisible red flag popped up in front of his navy blue eyes, 200-pound muscular, long-legged frame, and size twelve, thick-soled black boots. Porter and Hawkins sensed the bad vibrations pressing down on them.

Very hungry, Lem was ready to devour a big breakfast following the hard, speedy ride from Kennesaw (Big Shanty). Lem found a horizontal wooden pole onto which he tied his beleaguered white horse. Joining Chief Jones, was Clarence Bilbo, a round-faced, heavy-set, five-foot-five-inch man with a protruding belly. His eyes were brown; his face, clean shaven.

Sitting down at the Chief's table, Clarence asked, "What's eating you?"

"I have a question. Who are those two strangers sitting at that table?" asked Chief Jones.

"Hmm... I saw them get off the train last

night…Hey, but I didn't see them get on the morning train. I know they and the other strangers bought tickets to different towns," said Clarence.

"Something funny is going on. It don't add up," said Chief Jones.

"I think all those men were together. Why would they buy separate tickets?" asked Clarence.

"Clarence, you stay right here. I'm going to question those men," said Chief Jones. "Oh – go get my two deputies, Joe Morgan and Ed Beck. Don't waste any time."

Sauntering toward the table occupied by the two left-behind, obviously smelly, unwashed men wearing very dirty civilian clothing, the curious Chief of Police addressed the men.

"Did you ride the midnight train from Chattanooga?"

"Yes," responded Porter.

"Did you buy tickets for the outbound train?" asked Chief Jones.

"Yes sir, we did," said Porter.

"Show me your tickets," demanded the Chief of Police.

"Porter and Hawkins nervously reached into their pockets and placed their tickets on the table, in front of Chief Jones.

Chief Jones crowed. "Ah ha!! Both of you bought tickets to different places – one for Resaca and the other ticket for Chattanooga."

"Is something wrong?" asked Porter.

Walking at a frenetic pace through the door

were two deputies, and behind them was Lem, who had paused for a couple of minutes to gaze at the scenery and catch his breath. Noticing a small group of people gathering outside the general store, Lem called out impatiently, "Where is the police chief?"

A citizen replied, "He's in the restaurant."

Lem rushed into the restaurant and asked, "Where is the Chief of Police?"

"I am. What happened?" asked Chief Jones.

"Some men stole our train early this morning at six-thirty," said Lem.

"What?! Engine thieves?" asked Chief Jones in utter surprise. Then he said, "Wait a minute," while walking with his two young deputies toward the two civilian-clad Union soldiers.

"Stand up! You're both under arrest for suspicion of train theft and vagrancy," said Chief Jones.

Hawkins and Porter swallowed hard. The deputies immediately handcuffed and began searching the suspects from head to toe.

"What's this? Yankee revolvers! Were you going to kill us?" asked Chief Jones. "All right, men, take them to jail. Mr. Kendrick, thanks for your help. As a courtesy from the City of Marietta, the mayor has authorized a free night in the Fletcher House and free meals. Then you can be on your way in the morning. We'll transfer them to Big Shanty."

"Thank you, Chief. Come visit us at the Lacy Hotel in Kennesaw. I used to be a co-owner with a woman owner, but I decided to sell out. The hotel restaurant business was tying my life down," said Lem.

"I'd rather catch Yankees and crooks than deal with a bunch of annoying, picky people," said Chief Jones.

"After a hard ride, I'm ready to relax," said Lem.

"Mr. Kendrick, the City has also paid for horsefeed and livery stable fees. You're in high cotton today. We should give you the key to the City," said the smiling Chief of Police.

"Once again, thanks a lot," said Lem.

Farther up the road, the greatest railroad event was in progress, as Fuller, Murphy, and Cain were frantically puffing out their lungs in their efforts to reclaim a stolen locomotive. Captain Fuller was a robust, sinewy farmer born in Henry County, Georgia, a section of which was later annexed to Clayton County, Georgia.

The three pursuers: Fuller, Cain, and Murphy, ran at top speed for two and one-half miles from Big Shanty to Moon's Station, where section hand foreman Jackson Bond and his several men informed Fuller that some strangers had used the railroad crowbar and other tools.

"Mr. Fuller, some men were riding your train and stole our tools. They ripped up the track and cut the telegraph wire – not just that – look at those ties they left on the track. They were hoping to derail you," said Bond.

Angered, Fuller said, "That's a Yankee trick. They are not deserters. Yankees stole my train."

"Take this hand car," said Bond, an average "Joe", probably five-feet-eight-inches tall with short blond hair and a goatee.

"Thanks," said Fuller.

All three pursuers pressed the two poles against the ties on the track, to propel the hand car down a dangerously steep grade toward the bank of the Etowah River. A nasty surprise awaited the pursuers.

"Look out men – jump!" exclaimed Fuller as he saw a gaping hole, the result of a missing rail and cross ties scattered along the track. Fuller's party got up, brushed off their trousers, and noticed on the bank of the Etowah River a locomotive under steam, the "Yonah". It was commonly called "Cooper's Engine", which the Western & Atlantic Railroad leased to the Etowah Iron Works, set back a short distance on a spur track, away from the main railroad line.

Having a smaller wheel diameter and stroke, the "Yonah" would be adequate for short-haul trips to and from the Etowah Iron Works. However, Fuller was glad to use any available locomotive to continue the pursuit of the Union men riding aboard the "General".

Presently, at Camp McDonald in Kennesaw, Sergeant Marvin Brimstone was dressing down Corporal Henry W. Whitley of Company F, 56th Georgia Regiment, for dereliction of guard duty.

"Corporal Whitley, do you have two eyes?" asked Sgt. Brimstone, a dark-haired, five-foot-six-inch, blue-eyed, 180-pound career sergeant.

"Yes sir," said the recruit crisply.

"Did you see those men stealing the train?" asked Sgt. Brimstone.

"Sir, I assumed they were moving the commissary supplies to the hotel," said Corporal Whitley.

"Corporal, you ass-sumed," declared Sgt. Brimstone.

"Sir, all I had was a pike," said Corporal Whitley.

"You should have yelled for help," said Sgt. Brimstone.

"Yes sir," said Corporal Whitley.

"Corporal, double time it to the hotel. I'm putting you on K.P. right now," said Sgt. Brimstone.

"Yes sir," said the red-faced enlisted man, who then hastened across the tracks to the Lacy Hotel.

Meanwhile, Fuller's party was approaching an under-steam locomotive, the "Yonah". The raiders had differed with Andrews about the issue of destroying the "Yonah", to prevent its use as a chase vehicle. Simply stated, James J. Andrews was unwilling to risk being captured.

"Boys, if we take time to disable that engine, we might have to wait in Kingston longer than we should. We had best keep going or risk being caught." A half-moon shaped turntable had been conveniently positioned for an easy, unchallenged getaway.

Irritated, Campbell said, "Mr. Andrews, we're making a big mistake – believe me. The enemy will follow us in that engine."

"Mr. Campbell, it won't make any difference in our overall plans," said Andrews with finality. Even Pittenger realized it was useless to argue with their civilian leader. No one else said anything.

"There's a wood-and-water station up ahead," declared engineer Knight.

"Good. I figured it was time to refuel," said Andrews, as the stolen train was slowing to stop at Cass Station, where the attendant William Russell warily eyed the three cab occupants.

"Hey, how come Fuller and his men aren't on this train? What happened to the cars?" asked Russell.

"Sir, we're taking this shipment of powder to General Beauregard at Corinth. This is an emergency," said Andrews.

"By golly, I'd be glad to give him the shirt off my back. I think what you're doing is very noble," said Russell.

Seven miles north of Cass Station was Kingston, where several unexpected freight trains would delay the Andrews party for one hour and twenty minutes. Andrews had underestimated the repercussions of General Mitchel's capture of Huntsville, Alabama. Driven by fear and panic, the southbound freight trains arrived one right after each other in Kingston.

A red flag on the end of a train would indicate the impending arrival of a subsequent train originating from Chattanooga.

The presence of these trains sent an urgent message to Andrews.

"Mr. Switchtender, I have an emergency powder shipment that I have to get to General Beauregard as soon as possible," said Andrews.

"Mister, what makes you think you can come here and tell me how to run my railroad? I've got several trains coming from Chattanooga. What chance do you think you have of leaving this station?"

"The longer I stay here, the longer it's going to take to help the General," said Andrews.

"Where are your papers?" asked the switchtender.

"I have none," said Andrews.

"That does it! I ain't letting you out of this station until I get a clear track. Anyway, you can't just charge out of here and wreck another train, unless you're crazy." said Uriah Stephens, a tall elderly man.

"Is this your final answer?" asked Andrews.

"The answer is no! You ain't going to tell me what to do. You can't prove who you are or anything else," said Stephens in a gruff, irritable tone of voice.

Brazenly, Andrews plucked the switch keys from the switchtender's office, and immediately switched the one-way track in the northerly direction toward the next town of Adairsville. Stephens was hot under the collar. Andrews said he would return the switch keys – but he never did return the keys.

The Kingston depot was a stone-and-wood structure with an encompassing wooden platform, and the building was sixty feet long and twenty feet wide, as the raiders had observed upon leaving the station. On the north end of the building was the agent's office on one side, and the passenger waiting room occupied the opposite side of the depot. Sandwiched between these two rooms was a ticket window. The roof overhung the platform on each of the four sides of the depot.

Three and one-half to four-foot-high wooden steps ascended from the ground level to the north border of the wooden platform. A restaurant occupied a small-frame building with northern and southern ends. A local militia was conducting close-order drill on a vacant lot, but it was perhaps about a quarter of a mile and not visible from the Kingston depot.

While in Kingston, most of the Andrews Raiders were cooped up, waiting very impatiently inside three Confederate boxcars that would have been sent empty to Chattanooga to be filled with commissary supplies, in exchange for cannons, cannon balls, ammunition, and other items.

As soon as Andrews received the shocking news of the first southbound train from Chattanooga to arrive at Kingston, he quietly approached and discreetly whispered to engineer Knight.

"Walk back and tell the boys we have to wait for a later train. Be ready for anything – even a fight. I'll signal if anything is coming down," said Andrews.

Knight approached the boxcars and softly spoke to the men. "Boys, Andrews said to be ready in case of trouble." Nerves were becoming frayed, and the men were anxious to hasten the trip northward.

Peering out of a crack inside one of the boxcars, Brown noticed a man presenting Andrews a bulging envelope that probably contained a substantial amount of cash, which Andrews inserted inside his breast pocket. Apparently, Andrews was smiling due to the conclusion of a probable financial transaction related to his contraband goods sales. In any case, the one-hour-and-twenty-minute wait in Kingston was essentially peaceful. The raiders found it to be unnecessary to use their revolvers.

At this point in the railroad chase, the raiders probably breathed a sigh of relief at the passage of their first hurdle, but little did they know, the pursuers were rapidly gaining on the Union men. Evidently, Andrews had blundered again by neglecting to lift another rail at another location – between Etowah and Kingston, shortly after passing the "Yonah" in a ready-to-take-off mode. The long delay in Kingston merely shortened the window of time to only a few minutes between the pursuers and the pursued.

As the "General" sped northward from Kingston

toward Adairsville, Fuller and his party arrived in Kingston shortly thereafter. Although the "Yonah" had a good, strong engine, it was not actually designed for a long high-speed railroad chase, due to its smaller wheel size as compared to the larger wheels of the "Texas" and the "General". What might have been viewed as a setback in the chase, turned out to be a blessing in disguise, when Fuller had to abandon the "Yonah", due to the congestion of several southbound trains on the Kingston track, in search of another locomotive.

Murphy said, "Mr. Fuller, it is clear that we must give up the 'Yonah' to its engineer and find another locomotive."

"You're right, Mr. Murphy," said the conductor, who was resigned to the reality that their pursuit had encountered a glitch, but Fuller was a man who never accepted the word "can't." Undaunted, the wily, determined conductor exited the low-wheeled locomotive and seized a mule, bereft of a saddle and a rope bridle, and mounted the animal to ride around the obstructing southbound trains toward Kingston.

"Cain exclaimed, "Now I think I've seen everything – riding a mule, of all things. I never figured Fuller for doing that sort of thing."

Murphy said, "Mr. Cain, you don't know that man as I know him. Mr. Fuller is head and shoulders above the crowd – a fine lad indeed. I would bet my shalalee on him any day of the week," said the Irish-born Foreman of the Western

& Atlantic Railroad.

"Mr. Murphy, it seems to be a coincidence you were available on this day – of all possible days," said Cain.

"My lad, due to my position as Foreman of the Road, my job today was to examine an engine and find out if it could produce enough power to cut wood and pump water for the locomotives at Allatoona."

"I still think it's such an amazing coincidence you are with us today, and I want you to know I'm glad of it."

"Well, Mr. Cain, I'm flattered, but truly I must say that I merely rode with Mr. Fuller, because I am strongly committed to my duties. I am a company man, and I do not apologize for doing my duty," said Murphy in his Irish brogue.

"I respect your setting the example for the rest of us, Mr. Murphy," said Cain.

"If I were a leprechaun, still I would do no less than my duty," said Murphy with a friendly wink in his eyes. "Now I must hurry to catch up with Mr. Fuller. He's hard to keep up with."

Without another word, Murphy stepped down from the "Yonah" and proceeded on foot behind Fuller and the mule.

Parked on a siding of the main track, was the Rome Railroad locomotive, the "William R. Smith", in a state of readiness. Reluctantly, Fuller waited for Murphy and Cain to rejoin him on the second pursuit locomotive. Kingston was where the

Western & Atlantic Railroad connected with the westward rail line known then as the Rome Railroad.

In a few minutes, the pursuers rode out of Kingston, imbued with a renewed vigor upon learning that they were closing in on the "General".

The startled switchman, Uriah Stephens, said, "Mr. Fuller, what's going on?"

"Mr. Stephens, Yankees stole my train, and I intend to get the train back," replied Fuller.

"Where did it happen?" asked Stephens.

"I was sitting about a hundred feet away from the "General", when I had just sat down to eat breakfast in Big Shanty," said Fuller.

"You've got to be kidding!" exclaimed Stephens.

"Mr. Stephens, I can't change what happened – but darn it, I'm going to get my train back, if I have to go to Yankeeland to do it," said Fuller, his inflection rising.

"Take that locomotive on the siding. That's the 'Smith'. Wait until I throw the switch. Then you and your crew can pull out and chase those confounded skunks," bellowed the elderly switchtender in the sudden crimson change in his face.

"Thank you, Mr. Stephens. I won't disappoint you. I've got my job to protect, and I am responsible to Governor Brown for my train," said Fuller.

"You're all set," said Stephens, as he threw the

switch to allow Fuller's party to run on the one-way track from Kingston northward to Adairsville.

Aboard the "William R. Smith", the engineer and the new riders introduced themselves to one another.

"I'm W. A. Fuller. Meet my engineer, Jeff Cain, and this is Mr. Murphy, the Foreman of the Road."

"Oh yes, I've heard good things about you, sir. By the way, I'm Oliver Harbin. Glad to meet y'all," said the "Smith's" engineer.

"Likewise, Mr. Harbin....All right, men, let's go," said Murphy.

Oliver Wiley Harbin set the wheels in motion, and the steam escaped while the wheels resolutely engaged the track. Without explanation, engineer Jeff Cain decided to drop out of the chase. Ten miles north of Kingston, the crew spotted danger on the track.

"A missing rail!" exclaimed Harbin, who was forced to apply the brakes to the "William R. Smith" to prevent a collision. Without missing a beat, the chase had to go on. Fuller and Murphy, with old, rusted guns, ran very quickly for three miles toward Adairsville, where they met another southbound locomotive, known as the "Texas". Its staff included Peter J. Bracken, a 140-pound, five-foot-nine-and-one-half-inch engineer with dark hair, long chin whiskers, and a mustache. Wearing a gray flannel shirt and dark gray clothes, including a vest that was open low down, Bracken applied the throttle and reverse lever to the "Texas". He wore a hat and boots during the chase.

Alonzo Martin was the woodpasser for the "Texas". He was a heavy-set, sandy-whiskered man with a luxuriant head of auburn hair, large blue eyes, and wore civilian clothes. His role in the chase was to pass a load of wood from the tender to Fleming Cox (unknown physical characteristics), who functioned as a fireman stationed on the footboard between the engine and the tender. Martin's other duty was to remove remaining crossties from the track. Henry Haney was responsible for putting wood in the furnace.

Anthony Murphy wore brown pants, a dark vest and coat, and a large-brimmed dark, soft hat. He had a smooth face, long-cut brown hair, a brown collar, and a tie whose bow knot was not large. For unspoken reasons, the other "Texas" engineer, Samuel Downs, chose to get off the "Texas" at Adairsville, rather than to continue the famous railroad pursuit.

During the course of perhaps ten minutes, Fuller and Murphy stopped the "Texas", which discharged its twenty-one freight cars to a siding, and the pursuers used the recently serviced "Texas" to resume the pursuit – this time in reverse – as they hastened to Calhoun, Georgia. Fuller was brandishing an old, rusty gun when he approached the "Texas" two miles north of Adairsville, on the northward thrust to Calhoun.

"Yankees stole my train," said Fuller to the "Texas" crew, after signaling this south-bound train to halt on the single track.

"Get in!" said Harbin.

From Adairsville to Calhoun, the railroad bed follows the Oothcaloga Valley for a ten-mile stretch of track amid the mountains of North Georgia. The Andrews Raiders were still ahead of Fuller's party, but the gap between them was narrowing. Fuller had placed his gun on the wood in the tender so that no one outside the locomotive could see the weapon. Fuller's hair was easily blown by the wind while the "Texas" reached speeds of up to 65 miles per hour. He bounced a foot high off the buffer. For the next fifty-seven miles, Fuller stood erect on the buffer, a long section of heavy timber running across the rear of the tender. He tightly gripped two metal J-hooks that had been skillfully riveted to the rear end of the tender, near the corner and slightly beneath the flange, or flared rim. With his left hand, he would alert the engineer of dangerous objects such as crossties thrown on the tracks. According to Wilbur Kurtz, the tender's spark catchers were actually stove pipes six or seven inches in diameter, and six or seven feet long, to prevent sparks and ashes from coming into contact with the locomotive's machinery, after the debris is released from the bottom of the smokestack. Each engine usually had one available spark catcher, unless the railroad men forgot to bring them from the shop, and on April 12, 1862, the sparkcatchers were absent from the "Texas" (See W.G.K. papers, Vault #2 Notebook, Atlanta History Center).

THE RUNAWAY TRAIN

The flags of the "Texas" were fourteen inches by eighteen inches, and were attached to an eighteen-inch-long staff. The two staffs were secured to the front bumper slightly above the cowcatcher – one at each end of the timber. Each flag was furled and covered by a brass sheath.

It must have seemed very peculiar to see a locomotive running in reverse at higher speeds, simply because the surprised onlookers had no inkling that a train theft had taken place. Fuller was constantly focusing his eyes on the track to look for dangerous items that could derail the "Texas". Within a few more minutes, the engineer, Peter Bracken, slowed the train at the Calhoun station, where Fuller shouted to pick up young 17-year-old Edward Henderson, a Dalton telegraph operator whom Fuller pulled onto the train without uttering a word.

The engineer resumed traveling speed. "Good afternoon, Mr. Fuller. Why are you riding a different train?"

"Today's an unusual day, son. Yankees stole my train, and you are going to help us catch those rascals," said Fuller, as the engineer increased speed.

"How?" asked Henderson, expressing marked surprise.

"I'm fixing to write a telegram for you to send to Chattanooga for help," said Fuller.

"Yes sir. You bet I'll do it – for The Confederate States of America," said Henderson with a smile.

"Edward, you are a fine, patriotic boy," said Fuller. "Let's go, Mr. Bracken."

Henderson wore a stiff-brimmed black hat that had a low crown, and the young telegrapher sat near Fuller on the wood in the rear of the tender. Henderson, a current resident of Baconton, Georgia, sat close enough to receive verbal instructions from Fuller, who sat as comfortable as could be expected, on a tool box or a tank, according to Anthony Murphy in an interview with Civil War Historian, Wilbur G. Kurtz, Sr., roughly forty years later.

"Now, Edward, listen carefully. I'm writing the telegram I want you to send for me. If you can send it before the Yankees cut another telegraph wire, then we'll get to fight this war longer," said Fuller.

"Yes sir," said Henderson, excitedly.

Fuller penned the following telegram:

**TO GEN. LEADBETTER,
COMMANDER AT CHATTANOOGA:
My train was captured this a.m. at Big Shanty, evidently by Federal soldiers in disguise. They are making rapidly for Chattanooga, possibly with the idea of burning the railroad bridges in their rear. If I do not capture them in the meantime, see that they do not pass Chattanooga.
WILLIAM A. FULLER**

Barely finishing the written telegram, the train

was slowing down at the Dalton train station.

Fuller said, "When the train slows up, jump to the platform and get this message to Chattanooga. Don't speak to anyone. This is urgent."

"Yes sir," said Henderson.

"Whoa! I see a rail sticking up in the air," said Fuller as he peered out the cab, when the pursuers had run the "Texas" three miles north of Calhoun. "They cut another telegraph wire," said the astonished conductor.

The raiders were struggling to remove a rail, upon hearing the unsettling sound of the whistle of the "Texas". Fortunately for the pursuers, the raiders were running out of time, unable to remove one end of the rail, which they had propped up with a fence rail. How was the engineer to deal with a loosened rail?

Engineer Peter Bracken reduced the "Texas's" speed, and mounted the rail back into its normal position on the track.

"Whew! That was dangerous," said Fuller, wiping his sweaty brow with a white handkerchief.

"Take it easy, Mr. Fuller. I looked a long time before I hired all my engineers. Believe me, I'm very particular. I hire only the best," said Murphy.

"I wouldn't have ever thought anything at all to the contrary, Mr. Murphy. I feel sorry for the families of the boys who died of measles at Camp McDonald. Too many soldiers cramped in that one camp. That is a shame," said Fuller.

Murphy added, "It's bloody stupid, when those

knuckleheaded leaders in the State Legislature poked fun at Governor Brown's military expenditures."

"Yes, and that's why the stingy legislature forced Brown to order pikes instead of muskets," said Fuller.

"Oh, but the lying newspapers wrote about a sure victory over the Yankees in six weeks. This is going to be a long war," said Murphy.

"I agree, Mr. Murphy," said the wily conductor.

"Boys, look at this. There's the "General". They let go of a car," said Fuller, while noticing the position of the "General", south of the Oostenaula River Bridge.

"It'll couple up to our train," said Bracken confidently.

"They are getting desperate," remarked Fuller, as the "Texas" was crossing the bridge. Moments later, Fuller exclaimed in surprise, "Look! They let go of another car."

"I'll take care of this one too," said Bracken without raising an eyebrow. The cars would be soon switched to a side track in Resaca, while the "Texas" was still running in reverse.

"They tried to burn the cars," said Fuller.

Murphy said, "Those idiots should know it's too wet to burn bridges."

Soon, the "Texas" stopped in Resaca to take on ten Confederate troops commanded by Captain William J. Whitsitt, who had traveled from Ringgold, Georgia, with his ten fresh troops for an assignment in Mobile, Alabama.

"Hey, what's wrong, Mr. Fuller," asked the stationmaster. "Your train just passed us by and didn't stop."

"Yankees stole my train, and I'm chasing them," said Fuller.

"Well, good luck, Mr. Fuller. Catch'em, dagnab it. Catch'em," said the stationmaster, with his fists clenched.

Only a short while ago, telegrapher Edward Henderson's telegram had just gotten through to General Leadbetter – but only part of it. Andrews Raider, John Scott, had climbed the last telegraph pole in his life, and barely at the moment Scott cut the wire, the telegrapher, Paul Folsum, was transcribing the message, with raised eyebrows.

"Hmm.....it says.....'My train was captured this a.m. at Big Shanty, evidently by Federal soldiers...' Oh, no, the line went dead." Quickly he ran from the telegraph office down a dirt street about 300 feet to General Leadbetter's headquarters.

Quickly opening the headquarters building door, Paul Folsum said, "Urgent message. Yankees stole Fuller's train at Big Shanty."

At the front desk, Lt. Rosecrans Lookout rose smartly, took into his hands the hot telegraph message. Following a quick reading, he stepped into the office of General Danville A. Leadbetter, who already reeked of foul cigar smoke.

"General Leadbetter, here is a very important telegram, sir," said Lt. Lookout, while standing at attention three feet in front of the General's solid oak desk.

The prematurely aged, craggy-faced General riveted his eyes on the dispatch, as though he had been a dormant volcano that suddenly came to life, with the dancing and glistening of his tired, worn-out eyes, including his war-weary body.

"This is momentous news. I wonder if this train theft is related to General Mitchel's campaign to take our town. Those cannons speak for themselves," said General Leadbetter.

"It could be, sir," said Lt. Lookout.

"I believe the Yankees are trying to pull a pincer movement on us by wrecking the railroad and cutting off additional troops, supplies, and weapons from Atlanta," said the old, crusty, seasoned Confederate general taking another meditative puff of his half-smoked cigar, which he laid on his desk top, without regard to previously-made cigar stains.

"Thank you, Lieutenant Lookout. I'm calling an emergency staff meeting in thirty minutes in the War Room," snapped the General, with a pronounced gleam in his eyes. The unprecedented event of a train hijack had undoubtedly awakened a sleeping giant.

The Lieutenant saluted and executed an about face, leaving General Leadbetter's office. The headquarters' clerk was curious about the contents of the telegram and sensed his workload was about to be kicked a few notches higher.

"Sergeant Sprayberry," said the General, "cut orders for a cavalry regiment. They're going hunting for some Blue Bellies who stole Mr. Fuller's engine.

"Yes, sir, General Leadbetter," said the obedient, five-foot-eight-inch, black-haired, 150-pound, fair-complexioned Sgt. Will Sprayberry.

Thirty minutes later, General Leadbetter's faithful retinue assembled in the War Room, and the General barked the command, "Seats".

"Officers, I have just received a disturbing telegram about a stolen train in Big Shanty, Georgia. My educated guess is that the engine "General", as it is called, is in possession of the enemy somewhere between Dalton and Ringgold," said General Leadbetter, while standing in front of a large wall map of Tennessee, Georgia, Alabama, and Mississippi.

Using a splintery wooden pointer stick, he indicated the probable search area for a cavalry expedition.

"I am authorizing the dispatch of a hundred cavalrymen from Colonel Shotwell Jones's regiment. Gentlemen, your orders are to search for the train thieves and spread out in all directions. Do everything in your power to apprehend these men. It sounds like the train has been speeding, since it was stolen in Big Shanty, and furthermore, I believe they will run out of steam and have to abandon the train. Any questions?"

"Sir, do we notify the civilian authorities?" asked Col. Jones.

"Excellent question. As you ride through each

town, take time to notify each Provost Marshal. The civilians may catch the thieves before we can. If there are no more questions, I declare this meeting adjourned," said General Leadbetter, as the officers rose from their seats at the position of attention, courteously waiting for General Leadbetter to leave the War Room; which resembled a rundown structure of exposed supporting timbers, hastily constructed as a makeshift headquarters site, perhaps due to President Jefferson Davis's budgetary constraints.

Meanwhile, farther south in Dalton, one of its residents had gotten into trouble with the local authorities. When the raiders had speedily departed Dalton, Fuller's pursuing party was closing in on them. A Dalton citizen named Benjamin B. Flynn observed the high speed of the "General", and instinctively raised his hand in disapproval of the excess speed. He stated to another observer that the engineer should be fired for driving in a very unsafe manner.

Unfortunately, for Mr. Flynn, someone reported him to the local Provost Marshal, who led a regimental detachment which arbitrarily and heavy-handedly stormed Flynn's house, pulled and dragged the defenseless man from his bed, and then tied him up for a near-fatal flogging. The tattler had erroneously thought Flynn was urging the Andrews Raiders to speed up the engine "General", as an act of abetting the train thievery.

Six miles north of Resaca, Georgia, the raiders

stopped long enough at Tilton, to take on their last supply of wood and water at Green's Tank and Woodyard. Before their approach to the refueling stop, the raiders placed a loose rail in a diagonal position across the track, to serve as a futile delaying tactic.

"You must be Mr. Green," said Andrews to the refueling station's owner.

"You're speaking to him. What in blazes are you doing in Mr. Fuller's train?"

"We're carrying a powder shipment to General Beauregard," said Andrews.

Noticing the large holes at the front and rear ends of the remaining boxcar connected to the tender, Mr. Green became immediately suspicious of probable wrongdoing.

"Sounds like a tall tale to me, mister."

"Mr. Green, we have to get the powder to the battlefield. It could spell the difference between winning and losing the battle. Now, what do you say?" asked Andrews.

"All right, get out of here before I change my mind," said the agitated station owner. The purpose of each boxcar hole was to pass wood from the tender to the boxcar, and in turn to toss the wood onto the tracks to obstruct the pursuers.

Instantly, the engineers, Brown and Knight, with Andrews, climbed back into the cab of the "General" while the remainder of the men were still hidden inside the sole surviving boxcar. Within a few minutes, the raiders were approaching Tunnel

Hill where a darkened tunnel lay before them.

As the "General's" engineers reduced speed before entering the tunnel, a brief discussion ensued.

"Mr. Andrews, this is a good place to ambush those men," said Campbell.

"No, Mr. Campbell, it's too risky. Our mission is to get this train to General Mitchel," said Andrews.

"Are you afraid to fight?" asked Campbell.

"No, we must stick to our mission," said Andrews with finality in his voice.

Behind the "General" and almost nipping at the raiders' heels, were the tenacious Captain William A. Fuller and the "Texas" crew.

"Mr. Fuller," said Murphy, "it is unsafe to go through the tunnel. They may be waiting to shoot us all."

"Let's go," demanded Fuller. "We must save the railroad. Get ready. We're going through."

"We may regret it," said Murphy.

Both parties successfully dashed through the tunnel without incident. Perhaps the raiders could have stopped the pursuing "Texas" and the pursuers, but such a desperation tactic would have simply been in vain. A gun battle, however, could have bought the raiders more time, but the outcome of the chase would have probably remained very much the same.

CHAPTER 6
MISSION ABORTED

As things stood at this moment, the "General" was losing speed, having run short of wood and water since refueling stations were spaced far apart, in relation to much slower regulation travel speeds of fifteen to eighteen miles per hour. Time had also run out for the Andrews Raiders, as their last-ditch effort manifested itself in the release of the last boxcar with the uncoupling of the pin. The attempt to use blazing embers from the engine's fire box failed to set fire to the boxcar that the raiders then released to roll toward the Fuller party in the "Texas". A sudden burst of heavy rain easily extinguished the weak fire in the backward rolling boxcar of the "General". Reaching a summit, the "General" uttered its last gasp and came to a screeching halt. Andrews told the men to jump from the train and scatter into the woods, while the pursuers could see the fugitives make their getaway, two miles north of Ringgold, Georgia in Ringgold Gap.

As William Pittenger jumped from the train, he became disoriented and unsure of what direction in which to run, having lost sight of three of his comrades who had run very far ahead of him. Even though the very thick mud made running to be difficult, Pittenger succeeded in eluding Fuller, who had been climbing a fence not far behind Pittenger in the Ohioan's ascent on a wet wheat field. Pittenger easily escaped through a brook, soon crossing the Chickamauga Creek, before scaling a formidable land formation, the Chickamauga Precipice. Not surprisingly, Pittenger was languishing from the tiring flight toward Union lines, which would prove to be a very elusive goal, due to the constant cloud cover, mostly incessant rainfall, and the lack of a compass. Of course, he could have found his way back to his former military camp, if only he could have seen the sun and the North Star to point him in the desired direction – northwestwardly from Chattanooga.

For an undetermined length of time, Pittenger had been hearing the sound of hostile gunfire, shouting pursuers, and the loud barking of hunting dogs. He shuddered at the thought that one or more of his army buddies might have been victims of the distant gunshots – obviously, he was in bondage to fear rather than grabbing hold to faith to ward off adversity. Interestingly enough, these trials of military service would prepare him for his future career of being an ordained minister of the gospel.

Crossing rolling hills and valleys full of lightly

wooded timber, he descended a very steep incline leading to a bend in the Chickamauga Creek, a small body of water that flowed into the Tennessee River, a relatively short journey from Chattanooga, the military headquarters of Brigadier General Danville A. Leadbetter, C.S.A., whose rugged facial exterior revealed a man in failing health – such that he died of natural causes in 1866, four years after the Andrews Raid.

Much later in life, Pittenger would learn that he had been wandering around in an area close to Missionary Ridge, where Brigadier General Danville A. Leadbetter ultimately received an appointment as chief engineer of the Army of the Tennessee. Moreover, Leadbetter would be instrumental in laying out General Braxton Bragg's siege plans along Missionary Ridge near Chattanooga in 1864.

Far from desirable and convenient traveling terrain, Pittenger had to endure constant hunger and fatigue, while looking for a way out of his disoriented course of flight to avoid imprisonment. Needless to say, the heavy rains over a period of at least one week, yielded very little encouragement in a strange, unfamiliar land for which Pittenger did not have a map, let alone a compass. But such was the swollen, rocky Tennessee River whose inhospitable current forced him to hold securely in his left hand the Union army-issued revolver with ammunition, and with his right hand, he grabbed hold of rocks and swam single-handedly in the

Tennessee River, until reaching its other side.

The Chickamauga Precipice, as previously mentioned, was over 100 feet high, and a marksman or sharpshooter could have easily picked him off during the ascent of the formidable, almost absolutely vertical slope. Having arrived at the summit, Pittenger involuntarily fell to his knees at the base of a tree to catch his second wind. Suddenly, he heard the sound of aggressive bloodhounds for the second time, and then rose from his temporary rest break, to resume running over hills and streams, until the canine sounds were out of earshot.

And then another frustration kicked him in the teeth: Pittenger ran down into a sparsely populated valley and encountered a young, wiry, stocky man, who was feverishly hoeing a garden and getting ready to plant vegetable seeds, while standing beside his primitively constructed house of hewn timbers and notched logs, in resemblance of a Lincolnesque log cabin.

"Excuse me, sir, can you tell me how far Chattanooga is from here?" asked Pittenger.

"Eight miles," the rural resident replied.

The desired escape route lay in a northwesterly direction from Chattanooga, but the clouds stubbornly remained in place, and Pittenger's hopes seemed to hang on acquiring information from human sources, especially in the light of the return of dreadful torrential rain; which occurred after Pittenger had previously walked twice in circles, crossed a number of logs, and obtained what little sense of direction from occasional breaks in the cloud cover, revealing the First Quarter phase of the moon.

Toward the beginning of darkness on April 12, 1862, Pittenger spoke to an African-American horse-drawn wagon driver who said Chattanooga was four miles away.

If it had only been daylight, the exhausted, frustrated fugitive would have found the way to safety and security by walking around the west side of Lookout Mountain, in the northwesterly direction away from Chattanooga, but not even more detailed directions from three horsemen would be enough, as the sky was so dark that he could not even make out the horsemen's faces – quickly losing sight of them in the darkness. Consequently, he became so confused that he ended up taking the wrong highway – back to Ringgold, the area from which he had begun his escape from the "General". Even though the moon showed its shiny First Quarter phase again, yet it disappeared behind the clouds a half hour later, serving as an additional source of discouragement in his flight to Union lines.

Finally giving in to exhaustion, Pittenger found a huge log under which he lay down to sleep, undisturbed by the adverse weather, while temporarily concealing himself. The cold wind and heavy rain drenched this fugitive to the point of much discomfort, especially due to the lack of a raincoat, rain hat, and rubber boots.

After emerging from underneath the huge log to

walk a few more miles, Pittenger spotted two burly men in the act of roasting a pig with the aid of a very bright, glowing open fire, which would have been enticing under normal circumstances. Suddenly, he lost his balance and slumped to the ground alongside a fence where he slept, until a very cold wind jarred him from his sleepy state. Continuing his travel, he inexorably lunged into a pile of corn fodder inside a shed. In due course, a man awakened him.

"Who are you, mister, and what are you doing here?" asked the property owner.

"The Yankees took over Fleming County, Kentucky, and I've come to enlist in the Confederate army," replied Pittenger.

"This war stinks. I wish all our boys could come home. We need to get this war over with…Follow me, son. I know you want some victuals. You look very hungry," said the property owner.

"I would appreciate it so much," said Pittenger, who had not eaten anything in 36 hours.

As the famished Union soldier finished his meal, the stranger said, "Don't you dare tell anybody you stopped at my house."

"Yes sir," replied Pittenger, as he walked out of the house toward the next Georgia town, a place called LaFayette, where Pittenger asked someone for directions to Rome, Georgia and Corinth, Mississippi.

"I'm looking for the road to Rome. I'm trying to get to my regiment in Corinth, Mississippi," said Pittenger.

"Mister, take the first road about two miles west

of town and keep going," said the town resident.

"Thank you," said Pittenger.

"You're welcome," said a short, long-haired, 50-year-old, brown-eyed man.

When the traveler had gone two miles west of LaFayette, an overbearing, 45-year-old, 200-pound, blue-eyed Confederate Army officer, the notoriously surly Major Lofty Rakestraw, approached the disguised Union corporal.

"Stop right there! Don't move a muscle," shouted the officer.

"What is it?" asked Pittenger.

"We want to talk to you for a little spell. We just want to find out who you are. Strange things have been going on in these parts," said Major Rakestraw.

"What do you mean?" asked Pittenger.

"We've been searching for some Yankee engine thieves. We've sent men and dogs to look for them," replied Major Rakestraw.

"I didn't know that," said Pittenger.

"Identify yourself," demanded Major Rakestraw.

"I'm William Smith. I'm from Fleming County, Kentucky, and I'm going to join the Confederate army. The Yankees ran me out of Kentucky," said Pittenger.

"Why didn't you go straight to Corinth?" asked the infantry officer.

"I wanted to prevent capture by Mitchel's men," said Pittenger.

"That makes sense," said Rakestraw.

Wearing a hat covering his forehead, a dark-skinned man said, "Sounds like he's telling the truth. Mister, we want to take you to the Goree House."

A few minutes later, the men ordered Pittenger to sit down and submit to additional questioning.

"Mr. Smith, how many of the surrounding Kentucky counties can you name?" asked the interrogator.

"Walton, Green, and Sewell," said Pittenger.

"You're incorrect," said the interrogator.

"Sir, how many of the adjacent counties can you name in your area?" asked Pittenger.

"Hmm…You've got a good point. Forget that question," said the interrogator. "What can you tell us about your trip from Kentucky?"

Pittenger gave a lengthy explanation, and then the interrogator said, "That's enough. We'll get back with you in a few minutes."

For the next four hours, Pittenger had to field many more questions until an abrupt ending – a crowd was shouting in front of the largest hotel in LaFayette.

"They caught the Bridge Burners," said one man who stormed into the Goree House.

"What are their names?" Where did they come from?" asked an impatient Major Rakestraw.

The anonymous man replied, "Every last one of 'em said he was from Fleming County, Kentucky."

Major Rakestraw commented, "Very interesting." The men looked down their noses at Pittenger, who was feeling very uncomfortable by this time. Every fiber of his being wanted to escape the vindictive populace.

Pointing with hostility and clenching his teeth, he said to Pittenger: "You're going to jail."

Sitting in a chair near the window, Pittenger immediately stood up to be escorted to the LaFayette, Georgia jail.

Campbell, Slavens, and Shadrach were the first raiders who jumped off the "General", when the pursuers were within sight distance of the fleeing engine thieves. No raiders had been equipped with a compass or military maps of the surrounding countryside, an unbelievable omission on the part of General Mitchel, a supposedly well-educated man schooled in astronomy and other science subjects.

All of the Andrews Raiders were captured within one week after the end of the famous railroad chase. Near Ringgold, Georgia, not far from the site of the abandoned "General", the local authorities with canine assistance, located Jacob Parrott and Samuel Robertson; who, like all the others, were accosted by a howling mob and cries for immediate hanging.

Jacob Parrott had experienced cruel and unusual punishment for withholding significant information about the other apprehended train thieves. To eventually extract a verbal confession, a lieutenant and four other soldiers completely stripped Parrott naked and administered 150 lashes with a whip, as they held him in position on a rock at Tunnel Hill, Georgia. However, according to railroad historian, James G.

Bogle, no one has actually admitted divulging the identities of the other raiders.

Governor Joseph E. Brown lived in a house located near Camp McDonald (now Canton, Ga.). Six days after the Andrews Raid had occurred, Governor Brown had received a letter dated April 13, 1862, from the Superintendent of the Western & Atlantic Railroad, John Sharpe Rowland, in Dalton, Georgia.

Sipping a hot cup of coffee at the dinner table, the 41-year-old, dark-haired, balding, homely-looking Georgia Governor Joseph E. Brown was perusing a neatly written letter that instantly raised his hackles, on a face that was showing telltale signs of stressful wartime political cares.

"Confound it! Some men stole one of our locomotives. This is an outrage," said the Governor to his wife, while tugging at both of his curly locks of hair – one alongside of each ear.

"Why would anybody steal a train, Joseph?" asked his wife, Elizabeth G. Brown.

"That's a good question, and I'm going to find out," said Governor Brown resolutely. "Now, I want to read to you part of this letter:"

...They, getting out of wood and water, and seeing they would be taken, jumped off the car [actually, the engine] and took to the woods, but were pursued and three of them taken last night and are now in custody here [in Dalton].....One of them took 150 lashes at Ringgold [actually at Tunnel Hill] before he would acknowledge and then said there were sixteen [twenty was the actual total participating in the raid] of them sent as spies to burn our railroad bridges. Five made their escape from the cars last night that have not been caught. But Col. C. Philips and others [that included Col. Jesse A. Glenn of Dalton who organized a special regiment and 100 civilian pursuers added to Philips' twenty men] went after them when I left Ringgold.........

"Honey, that's quite a letter. I never thought I would live to hear about a stolen train," said Mrs. Brown.

"Well, strange things can happen during a war," said Governor Brown. "I would bet my paycheck that was Captain Fuller's train. Whoever started the chase deserves public recognition."

"Joseph, is anything else bothering you?" she asked.

"Yes – as a matter of fact – the Yankees took Fort Pulaski."

"How did they do that?' asked his wife.

"The Union navy blew the fortress walls apart with a rifled cannon – a new type of cannon just invented," said Governor Brown.

"What's a rifled cannon?" asked Mrs. Brown.

"Each raised metal surface is called a 'land', followed by a groove to enable a cannon ball to make a direct, solid strike on its targets, without wobbling around in the air as it leaves the cannon. This is the first time in military history that cannons have knocked down walls that were once thought to be impregnable," said Governor Brown.

Coming on the heels of the Federals' capture of Fort Pulaski, in Savannah, on Friday, April 11, 1862, the passage of President Jefferson Davis's Conscription Act thoroughly enraged Brown since it adversely affected the available state militia manpower.

"Jeff Davis is an incompetent leader. Now he's making it hard on me to recruit soldiers to defend my railroad, its bridges, and the people of Georgia. Richmond is no better than the Lincoln Government in Washington. Why are we fighting this war? Richmond is simply another oppressive central government. If Jeff Davis had a brain, he'd take it out and play with it," said Governor Brown.

"What else is happening in Georgia?" asked Mrs. Brown.

"As if we didn't have enough trouble, the latest problem is a stolen train – probably the work of Yankee thieves. I need to recruit my own soldiers to guard our state-owned railroad, because it has been and is a terrific moneymaker for the state. Also, the W&A is vital for the efficient flow of commerce, the transport of troops, and the shipment of raw materials to make our cannons, weapons, and ammunition," said Governor Brown. "Come to think of it, I've a mind to tell all our young men to defy Jeff Davis's Conscription Law. Yes, I will do just that (and he was true to his word)!"

"Sweetheart, go take a nap. You must be tired."

"That's a good idea, Elizabeth," said Governor Brown.

In due course, the authorities captured four more raiders: Daniel Dorsey, William Bensinger, Robert Buffum, and George D. Wilson. Knocking on the door of a log house, the owner feigned sickness to avoid giving food to the suspicious strangers at such a late hour of the evening. Dorsey readily perceived the owner was not actually ill. With Dorsey, Wilson hobbled on an injured foot. At the next house, the resident refused to feed them, but as they walked off the wooden porch, the men took advantage of an opportunity to drink from a bucket of milk that was left out overnight, exposed to the elements.

A short while later, a search party of fifty men encircled the raiders after having observed them from a hillside. One pursuer positioned his pistol against Wilson's head to signify the intention of shooting the raider. Another captor presented a ready-made noose.

Dorsey said, "If you're going to send us over the Jordan, can we at least eat our last meal?"

"Heck, yeah. You should eat your last meal," said a search party member, a five-foot-nine-inch, 180-pound, bearded, 45-year-old, gray-haired man with big feet and wide ears. The major told the pistol bearer to put away his weapon and transport the men to jail.

Before the authorities led the men to jail,

another man placed a double-barreled shotgun against Daniel Dorsey's chest.

"You'd better tell the whole truth or I'll blow you away," declared the second weapon bearer, a red-headed, freckled-faced, brown-eyed, 200-pound, five-foot-six-inch bearded man.

"Why don't you get it over with? Put your money where your mouth is," said Dorsey, an ex-school teacher from Ohio.

* * *

At a different location, but not very far from the abandoned engine "General", searchers placed Andrews, Ross, and Wollam in heavy irons, after men and dogs had surrounded the escapees. The search party leader, a strapping, muscular, blond six-footer with blue eyes and a mustache, became very angry that Ross had fired a revolver at the search dog.

"Drop that gun or I'll fill you full of lead. Search him," said a six-foot-one-inch, 170-pound, 45-year-old, blue-eyed search party leader.

Conducting a thorough body search of the captives, the captors found $2,000.00 and some compromising papers on Andrews's person.

"So you're James J. Andrews, the famous blockade runner and spy – and now, an engine thief. We have plans for you, Mr. Andrews," said the leader.

* * *

THE RUNAWAY TRAIN

Elsewhere, Knight, Reddick, Scott, and Mason had just climbed a hill, feeling certain they had made good their escape. Seemingly out of nowhere on the top of a hill, two dozen horsemen closed in on the fugitives in a matter of moments, after the raiders had been refused food at a nearby house. Supposedly, the owner had sent his son to plow a garden for a neighbor, but the appearance of cavalrymen a few minutes later, revealed that the householder had deceived the raiders.

The cavalry major halted the four hungry men and smartly raised a saber in the air, as a gesture of authority.

"Where are you from?" barked a Confederate major.

"Fleming County, Kentucky," said Knight.

"Oh, yeah?" Do you have a pass?" asked the officer.

"No," said Knight.

"Let's go to Bridgeport," said the leader, with a sadistic smile on his face. Apparently, he had something else in mind – arrest and confinement in Chattanooga.

* * *

In another location, in North Georgia, J. A. (Alf) Wilson and Mark Wood were faring much better, at least for the present time. The men found a hiding place under an old, rotten log with some leafy limbs; but later, two armed Confederate civilian searchers saw these fugitives fleeing within fifty feet of their log hiding place.

One searcher was overheard to say, "Two men – no guns. Let's get 'em." Wilson and Wood lay low until it was prudent to vacate their cramped arboreal hiding place, to take it upon themselves to travel all night, in search of some bundles of corn fodder under which to hide during the daylight hours. Suddenly, two young women hunting for eggs were shocked when one of them touched Alf Wilson's hand, which was resting near the edge of the corn fodder pile, following six hours' rest.

Rushing frantically into the house, the two young women were upset by this unusual incident, in an unexpected place: a hole where chicken eggs would have normally been laid. While leaving the corn fodder storage area in the barn, the two men brushed off from their clothing some of the chaff that had stuck to their rain-soaked clothes, and went to apologize for frightening the young women.

"Ladies, we're looking for the train thieves. We slept in the barn so we wouldn't wake you up. By the way, would you be so kind to give us something to eat?" pleaded Wilson.

"All I have is a pitcher of buttermilk and some cornbread. Hope that's o.k.," said one of the women.

"We appreciate your kind hospitality," said Wilson.

"One hour later, Wilson and Wood approached and temporarily hid in a dense, wooded area full of underbrush. With uncanny timing, as soon as the men took cover, they heard some shouting Confederate cavalrymen.

"Lieutenant, keep looking for those S.O.B.'s. I know they're here somewhere," said Cavalry Major Ben S. Grogan to Lieutenant Samuel Tinsley. Both men looked almost like twins, being of the same slender 180-pound frame that included impressive biceps, blond hair, and muttonchops sideburns. The former spoke in a deep base voice, and the latter had a conspicuously raspy voice, due to many years of cigar smoking. Both men were born on March 14, 1836, only two hours apart in different states. A long oval face, a mouth of healthy, white teeth, and narrow ears were other descriptive features of these staunch Union officers possessing fair, unblemished complexions.

On Sunday, April 13, 1862, Wilson and Wood ate their lunch, the second meal of the day, at a Union couple's small, isolated log cabin situated at the base of a mountain.

A short, heavy-set woman answered a knock at the door.

"May I help you?" she asked.

Wilson replied, "Please. We are tired, hungry, and lost."

"First, let's get you fed. Then I'll help you find your way," she said matter-of-factly. "Now, I don't have nothing fancy, but you're welcome to what I can give you. I'm not the best cook in the world, but if you can stand my cooking, more power to you."

The lady of the house was proud, down-to-earth,

and wore an ordinary, homespun dress.

"Gentlemen, be seated and make yourselves at home. I have ham, eggs, cornbread, and rye coffee. Is that all right?" she asked.

"Sounds fine, ma'am. We sure appreciate it," said Alf, with sincerity in his voice.

While cooking the breakfast, she carefully studied the speech, mannerisms, and how the men carried themselves.

"I would bet my house that you two are Union men," said the unusually perceptive 40-year-old, brown-eyed, five-foot-five-inch, hefty brunette, whose shoes had wooden liners to add more life to her footwear.

"What can I say," said Alf, admitting his allegiance to the Union.

"Ah ha! Confession is so good for the soul. Now, don't you feel better when you tell the truth?" she asked.

"Yes ma'am," said Alf, acting as the pair's mouthpiece; moreover, Wood was not a person given to making small talk.

"I don't mind telling you my husband and I are the neighborhood black sheep. Because we are for the Union cause, other people around here don't even give us the time of day," said the woman.

"God bless you," said Alf.

"Now, another thing: I can read people, and I can smell a Union man a mile away. I take it you're on your way to sign up with the Union army," she said.

"Well, kind of," said Alf.

THE RUNAWAY TRAIN

A few moments later, a puzzled man came into the dining room, wearing a sober, all-business look. Her husband was unquestionably a rather handsome man for a 45-year-old male, who was five-feet-eight-inches tall with brown eyes, a big mole below his left ear, and varicose veins in his legs, perhaps due to extended periods of woodchopping.

"What do we have here – new neighbors in the valley?" asked the husband.

"Sir, we want to pay you for the food," said Alf.

"Nope. It's on the house. Any Union men are friends of ours. The sooner our men in blue can get here, the better it'll be for us," said the man of the house.

"Thank you, sir," said Alf.

"Let me warn you about old Snow's Cavalry. He's got an eagle eye for deserters. He is so slick he'll sneak up on you like snake on stink," said the man of the house. "If Snow catches you, tell him you men are sons of Benjamin Smith. Snow don't know their names."

"Appreciate the warning," said Alf.

The man provided directions, but before long, Wilson and Wood ran into Snow's trap in a somewhat populated valley. The best laid plans had faltered at the unexpected appearance of the cavalry.

"Halt or I'll shoot out your brains," said a potentially trigger-happy Confederate Captain armed to the teeth.

"Identify yourselves."

"I'm Benjamin Smith, Jr.," said Wilson.

"I'm Triple O. Smith," said Wood.

"We're sons of Benjamin Smith, and we're from Harrison," said Wilson.

"Well, how is Benjamin?" asked the Captain.

"He's doing pretty good, thank you," said Alf.

"That's good news. I respect good people – what few we have left in this world.... Boys, I think you're trying to wiggle out of military service. You should be executed."

"No sir. We support Jeff Davis," said Wilson.

"Look here. I know Benjamin Smith, and that's good enough. So, you must be o.k. They're fine pillars of the community, and have been for many years. Otherwise, I would arrest you two for being part of the Bridge Burners."

"I understand, sir," said Alf.

"Follow me to the Chief Valley C.S.A. office. I want you to meet some of my friends," said Snow.

Alf Wilson and Mark Wood had a very uneasy, shaky feeling as they were being benevolently escorted to another typical log cabin house, for this was apparently not a house meant for the exercise of southern hospitality. If these valley residents had been sophisticated, educated people with a sense of humor, they might have spontaneously taken it upon themselves, to affix a temporary sign above the front door of the cabin to read the following:

"Relinquish All Hope Ye Who Enter Here"

The Cavalry Captain had a grim, serious expression on his face, while an old, hateful snaggle-toothed woman, six-feet-one-inch tall, was breathing fire like a dragon anxious to devour his prey.

The woman said, "Welcome to my lecture on Southern Rights and Northern Atrocities." Seething with rage as her face turned red, she said, "Before you leave this house, you will take the loyalty oath to the Confederacy. The Lincoln government has sent stormtroopers into our homes to rape our women and loot our homes. Yankees have murdered innocent civilians and upset our fine, respectable plantation system based on slavery. It is high time we stand up against the Great Satan of the North. We will fight for States Rights until the last Southerner bites the dust."

The old woman ranted, seethed, and carried on her harangue for two hours, as the two Andrews Raiders, Wilson and Wood, listened with their ears burning. Then it was the Captain's turn to deliver his own hostile lecture.

"Lincoln married a Confederate woman, Mary Todd Lincoln. For that we cannot show him any respect. She should have not married a Yankee, so we have disowned Mary Todd Lincoln for that reason. We have no use for either one of them. As for the South, we will live free of Lincoln rule or we will die. No matter what happens, the South will rise again," said the serious Captain. Finally, his lecture ended with a thud and a bang with his hand coming down on a writing desk.

"Oh, Captain......if you need our help, just give

221

us a holler and we'll come a-running," said Alf Wilson, in a folksy tone of voice.

"I'll come look you up, but first I want you to keep your butt straight," said the Captain.

"Yes sir," responded Alf.

With joy in their hearts, Wilson and Wood departed for the mountains where they snoozed for the rest of the day, until the sun went down. A challenge awaited them. Pressure was brought to bear to locate a boat and sail down a river to avoid running into Snow's Cavalry again.

Wilson said in a reclining position, among the leaves and twigs under a mountain blue sky, "We have to find some more food for our next meal, or we'll sicken and die in this stinking Rebel wilderness."

Wood replied, "Survival is the key word."

It was late, probably 10:00 p.m., when Alf Wilson quietly strolled up toward a log cabin, where he knocked on the door. Mark Wood remained hidden some distance away from the cabin.

"There's someone at the door," said a five-foot-five-inch, stocky, 150-pound, blue-eyed, round-faced, blonde woman. An unexplainably eerie stillness prevailed on the evening of Thursday, April 17, 1862. This twosome had been on the lam for six days.

Pointing a loaded, cocked rifle at the unexpected visitor, the woman slowly opened the door.

"Ma'am, may I talk to your husband outside?" asked Wilson.

"All right. Jeb, go see what he wants," she said to her husband.

"He'd better not be one of them Rebel stormtroopers," said Jeb.

"What do you mean?" asked Wilson.

"Every so often them darn Rebels go around knocking on the doors of Union sympathizers," said Jeb.

"Oh, I see," said Wilson, without showing reaction on his face.

"Ma'am, I need to speak to your husband outside," said Wilson.

"All right, mister, but make it quick," she said, while still pointing the rifle at the two strangers.

Walking circumspectly away from prying ears, Wilson asked, "I'm a Union man in distress. I need your help." Both men feared being shot on sight, while engaging in very secret conversation.

"Very well. Lincoln is number one in my book. Jefferson Davis can't even govern the Confederacy, let alone the entire United States," said the cabin owner.

"Sir, I appreciate it. I'm between a rock and a hard place," said Wilson.

"Raise your right hand. Repeat after me. I solemnly declare, as the Lord is our witness, to uphold, protect, and defend my new friends against all evil forces to the best of my ability." At the end of swearing the oath, the Union sympathizer and Wilson amicably shook hands, and the man led the two fugitives to a vacated house on the outer perimeter of the cabin owner's property. Sixteen square feet of trap door separated a hidden basement that had some comfortable quilts on which to sleep with the utmost comfort, in contrast to sleeping on the ground in the wilderness, exposed to the elements.

"Gentlemen, this is just a temporary sanctuary until I can whisk you away in safety from this neighborhood. Rest assured, I will not reveal your location to anyone, because I don't trust nobody around here," said the male householder.

"Thank you, sir," said Wilson, with an humbled expression on his care-worn face, that looked as though he had recently aged.

At the dawning of Friday morning, April 18, 1862, the men were awakened by the man calling the hogs to eat their first meal of the day. Shortly thereafter, the wife hurriedly arrived, at her own risk, carrying a basket that appeared to be crowded full of corn, but actually it served as a ruse to deceive anyone who was watching everything that was going on at the abandoned cabin.

Removing the layer of straw covering the trap door and sliding a big overlapping piece of wood covering the trap door, the woman lowered the basket down the four-foot-square trap door hole to the recipients' hands. They removed their breakfast from the basket and relayered the corn in its original position inside the basket, and began to eat the food in a very small bedroom, with barely enough legroom.

THE RUNAWAY TRAIN

The woman said, "Boys, I figured you were Union men. I sized you up right away. It's too bad you couldn't burn those bridges."

"Retribution will be coming to the South," said Wilson.

"I agree with you," she said.

For several days, Wilson and Wood rested their tired, sore feet and exhausted bodies, while the pursuers would perhaps give up the chase.

"My brother lives about two days' travel from here, and he comes to visit us at about this time every week – just to check up on us. He can guide you to the river by taking a winding, twisted road through a rocky area. The Rebels do not normally travel there. You should be all right," she said.

* * *

For some mysterious reason, the night sky was almost as light as the daytime sky, a definite disadvantage to the fugitives. The route to be taken was probably a tributary of the Tennessee River known as the McLarimore Creek, where Wilson called out to a boatman to ferry them across the creek. It was now three days later.

"Hey, mister, can you change a five-dollar Confederate note?"

"Sorry, I can't do it," said the boatman.

The men had no recourse but to walk deep into the woods where they discovered a boat tied up to a tree in extreme darkness amidst persistent rain.

They walked the boat to the creek and lay inside it while a Confederate patrol boat glided past the Union men, who began to face river obstacles such as, a very swift current and bunches of driftwood, ranging from the smallest to rather large quantities. At this time, the rain intensified and the creek was becoming flooded. Despite poor visibility, high winds, treacherous currents, and chilling rains, Wilson and Wood luckily found a small, calm, peaceful island, on which they could seek refuge from the inhospitable sleet and hail, penetrating the body to produce a distinct chill.

Much later, the men noted a cabin and its stone chimney billowing with smoke, almost as if it were sending smoke signals to an Indian tribe. Located on the shore of a creek was an unattended boat. The male householder asked the men, "Who are you and why are you here?"

"We're looking for abandoned boats so no draft dodgers and deserters can use them," said Wilson.

"That's great," said the resident.

"Have you seen any more boats around here?" asked Wilson.

"No, mine's the only boat," said the resident.

"Sir, can you help a couple of poor soldiers with a bite to eat?" pleaded Wilson.

"Sure, you're fighting for Abe Lincoln, aren't you?" asked the resident.

"Yes sir," chorused both men in unison.

"Then sit down at the kitchen table. You certainly deserve no less than to be fed," said the resident.

THE RUNAWAY TRAIN

The man's wife smiled sweetly as she subjected a skillet full of grits to a boil, and picked up the cooking vessel by the handle to place on the table, which had no tablecloth resting on top of the oakwood kitchen table.

"Enjoy. I'll get you some scrambled eggs in two shakes of a lamb's tail, gentlemen," said the giggling young wife of the householder.

After the meal, the travelers dried their clothes on a wooden bench near a hot, blazing fire inside the fireplace. When the clothes were sufficiently dry, Wilson and Wood said goodbye to the couple, and Wilson said, "Be looking out for more boats."

"You can count on me," said the male householder.

"Thanks for the food, mister," said Wilson, as he exited the front door of the humble cabin. "We need to row hard down the river. The enemy is nipping at our heels. It's a strong feeling I get," said Wilson.

"Alf, you're right. The sooner we get out of this area, the better," said Wood.

Later, the clouds parted to give way to mostly azure blue sky and abundant, warm sunlight. Two hours later, the twosome decided to hide inside some thick, luxuriant bushes for some needed relaxation.

"Paddle over to those bushes, Mark, and park the boat on the shore," said Wilson.

"Aye, sir," said Wood with a wry smile.

Quickly, the men disappeared behind the bushes, but yet they were still able to keep watch over their immediate surroundings.

"Mark, if you had it to do over again, would you have participated in a train stealing mission?" asked Wilson.

"Alf, I learned a valuable lesson about military life. Never volunteer for anything," said Wood.

"My sentiments exactly," said Wilson.

"What the.........Look, two men approaching our boat. Let's go see what they're up to, Mark."

"What's going on here?" demanded Wilson.

The father and his son were stunned to find the boat users near the parked boat. "Oh, we were looking for a boat to take us to town. We're low on food," said the adult who had a 12-year-old, red-headed, brown-eyed, five-foot-five-inch lanky son. The father stood at five-feet-eight-inches and had long black hair, an unshaven face, and a pronounced beer belly. He was thirty-five years old and his wife had recently died of tuberculosis. Secretly, he was evading the State conscription law enacted on Friday, April 11, 1862, during the previous few days, not knowing for sure if he would be granted an exemption for military service, since he was the sole surviving parent.

"Can't do it. This is a Government boat – for official business only," said Wilson.

"Really?" said the father.

"Our job is to chase down draft dodgers and prevent them from getting away," said Wilson.

"I see," said the father.

"Do you think the wind has settled down?" asked Wilson.

The father replied, "Don't try it. The wind is still too strong for boating. Why don't you stay with us at the house? Go make yourself at home."

Arriving shortly at the front door of the cabin, the man's sister, a short, wiry, rather healthy, 28-year-old woman who had the gift of gab.

"Who are you?" she asked.

"Ma'am, the man invited us to stay for a spell at your house, since the river current is too strong to row a boat," said Wilson.

"You've got that right, mister. Are you men in the army?" she asked.

"Yes, ma'am. We're from Kentucky and looking to sign up at a regiment in Alabama," said Wilson.

"I just got a letter from our son; being a soldier is a tough row to hoe. He's been going through a lot of hard knocks. He had the flu for a couple of weeks, but now he's much better, thank the Lord," said the chatty woman.

"That sounds just like the army," said Wilson.

"I pray the Lord will see you safe and sound. Won't you stay for the night?" she asked sincerely.

"If we didn't have to report to camp, we'd oblige you, ma'am," said Wilson.

"By the way, you're five miles north of Chattanooga," said the young woman.

"Thank you kindly," said Wilson. Without delay, the men shoved off in the boat and navigated the river for a while, until they encountered a stray log that slammed into the left side of the boat, thus slowing down the boat.

As the sun rose on the morning of Saturday, April 19, 1862, a man beckoned them to row their boat ashore.

"The water is too rough. Even more seasoned men have drowned," said the stranger.

"We'll pay you three dollars if you'll be our guide," said Wilson.

"All right, hand me that paddle. I'll show you how to get through Devil's Gorge." All three men paddled downstream in unison as the current continued its turbulent flow. Water splashed all over the three rowers, and a few loose small limbs bounced off the side of the small boat. A few minutes later, the skilled oarsman safely guided the fugitives through the dangerous, narrow gorge.

"Thanks, mister," said Wilson.

"Don't mention it," said the stranger.

About one hour later, a scouting Confederate cavalry squad leader shouted at the boaters to come ashore.

Wilson and Wood merely ignored the horsemen and kept rowing the boat gently down the river. The current had moderated, and fish were playfully jumping up and down in the water. Much to their advantage, the travelers were beyond musket range.

Ten miles later, the Northern twosome crossed into Alabama, and soon floated undetected by a Confederate bridge guardpost.

"Mark, stay in the boat while I go to town. Got to make sure our army has taken Bridgeport," said Wilson.

"Good idea. I'll stay here," said Wood.

After walking only a few minutes, Wilson received a rude awakening, as he cringed at the unexpected sight of the butternut-colored uniforms inside the city limits of Bridgeport, Alabama.

"Great Jehosophat!" whispered Wilson to himself. Without hesitation, he hastened back to the canoe to break the news to Wood.

"Mark, I saw Rebs in Bridgeport. Let's get out of here," said Wilson.

"I'm with you," said Wood.

The two men rowed the boat all night, hid their canoe, and stopped to ask for food at a man's cabin.

* * *

"Sir, we're trying to get back to our outfit in Corinth. We decided to join up again. Could we have some food to eat?" asked Wilson.

"Why, sure. Come in and sit down at the table. Annie Mae can cook a right smart rip-roaring breakfast. You must be Johnny Rebs," said the male householder.

"Yes sir, we're mighty anxious to whip them Yankees. Even though it's hard work, we know we can do it," said Wilson.

"Now, I like your hearty spirit, young man. Let's see...How about some scrambled eggs, sausage with biscuits and gravy, and some hot grits?" asked the male householder.

"Sounds great to me. Right, Mark?" asked Wilson.

"Yes," said Wood.

"I want you guys to know the Yankees have

taken Stevenson. They're thick as thieves and they're covering every inch of that town," said the male householder.

Wilson said, "I appreciate the information."

Several hours later, the pair encountered a Confederate squad of soldiers that had hurriedly escaped Stevenson.

"Yanks have Stevenson, lock, stock, and barrel." The two found it rather odd that these Confederate troops did not question their identities or their destination, and likewise the next company of Confederate troops leaving Stevenson was mainly concerned with their march to another location assignment.

"I think we'll be all right, Mark. Tie up the boat in the woods. Let's cross the stream and head up that steep hill."

After struggling up the incline, Wood said, "This looks like Stevenson."

Shocked, Wilson said, "Oh my God, those are Confederate soldiers." The men were unaware that General Mitchel and his engineering troops were repairing a bridge located on the western side of Stevenson, with the intention of returning to the town.

"Since we're in town, let's buy some tobacco at the store," suggested Wilson.

"Why not? Now's our chance," said Wood.

Outside the tobacco store, a Confederate lieutenant had been scrutinizing the two suspicious tobacco store customers entering the establishment. Alarm bells went off in his mind. Curiosity drove him to buttonhole the disguised Union men.

"Pardon me, gentlemen. I need to talk to you," said the keenly observant Confederate officer.

"Yes sir," responded Wilson.

"What are y'all doing here?" asked the Confederate officer.

"We bought some tobacco," said Wilson.

"Are you enlisted men?" asked the officer.

"Yes sir. We are from Fleming County, Kentucky. Yanks took control up there, so we're going to Corinth to join up with a regiment in the Confederate army," said Wilson.

"You're all right," said the officer.

"Officer, that man was here last night. He's been loitering," said an alert watchdog resident.

Needless to say, the sudden arrest of Wilson and Wood created such a stir that a brief period of civil unrest ensued. The gathering of numerous, curious, angry onlookers had significantly disturbed the city's routine. Wilson used the chaotic circumstances to rip up the travel map into very small chewable pieces, some of which he eventually swallowed while other fragments sporadically and skillfully disappeared from the watchful eyes of the local authorities. Quickly the throng surrounded the arrested men.

"Look, we're just good ol' country folks not bothering anybody," said Wilson.

"You're under arrest....Sergeant, chain these men to a hand car. Take them to jail," said a five-foot-nine-inch, 180-pound, blue-eyed, freckled-faced, long-haired lieutenant.

Upon their arrival at the jail, a five-foot-five-inch, stocky, brown-eyed, short, blond-headed, bearded sergeant began to strip-search the captured Union pair. In spite of searching every item from hats to socks and boots, no extraneous items had been found. After a long, uneasy silence, another man abruptly showed his face and shouted, "These men are mixed up with the other train thieves. I was a passenger on the down train from Chattanooga. I never forget a new face; and besides, he's wearing the same smelly, dirty clothes."

On Saturday morning, April 26, 1862, Governor Joseph E. Brown was gingerly sipping a ceramic cup of coffee lovingly prepared by his wife, Elizabeth.

"Honey, the 'Southern Confederacy' has an interesting article on the latest events surrounding the Andrews Raid on our railroad."

"Joseph, have they been catching those engine thieves?"

"Yes, my dear. The paper says they caught two more Bridge Burners near Chattanooga, and the authorities took them to the Chattanooga jail two days ago – that would make it the 24th. Furthermore, the newspaper states that one of the engine thieves is still at large or has escaped to enemy lines," said Governor Brown.

"Oh, so one engine thief is still on the loose," she said, while cooking some soft-scrambled eggs, grits, and bacon on the Browns' kitchen wood stove.

THE RUNAWAY TRAIN

"Yes, but I have to say that we should have had musket-armed security personnel at every train station, but the Georgia legislature has been poking fun at my military budget, and that's why I had the State purchase the pikes. But I see now that hindsight is better than foresight. It's darned if you do and darned if you don't."

"Oh, Joseph, you're a hard-working man, and God will richly reward you one day," said Elizabeth.

"If I don't die in office, it'll be a miracle," he said with seriousness on his homely, unsmiling, unshaven, anxiety-ridden face.

* * *

Meanwhile, a short distance northwest of Canton, having been placed under arrest, William Pittenger began walking in chains between two armed soldiers followed by a hostile, yet inquisitive gathering of townspeople looking for relief from their monotonous daily routine, in a very small, obscure town. Pittenger became immediately penniless upon surrendering his wallet to his captors, who led him to be confined inside of an iron cage, on the second story of a large brick building, located on a side street in LaFayette, Georgia. The two-story brick jail was made up of broad metal slats arranged in a grid pattern, which included one side of the cage that had a small space between itself and the walls of the room. The jail had a heavy key-locked iron door and a solid-iron floor.

While Pittenger was mulling over the circumstances of his captivity in an iron cage within an established structure, the arresting officer was talking with one of his subordinates, Sgt. Alvin Gentry, a five-foot-six-inch, blue-eyed, blond, 180-pound, clean-shaven, rugged complexioned, large-torsoed man.

"Alvin, I have an assignment for you. I'm going to have you pose as another prisoner with that Yankee. Get him to talk about the train theft and bridge burning stuff. I want you to find out as much information as you can about him," said Lieutenant Jack Verner, a stocky, five-foot-eight-inch, 200-pound, blond 23-year-old man.

"Yes sir," said Sgt. Gentry.

"In my opinion, there was another reason for stealing the train. They were probably planning to invade Georgia, if they had succeeded in tearing up the track and burning the bridges," said Lt. Verner.

"Sir, I'll start talking to him," said Sgt. Gentry.

"You do that, sarge. Did you want a furlough?.....Well, if you can get him to talk. You know what I mean?" asked Lt. Verner.

"Yes sir," said Sgt. Gentry.

"Change into these civilian clothes as a disguise," said Lt. Verner, who then took Sgt. Gentry as a pretend prisoner to Pittenger's cage inside the LaFayette jail on the second floor, which was one floor above the jailer's quarters, on the first floor of the City jail. The two-story jail consisted of four rooms. The jailer had two on the ground floor, and two other rooms were on the second floor for the use of prisoners.

"Mr. Pittenger, this is 'Mr. Jones', your cellmate. He will keep you company," said the Lieutenant in charge of the jail.

The cellmate immediately struck up a friendly conversation.

"Pittenger, what did you Yanks expect to gain by coming down here and stealing a train?"

"We want to win the war," replied Pittenger.

"If you Yanks had gotten away with this, what were you planning to do next?" asked the "plant".

"To win the war," replied Pittenger again.

"How many troops does General Mitchel have?" asked Sgt. Gentry.

"So many it would make your head swim," said Pittenger.

"Where is General Mitchel?" asked Sgt. Gentry, the undercover cellmate.

"In an unknown location," said Pittenger.

"Where do you think you are?" asked Sgt. Gentry.

"In jail with an informant," responded Pittenger.

"Jailer, come here!" demanded Sgt. Gentry.

An eavesdropping red-haired, five-foot-six-inch, slim 22-year-old private named Bradley J. Coker, stepped forward to unlock the iron cage door to release the "plant". Pittenger had sensed a plot to pump him for secret information.

After the jailer and informant had left this second floor room of the City jail, Pittenger noticed that the other prisoner's plate of food was still intact. The extra jail food, while not the best cuisine in the South, nevertheless surpassed the hunger pangs that he experienced most of the time, during both the train chase and the flight from the engine "General". One could safely say that all the Andrews Raiders very likely lost much weight, since their previous meal at the Crutchfield House in Chattanooga on Friday, April 11, 1862.

Being incarcerated inside of the iron cage was, at the least, a very humiliating experience, particularly in the light of mercilessly inflicted public ridicule and name calling, referring to Pittenger as the "Beast in the Cage". Before very long, he reached his breaking point, so that he was compelled to assert himself by requesting to have an audience with the Vigilance Committee.

"I must see the Vigilance Committee," said Pittenger to the guard on duty.

"Sit tight, Yank. I'll be back," said the guard.

Within a few short minutes, two armed guards returned to accompany Pittenger to a certain building to face questioning from some lawyers.

"I'm ready to come clean," declared Pittenger, as the audience waxed silent as a tomb. "My real name is Corporal William Pittenger. You already know I'm a Yankee."

Laughter broke out as one very thin, six-foot, blue-eyed, black-haired attorney approached a pine desk directly facing Pittenger, who was handcuffed in front of his body, while seated in an old wooden chair.

A manifestation of the ill effects of the federally imposed naval blockade, were the attorney's malnourished, sallow cheeks. His shoes had holes in the soles, and the trousers were frayed at the bottoms.

"You people seem to be smart and sophisticated. If you are truly loyal and decent patriotic people to Jeff Davis, you will transport me to your nearest military installation," demanded Pittenger.

"Where is your trust?" asked the lawyer.

"Only the military have jurisdiction in military judicial matters. In plain language, because I'm a soldier, I should be tried in a military court for the things I've done against the South," said Pittenger.

"Does that mean you aren't going to answer our questions?" asked the blue-eyed, handlebar-mustached lawyer. Due to a dearth of scissors on the market, the barber had only a long, sharp knife with which to cut the attorney's hair. His shirt was unstarched, as evidenced by his unruly collar, making the lawyer look less professional.

"I will testify only before a military court," said Pittenger.

"So you think you can hold out on us. We have methods of extracting information from you."

"Please do not take it personally, Mr. Attorney," said Pittenger.

"All right, you win, Corporal. What you've said is logical. You're going to Chattanooga today," said the attorney.

"Thank you, sir," said Pittenger, with obvious relief on his face.

After dinner, men led Pittenger from the jail to be chained at the public square to a horse-drawn carriage, with an armed Confederate guard riding a horse on each side of the transporting vehicle, which was embarking upon the twenty-seven mile journey to General Leadbetter's Regional Confederate Headquarters in Chattanooga.

From a large, furious mob, a man blurted out, "You will be hanged just as soon in Chattanooga as you would be here, Yank."

Another heckler shouted, "You piece of crap. How dare you steal our train and burn our trestles."

"The only good Yank is a dead Yank," said another.

"Foreigners like you should stay in your own backyard," said one pleasingly plump woman. "I say you damned Yankees have no right to tell the South how to live its life," she said. "Let's be done and over with it."

"Times a-wasting," said a scowling old man.

"You're worthless scum crawling out of Lincoln's butt!" said another old man.

Looking around for a reasonably intelligent citizen, Pittenger chose to crack a joke. "How many Yankees do you need to fire a musket?"

"You tell us, Yank," said one onlooker.

"One holding the front of the bore; a second holding the trigger; and a third one steadying the butt of the musket," said Pittenger.

"That's rich," said the Mayor of LaFayette laughingly. "No wonder the Yanks lost so many men at Corinth."

I'll bet you've never seen a caged Yankee before," said Pittenger.

"And we've never seen a caged subhuman, either," said another man.

Another bystander remarked, "It's a darn shame he's a Yankee. If I didn't know any better, I'd say he looks a lot like a preacher."

The soldiers padlocked his neck with a nine-foot-long chain, secured the opposite end of the chain under the carriage seat, and another padlock immobilized one of Pittenger's feet, so that he could not stand straight up on the horse-drawn conveyance. Needless to say, the Confederate soldiers had secured their prisoner for transfer with an elaborate restraint system, which also entailed handcuffing and the use of additional ropes that confined his elbows to their respective sides of the prisoner's body.

What ensued was a very unsettling ride over extremely muddy roads and plentiful rocks, and the tightened chains pressed unforgivingly against Pittenger's frame, as the Nineteenth Century version of the modern-day automatic seatbelt – without a manual release button. The weather improved as the clouds had lifted during the previous evening, when Pittenger was pondering capital punishment at the end of a rope. Certainly, he knew he would not have received a fair trial in LaFayette, for he sensed their vindictive, hateful attitude. He reasoned that the Confederate military would at least grant him a trial, with the probability of a prison sentence, in lieu of a mob-induced hanging in LaFayette. Slowly and inevitably, he was, to a greater extent, relying on God to deliver him from the depressing day-to-day life of captivity in a faraway place, with the hope of returning to Steubenville, Ohio, as a newspaper reporter. Reluctantly, he was beginning to accept the reality that God was surely in control of his life, not William Pittenger.

Before the lapse of much more time, Pittenger's wagon was traveling to the northeast of Lookout Mountain, having crossed the Georgia border into Tennessee. At this point, an officer shouted, "Stop on this hill. I have to obey the call of nature."

Another officer said, "When you come back, it'll be my turn."

"I think you and I drank too much coffee before we left LaFayette," said the remaining officer at the wagon.

"You've got that right," said the officer walking quickly toward the bushes.

An hour later, the City of LaFayette's horse-drawn vehicle crossed the city limits into Chattanooga. The officer riding on the right side of the wagon said, "Stop at the Crutchfield House."

THE RUNAWAY TRAIN

The Confederate army had recently seized the Crutchfield House to establish their regional headquarters, whose commanding general was General Danville A. Leadbetter.

CHAPTER 7
DOWN IN THE DUNGEON

As William Pittenger arrived with armed Confederate guards, an angry mob appeared near the Crutchfield House to spew hateful, mean-spirited epithets at the transferred Union prisoner.

An especially dignified-looking elderly resident looked condescendingly down his nose, as his glasses slipped several notches down his nasal bridge. The elderly man walked stiffleggedly, as the result of a serious leg wound sustained during the Mexican War in 1845. He was a gray-haired, gray-bearded, 60-year-old, dark-complexioned, five-foot-eight-inch, 185-pound man, who was probably a college professor of Theology.

The man arrogantly growled, "What is your age, son?"

"Twenty-two," replied Pittenger.

"You moron. You look so much like a schoolteacher. If you're lucky to live long enough, you'd be wise to return to your own backyard and leave the South alone. You Yankees are a pain in the buttocks."

The gruff old man pivoted on his left heel, blending in with vocal locals, who then cheered in response to this public tongue-lashing of the subdued, tired prisoner.

An unidentified bystander commented, "This Yank looks like a professional jailbird. He has that hardened look on his face."

William Pittenger writes that General Leadbetter was a Northern-born, notoriously cruel, cowardly man, based upon the other soldiers' observations. Meanwhile, the two armed Confederate guards unfastened the chains and led Corporal Pittenger from the horse-drawn wagon to General Leadbetter's office.

"I understand you have been withholding some vital information. Let's hear it," said General Leadbetter demandingly, as he curiously eyed Pittenger standing in front of the General's desk.

"I was on a special detail for unspecified duty in an unknown location," replied Pittenger.

"What was the engineer's name?" asked General Leadbetter.

"I decline to comment," replied Pittenger.

"And what was the scope of your mission?" asked the General.

"To steal a train and burn bridges," replied Pittenger.

"What is General Mitchel's troop strength?" asked the General.

"More than 60,000 troops – enough to overpower Chattanooga," replied Pittenger.

"Hmmm.....do tell! Name the number of men on the stolen train and tell me about them," asked the General.

"I'm a United States soldier not wishing to divulge sensitive information regarding my compatriots," replied Pittenger.

"Really, now. Perhaps I'm being too rude for being so nosey," commented General Leadbetter.

"Yes sir," said Pittenger.

"Perhaps I should enlighten you. I am very much informed about your leader known as James J. Andrews. Tell me what I don't already know about him," said the General.

"I'll say one thing about him. Chances are slim and none of catching him," said Pittenger.

With a triumphant, victorious smile likened to the cat that ate the canary, General Leadbetter began to lower the boom on the unsuspecting captive. "That will be all," he said. Turning at an angle toward the doorway at detainees Andrews, Ross, and Wollam, all standing while chained in heavy irons, the crusty, weather-beaten-faced General snapped, "Escort this man to the 'Hole' without delay." The General returned a salute to the Captain, who accompanied the unexpected additional prisoners. Pittenger was aghast.

The "Hole" was known as the old Swims Jail, once used to incarcerate slaves at Lookout Street, between Third and Fourth Streets. The jail was constructed into a hillside, and the structure was a small masonry building encircled by a very wide, high fence. Eight guards dutifully linked their elbows with the prisoners during the transfer to the Swims Jail front door opening on level ground. The walls and floor were of solid oak.

The jailer, Mr. Swims, was a 60-year-old white-haired man, whose face showed many care-worn years, perhaps due to a very hard life. His voice was characterized by an obnoxious whining sound, and he habitually responded to water requests with a hoarse scream. Swims viewed Yankees and slaves as the lowest forms of humanity. He and his family were quartered on the upper north end of the building, and the prison rooms were located on the lower floor on the south end.

Pittenger easily felt the sharp end of forceful bayonets, while standing at the dark entrance to the "Hole", accessible only by a stepladder easily lowered and raised at the jailer's pleasure. Pittenger sensed a figurative descent into hell while bound by handcuffs. Only thirteen square feet of space separated each inmate, and everyone's greatest fear was death by asphyxiation, and one of the worst irritants was the lingering stench of unbathed inmates some of whom were runaway slaves flogged for advertising their resale.

When raised, the lower side of the trap door had bolted huge iron strap hinges previously hand-forged on an anvil. Each of the seven boards had two bolts fastened to the trap door. The four-inch-thick wooden trap door had two locks, one on the upper left side and the other lock on the upper right side, opposite the hinged side.

All of the prisoners were chained together and crowded like sardines in a can. Whenever a prisoner had to go to relieve himself of bodily wastes or to go for a drink of water, it became necessary to drag by chain, several other prisoners along with him. One can easily imagine the interpersonal conflicts that arose as prisoners stepped on one another in unbearably crowded conditions.

Sometime during Monday evening on April 21, 1862, Andrews, Ross, and Wollam climbed down the portable ladder to the "Hole" to join Pittenger. As long as the trap door was open during the entry of additional prisoners, the introduction of cool, fresh, unadulterated air presented a welcomed relief to all the inmates below the trap door. Even before the sound of chains had ceased, Swims closed the trap door to once again leave the lower floor of confinement in virtually total darkness.

"Boys, we've just been questioned upstairs. We gave certain answers, and I want you to listen carefully to what I tell you. You are to tell them you were commanded to go on the mission to steal the train. Unfortunately, I can't say that since I led the raid – that won't be at all convincing," said Andrews, as he talked to his associates near the two lighted small ground floor windows, one of which was located under the stairwell leading to the exterior of the building. "One more thing, boys:

don't tell them the engineer's name and don't mention that Campbell is a civilian."

Most of the Andrews Raiders had arrived to be imprisoned at the Swims Jail by Tuesday, April 22, 1862. George D. Wilson, Daniel Dorsey, Robert Buffum, and William Bensinger clanged their chains upon descending the portable ladder to the "Hole".

Previously, these raiders were apprehended and transported to Ringgold, before being taken south to Marietta for a brief confinement, but military cadets were experiencing a difficult time in protecting these men from a very angry gathering of local citizenry. It then became necessary to move the prisoners northward to Dalton, where local women fed them dinner with the assistance of servants. The men were chained around their necks in pairs and were, of course, handcuffed. Dorsey received a rose from one of the women. Evidently, the food preparers of the delicious home-cooked dinner were tearfully sympathetic with the prisoners' awkward situation of trying to eat, while irons and chains severely restricted their movements.

Later, in Chattanooga, prior to their transport to the Swims Jail, a benevolent hotel landlord treated them to a complimentary breakfast.

After the men were taken to the Swims Jail, the jailer opened the trap door and said, "Corporal Pittenger, report to the Judge Advocate." As he carefully climbed up the swaying ladder, two armed guards disconnected his chains from William

Bensinger, who had been attached by one handcuff to Pittenger. The guard had earlier connected Bensinger by a chain to Buffum.

Having then been taken outside to the prison yard, six guards very closely watched Pittenger.

Within a few minutes, a captain ordered the six guards to take Pittenger to the Crutchfield House to submit to questioning from the Judge Advocate, who said, "Pittenger, we'll let you have immunity from prosecution if you'll answer all our questions."

"I respectfully decline to comment on the grounds it might incriminate my compatriots. As an American soldier, I am sworn to do my duty to my country," replied Pittenger.

"You are free to return to jail," said the Judge Advocate. When Pittenger returned to the Swims Jail, the guards held Pittenger outside in the jail yard, where he noticed the jailer eagerly reading a newspaper article. Swims left the newspaper on the window sill without thinking; and Pittenger seized the golden opportunity to hide the newspaper inside his shirt, before quickly relaying it through the triple window bars of the close-to-the-ground window.

Suddenly, a tall German-born Confederate soldier shouted vehemently, "Move away from the building!" Two guards followed with fixed bayonets. One guard said, "One more foolish move and you're dead." The jailer was unable to retrieve his newspaper.

General Mitchel's forces were already attacking

THE RUNAWAY TRAIN

Bridgeport, Alabama, on Tuesday, April 29, 1862. Perhaps General Mitchel would have taken Chattanooga, if only he had been equipped with intelligence information regarding the understaffed defenders of Chattanooga.

While lowering in a basket the men's limited breakfast menu items, Mr. Swims drunkenly stated, "Boys, I hear tell General Mitchel is coming." The sound of distant cannons confirmed the welcomed news to the inmates. To prevent the Union Army's rescue of the twenty-two prisoners in Chattanooga, the decision was made to remove them to a more secure place to retain the prisoners for trial as spies.

A few minutes later, the trap door opened as a guard shouted, "Everybody up the ladder." The guards carefully inspected all the chains to which they added some new connectors for additional strength.

"Listen up, inmates. We're taking you somewhere else, since the Yankees are getting too close to us," said a captain. All the Andrews Raiders were taken to the Chattanooga train depot for temporary relocation to Madison, Georgia. During this trip, a crowd of angry bystanders confronted the prisoner transport train while stopped at Ringgold, Georgia.

Later, in Atlanta, a very angry mob demanded that the authorities hang the Andrews Raiders immediately. Several members of the mob were injured in their attempt to draw close enough to the barred train windows. One man managed to reach a barred window through which he shoved a current newspaper. The man simply said, "A friend," and quickly disappeared in the crowd. The headlines declared the federal capture of New Orleans, a very interesting, morale-boosting tidbit of good news to the raiders.

Dorsey and Porter were showing signs of fatigue and irritation during the long train ride from Chattanooga. The two men started having words.

"Porter, this is the first time you've ridden a train since you went south to Marietta," said Dorsey.

"Just what do you mean by that crack?" asked Porter.

"You didn't show up when we stole the train," said Dorsey.

"Yeah, I know. I overslept," said Porter.

"If you had managed your money, you could have paid some hotel employee to wake you up," said Dorsey.

"Why don't you shut up," said Porter, very irritated.

"Make me, sleepyhead," said Dorsey. Suddenly, Porter jerked and tried to twist Dorsey's neck chain, and Dorsey retaliated by twisting Porter's neck chain with the intention of strangling Porter, resulting in a stalemate.

Andrews intervened and said, "All right, boys, no more fighting. Save your energy for the Madison jail."

The Andrews Raiders arrived by train on May 2,

THE RUNAWAY TRAIN

1862 to be immediately locked up in the Morgan County, Madison, Georgia jail for three days. It was a very depressing stone structure, occupying the southern half of the same site of a 1930's automotive repair business, the Ben S. Thompson Garage, according to Civil War Historian, Wilbur G. Kurtz.

Several hours after admitting the prisoners to this jail, a man dressed in a Confederate uniform, disguised as a jail guard, whom Andrews recognized as a former espionage colleague under the auspices of the United States Secret Service in Kentucky. Without hesitation, Andrews used sign language to inform the "visitor" that the hijack of the "General" led to their imprisonment in Chattanooga and temporary captivity in Madison, due to General Mitchel's military threat to Chattanooga. The spy appeared surprised and hand-signaled he had to leave town in a hurry. Andrews manually signaled, "Goodbye and be praying for me and my boys."

Rushing away from the Madison telegraph office, the Provost Marshal appeared to be carrying a hot potato in his hands, but it was actually a telegram hot off the telegraph wires with an urgent message.

Entering the jail, a long brick building providing much better conditions of confinement, the Provost Marshal shouted, "Guards!"

"Yes sir," said one guard.

"This telegram says there's a Yankee spy in

town," declared the Provost Marshal.

"Sir, there he goes down the street. The first guard fired a shot at the spy, who feigned being wounded and fell to the ground. The bullet whizzed within an inch of the spy's right butternut uniform sleeve.

"Come on. He's down. Let's catch that Yankee," said the Captain of the Guards.

One guard grabbed the spy by the right elbow, after realizing the man was still alive and unscathed.

"Oh, so you were playing possum," said the Captain of the Guard gleefully.

"Listen, I have papers proving who I am," said the spy, as he rose up from the prone position on the ground.

"How dare you wear the Confederate uniform, you skunk," said the Captain of the Guard in a very hostile tone of voice.

Running his hand nervously through his hip pocket, the Confederate imposter said, "I know I have the papers."

"Let's see 'em. We don't have all night," said the Captain of the Guard.

The spy quickly kicked the captain in the groin, pushed another guard to the ground, and away the Yankee spy ran like a marathon runner, to grasp the hand rail attached to the final passenger car of an accelerating train, departing the Madison, Georgia train depot.

A few minutes later, the Captain of the Guard, still writhing in pain from the unexpected kick to his private parts, said to Andrews, while delivering the dinner food to the inmates, after unlocking the cell door with an old-fashioned handmade key, "Guess what."

"Begging your pardon, sir?" asked Andrews.

"There was a Yankee spy in town. We were fixing to arrest him. He kicked me in the crotch, and caught a speeding train out of town," said the Captain of the Guard.

"I'll bet that hurt," said Andrews.

"Big time!" said the Captain.

The guard locked the cell door and the raiders began to eat their evening meal. Andrews was smiling and said, "Boys, our secret agent and I used sign language. Thank God he got away. I told him about our special ride from Big Shanty. He'll get the word out up north," said the Andrews Raid ringleader, with his mouth half full of cooked potatoes.

On the third day of imprisonment, the Captain of the Guard approached the cell and said, "All right, you men, you're riding the train back to Chattanooga. Don't try anything stupid." Apparently, General Mitchel did not carry out his planned attack on Chattanooga, because the raiders and the stolen train could not meet Mitchel in Huntsville, Alabama.

One chain after another could be heard clanking, as the raiders filed out of the jail and boarded a horse-drawn wagon to be taken to the train station in Madison. As the last raider ascended the steps to the outbound prisoner transport passenger car, a loud thud was heard as a thrown rock barely missed Porter while striking the door jamb of the car.

"Whew, that was a close one," said Porter in utter astonishment. "Somebody doesn't like us."

The guard interjected, "That's because they don't like train thieves and Bridge Burners."

You're not just whistling 'Dixie', Reb," commented Porter, as he walked toward his seat in a filthy, roach-infested, wet railroad car.

As the train lurched forward, perhaps due to poor lubrication and maintenance practices, an idea was cooking in Andrews's mind. He was recalling the pleasant days in Flemingsburg, Kentucky, during his evening lessons as a music instructor, and now he was thinking about the possibilities of escaping the Swims Jail in Chattanooga. But for right now, he decided to utilize the travel time constructively by leading songs for his men to sing. The idea was not to impress the guard, but rather, it was meant to be a good morale-booster.

"Boys, I used to teach music. I want you to learn how to sing "Dixie", since we have some spare time," said Andrews.

"Are you kidding? We're Yankees. What business do we have with Southern songs?" asked Campbell.

"Relax, Mr. Campbell, and enjoy the music practice session," said Andrews with a pasted-on smile.

The guard listened intently throughout the

singing of the popular Southern song and then remarked, "You men can sing. It's too bad you messed up your lives. You could have gone places."

"Oh, we've been going places," said Campbell with a lighthearted chuckle.

"That's not what I meant. You know better than that," said the train guard.

"I'm just joking," said Campbell.

The trip through Atlanta and other towns was essentially a repetition of the earlier trip to Madison; it was simply one unfriendly set of station greeters after another – hecklers and catcallers galore – at each train stop during the return trip west to Atlanta and north to the Chattanooga train station.

For some unexplainable reason, the 25-year-old Captain of the Guard, Captain Laws, permitted the Andrews Raiders to be quartered in the upper room of the Swims Jail, while the fourteen East Tennessean prisoners were relocated to the dark, unpleasant dungeon. In contrast to the "Hole", the raiders reaped the benefit of visible outside scenery, seen through one high row of barred windows.

Even though their prison conditions slightly improved, the warden tightened security with armed guards placed virtually everywhere, including the stairwell entrance. One guard on perimeter patrol and two rows of bayonet-bearing guards always accompanied the food distributor when delivering meals to the Andrews Raiders.

Despite routine body searches, Knight would

adroitly conceal a pen knife by turning his arm in a certain manner, to avoid discovery of the sharp instrument, which he had planned to use to whittle, cut, and shape pieces of chicken bones as keys, to unlock the locks on the chains confining their bodies. The raiders must have realized that their above-ground location of imprisonment presented a golden opportunity for escape to Union lines. A particularly disturbing incident occurred to motivate efforts for planning an exit to the outside world.

Andrews received from an unidentified officer, a sealed document during a rest period in the jail yard. Curiosity prompted Andrews to break the seal, and to his utter surprise, it was his death warrant, which immediately changed his prison status to reconfinement in the dungeon. His skin turned very pale. Saturday, May 31, 1862, was the next to the worst day of Andrews's life, which was scheduled to end by execution on Saturday, June 7, 1862.

The distraught, dejected ringleader walked discreetly toward his engineer, William Knight, and quietly whispered, "They're going to hang me next week. We must get out of here by dawn. Pass the word along."

"So that's what the paper was all about," said Knight.

"Exactly," said Andrews.

"I've got a plan to escape," said Knight.

"Let's do it, Knight," said Andrews resolutely.

"Tomorrow at dawn when the jailer makes his visit," said Knight.

THE RUNAWAY TRAIN

"Good plan," Andrews said.

All night long the raiders kept singing to entertain and distract the guards while Knight cut away with his pen knife an opening above the ceiling, to loosen mortar and bricks on the outside wall to the jail yard. In the process, Knight had to first cut through the ceiling plank to be in position to create the escape hole to the outside of the building.

Knight said to one of his compatriots, "Pass the word around. All undergarments must be collected to make a swing-out rope from the hole I'm making."

Campbell relieved Knight and cut the rest of the plank until it broke in two. "Hey, Knight, you take a break. I'm going to finish the rest of the job, because I have the muscle-power," said the burly civilian member of Company "G" of the Second Ohio. Later, he cut the lock from the trapdoor.

Finally, as the dawn broke, Knight lowered a makeshift ladder composed of undergarments tied together for Andrews to ascend to the upper floor of the jail. The stage had been set for immediate flight. Andrews was the first one to descend the rope to the ground. A strong, bearded young backyard prison guard appeared as a murky, grayish, indefinable shape, that was soon firing his musket at Andrews, who quickly escaped by scaling the jail yard wall.

As Andrews descended the rope from the gabled end of the jail to the ground, the noise of a fallen brick alerted a patrolling guard. As Andrews swung

259

out from the building, a bullet whizzed by his head and frightened him so much, that he lost his grip on the boots and ran away without the mandatory footwear – much to his detriment.

John Wollam was the second escapee to face musket fire, but neither man was hit. Wollam instinctively ducked his head during the risky plunge from the pen knife-carved opening to the ground. The early morning semi-darkness and the difficulty of shooting fast-moving targets caused the guards to shoot wildly with their muskets.

Daniel Dorsey had tried to escape, but one guard brandished a cocked musket and a fixed bayonet. "It's no use, men. We can't make it," said Dorsey.

Somewhat later, another prisoner – not one of the raiders – approached a barred window through which he thrust the Wednesday, June 4, 1862 issue of the Knoxville Register, which contained an advertisement: ONE HUNDRED DOLLARS REWARD FOR THE CAPTURE OF JAMES J. ANDREWS.

Meanwhile, Andrews spent the entire day high up in a well-foliaged tree, located very close to a railroad track. Time after time, trains sped past his temporary arboreal refuge, and one passerby wasp buzzed over Andrews's head without any intention of harming him.

A little while beyond sunset, perhaps about 8:30 p.m. that time of year, Andrews climbed down the tree and decided to swim over to the other side of a fast-flowing river current, but he lost, in addition to his boots, his hat and coat. His socks were no match for the very sharp rocks on the river bed, and it was a futile exercise in frustration to cover his bloodied feet, with what little clothing he had left to bind his feet for protection.

In the twilight, people observed Andrews walking through an open field, swimming to Williams Island, a relatively small island, where he hid himself in a pile of driftwood on the northern tip of the island. But searchers spotted Andrews and followed him to the opposite end of Williams Island, where two boys accidentally noticed him in a tree. Having ridden a skiff, searchers recaptured Andrews at 2:00 p.m. on Tuesday, after a two-day absence from the Swims Jail.

The other escapee, John Wollam, was very skillful in the art of throwing the pursuing hounds off his trail, at least for a week. By walking a short distance into a river after tossing his coat and vest beside the river bank, Wollam was able to gain some time, since the hounds were no longer able to trace the fugitive's bodily scent. A little while later, the pursuers and the barking hounds walked very close to Wollam's hiding place in some bushes.

One aggressive searcher said, "By golly, we're going to catch the scoundrel."

"Look! He dropped his clothes near the river. We've been all over this place – up, down, and all around. I think he drowned," said the second pursuer.

"Serves that Yankee right," said another

pursuer, also giving up the pursuit.

However, Wollam had been fortunate to get a new lease on his freedom, which was not without its nettlesome problems: the stress of flight, the uncertainty of his direction of flight, and the failure to identify a gunboat, passing by a canoe which he had stolen from a mountain resident, before rowing down the river. Unfortunately for Wollam, he was unable to discern whether the gunboat was either Union or Confederate. Perhaps, a genuine risk-taker would have hollered at the gunboat, but alas, it was not to happen, for the outcome was nothing more than "two ships passing in the night" – probably a lost opportunity to escape to Union lines.

Fear of recapture took the upper hand in his mind. Interestingly enough, General Mitchel, a master engineer, had taken the initiative to build a Union gunboat, an activity of which Wollam was unaware.

Wollam had perhaps rowed very close to a Union gunboat in the darkness, but one will never know whether or not the hull of the gunboat bore any clearly identifiable military lettering, such as "U.S." or "C.S.A".

A short while later, perhaps during the following day, a Confederate cavalry unit had been dispatched to look for John Wollam. To pursue him by water, three of the cavalrymen dismounted and commandeered a boat that had been chained to a tree near the river bank. With the aid of three cavalrymen utilizing three oars, they soon recaptured John Wollam, whom they transported back to Chattanooga. Coincidentally, Lt. Edwards, a tall, lanky, 25-year-old, blue-eyed, blond officer, readily recognized John Wollam as the very same man captured about two and one-half months earlier, at the end of the locomotive pursuit phase, of the Confederate military roundup of the Andrews Raiders.

Sometime in late May of 1862, the Captain of the Guard called the prisoners to fall in for an informational briefing in the jail yard of the Swims Jail in Chattanooga.

"Listen up, inmates. Twelve of you have been selected to attend a court-martial proceeding in Knoxville, Tennessee. I guess we must have twelve privileged characters in this jail. The train will leave in thirty minutes. Fall out!"

Some of the engine thieves were practically at the point of severe sweating, upon hearing about this new development. The first logical question was: Why were those particular raiders chosen to stand before a court-martial, and the second question was: What were the charges? And thirdly, what type of punishment would be meted out, and when would the punishment be carried out? Worry had stricken them like an imaginary flame searing their flesh.

James J. Andrews was not included among the "Knoxville Twelve", since the Swims Jail kangaroo court had summarily issued the ringleader a written death warrant, and the jail's blacksmith had been called to rivet heavy iron fetters on Andrews's feet, as his legs and feet were placed across the blacksmith's anvil, on which he vigorously hammered the fastening devices, to ensure the difficulty of a further escape attempt. As an additional physical restraint, Andrews's hand had been as tightly restricted as his feet. The countdown continued, as only four days to Andrews's execution remained. He had written his will to be administrated by a probate attorney in Flemingsburg.

Elsewhere, in Eastern Tennessee, a court-martial was in progress. During a recess, Confederate officers were reading newspapers, chewing plugs of tobacco, smoking cigars, and talking softly to each other. Such was the lack of decorum in the military tribunal in Knoxville, during the first week of June, 1862.

"Corporal Pittenger, report to the Judge's chambers – front and center," snapped a young, slender second lieutenant with ruddy cheeks, a five-foot-eight-inch stature, weighing 150 pounds. He had a tattoo of Jefferson Davis on the left wrist; long, wide sideburns and a handlebar mustache rounded out his physical features. The large waiting room became all of a sudden as quiet as a funeral parlor.

"I'm Judge-Advocate Holt. I'm going to ask you some questions. Answer truthfully."

"Yes sir, responded Pittenger.

"Why did you travel to the South and what was your mission?"

"Your Honor, I was ordered to go on a mission under duress, and no one told me the purpose of it. I had no choice in the matter. I was simply following orders," said Pittenger.

"Corporal Pittenger, who was your engineer?" asked Judge-Advocate Holt.

"I am not privy to that information, sir," said Pittenger.

"Isn't that rather strange?"

"This was a unique and strange mission, sir."

"What is your duty classification, Corporal Pittenger?"

"Your Honor, my responsibilities included building bridges and functioning as a company clerk."

"What outfit were you in?"

"Company "G", 22nd Ohio Regiment."

"I guess that would make you a Yankee."

"Absolutely, your Honor, and proud to be an American."

"You mean I'm not an American?"

"You were until your state seceded from the Union, to become the Confederate States of America."

"Oh, my, I'm really getting educated."

"What did you do before you joined the Army?"

"I was a reporter for the Steubenville, Ohio Herald."

"Oh, what a bright young lad you are, and it strikes me rather odd that you don't know your engineer's name, or the exact purpose and nature of your expedition into Georgia...All right, last question: Who was your leader who brought you to Georgia?"

"Due to the confidential nature of the mission, we did not use names."

Obviously irritated and frustrated at getting nowhere in the line of questioning, the Judge said, "Soldier, no jurist in the country would accept your answers. That is all. You can go."

One after the other, each raider had to submit to questioning in the Judge's chambers, during a very long day that included catered meals for lunch and dinner from the Distended Belly Restaurant, which was located across the street in this mountainous area of Eastern Tennessee.

Later, William Campbell quipped, "That judge kept trying to pick my brain, but I just kept boring him with details about my upbringing and the time I murdered a whorehouse owner."

"That's news to me," said Pittenger.

"What did the judge ask you?" asked Campbell.

"He tried to get me to name our engineer, but I played dumb and said we didn't call each other by name, due to the secrecy of our mission."

"Outstanding, Pittenger, but I doubt we'll be let off the hook. One of our men is bound to spill the beans," said Campbell with a sigh.

"It's all in God's hands. We have no control over this situation and our ultimate disposition in this whole mess," said Pittenger.

Unexpectedly, a junior officer put a newspaper in Pittenger's hands and said, "No more talking, Yanks. I know you men can read newspapers, and that's all I want you to do."

THE RUNAWAY TRAIN

As the officer walked away, the headlines immediately hooked Pittenger's attention. The bold headlines read: **"TRAIN THIEVES TO FACE COURT-MARTIAL"**. Pittenger and Campbell raised their eyebrows and whistled in astonishment.

"This is big local news," said Campbell.

"Yes, we'll be lucky if some angry mob doesn't tear us apart limb from limb," said Pittenger.

On the other side of the large room, two senior officers were conferring with one another while smoking cigars.

"Lt. Jones, I've got a feeling we need to wrap up our proceedings shortly. I've just received intelligence about a group of saboteurs not too far from here," said Major B. R. Smith.

"What is our game plan?" asked Lt. J. O. Jones.

Major Smith replied, "When the last defendant leaves Judge Holt's chambers, alert the riot squad to line up on both sides of the Bridge Burners, and make sure they are properly chained to the horse-drawn wagon and whisked away to the train station, as soon as possible, so we can get back to protecting Eastern Tennessee. If these men had succeeded, General Mitchel would have been an additional pain in the neck for us."

"Yes sir, consider it done," said Lt. Jones.

"Lieutenant, there's another reason for getting rid of the hot potatoes," said Major Smith.

"What's that, sir?" asked Lt. Jones.

"That train conductor named Fuller was poking his nose into our business yesterday, and inquiring about the proceedings," said Major Smith.

"Is that right, sir?" asked Lt. Jones.

"Fuller had placed an ad in the June Fourth Knoxville Register for a one-hundred dollar reward for the reincarceration of Andrews. He might start harassing these prisoners. He appears to be a persistent seeker of justice – the type of man who never sleeps until justice is served," said Major Smith. Both were of medium height and were heavy-set, hard-drinking officers, who appreciated the finest available cigars from which the military brass derived great pleasure.

Finally, after another thirty minutes, Judge Holt had concluded the questioning of all twelve selected Andrews Raiders.

It was still daylight as the raiders boarded the train, but three hours later, darkness fell upon the land. Four train guards were seated with muskets, after having eaten a very delicious heavy meal with smuggled European wines at the Distended Belly Restaurant. As the night wore on, the guards were gradually becoming very sleepy.

Campbell whispered to Pittenger. "Look. The guards are asleep. Now's our chance to escape."

Immediately responding to the well-meaning elbow nudging, Pittenger opened his eyes and said, "I wouldn't recommend it. None of us are prepared to survive in these rugged hills, especially since there are Cherokee Indians ready to kill any white man who even sets foot there."

"Oh, I didn't know that," said Campbell.

"And besides, the Cherokees were run out of Georgia when Andrew Jackson was President of the United States, and those that remain are well hidden in the hills. Jackson hated the Cherokees because they were allies of the British soldiers, who forced Jackson's parents to quarter the troops in the Jacksons' home – without their consent. So, that's why Jackson pushed the Cherokees out of Georgia," said Pittenger.

"Oh yeah, it was called the 'Trail of Tears'," said Campbell. Well, we'll find a way to escape later. I have to hope, anyway."

"Never give up hope, Campbell. Our faith is being tested," said Pittenger.

It was probably early Sunday morning on June 1, 1862, when the Swims Jail authorities put the Andrews Raiders on a southbound train from Chattanooga, Tennessee, to be transferred to the Fulton County Jail in Atlanta, Georgia.

As the men were boarding the train, William S. Whiteman entered the raiders' car and said to the ringleader, "Mr. Andrews, how do you account for the $10,000 I gave you to purchase medical supplies and other items?"

"I'd rather not talk about that subject right now," said Andrews softly.

"I heard what a foolish thing you did. You shouldn't have stolen that train," said Whiteman disdainfully.

"Good day, Mr. Whiteman," said Andrews.

Angered and red-faced, Whiteman pivoted on

his right foot and stormed out of the railroad car in a huff. Andrews's compatriots were very puzzled that he did not ever discuss the business relationship between him and Whiteman. As far as Andrews was concerned, he broke his partnership with Whiteman the moment the adventurous blockade contraband merchant conferred with the Ohio volunteers on the Wartrace Road, at the outset of the trip southward to steal the "General". Perhaps the two men had been previously bickering about how to conduct the business.

CHAPTER 8
THE GREAT JAIL BREAK

The railroad trip southward to Atlanta would be the longest and the last one for James J. Andrews, the leader of the failed Andrews Raid. Since February, 1862, he had no further contact with his fiancée, Miss. Elizabeth Layton, who was probably in a continual state of anxiety, without even so much as having received a letter from Andrews. The couple would have been married on June 7, 1862. One can only imagine the types of thoughts that were racing through his mind, as he viewed for the last time on the earth the beautiful green mountain scenery of North Georgia, serving as a grim reminder of his aborted mission to advance the cause of aiding his country, in response to President Abraham Lincoln's public declaration that the Union must be preserved. Apparently, Andrews put his country first over his plans to marry Miss Layton, a selfless act of patriotism.

Several of the raiders were nervously chewing their plugs of tobacco, while looking out the windows of the passenger rail car, halfway through the trip to Atlanta. Shifting mental gears from the deep-in-thought mode, Andrews made an off-the-wall remark about his future: "Boys, I wonder what it'll be like to be on the other side of the Jordan. There's one sure thing: I'll find out very soon."

Pittenger responded, "Mr. Andrews, we all eventually die and leave this earth. It is my prayer you will be ready to meet God."

Campbell broke in and said, "When you get to Heaven, don't tell God about our failure to steal a train. He might think twice about letting you go past the gate." The others laughed heartily and Wilson almost swallowed his plug of chewing tobacco while laughing so hard.

Momentarily, the engineer slowed the southbound train as it neared Dalton, Georgia. The telegrapher stepped out of the telegraph booth and stared at the raiders' car.

"There's the telegraph boy. I'll bet he was the one who squealed on us. If we had only cut the wire a minute or two sooner, we wouldn't be wearing these wretched chains," said Campbell angrily.

Seventeen-year-old Edward Henderson had indeed noticed the deboarding chained prisoners proceeding to queue up at the only outhouse, a separate wooden structure with a roof slanted toward the door, which opened and closed with the aid of a long spring, attached by a horseshoe nail.

Henderson asked the stationmaster, "Who are these men?"

THE RUNAWAY TRAIN

"Train thieves being transferred to the Atlanta jail."

"This is interesting," said Henderson, dressed in a pink-and-black-checkered Western & Atlantic Railroad shirt and blue trousers.

"Your hustling that telegram sure paid off – there's living proof of it," said the stationmaster.

Hmmm...Look how they're chained together. I don't see how they're going to use the outhouse," said the amused stationmaster, chuckling to himself as he watched the men taking turns using the primitive sanitary facility, the door closing on each subsequent connecting chain segment.

A curious crowd was forming near the line of chained men; instantly, one person threw a rock, narrowly missing Campbell, who quickly picked up and hurled the dangerous missile back at the hostile crowd.

"Come here you damn cowards. I'll bash your heads in two," growled an irascible Campbell. His angry, intense tone of voice was full of hatred; the crowd hastily dispersed, as they detected the presence of an evil spirit permeating the outhouse and railway station – during the very hot summer morning of June 1, 1862. This misbehavior reflected Campbell's dysfunctional family background, as previously detailed.

"All right, men. Let's ride," said the officer in charge, when the last raider had left the outhouse.

"Phew!" exclaimed Dorsey, "There has to be a better facility than this smelly thing, and whoever improves upon this stinkhouse will become a rich man."

"No more talking," said the officer. "Get on the train. Time's a-wasting."

The crowd turned around and again approached the captive transferees just before the officer in charge fired his musket in the air, as a warning shot to the unruly crowd, that had been hanging around the Dalton train depot.

Pittenger said to Campbell, "That certainly got their attention. Who wants to go where he's unwelcome? Let's shake the dust off our feet and board the train."

"You've got that right, Pittenger," said Campbell with a belly laugh. "That's scriptural."

Five adult women members of a Dalton church, gave the prisoners some cornbread and apples to carry with them as travel snacks, and one neatly attired, well-suited man bumped into Andrews and thrust twenty dollars into the condemned man's shirt, to share with his compatriots – just in case they might escape the Atlanta Jail and have a need for the money. The unknown benefactor simply said, "God bless you," quickly disappearing.

In addition to the prison rail car, four civilian passenger cars were also hooked up to the engine "Texas", which was ironically the engine used by Fuller and his men to pursue the Andrews Raiders.

Naturally, the reappearance of the "Texas" stirred up stored emotions in the minds of the Andrews Raiders, like prematurely removing the scab from a cut on the leg. Pittenger thought this train might be an instrument to rub salt in their psychological wounds.

Almost two hours later, the "Texas" engineer, Peter Bracken, slowed the iron horse at the Big Shanty train depot.

Dorsey commented, "Oh God, no. This is where we stole the "General".

"Big Shanty, twenty minutes for supper!" cried the conductor, whose face was new to the prisoners. "Everybody goes to eat – especially you train thieves. Believe me, you Yanks will never steal any more of our trains, including this one."

"Mighty big talk for a young man," said Dorsey. "Remember, sonny, pride goes before a fall. That's what my mother taught me when she read to me from the Good Book."

"We're going to win the war," said the young baby-faced, five-foot-five-inch, 150-pound, blue-eyed, blond conductor.

"Your plantation system will soon be destroyed. We have God on our side," said Pittenger matter-of-factly.

"Fat chance, Yank. The South is going to live forever," said the conductor.

Pittenger said firmly, "Remember this conversation. God will bring judgment upon the South against their pride, arrogance, and spirit of rebellion."

"Get out of here before I change my mind, Yank. You'd better get some supper," the conductor whined.

275

"Nice chatting with you, boy," said Campbell with a sardonic smile.

The head waitress of the Lacy Hotel was alarmed at the strange sight of chained prisoners walking toe-to-heel across the dusty front lawn, to the water troughs to wash their hands before eating supper. The sound of the clanking chains grew louder and louder, as the traveling prisoners entered the front door of the Lacy Hotel.

Recognizing James J. Andrews in chains and handcuffs, the head waitress said, "Mr. Andrews, don't you think you should have eaten breakfast instead of doing something else in April?"

"No, not at all. I wanted to do my part to preserve the Union, no matter what the cost may be for me. I'm ready to die for my country," said Andrews.

"Very well, Mr. Andrews. You made your bed and you'll have to lie in it," she said.

"I accepted the risks. You'll find out there will be hell to pay. You people will always be looking over your shoulders. Before too long, Blue Bellies will be marching through Georgia, pillaging your farms and destroying your factories and railroads."

"Talk is cheap, Mr. Andrews. We shall see," said the head waitress, with a self-righteous, haughty countenance.

"Well, so much for the war. We'll eat whatever you have," said Andrews.

"You are so privileged. The Confederate government is paying for yours and your men's meals, since you are their traveling guests. I'll be out with the food in two shakes of a lamb's tail," she said, walking swiftly toward the kitchen.

"Wow, I didn't think Jeff Davis had any money left to feed us. He can't even afford enough muskets, bullets, clothing, shoes, and food for their own army," said Pittenger.

Andrews responded, "Don't talk too loud. Be thankful to the Lord for the food, even if it comes from the evil Confederacy's coffers."

Gliding out of the kitchen as if she were walking on cloud nine, the head waitress beamed with delight, while bringing the first round of double-stacked wooden breakfast plates with wooden spoons, forks, and knives.

Pittenger whispered, "Fellows, notice the lack of silverware. They're afraid we might open the chain locks and take the waitresses as hostages. No such thing as a dumb Southerner."

Andrews laughed and said, "Oh, that's so funny."

When the twenty minutes ended, the conductor barked, "All aboard!" Soon the Lacy Hotel employees and foodservice personnel closely watched the train depart the Big Shanty station, with escaping steam and the accompanying "CHOO-CHOO" sound.

From the modern-day location of Canton, Georgia, the location of Governor Brown's home, the Browns took it upon themselves to ride the State Government horse-drawn wagon driven by one of his personally selected bodyguards, 40-year-old Sgt. Frank W. Irons, a handsome, clean-shaven, bald, brown-eyed, 200-pound burly man, who stood nearly seven feet tall. His hands were larger than a sixteen-inch neck, and he had a voracious appetite for Brunswick Stew.

Andrews and his fellow prisoners failed to recognize Governor Brown and his wife Elizabeth, when the prisoners were boarding the train.

"Sweetheart, I never thought I would ever get to see the train thieves. I'm surprised they haven't been hanged yet."

"Joseph, the wheels of justice may seem slow, but eventually justice gets served."

"Their sins have found them out. I shall remember this sight not only as an historic event, but also it means so much to me personally, to see those spies on their way to the Atlanta jail and the gallows," said Governor Brown.

"Darling, I see all of that as a distinct probability."

It was about 9 p.m. on Sunday, June 1, 1862, when the engine "Texas" pulled into the Atlanta train station at the old car shed.

"Get in the wagons, inmates," shouted the Officer in Charge. "We're taking you to your next home."

The wagons rolled perhaps a few blocks, in downtown Atlanta to the Fulton County Jail, an old well-guarded, sturdy brick structure, located at Fraser Street and Fair Street (now Memorial Drive), not far from Oakland Cemetery, Atlanta's first public cemetery, which opened in 1885.

During the first morning at the jail, the raiders created their own means of entertainment. Using a nail, an inmate scratched a good likeness of a checkerboard on the jail floor. But the most enjoyable activity was the opportunity to conduct debating contests. The men unanimously agreed to discard the playing cards, removing the temptation to gamble.

Saturday, June 7, 1862 arrived much sooner than Andrews would have liked. The Provost Marshal of the Military Post of Atlanta, Colonel Oliver H. Jones, entered the Fulton County, Atlanta, Georgia jail with four armed Confederate guards.

"Mr. Andrews, we have arranged for a carriage. You will be hanged in one hour," said Colonel Jones.

"Boys, I've been curious about what it's going to be like on the other side of the Jordan," said Andrews.

"Let's go," replied Colonel Jones, impatiently.

Andrews immediately sprang to his feet from his bed and stood erect, his jawline taut. The other inmates, including Pittenger and Dorsey, observed the guards escorting Andrews, the first condemned man, to the Fulton County Jail carriage, parked in front of the jail on Fair Street.

"Oh my God," said John Scott, who had participated in cutting telegraph wires. "Just as sure I'm standing here, I'm going to find my name on one of their ropes."

Campbell said, "Men, you know what we've got to do, but we've got to carefully choose the time."

Pittenger remarked, "Time is getting away," as he looked down the long hallway of the jail that ran north to south. Forty years later, two yellow houses would be standing on the original site of the jail.

Five minutes later, the carriage driver picked up the pace, as the horses advanced forward at the crack of a whip. People looked out of windows and stared at the horse-drawn wagon rolling along Fair Street. It was a gut feeling that Andrews was not out for a joy ride, for they sensed that an execution was about to take place. Curiosity seekers mounted their horses and got into horse-drawn wagons to slowly follow the escorted carriage, in which Andrews was handcuffed, and two long chains secured him to the conveyance, while sitting upright.

Down the street, the Rev. W. J. Scott, a man of average height, lived in a small, modest wood-frame, one-story house, which probably served as a parsonage maintained by Wesley Chapel, where he served as its full-time pastor, in addition to his chaplain duties at the jail. Wesley Chapel later became the First Methodist Church of Atlanta.

"Stop the carriage at Rev. Scott's House," demanded the Provost Marshal. A dozen Confederate cavalrymen flanked the right and left sides of the carriage, which soon halted in front of Rev. Scott's house.

Colonel Jones dismounted, smartly marched toward the clergyman's front door. Perusing his study notes in preparation for the upcoming Sunday sermon, the Rev. Scott was distracted by the unexpected knock at the front door.

"Rev. Scott, I need your services now to officiate at a hanging," said Colonel Jones.

"Very well, sir. I will go with you," said the chaplain reluctantly.

Mounting the running board of the carriage, he said to the Provost Marshal, "Sir, I really am not comfortable about witnessing executions."

Andrews then responded in a poignantly subdued voice, "I would be pleased to have you go with me, Reverend."

"Since you have made a request, I cannot refuse to honor it," said Rev. Scott, sitting next to Andrews, as the driver put the carriage in motion and glided past persons of various races, colors, and creeds; also included were the lame, the crippled, disabled Confederate soldiers, mothers pushing baby carriages, and groups of African-American slaves, among the curious multitude following from a respectable distance the military-escorted carriage. This must have been a very interesting, exciting event to behold, as the entire scene resembled a mass exodus of refugees leaving an invaded area, or even a naturally devastated area.

"Mr. Andrews, tell me about yourself," asked Rev. Scott.

"I know I'm a sinner, but I feel I did right to take a train in the service of the Union army. I uphold its legitimacy. I would have received

$5,000.00 each month in goods if the mission had worked out. I was engaged to marry a woman from Flemingsburg, Kentucky. Well, that won't happen. I've never joined a church, but I have been seeking God."

"Mr. Andrews, may I explain to you how you can receive eternal life in Jesus Christ?"

"I'm listening," said Andrews, as the carriage wheels kept inexorably rolling toward the site of the gallows.

"Do me a favor, preacher."

"Certainly, Mr. Andrews."

"Please make a statement on my behalf before they hang me."

"I'll do that," said Rev. Scott.

As the carriage coasted to a standstill, the Colonel said, "Escort the prisoner to the gallows." During the walk to the site of certain death, Andrews readily noticed a very thick, strong rope encompassing the perimeter of the site of the gallows. The upright boards were four feet by six feet, and the top crosspieces were four feet long and four feet wide.

Serving as the condemned man's mouthpiece, Rev. Scott stepped up to face the crowd to deliver Andrews's pre-execution statement.

"Mr. James J. Andrews asked me to speak on his behalf. He does not apologize for stealing the train. He has accepted Jesus Christ as his Savior. At this time, I'm going to call on Rev. Conyers to pray."

"Oh, mighty God," said Rev. Conyers, "Our

THE RUNAWAY TRAIN

help in ages past and our hope for years to come and our shelter from the stormy blast of this difficult, miserable temporal earthly existence. Lord, I ask you to comfort this man's fiancée and family members. Give them the strength to press onward and mount up their wings like eagles. We pray Your blessings upon Mr. Andrews, who has responded to John 3:16, as a genuine convert to your kingdom, Lord. In Jesus' Holy name we pray. Amen."

Andrews's carriage traveled northward to Peachtree Street to the site of his execution, now located at the intersection of Juniper Street and Third Street. Andrews had stated he would receive from the Union army a tidy sum of $5,000 worth of contraband goods every month, as a reward for stealing the engine "General". He insisted he was not an enemy of the South, its government, or its people, and he adamantly stated he had no intentions of burning any bridges.

Two Western & Atlantic Rounders had come from the W&A Round House, where trains turned around to change directions. These men were James Squires and J. J. Adcock who were engineers. Both men listened to the speech of Rev. Scott and Rev. Conyers's prayer, while perched in a small hickory tree in an adjoining wooded area, from which they could conveniently view the scaffold, consisting of two upright timbers, a platform, and a spring-operated trap door. Suddenly, Andrews's feet touched the ground. The executioner, Colonel

Oliver H. Jones, then approached Andrews's dangling body, against which he pushed and stood while shoveling away the dirt, ultimately leading to the intended death of Andrews by strangulation. James Squires did not remain for the burial at the intersection of Juniper and Third. Some years later, Andrews was reinterred, in 1887 in the National Cemetery in Chattanooga, Tennessee.

While dining early on the evening of Wednesday, June 18, 1862, a jail messenger knocked on Rev. Scott's front door.

"Here is a message from the Provost Marshal. It is urgent."

The message was that the minister was instructed to report to the jail to counsel seven Andrews Raiders, scheduled for execution that very same day. Colonel Foracre was unavailable, due to an emergency assignment, perhaps of a secret nature, and only a clerk was manning the office of the Provost Marshal.

Rev. Scott put his dinner aside and walked to the parsonage, where the pastor of Trinity Church, Rev. G. N. McDonel, was living.

"Rev. McDonel, I want you to go with me to the jail to talk to some condemned men – about to be hanged."

"All right, but you must be the one to do all the talking," said Rev. McDonel.

Thirty minutes later, the two ministers entered the jail cells of the prisoners. The inside of the jail contained an iron grating, and crossed boards constituted the front door of the jail, which swung toward the outside of the building. Down the long hallway proceeded the two local clergymen with a Confederate officer carrying a key in his hand.

"Gentlemen, I'll lock you in for fifteen minutes – that's all the time we can give you," said the officer.

Inside the locked jail cell, the ministers conferred with the seven men marked for death.

Rev. Scott said, "Boys, I hate to be the bearer of bad news. The army has issued orders to execute all seven of you."

"Preacher, how are they going to execute us?" asked Campbell.

"By hanging," said Rev. Scott, with a solemn facial expression.

"We should be shot – not hung like dogs. It's a dirty shame," said Campbell with rising indignation.

Another man whispered, "When?"

"In about two hours – maybe less," said Rev. Scott. "Now boys, let's get one thing straight: We are not here to discuss whether or not capital punishment is just or unjust, but we are here to prepare you for death with counsel and prayers."

The following Andrews Raiders would be hanged at the intersection of South Park Avenue and Fair Street (now Memorial Drive): George D. Wilson, John Slavens, John Scott, Marion Ross, Samuel Robertson, Perry G. Shadrach, and William Campbell, a civilian.

Before these men were escorted from the jail to

the horse-drawn wagon, Rev. McDonel closed with a prayer.

"Oh, mighty God, I pray that You would spare these men, if the Confederacy approves of it.....Amen."

A hush came over the seven condemned men, who were irritated by the holier-than-thou prayer from Rev. McDonel, an inherently insensitive person, who lacked the love of Jesus Christ in his spirit. Motivations for entering the ministry are many and varied, and perhaps Rev. McDonel had pursued Seminary training to avoid physically demanding secular labor, which was beneath his dignity.

"I could care less what you think of what we did for the Union," said Pittenger to Rev. McDonel, "but the hanging of Andrews was cold-blooded murder – nothing more, nothing less. God will ultimately judge the persons responsible for his death."

"Mr. Pittenger, I must tell you that you are really not in a position to speak your mind so freely, especially in the presence of the powers-that-be in this jail. However, I hasten to add that because of the confidentiality of a clergy-client relationship, what you have said to me will go no further than my ears, and will certainly never leave my lips to satisfy the itching ears of other people," said Rev. McDonel.

"Thank you for your open-mindedness, Reverend," said Pittenger.

THE RUNAWAY TRAIN

"I'm sorry, but I must go with Rev. Scott to accompany these compatriots of yours," said Rev. Scott.

"Men, God will honor you for working against a persistently rebellious South, that shake their fist at God every waking moment of their lives," said Pittenger with candor and fervor in his voice.

Neither preacher wished to being a party to a debate, due to the circumstances of the jail visit. Preaching a funeral would have been preferable to their involvement with marked-for-death men.

"Goodbye, men. Godspeed," said Rev. Scott sincerely.

As soon as the crossboarded front door of the Fulton County Jail opened, a crowd began to gather like a colony of ants advancing upon a decaying dead animal. Two files of Confederate cavalrymen each took left and right sides of the prisoners' wagon, even though the seven men were restrained by handcuffs and chains attached to the undercarriage as well as their legs, by means of key-operated padlocks. Nearby residents peered curiously out of windows and passersby, both black and white, empathetically looked on with helplessness, as indicated by their body language.

From the head of the wagon, the Captain of the Guard commanded, "Draw.....Sabers!" Then he issued the command to the driver. "Forward, march!" The procession seemed to be similar to a funeral procession – but the only difference was that these men were not yet dead.

HENRY H. KURTZ

The sight of the gallows was in the vicinity of Oakland Cemetery, where the graves of many Confederate soldiers and twenty Union soldiers may be seen.

At the execution site, Rev. Scott opened with prayer.

> Almighty God, we ask Your mercy upon the souls of these men who are about to depart this life, through the door of death to the Glory of Eternity. We pray Your blessings upon our brave fighting men in faraway locations from families, friends, wives, and girlfriends. May peace soon come and may the North turn from their wicked ways, so that you, Lord, will heal our land of iniquity. Amen.

William Campbell was incensed at the slanted prayer, and Marion Ross also perceived the openly haughty attitude to be clearly biased and bereft of political neutrality.

Campbell was the first to be roped around the neck, and as the trap was sprung, Campbell unexpectedly broke the rope due to his heavy weight; but on the second try, he was dead. Samuel Slavens, also overweight, was hanged on the second attempt. As it was during Andrews's execution, the audience was quiet, respectful, and did not heckle, jeer, or shout inappropriate words; and above all, they uttered no profanity.

THE RUNAWAY TRAIN

William A. Fuller observed very closely each execution, without speaking to anyone. Perhaps he felt a great sense of satisfaction, now that Andrews was taken out of the equation, after the conductor had paid one hundred dollars to Samuel Williams, the captor of James J. Andrews, and the owner of Williams Island. According to Historian Wilbur G. Kurtz, Sr., the seven executed men had been adjudged guilty of lurking as spies in civilian clothing, and no mention was made of a train theft. Such was their court-martial charges in Knoxville, Tennessee. In early July, 1862, the fourteenth prisoner, John Wollam, had been recaptured and imprisoned at the Fulton County, Atlanta jail with the surviving Andrews Raiders. As of June 18, 1862, a total of eight raiders had been hanged.

During one hot summer day in 1862, a visiting preacher asked the fourteen inmates, "What in the world ever possessed you Yanks to invade the South and threaten to take over the Confederacy?"

"Reverend, why do you contradict yourself? You are supposedly a minister of the gospel opposing sin, yet you condone the sin of slavery," said Pittenger.

The preacher steamed indignantly as if Pittenger had struck him in the jugular vein. "Slavery is the backbone and lifeblood of the Southern economy, and you Yanks have been sticking your noses in our business. We were doing fine until you Yanks upset the apple cart. Besides, the Lord gave us slaves due to the black man's inherent inferiority."

"Oh, really. What makes you think you're better than black people? Every person in the world was created in the image of God. Sounds like you have thrown out the Book of Genesis, but my Bible just happens to read the same as yours. Blacks had no more control of their skin color than you or I," said Pittenger.

"God will get you for your wrong beliefs," said the angry preacher.

"Preacher, you are a hypocrite. God will especially judge you for defending the cruel, unjust treatment of buying and selling human beings while separating husbands from wives, and abducting children from their parents," said Pittenger.

"You're wrong, wrong, wrong," retorted the preacher.

"And you sir, have no conscience, and you lack a sense of guilt or sensitivity to the cruelties of human bondage. Your values are twisted – not mine," said Pittenger, pointing his finger at the double-minded clergyman. "You call yourself a Christian, and yet you do not have God's love in your heart."

"May the Lord have mercy upon your sin-sick Yankee soul," said the departing preacher.

"Second Chronicles 7:14 says: 'If my people who are called by my name shall turn from their wicked ways, then I will heal thy land'," said Pittenger.

"I have to be going now," said the unknown visiting preacher, who seemed ready to spit nails at Pittenger.

One day during a testy, emotional debate on whether or not it was preferable to go to Cincinnati or to Heaven, a prisoner from the recently admitted Wisconsin army unit had surreptitiously sent a written message attached to a string on a stick, passed through a hole at the chimney pipe connection – it was perhaps a loose connection. The message had been delivered by a seemingly overzealous horseman, who might as well had been a horseman of the Apocalypse, as he was carrying a very sobering message from Richmond, Virginia, the capital of the Confederate government. The message taken from the string-on-the-stick homemade device read the following: "Bad news – More nooses to come."

Meanwhile, the horseman was riding quickly, until he stopped at the gate to deliver the death warrant, for the execution of each remaining Andrews Raider in the Fulton County Jail.

"Boys, let's get real. We must escape or we'll be dead ducks. That message means we're marked for hanging," said Pittenger. I've just been talking to George W. Walton, one of the Wisconsin men behind this hole in the wall."

"I'll bet that was a 'Holey' conversation," quipped Campbell with a grin.

"This is serious business. Our lives are on the line. This is no time for levity, Campbell," said Pittenger, grimfaced.

The jailer, Mr. Bob Turner, heard the courier shout, "Turner, come here!" The sun shined so brightly, causing a glaring refection on the galloping courier's belt buckle.

"Turner, where is the nearest blacksmith? My horse has a broken left hind shoe," said the horseman.

"Go two blocks west on Fair Street. Daniel Bellows is the best, most reasonable blacksmith in the city of Atlanta," said the jailer.

"Thanks, Turner. That's a hot message. Take it to your commander as soon as possible. The courier cracked his whip on the wooden hitching post crosspiece, with the comment, "To the Confederacy. Long live Jeff Davis."

"Victory will be ours," said Turner, a jubilant, old, tired, 63-year-old, craggy-faced man.

George W. Walton could sense an air of imminent danger. Mark Wood and Daniel Dorsey had been languishing from the lack of medical care at the jail, and no light at the end of the tunnel had revealed itself. Only hopelessness reigned supremely and unchallenged – or so it seemed.

Everyday, no more than, and no less than seven guards were on duty at the jail. In the front room of the jail were four POW's and one Rebel prisoner, a convicted Union sympathizer. The rest of the rooms comprised ten or twelve POW's. Mr. Turner's watchman, Thoer, a grouchy, unhappy five-foot-three-inch, 100-pound, brown-eyed, blond man, was mysteriously absent from the jail.

Suddenly, some prisoners rushed the black women, who were in the act of distributing the bread pans as part of the meager rations. Captain Frey, a Wisconsin unit officer, said, "Are you enjoying your evening, Mr. Turner?"

"Yes sir," said the jailer.

"We need some exercise. I hope you don't mind," said Capt. Frey.

"Can you shake the guards?" asked Turner.

"Mr. Turner, don't sweat the small stuff," said Captain Frey.

Turning remarkably white as a sheet, the shocked jailer was alarmed at the Captain's brazenness and unrestrained courage.

"Hand over the keys, Mr. Turner. I don't have all day," said Captain Frey sternly.

"GU-GU-GUA," said Turner, as Pittenger quickly and forcefully covered the astonished jailer's mouth, preventing him from sounding the alarm. Capt. Frey wrapped his arms completely around the defenseless jailer, and instantly, Robert Buffum seized the jailer's hand-held keys; Turner bit down in vain on Pittenger's right index finger.

Cautiously inching his way along the stairway, assuming that the guards might have heard the shouts of the jailer, William Knight waited until John R. Porter slammed a guard against the floor, to successfully disarm the sentinel before escaping through the back door of the jail. William Bensinger managed to knock out another guard by perhaps rendering a concussion. Another raider subdued a guard in the front yard, while Robert Buffum had tried without success to open the last jail cell door. Consequently, a jail guard foiled Buffum's escape attempt, at gunpoint.

HENRY H. KURTZ

As for another prisoner's escape attempt, Capt. Frey pretending to have been killed, fled to Union lines. To make up for extreme fatigue, Capt. Frey hid in the woods for twenty-one consecutive days, resisting the temptation to lodge with strangers. Later, he achieved the promotion to the rank of Colonel, and eventually returned to Kentucky.

William Pittenger failed to escape, due to the very bright sunlight from which he was unable to adjust his vision; it was nevertheless a probable case of deficient eyesight, even with the aid of eyeglasses, a product of primitive optometric standards of his day. As Pittenger ran for the front gate, a guard hastily fired his musket but missed Pittenger, who was directed to halt or be killed.

A short while later, a plantation owner held a gun on Bensinger, until a cavalry company arrived to return the escapee to the Fulton County Jail. Eight raiders escaped, but the Confederates reincarcerated six raiders. In a tragic incident, an 18-year-old Tennessean prisoner broke his leg while attempting to jump a fence, and later died on account of the jailer's unwillingness to provide essential medical treatment for the broken leg.

Colonel Lee exclaimed, "Shoot the Blue Bellies in the back. Leave 'em in the woods. Captain Troglin, assign guards at all ferry and railroad crossings." None of the raiders was killed or wounded, but yet it must be taken into consideration, that moving human targets pose difficulties even for well-trained shooters firing multiple shots.

THE RUNAWAY TRAIN

A five-foot-eight-inch, bearded, blue-eyed, gray-haired 51-year-old Confederate prison guard laughed gleefully when he said, "I'll say one thing about them Yankees: They can run like warthogs."

A thin, 30-year-old sergeant with brown eyes and a goatee added, "They're experts when it comes to running away from the battlefield." He took in a fresh plug of chewing tobacco while the latter guard spat his tobacco juice onto the grassless prison yard, as the sun bore down on each person outside the jail walls. The jail's feline mascot, "Musket Ball", was busily chasing a fat rat around the backyard, in a vain attempt to grab a snack. An annoying fly buzzed and collided with the latter guard's forehead, prompting him to say laughingly, "Just wait till I catch up with that fly. His days are numbered."

About ten feet from a jail window, a prisoner was relaxing while listening to two guards talking about the jailbreak. The prisoner's hammock started swaying back and forth, as a demonstration of his anger at the guards.

At nine-thirty on the next day, William Pittenger spoke to the jailer, making his early morning rounds.

The jailer said, "Pittenger, when you boys broke jail, somebody put his hand over my mouth. I'd like to string him up."

"Maybe you'll find out," said Pittenger.

"I have no clue, Yank. I got so surprised. I couldn't get a good look at him." The jailer never found out the mystery mugger who had caught the jailer off guard. Mr. Turner, the jailer, probably Thoer's replacement, made what he thought was a true statement. "Those men who got away think they're going to be better off than you men. I just don't think it makes any sense to be so ungrateful. You know, I bend over backwards to treat them like I would want to be treated," said Turner.

As Pittenger and Turner were conversing, miles away toward the east, William Knight, Elihu Mason, Daniel Dorsey, and Martin J. Hawkins had teamed up as a group of escapees; but unfortunately, Mason was so ill that his fellow raiders reluctantly left him behind to fend for himself in the woods.

As the trio of Knight, Dorsey, and Hawkins penetrated deeper into the woods, they came upon an old, modest, rustic cabin. The owner of the cabin professed to be a Union sympathizer.

Answering the unexpected knock at the door, a burly, bearded 250-pound, brown-eyed, five-foot-ten-inch man wearing blue overalls looked suspiciously at the visitors. "State your business. I'm getting ready to feed my dogs," he said.

The trio spokesman, Daniel Dorsey, a former Ohio schoolteacher, asked the man, "Sir, we would appreciate a bite to eat. We're soldiers from Fleming County, Kentucky. We're looking for a regiment to join."

"Oh, you're Yankees, aren't you? I'm on your side, boys. I'm against slavery and I hate Jeff Davis.

He's a no-good, incompetent leader. He can't even lead a horse to water. We're better off with Lincoln."

The men listened politely but made no comments, since silence was golden at this juncture in the conversation.

"Well, come in. We'll rustle up some sausage, biscuits and gravy for you. We can't let you starve out there. This is my wife, Matilda. I'm Horace Goad.

"Boys, I'm the best cook this side of the Mason-Dixon line. I hope you like my cheese grits and sausage and biscuits," said the owner's five-foot-five-inch, stout 40-year-old wife. "Give me a few minutes, and then you can sit down to some good eating."

Horace said, "I want you to meet my three dogs: Growly, Howly and Prowly. Prowly hardly ever barks – he just looks and listens and walks a lot." Growly snarled while Howly yelped.

"Boys, breakfast is served. Now sit yourselves down at the table. Dig in and enjoy," she said smilingly, thirty minutes later.

"I'm going to tell you boys something: We've got nosey neighbors. If they see you, they're going to think you're Yankee deserters or those train thieves," declared Horace Goad, licking his lips, saturated with cheese grits.

Matilda Goad chimed in, "Have a cup of Yankee coffee. My husband sneaked a bag of coffee when he last went up to Knoxville."

"Thank you, Matilda. This is great coffee, and you are an excellent cook," said Brown with sincerity in his voice, while initially sipping the hot caffeinated beverage.

"The coffee's a year old, but it's still pretty good," said Horace with a wide, toothy grin.

Upon ingesting the last bite, the three escaped prisoners thanked the hosts and walked out the front door of the cabin.

Suddenly, three middle-aged men boldly approached the three raider escapees. One of them said, "Did y'all break jail?"

"Yes," replied Brown.

"You don't have a snowball's chance in hell of getting away. Besides, soldiers have already shot up your three buddies. They have sealed off every ferry and bridge. There's no escape," said one of the neighbors.

As an act of betrayal, Horace Goad released his three dogs to attack Dorsey and his comrades. Instinctively, the men picked up rocks and threw them at the dogs, producing direct hits. The dogs barked in pain, and the three men eluded the hounds by traveling along the bed of a stream. Later, the three men reached a point beyond the north side of Stone Mountain, located eighteen miles east of the 1862 city limits of Atlanta.

Hiding in the grass by day, they traveled only at night for twenty consecutive days, subsisting on nuts, bark, buds, two ears of corn, and a mountainside goose. However, the men lacked the means to cook and prepare the goose; nevertheless, they ripped off the goose's legs and devoured the avian species raw.

On the morning of the tenth day, the trio found two fence rails, which they soon used to build a makeshift raft reinforced with cut tree limbs, to provide a convenient mode of transportation down the Chattahoochee River.

Before embarking down the river, the men collected some sour apples found in an apple orchard and some leftover tobacco strips. Knight noticed a pig running aimlessly around the area, and Brown picked up an available, pre-sharpened shovel, used to slice the pig in segments, over a previously burning fire in a back field. The pig became pork after Knight led the pig toward a tree, before Brown slammed the shovel against the pig's head. Undoubtedly, the roasted pig was the answer to their persistently gnawing hunger pangs, after hours of rowing downstream.

Later, the escapees accosted two armed-to-the-teeth mountaineers, somewhere in a deep North Georgia valley. Both groups exchanged friendly handwaves and walked away in separate directions without incident. One hour later, Knight's group purloined two ears of corn from a mountain dwelling by going down and coming out of its chimney with the corn. Knight found a burning stump on which he roasted the stolen food items.

As the following day dawned, the escaped trio proceeded downstream, negotiated a sharp bend in the river, and were pleased to see two men seated on the front porch, in from of a rather large, spacious two-story wood-frame house.

"Hey, how far to Cleveland (Tenn.)?" asked Brown.

"Every bit of sixty miles," said one of the blue-overalled men smoking pipes, obviously contented, with their rural surroundings on a hot morning.

"We're not feeling well. We're hungry soldiers. May we have something to fill our bellies?" asked Brown.

"God love you. We hate this war," said one of the residents, a tall, lanky, 150-pound, long-faced, long-nosed, gray-bearded 50-year-old man chewing a fresh plug of tobacco. He had five missing lower teeth and a healthful suntan. His name was Walter Strickland, a neighbor sitting in a rocking chair on an old, rickety wooden porch.

Also present were a young woman, and a very outspoken female senior citizen who never pulled any punches when she spoke her mind on any subject.

She said, "I hate this war so much. I want it to be over so I can get some Lincoln coffee, and I'm sorry I don't have any to share with you gentlemen." Then the elderly woman looked penetratingly at the three men.

"Where are you men from?" asked 87-year-old Effie Cabe, Robert's mother-in-law.

"Ma'am. We're from Kentucky," responded Brown.

THE RUNAWAY TRAIN

"You look like Yankees. I sized you up the minute I laid eyes on you," she said, as the guests seated themselves at the dinner table in the dining room.

"Yes ma'am, we are Yankees," said Knight. "We are the engine thieves."

"Ah ha! I thought so. I know all about what you did, and I'm very proud of all of you. Will you stay a week with us and rest your weary bones?" asked Effie.

"We would be humbled," replied Knight.

"You need not worry at all. We have a nice, cozy hiding place so the Great Rebel can't catch you. You need to get your strength back. Our big dog will protect you from the hounds and hunters," said Effie.

Knight said, "Let's sing some Civil War songs. I will lead the song entitled "Tenting Tonight...Tenting tonight, tenting tonight, tenting on the old camp ground. Many of our hearts are weary tonight, waiting for the war to cease..." Suddenly, someone knocked on the door.

Entering the large house, the dog's master clearly conveyed an attitude of genuine warmth and hospitality toward the strange visitors.

"Father, these guests are Yankee soldiers. They're feeling right pitiful and weak, and we're having them stay a week with us – if that's all right," said the tall, muscular, 35-year-old man named Lofty Peak. Everyone shook hands.

"My heart goes out to you men. All of us love

the Union, and townspeople have cussed, spit on me, and overcharged me at the store. I love the Union. I have no use for them people in town," said Robert Peak, a five-foot-eight-inch, 180-pound, muscular, brown-eyed, blond 45-year-old farmer. The raiders felt at ease to be in a Union-friendly home, relieved beyond the shadow of a doubt.

"Robert, I told your wife that we were train thieves. I also want you to know we broke out of the Atlanta jail and walked to the north side of Stone Mountain on our way over here," said Knight.

"For your information, Stone Mountain is the largest mass of exposed granite in the whole world," said Robert.

"I'm not at all surprised," said Knight, chewing ravenously on a piece of roasted chicken.

Later, Robert's older son, Jeb, led the raiders toward a large secluded cave, located at the base of a steep mountainside at the end of another ravine. After five days of three nutritious meals, the men had finally recuperated from extreme fatigue and hunger, and they were ready to travel with a local guide over the mountains.

A few hours later, the guide noticed a candle burning inside a mountain cabin where Union sympathizers were present.

As the guide escorted the escapees to the front door of the cabin, the Union sympathizers stood shoulder to shoulder in silence. An elderly gentleman looked kindly upon the civilian-clad soldiers and asked respectfully, "Are you carrying any money?"

Knight replied, "No."

"You men could definitely use some decent clothes," said the anonymous man.

He spoke to the other men assembled in the rural house. "These men need clothes and money." Within a few minutes, every raider received ten dollars and some decent clothing before starting a three-night trip for a thirty-dollar charge, to pay the travel guide on the final leg of the journey.

The senior citizen was five-feet-eight-inches tall, weighed 195 pounds, had a double chin, and ten teeth were missing. He had blue eyes, cauliflower ears, and a long nose with flared nostrils. He walked with a cane due to a Mexican War injury in 1845, while fighting General Santa Anna's Mexican Army at the Battle of San Jacinto, where he took a musket ball in the left leg.

"Good luck, boys. I fought for the Union when I served in the Mexican War. I'm glad you're doing your part to get the Union back together again," said the old man.

"Thanks for the clothes and money. I wish we could repay the favor," said Brown.

"It's our pleasure. You men are true American patriots. Have a safe trip," said the smiling old man.

CHAPTER 9
FOUR ESCAPE STORIES

As the first pair traveled northward each night, with the aid of the North Star, and a knowledge of astronomy, their ability to maintain their direction was indeed assured. It took Brown and Knight forty-seven days and nights and asking cabin residents for directions, until safely reaching Union lines.

The second pair of fugitives, Daniel Dorsey and Martin J. Hawkins, encountered four African-American males in their early twenties.

"Hey, men, will you take us across the river for five plugs of chewing tobacco?" asked Dorsey.

"We sho can, boss man. Come get right on our little boat, and we'll go to the other side of the river," said one young, muscular African-American man.

Another young man said, "I hope you ain't running from the law."

"Young man, we are Union soldiers. We're fighting the Rebs so we can make it possible to have freedom," said Dorsey.

"Well lawdy mercy, hop on this boat. Youse men are our friends. We're tired of whips and picking cotton."

"We sure appreciate this ride," said Dorsey.

"My name's Bo. I don't rightly know my last name. I've been sold five different times. I'm tired of it."

"Bo, we're going to win this war, and Mr. Lincoln is going to set all of you free," said Dorsey.

"I want my freedom so bad, I could just taste it," said Bo.

"Be patient. The North is winning," said Dorsey.

"I sho praise de Lawd for that," said Bo.

"Well, we've reached the other side," said Dorsey.

"Gentlemen, thank you. May de Lawd bless you and keep you," said Bo.

Two hours later, the men approached a road, where five local civilians were walking around with loaded shotguns.

"I'll bet my week's pay those men broke out of the Atlanta Jail. Let's rush 'em," said one of the armed civilians.

Swift of feet and very quick to react, Dorsey and Hawkins fled into the nearest stand of trees, vanishing without leaving a trace. The pursuers' mouths flew wide open in amazement.

"Dadburn it, those Yankees got away!" said one of the weapons bearers.

"Where did the deserters go?" asked another man.

"We lost them," replied the leader of the search party.

Five hundred feet away, a five-foot-five-inch, sandy-haired, 18-year-old, blue-eyed, blond Confederate deserter spotted Dorsey and Hawkins, from his nearby hiding place, a luxuriant green thicket.

Hearing a bird call, the pair stopped in their tracks.

"What was that?" asked Hawkins.

"Sounds like a bird," replied Dorsey, "but it might not be a real bird."

"You're exactly right, mister," said the Confederate deserter unabashedly.

"Where's your musket, Reb?" asked Dorsey.

"I left it in camp when I ran away. I ain't liking this crazy, mixed-up war at all," said the Confederate deserter.

"What's your name?" asked Dorsey.

"I'm Corporal James Raines," said the young naïve, misguided man.

"It seems we all have one thing in common. We're all running away from something," said Dorsey.

"You know about me. What about you guys?" asked the deserter.

"We are Union soldiers. We stole an engine, got arrested, and broke jail," said Dorsey.

"Let's make a deal. I've got an uncle in

Washington, D.C. Nobody'll bother me up there, because lots of Confederate sympathizers live there," said Raines, the deserter.

"All right, James. We might as well work together so none of us gets caught by the Rebs," said Dorsey.

"Great. Where are you guys going?" asked the Confederate deserter.

"Reb, we're going to Tennessee," said Dorsey.

"I can direct you both to LaFayette, but don't go into that town – go around the left side of it. Then you'll go northwest to the Tennessee River," said Raines.

"O.K., once we cross the river, we'll be safely into Union lines," said Dorsey.

"Yes, but I'll have to go northeast to get to D.C. I'm going to have to leave you now," said Raines.

"That's a mighty long distance to travel," said Hawkins.

"Well, I have no choice," said Raines. "So long." The Confederate soldier vanished quicker than a snake in the grass.

"So much for that Johnny Reb. Let's go find a place to hide until dark," said Dorsey.

Four days passed uneventfully – until another challenge faced these escapees.

"Here we go again, Hawkins. Let's beat it," said Dorsey.

The pursuers popped up again with the presence of their muskets. "We should have brung [sic] the dogs. Those Yankees don't care if they get shot," said one of the pursuers.

"Quit talking and run," said another musket bearer. The five men picked up speed, but the Northern twosome was simply too swift and cunning for the "Unmagnificent Five".

"Blast it! We lost them again. What rotten luck," said the leader of the pursuers.

"You should have listened to me. We needed the hounds. Muskets alone are not enough," said another pursuer.

The leader replied, "Thanks to the Union blockade, we couldn't get enough food to feed the hounds."

The "Unmagnificent Five" walked mindlessly past the lush thicket, under which Dorsey and Hawkins had stealthily isolated themselves from their surroundings. It would have been an additional feather in their hats, if they had been trained in the art of camouflage. Nevertheless, the wise strategy of hiding by day and traveling by night proved to be very beneficial in the long term.

"Look! Up ahead. There's a river crossing. Let's examine it," said Dorsey.

"If you look over to the right, you'll see a cabin," said Hawkins.

After the two men had measured the depth of the stream, they determined that it would be impossible to ford this formidable body of water.

"Forget it. Let's take cover and keep our eyes peeled on that house," said Dorsey.

"I wish we had binoculars. They would have

come in handy," remarked Hawkins, with disappointment written all over his face.

"Dream on, Hawkins. You know darn good and well. Only officers receive government-issued binoculars. The common, ordinary soldier operates without them," said Dorsey.

"I know, but it would still be nice to have them, especially now," said Hawkins.

"I see a black woman – probably thirty years old. She's taking clean clothes from the clotheslines. Pigs are running around in the yard," said Dorsey.

A few hours later, it became apparent that the woman was the only occupant of the cabin.

"Come on, Hawkins, we need to go ask for breakfast," said Dorsey.

From their hillside vantage point, the men briskly walked toward the rural dwelling, as though they routinely traveled the local area.

Dorsey knocked loud and decisively on the woman's front door.

"Who is it?" she asked.

"Ma'am, we're hungry soldiers. Could you spare some food?" asked Dorsey.

"Yes suh, I sho can. Come in," said the woman.

"We don't want to trouble you," said Dorsey.

"No – not at all, mistuh," said the woman.

"You're sure," said Dorsey.

"I'm sure. Now you gentlemen sit yourselves down. I've got dried corn, some scrambled eggs, chitlings, cornbread, and some Yankee coffee," said the hostess.

"Outstanding, ma'am," said Dorsey.

"I'm gonna say de blessing....Dear Lawd, bless this food and be with these soldiers as they go back to war. Amen," said the prayerful woman. Drawing a breath, she then said, "Now, why you men come to my house?"

"We are on our way to rejoin our unit in Tennessee. Can you direct us to a good ferry crossing?"

"Yes. Go two miles downstream. There's a right smart narrow crossing," she said.

"Thanks," said Dorsey.

An hour after breakfast, fatigue set in, as the men easily found a damp, uninvitingly cold sleeping place under some thick bushes, after having crossed the stream, according to the cabin resident's directions.

When nightfall came, Dorsey said, "Come on. Let's push on. I've got a good feeling we're going to make it back to our lines, but only if we stay alert."

"I couldn't agree more," said Hawkins, displaying his yellowed, unbrushed teeth, and thirsty, foul-odored mouth, including the rest of his body. Both men had not bathed in several months, a not-at-all surprising outcome.

An hour later, while on a road leading north from the Chattahoochee River, the men saw a number of fugitives and slaves that had been traveling for days from Kentucky.

Dorsey asked one of the traveling slaves,

THE RUNAWAY TRAIN

"Where is Bragg's Army?"

"I saw a right smart lot of soldiers moving mighty slow – about three miles back. Yah suh. Dey's carrying all their things. Lawdy mercy. I don't know where dey is goin'. Dey is like de weather. Can't tell what's goin' to happen next," said one of the black slaves with a puzzled look.

"Thanks for the information, young man," said Dorsey graciously. "This seems to be another shred of evidence that we are winning the war."

"Sounds like it, Dorsey," said Hawkins.

Further down the road, the men spotted a campfire site in a clearing, and from behind a thick bush, Hawkins winked at one of the slaves, serving as a cook for a Confederate army brigade commanded by Brigadier General Braxton W. Bragg. Within thirty seconds, the slave voluntarily snuck some freshly cooked sweet potatoes that had been placed inside of a covered skillet over a flaming campfire. Coincidentally, the slave cook had previously spoken with Dorsey regarding the location of Bragg's Army, and it then became crystal clear that the slave had been deliberately evasive, until he later realized that Dorsey and Hawkins were not likely Confederate soldiers, but were, instead, Union soldiers fighting to free all slaves.

Within twenty-four hours, the men had traveled from the camp to a point on the Hiawassee River in Northeast Georgia, and the next crucial leg of the travel would be necessarily at the confluence of the

Hiawassee River and the Tennessee River, the latter constituting the last waterway segment of their escape route from Georgia into Eastern Tennessee, Union friendly territory.

But in order to fulfill such travel plans, it became necessary to engage the services of a cooperative ferryman possessing a reliable, river-worthy boat to meet hazardous rowing demands.

The ferryman was a Confederate Army Corporal Wallace Riggs, whose military duty was to ferry passengers across the river, but in this particular case, Corporal Riggs, a five-foot-four-inch, brown-eyed, blond, 120-pound soldier, had to obtain a pass from his sergeant to transport Dorsey and Hawkins to the Tennessee River. This process took the ferryman twenty-four hours to complete.

Dorsey and Hawkins accosted the ferryman. Dorsey asked, "Sir, would you be so kind to ferry us across the river?"

"Gentlemen, I must ask for a weekend pass from my sergeant. I'll let you sleep in my hut until I get back," said the ferryman.

"I hate to trouble you," said Dorsey.

"It's just a formality to get another soldier to replace me, while I'm rowing you up the river," said the ferryman.

"We certainly appreciate this, Corporal," said Dorsey.

"Don't mention it," he said.

Setting off on the other side of the Tennessee River, the men later found a somewhat serviceable dugout canoe. In the meantime, Dorsey anxiously rowed the canoe to a riverbank, where they found a hickory tree from which they gathered some hickory nuts before resuming their night-time waterway travel; at dawn, the men hid the canoe under dry leaves.

After the men took turns sleeping, the twosome located a cabin inhabited by two women, who were naturally inquisitive about the identities of the strangers.

"What brings you men here?" asked the mother, who was standing beside her daughter at the door of an old, rustic cabin.

"We got laid off from a sawmill up in the hills, and we're headed for Chattanooga to find a job," said Dorsey.

"Be careful they don't put you to work in the army," said the mother.

"Not a problem. We happen to know General Leadbetter," said Dorsey. Dorsey and Hawkins sensed they might not be welcome, and discretion dictated a quick exit to the canoe tied up on the bank of the lake.

Shoving off from the riverbank, Dorsey declared, "Let's hope we can get past the tree stumps so we don't get a hole in the canoe." Soon, they made their way to deeper water, but a Confederate picket had seen the canoe and abruptly fired at the river-craft without asking questions.

"Duck!" shouted Dorsey, as shots whizzed over the pair's heads, forcing the men to remain in the prone position in the boat; apparently, the men acted prudently, as the ferry guard no longer fired shots at the moving boat, looking more like a free-floating log rolling downstream.

"Whew! He narrowly missed us. That was downright rude, if you ask me," said Hawkins. "That bullet almost had my name on it."

"Hawkins, we're getting fairly close to Chattanooga. We have to leave the boat behind. Don't bother to tie it up," said Dorsey.

"Yes sir," said Hawkins.

Several hours later, the men noticed fresh wheel and horse tracks – those of Brigadier General Braxton Bragg's troops in retreat from Kentucky.

Having spotted two teenage boys in the act of hunting a raccoon, Dorsey asked them a question. "Have you seen any Rebs around here lately?"

"Yes sir, Johnny Rebs have been crawling all over creation. We saw a lot of men pretty bad shot up – bandaged heads and bloody legs and arms. It was a terrible thing to see," said one of the boys, a five-foot-six-inch, blond 12-year-old boy with freckles, a short haircut, wearing a thin, blue homespun shirt and faded blue jeans.

"How long ago?" asked Dorsey.

"Ever since we've been there – maybe two hours ago," said one of the teenagers.

"Look!" exclaimed Hawkins. "Johnny Rebs."

"That must be Bragg's army," said Dorsey, looking intently at the pattern of campfires neatly, systematically spread across the foreground.

THE RUNAWAY TRAIN

As the dawn broke the next day, Hawkins warned Dorsey not to crack corn, so they would not blow their cover.

Suddenly, the snuffling of a horse announced the presence of a roving cavalry unit. The escapees automatically concluded that a Confederate picket was posted near their location – a very unsettling feeling.

"Shh! Here comes a cavalry unit. Stay under the bush. Keep quiet," said Dorsey. The men kept a vigilant eye on the steadily moving cavalry soldiers, until the two disguised Union soldiers could covertly cross over the road to a wooded area, that comprised a very nettlesome quarter-of-a-mile stretch of briars, through which the men crawled agonizingly on their hands and feet, while sustaining multiple cuts and scratches, particularly on the arms and legs.

"Hawkins, after we climb this next mountain top, we're going to be in a good lookout position," said Dorsey.

"Good idea," said Hawkins.

"I'm so hungry I'd kill a Confederate horse if I could get one. Hunger or no hunger, let's get our carcasses up this hill so we can see our way clear," said Dorsey.

"Watch that tree limb. Don't let it slap you in the eyes. We've got no doctors out in this wilderness," said Dorsey. "Always keep a sharp lookout for snakes." The hillside ascent was characteristically steep for the type of hills in the general area.

The men panted for breath while undertaking the uphill trek, a much more physically demanding feat, when one considers the men's sharply reduced food rations and virtually exhausted water supply. Their clothing needs were elevated, such that they stole from a clothesline a quilted skirt, near a ford on the Sequatchie River.

"Grab that skirt, Hawkins. We can make undershirts out of it," said Dorsey.

Fatigue and hunger were exacting a toll on the men as their desperation for relief increased. Three hours later, the famished, tired men met in a wooded area some curious lumberjacks.

"Hey, who are you people?" asked the tallest lumberjack in the group.

"We are patients from a Confederate field hospital, and we are planning to go back to our regiments," said Dorsey.

"Is that so? We ought to have you locked up for a spell," said the tallest lumberjack, who was six-feet-three-inches, weighed 200 pounds, had long blond hair, and an intimidating ax swing.

"I'm sorry. I lied to you. We are at the moment detached from the Twentieth Ohio Volunteers, and we're trying to find them," said Dorsey.

"We understand.....Here's some bread and deer meat stew. We're Union sympathizers. We were kind of scared of each other. You get my meaning of course," said the tallest lumberjack.

"Yes, we do. We all have to look out for ourselves," said Dorsey.

"You're well supplied with rations. It was nice meeting you," said the tallest lumberjack. "Don't run into any trigger-happy Johnny Rebs."

"We'll do our best," responded Dorsey, as he and his traveling partner departed the lumberjacks' working area. "Thank you for the food, gentlemen."

"Don't mention it," said the tallest lumberjack.

Twenty-four hours later, these Atlanta Jail escapees reached their military outfit's present location at Lebanon, Tennessee.

Walking into the Union camp, a man named James Jones exclaimed, "Dorsey! You're alive."

"James, you don't know how it feels to be back among friends," said Dorsey.

"I thought the Rebs had hanged all of you men," said James Jones.

"I have to tell you this: The Rebs hanged our leader Andrews and seven others. Some of us escaped – don't know who else got out," said Dorsey.

"That's a rotten shame. I feel very sorry for their families," said James, a five-foot-eight-inch, 180-pound, clean-shaven, blue-eyed, blond 28-year-old Union private.

"You'll never know what we went through in Confederate prisons. It was terrible – words can't describe how bad everything was," said Dorsey.

"Andrews was to be married. His fiancée will be very sad," said Dorsey.

"Andrews was an asset to the Union cause. What a tragedy. We'll beat the South yet," said Hawkins.

"James, we could sure use some money," said Dorsey.

"Dorsey, you're a friend in need. Here's five dollars. I want you to have it," said James.

"I owe you, James," said Dorsey.

"Forget it. If it were the other way around, I'm sure you'd help me out," said James.

On the next day, Dorsey and Hawkins were introduced to Major Ellis, a member of their regiment, and an Ohio United States Senator, Adam Brotherlin from Columbus, Ohio.

Having listened attentively to their unusual wartime experiences, Senator Brotherlin said, "I want you gentlemen to meet me at my house tonight at eight o'clock."

"We shall see you tonight, Senator Brotherlin," said Dorsey, who was undoubtedly curious about the invitation. Out of courtesy, he refrained from asking questions.

Sometime during late July of 1862, the happy ending of Dorsey and Hawkins' escape had finally come to pass; no one else would have probably shown such an act of thoughtfulness and appreciation.

Accompanied by Hawkins, Dorsey knocked on the front door of Senator Brotherlin's fancy two-story brick home in Columbus, Ohio. They had arrived promptly at 8:00 p.m.

"Gentlemen, so nice of you to come. I want you to meet someone very special to all of us," said Senator Brotherlin, who had taken off his sport coat and removed his tie. "Dorsey and Hawkins, this is Governor David Tod."

Dorsey responded, "Governor, we're pleased to meet you."

"The same," said Governor Tod. "Gentlemen, tell me about your exploits in the South. Senator Brotherlin has presented me with a thumbnail sketch, but I want to hear more about it from you both," said the smiling politician.

Hawkins said, "You tell him, Dorsey. You used to teach school. You're good at explaining things."

Sir, a civilian named James J. Andrews took us from our regiment as volunteers to undertake a dangerous assignment – to steal a Confederate train, wreck the railroad, and burn its bridges with the idea of doing a rendezvous with General Mitchel's troops at Chattanooga. Well, sir, we failed. Eight men were hanged, some of us escaped, and a few of our men are still in the Atlanta Jail. Congestion on the railroad with southbound passenger and freight trains, heavy rain, and fuel shortages contributed to our failure to accomplish our objective.

"I see. That is indeed an incredible story, Corporal Dorsey. I take it you were prisoners of war in at least one Confederate jail."

"Yes, Governor. We spent several months in the Chattanooga Jail, the one in Knoxville, for twelve of us attending a court-martial, and later transferred to Madison, Georgia – when Mitchel was threatening Chattanooga – and finally, at the Atlanta Jail where we escaped."

"Gentlemen, this is a very intriguing story. Mr. Dorsey, let's now go to the kitchen."

When Governor Tod led Dorsey into the kitchen, the influential dignitary intended to talk only with Daniel Dorsey.

"By the way, Corporal Dorsey, I am going to remember you. I will make every effort to find some way to reward you for your bravery and your successfulness in surmounting such formidable obstacles. You and others have shown the rebellious South how much we mean business to restore our Federal union at whatever the costs may be."

"I thank you, sir, for your compliments. I was just doing my duty as a soldier," said Dorsey.

"And you performed marvelously, regardless of the results," said Governor Tod. The main thing is, the Andrews Raid caused the South to sit up and take notice that we Unionists are not creampuffs."

"I agree, sir," said Dorsey.

"Gentlemen, won't you stay for some coffee and cake?" asked Mrs. Brotherlin, dressed in a long brown dress protected by an apron.

"Don't mind if we do, ma'am," said Dorsey. During the refreshments party, both Dorsey and Hawkins revealed more convincing, eye-opening details of the Andrews Raid, while Governor Tod leaned forward in his wooden chair at the kitchen roundtable and listened, while being spellbound into utter amazement at Dorsey's explanations of the absolutely deplorable treatment and inhumane prison conditions.

Within the ensuing six months of 1862, Dorsey received a Second Lieutenant Commission for his participation in the Andrews Raid, and he reported for duty at his military unit, at Murfreesboro, located thirty miles north of the camp from which he embarked to meet Andrews on the Wartrace Road.

What happened to the third pair of Atlanta Jail escapees in the midst of hastily fired shots missing every escapee? Women squealed eerily, men frantically ran, jail bells clanged, drumbeats punctuated the air, and dogs howled incessantly, perhaps sensing the unacceptability of a jailbreak. Only Heaven knows how close it came to having deaths caused by trampling amid the pandemonium.

Without missing a beat, John R. Porter and John Wollam ran very hard to escape the jail. Later, they hid themselves in a wooded area to rest their weary bodies. Being within earshot, they heard a homeowner's clock strike ten o'clock – the signal to resume travel, but only at night. The men had hardly eaten anything during the preceding twelve days, and as the sun dipped to its lowest position at the horizon, the pair located a rustic cabin somewhere in the hills of Northwest Georgia.

"Porter, I'll stay back out of sight while you ask for food," said Wollam.

"Good idea. They might get uneasy it we both go to their door," said Porter.

The householder, a five-foot-eight-inch, 55-year-old, gray-haired, bearded man with steely blue eyes, answered the knock at his door.

"What can I do for you, mister?"

Porter replied matter-of-factly, "I'm traveling to go back to my Tennessee regiment."

"My son-in-law is a member of Captain Smith's Regiment. Please look for him and write me about how he is getting along. I would appreciate it."

"Certainly, I can do that," said Porter.

"Before you go, let me give you some cooked ham."

"Thanks a lot," said Porter, his mouth watering for food.

A few hours later, hunger again struck the men. Approaching an unoccupied house, desperation drove them to resort to burglary by taking out a floorboard, gaining entry to steal meat and cornbread. Later in the day, they removed from the roof of another house several clapboards, while the occupants were not at home. The men hid wherever they could find convenient locations, such as a mountain cave or a dense thicket; at one point, they had to remove several hogs from their warm rest area.

During one late afternoon, Porter and Wollam reached a point on the Tennessee River about thirty miles south of Bridgeport, Alabama, on day twenty-two, since imprisonment in the Atlanta Jail.

THE RUNAWAY TRAIN

As they walked down one side of the Tennessee River, a padlocked chain around a boat secured to a tree seemed to leap out at them, as though it were an answer to a prayerful request for the fastest possible means of transportation.

"It looks like our boat has come in, Wollam," Porter said with a wry grin.

"Let's grab it," said Wollam.

"When I got caught after my escape from that awful Swims Jail, I said, 'self, I will do everything I can, so I don't get caught again.' As God is my witness, I'll never serve another day in any jail," said Wollam.

"I have one major regret: I wish I hadn't overslept in Marietta. I wanted so much to be with you boys on the "General".

"Don't be so hard on yourself, Porter. You'll drive yourself into an early grave. You can't change the past," said Wollam.

"I guess you're right.....Well, let's take this boat before anyone sees us," said Porter, while twisting a chain and subsequently springing the padlock loose.

"All right! Let's sail," said Porter. Much later, while paddling down the river, the men saw what appeared to be a vacant house on an island, in the middle of a section of the Tennessee River.

"Look! Beehives. We can use the honey to tide us over until we can get more food," said Wollam.

"Wow! Just what we needed," said Porter to Wollam. "Pull up to the shore. Walk softly and keep a sharp eye out," advised Porter.

Leaving the boat on dry ground, they located a crock into which the men poured some honey easily obtained from the beehives.

"This is a very lucky break. Nobody is in the house. That's enough honey, Wollam. Let's get off this island," said Porter.

Farther down the river, the appearance of a house attracted their attention. "Perfect opportunity to get more food. We'll cover up the boat with leaves and bushes," said Wollam.

Instantly, a woman opened her door in response to her barking dog. Shielding her eyes from the sun, she noticed two strange men slowly walking toward her house.

Porter opened the conversation. "Ma'am, we're sick soldiers. We just got out of the hospital. We'd appreciate some food."

"Come in and sit yourselves down. You poor souls. I'll cook you something really tasty. You men look so starved. What I have will tide you over for a spell."

"Thank you so much," said Wollam.

"This is just what the doctor ordered," said Porter.

"I'm glad to lend a helping hand to people in need," she said warmly.

"Thank you, ma'am," said Porter. "We need to be leaving. The food is so delicious."

"I'm so glad," she said.

A few minutes later, Porter and Wollam said good-bye to the woman. Once again, the Tennessee

River, their aquatic super highway, beckoned to this pair of fugitives.

"Let's paddle hard. We haven't time to stop and smell the roses," said Wollam.

"Right. We've got a much better chance of eluding the Rebs if we can hug the river as much as we can," said Porter.

And so they rowed very hard all night, making meaningful strides along a meandering, bending waterway, until they found a suitable resting place where they woke up some eight hours later, as the late afternoon sun had sunk low into the horizon – the signal to resume aquatic travel.

At lunch time, the men arrived at Muscle Shoals, Alabama, a point at which water transportation had to be discontinued due to unnavigable, rough water. Next, they walked forty-five miles to Florence, Alabama. Fortunately for them, they found a food stash in a tree located above a fence. However, the victims of the theft would later discover to their anger and disappointment, that their tin can full of lard, a king-size loaf of cornbread, three pounds of salt, some ears of corn, and five pounds of bacon, were no longer there.

"Wollam, this is a lot of food to carry in the double-sack, but we can do it. We'll take turns lugging this bag of food around. We could use a canoe. That's our kind of luck," said Porter.

"It's not all bad. At least we have plenty of food for a change. Let's get out of here before that fishing party comes back," said Wollam. Later, they found a skiff, but they noticed a hole in its bottom; nevertheless, their unshakable faith was later rewarded upon discovering a boat in good, river-worthy condition. Having rowed all the following night, they slept throughout the day and decided to explore the Florence area on foot. The daytime foot travel produced one interesting tidbit of intelligence information: an African-American male passerby asked the men if they had a light.

"Hey, gentlemen, do you have a match?"

Porter replied, "If you'll answer a question, I'll give you fifty cents."

"All right. Ask me."

"Are there any Yankee soldiers in Corinth, Mississippi?" asked Porter.

"There sho is. That place is covered with Blue Bellies. Yah suh," said the young, attractive man.

"Thank you. Here is fifty cents," said Porter. "I'll also light your cigarette."

"Thank you, suh. God bless you men."

"You're welcome. If we don't see you again, then we'll look for you in Heaven. By the way, what is your name?"

"I'm Arthur Ebony. I answer to 'Art'," said the five-foot-five-inch, brown-eyed, short, kinky-haired man, probably twenty-five years old.

"Nice meeting you, Art. So long," said Porter.

It was getting late in the afternoon on a hot, humid day, but nonetheless, the men pressed onward until reaching Hamburg Landing, the end of

THE RUNAWAY TRAIN

their waterway travels, for it then became necessary to continue the lengthy, arduous trek by foot. Corinth was eighteen miles from Hamburg Landing – a hard day's travel without wheels.

The quest for a shelter was the next order of business, and upon hearing the barking of a dog, a bolt of lightning illuminated the entire, partially overcast night-time sky, to reveal a single-story, unpretentious wood-frame house, that was unquestionably overdue for an exterior paint job – signs of cracking and peeling layers of white paint. In the next moment, a hard, torrential rain relentlessly descended upon the men, who were not dressed for rainy weather.

Cautiously, Porter and Wollam advanced toward the noisy, incessantly vocal canine creature, reacting to the human strangers setting foot on the animal's territory.

The door of the house flew open, and the man of the house, a tall, white-haired, 70-year-old, thin, blue-eyed, blond man, called out in a friendly, folksy voice, "Who might you be?"

"We're soldiers going to join up with our regiment in Corinth," said Wollam.

"Well, for goodness sakes, boys, come in and we'll feed you a good home-cooked meal. I'm Bill Washburn. That's Sally, my wife, the best cook this side of the Tennessee River, and you can tell by looking at me she can cook well," said the old man, who had shrunk three inches to his present height. His wife was happy, pleasingly plump, and stood at five-feet-two-inches, with eyes of azure blue with shoulder- length brown hair.

Sally Washburn commented, "You boys look a might sickly. Is the war that bad?"

"Ma'am, we got quite sick, but we're feeling better now," said Porter.

"I'll be glad when this war is over. I think the Lincoln government is going to beat us good. It don't look like we're going to keep our independence from Washington," said Sally.

Wollam interjected, "We won't give up, no matter what happens. We aim to see this war through – come hell or high water."

"That's the spirit. You're my kind of people," she said.

"Mr. Washburn said, "Boys, you can't be out in that rain. Stay here tonight and sleep in these two beds," at which he pointed a finger. "We'll be glad to sleep near the fireplace, because you can sleep better in a bed."

"Very well," said Porter. "We bid you a good night. We're so tuckered out," said Porter.

A few hours later, Bill Washburn placed some kindling wood in the fireplace and started a fire with a wooden match. Once the fire had become hot enough, Sally Washburn quickly threw together a delicious, wholesome breakfast as efficiently as a fast-food cook on a mission.

Sally made it a point to give some parting advice to the Union men traveling undercover as Confederate soldiers. "Now, you boys keep in touch with us and write us. We want to know how you're going to outfox them Yankees."

"I'll do that," said Porter, as he and his partner walked out of the house and discovered they would have to cope with wet, muddy roads, that would slow their progress. While walking away from a stand of tall trees, they came through a clearing – face to face – with the blue-coated Union troops of the Ninth Iowa on Saturday, October 18, 1862.

The sloppy attire and filthy appearance of unshaven civilian-clad men, presented an unconvincing case for being Union soldiers.

"Halt!" demanded a regimental Lieutenant. "Identify yourselves."

"Sir, we are from Joshua W. Sill's Twentieth Ohio Brigade, and we were jailed for stealing a train," said Wollam.

"And you expect me to believe that?" You look like rag-tag Rebels to me. Listen, I'm going to escort you men to the officer in charge. He will ask you some questions," said the Lieutenant.

About an hour later, several seated distinguished Union officers glanced up at the disheveled pair, walking smartly into the Provost Marshal's office in Corinth, Mississippi.

The assigned guard said, "These are two jail-breakers."

The eldest officer responded with irritation in his voice. "So, what do you propose that we do? Should we have a parade and sing "When Johnny Comes Marching Home?"

"Sir, we are true-blue, loyal Union soldiers from Joshua W. Sill's Twentieth Ohio Brigade. We and eighteen other comrades stole a train in Georgia, but we got caught and put in jail," said Porter.

"Where did you break jail?" asked the head interrogator puffing a cigar.

"We broke out of the Atlanta jail, but we had been transferred from the Chattanooga jail," said Porter.

"Why were you held in the Chattanooga jail?"

"Sir, we stole a passenger-and-mail train at Big Shanty, Georgia, while everyone else, including railroad employees, was eating breakfast at the depot restaurant."

"Go on, private."

"Our mission was to steal the train, burn the bridges in North Georgia, and tear up the tracks all the way to Chattanooga," said Wollam.

"So why did your mission fail?"

"Sir, we ran the locomotive so fast we ran out of steam and had to leave the locomotive behind, just north of Ringgold, Georgia," said Wollam.

"Hmmm.......that explains why you got thrown into jail. What happened to the remainder of your group?"

"Sir, eight of our men were hanged. Some escaped – don't know how many – and others are still in the Atlanta jail," said Wollam.

"What was the name of the stolen locomotive, Private Wollam?"

"The 'General', Sir."

The interrogator paused to confer in whispers with the other seated officers. "Gentlemen, our consensus is that you are spies."

"Sir, General Mitchel will vouch for us. He sent our leader Andrews to recruit volunteers to steal the train," said Wollam, "and Andrews was hanged a few blocks away from the jail."

"So you think we can telegraph General Mitchel and hear from him right away?" asked the first interrogating officer.

Another seated officer remarked, "Since you don't have any proof of identity or uniforms, how do you expect us to believe your story?"

"I have names of all Andrews Raiders who stole the train," said Wollam.

"And you think that will get you free?" asked the officer in charge.

The ex-prisoners set their faces like a flint arrowhead, exuding unshakable faith, assurance, and steadfast courage.

An indescribably nagging feeling of doubt seized the officer in charge. "All right, we will suspend final judgment and simply give you the benefit of the doubt, but I must emphasize that you are not yet free from suspicion of spying on the Union. For now, I order the guard to transfer these men to General Dodge's Headquarters for further questioning."

An hour later, Major General Grenville Mellen Dodge appeared at his desk in his headquarters, about five minutes after the officers in charge had seated Porter and Wollam. Dodge was attached to the Army of the Tennessee, 4th Corps, 16th Division, was later wounded in the Atlanta campaign of 1864, and eventually become a United States Representative from Iowa.

"Gentlemen, I'll make this inquiry as brief as possible. You are not on trial here. However, my duty is to follow up on the report from the officer in charge. State your names," said Major General Dodge, who continued to question the two escapees.

"Private John R. Porter. Twentieth Ohio Brigade, Company 'G', sir."

"Private John Wollam. Thirty-third Ohio Infantry, Company 'C', sir."

"Why are you out of uniform, Corporal Wollam?" asked General Dodge.

"Sir, we and eighteen other men stole a train at Big Shanty, Georgia. Our mission was to tear up rails, burn bridges, and disable the telegraph communications," said Wollam.

"Who is your commanding General?"

"General Don Carlos Buell," answered Wollam.

"What was the outcome of your mission?"

"Heavy rains delayed us so that we were behind General Mitchel's timetable. Because we failed, he did not attack Chattanooga, since we did not show up with the stolen engine. Unexpectedly, Confederates chased us with another locomotive, and later we ran out of steam and had to escape to the woods north of Ringgold, Georgia. Including Andrews, eight of the twenty Andrews Raiders were hanged; others like us escaped, and the rest of the survivors are still in the Atlanta Jail," said Wollam.

"Your story certainly agrees with newspaper accounts, but more importantly, no other persons could possibly provide such additional factual detail as I have heard from you," said Major General Dodge, reflecting for a few moments before speaking again. "Quartermaster, procure uniforms and blankets for these soldiers – as soon as possible. These men are to report again to me without delay," snapped Major General Dodge.

"Yes sir," responded the quartermaster, while saluting the general, immediately before conducting the men to the supply room; and one hour later, they donned a complete outfit of military clothing, including United States government-issued shoes, socks, and spanking-clean, neatly-pressed, professionally manufactured blue Union uniforms. Their new military attire sharply contrasted with the dirty civilian rags worn during the previous seven months, since the inception of the Andrews Raid on April 12, 1862. In addition to the new clothing issued, the men had received the invitational privilege to eat dinner with Major General Dodge.

Dining at the General's table, Porter said, "General Dodge, I feel like a million dollars, because I'm eating like a king. I want to thank you, sir."

"It is nothing, Private Porter. In the future, don't oversleep when on an important, daring mission. It could have gotten you killed."

"Yes sir," said Porter tersely, with curiosity spread all over his face.

"It's no reflection on your character. Always remember, bad news always travels fast," said Major General Dodge with a friendly smile.

"That won't ever happen again, sir. I hate jails. I need to keep both my weapon and nose clean," said Wollam.

"Correct. Obviously, you have been and intend to remain a good soldier. By the way, both of you are receiving travel pay – $5.00 each. I regret we can't disburse you additional funds. However, I hope our President will award all of you men the medals you deserve."

"My sentiments exactly, sir," said Porter with a gracious, humble attitude.

All eight escapees had left the Atlanta jail over the previous month and two days as MIA's. Understandably, Porter and Wollam wanted to go home and notify their families that these Union soldiers were still alive.

John R. Porter and John Wollam rode a passenger train from Corinth, Mississippi to Columbus, Kentucky and soon took passage on a boat to Cairo, Kentucky, but Porter could still not find a trace of his regiment. This trial-and-error search ended in due course at Nashville, where his former Twenty-First Ohio Regiment had been assigned Provost Duty. John Wollam had to travel eight miles further to rejoin his Thirty-Third Ohio Regiment, already stationed outside of Nashville, Tennessee.

THE RUNAWAY TRAIN

"Oh my God!" exclaimed Colonel Niebling, who hastened to warmly shake Wollam's hand and to extend congratulations to John R. Porter, who would later receive from the State of Ohio a letter of appreciation.

The fourth pair of Atlanta jail escapees, John D. Wilson and Mark Wood, took a southwesterly escape route from Atlanta, unlike the directions of travel of the aforementioned three pair of jail fugitives.

Wilson enabled himself and his partner to scale a jail wall by throwing bricks to distract two armed guards; and despite a burst of musket fire, both he and Wilson cleared the wall, disappearing into the dense woods, where they could easily conceal themselves in the green foliage, until it was safe to travel at night.

Confederate cavalry initiated the pursuit in skirmish formation, and strangely enough, one Confederate picket was stationed only fifteen feet away from the pine bush, under which Wilson and Wood were quietly hiding.

Another picket arrived to relieve the first one, but not before they had conversed with one another.

"I'd give my eyeteeth if I could recapture those stinking train thieves. They're the scum of the earth – worthless pig slop," said the sentry, being relieved of picket duty.

Somehow the pair later eluded the picket by climbing a nearby fence, and then located a desirable resting place on the side of a heavily

335

foliaged wooded hillside.

Following several hours of welcomed rest, Wood had a brainstorm. "We're going to do the unexpected thing. Instead of going north, we're going to go southwest."

"Good idea. The Rebs won't even suspect it. This time we're going to make good our escape. I'm not yet well. One more time in jail and I'll surely die. I would rather be killed in action," said Wilson, with unmistakable resolution in his voice.

"I'm game. 'The die is cast'," said Wood, from a famous quotation of Julius Caesar upon his decision to cross the Rubicon River before returning to Rome to become dictator for life.

"What we need to do is to locate a river that flows south into the Gulf of Mexico, and board a blockading Union ship. After all, our Navy controls all of the coasts and waterways. The Confederates have a very weak Navy and very little money to keep it up," said Wilson.

"Let's do it, Wilson."

"We'll use the North Star to guide ourselves southwest. We'll find that river – I know we will," said Wilson.

Hunger attacked their stomachs once again, but fear dominated their thinking, even though they wanted to stop at a house to ask for food. Since Wood was so ill, he could barely crawl on his hands and feet, but only for a short distance at a time.

"I feel like I want to lay down and die," lamented Wood, who was on the verge of giving in to his physical impediment.

"Come on, Wood. We're in this together. I tell you, we are going to be looking at the warm, beautiful blue water of the Gulf of Mexico. You've got to have the faith to believe it will happen. We can't quit now. We've been through so much misery, but I know that if we keep pressing our way, we will find freedom and a long rest," said Wilson.

Taking a deep breath and then exhaling, Wood said, "Let's go to the Gulf."

"That's more like it, Wood," said Wilson.

"Look over there. This stream ends and that's got to be a river," said Wilson.

Suddenly, the men heard a distant, shrill train whistle while rowing in this sparsely populated area in Georgia.

"That track probably goes to Columbus. I think we're right on course. It would be nice to have a compass, but we'll make do with the stars and the sun," said Wilson.

Soon, the men were feeling the practically unbearable pain and agony of sore, tired feet as a result of mile after mile of mostly constant foot travel.

"Ah! There's a skiff tied to a tree. I'll break the chain lock with a rock," said Wilson.

"Good job. Now we can go boating," said Wood with glee.

Far from being pleasant, a continual presence of pesky mosquitoes mercilessly bombarded the men during the entire southwesterly trip. In the North, they had not ever experienced the misery of mosquito infestation, their worst bane of travel, other than hunger, fatigue, and physical problems brought to bear by previous incarceration.

Overhead was a thick canopy of bowed trees that blocked out much of the sunlight, delaying the men from rowing in the darkest inlet, where mosquitoes and gnawing hunger pangs hindered a good night's sleep.

"I can't get a wink of sleep, Wood. Let's see if we can find some food. There's got to be a house somewhere," said Wilson.

"Let's beat it, Wilson," said Wood.

After additional rowing time, the men eyed a plantation, slaves, and some bloodhounds confined with chains to a wooden fence.

"Wood, here's where we're going to have to do some good lying to save our skins. If they find out who we are, we'll be dead ducks. Let me do the talking," said Wilson.

"Sure thing," said Wood.

Approaching the plantation's house, the slave owner easily detected the men's presence.

"Who are you?" he asked.

"We're very sick soldiers," said Wilson.

"You must be very hungry. Come eat with us," said the plantation owner.

"Thank you," said Wilson.

"Have a seat in the living room, and my wife will cook you a really nice big meal. You men seem all right. You've probably heard about the engine thieves. The authorities ought to hang every last one of 'em. I hear tell some of those men fought back even though they got shot," said the planter.

A few minutes later, the men partook of a delicious breakfast that included fried eggs, bacon, grits, and toasted white bread. When they finished the breakfast, the planter and his wife wished them well.

Paddling for a while down the Chattahoochee River, Wilson became frightened at the sound of an unknown animal making an awful, unsettling noise. What was it? They could hear it, but they couldn't get a good close-up look to make a positive identification of a potential travel risk.

"I see the rapids ahead. Once we go down, we should be able to get away from that beast – whatever it is," said Wilson.

"Watch out! There's a sharp rock. Turn left," warned Wood, as Wilson immediately reacted to the formidable river obstacle.

"I'm glad you saw that rock. It's so dark, it's hard to see anything. All right, hold tight. We're going down the rapids," said Wilson gritting his teeth.

Next day, the sun rose to provide a welcomed warm-up and relief from the pesky mosquitoes. It was time to park the boat ashore and sleep through the day.

Alarmingly choppy, turbulent waters and rough, hilly terrain became genuine travel challenges for

100 miles of steady, uninterrupted paddling. They passed a mill dam, and a short while later, abandoned the boat in a very deep, dangerous gorge, not conducive to boat travel.

Traveling on foot during the day, only five miles could be traversed. Very soon they could see Columbus, Georgia, around which it was necessary to detour and hide underneath some grapevines covering some driftwood. They happened to see the ironclad "Chattahoochee", which reputedly exploded at a later date.

When they saw a boat on the Alabama side of the Chattahoochee River, the pair successfully broke the chain lock with a sturdy stick, very quickly paddling away from the pursuing boat owner.

Next evening, the men received a rude awakening upon returning with some purloined farm food items such as, pumpkin seeds, and a couple of dozen ears of corn. While returning to the site where they had left the boat, the men were astonished to learn that the boat had been stolen.

They later wandered into a swamp and fortunately found a boat below the surface of the water, but increasingly rough water precluded the use of a boat across the half-mile turbulent stream where two rivers met. It was decided to build a flimsy raft from inferior materials tied together by grapevines. Surprisingly, the constructed raft was suitable to float, and the use of a found strong, sturdy stick, enabled Wilson to guide the raft, and provide protection against alligator attacks.

Downstream sometime later, the pair saw the wisdom to never leave a boat unattended. Paddling the boat along the Georgia side of the river, they picked up some Spanish moss to be used as a makeshift mosquito net, providing a respite from the discomfort of countless mosquito bites.

On the stolen boat were some fish hooks and two fishing poles that were a means to catch some catfish for much-needed human nutritional support. Unfortunately, due to a lack of matches, the men could not yet eat the catfish.

In due course, the enlargement of the stream showed there was light at the end of the tunnel. Plainly visible ahead was the town of Apalachicola, Florida; but first, Wilson had to take an abandoned pipe from the boat, and immediately rowed the boat ashore to ask a homeowner to light the pipe for him.

The homeowner, an old Scotsman, named Carlton F. McAfee, said, "You can have these matches, but you need to watch out. Some Union blockade ships are in the Gulf and are closely spaced to each other. I wanted you to know about it, me lads."

"Thank you, sir," said Wilson. "I appreciate your lighting my pipe."

"My pleasure, young lad. You be careful and take it easy. That water gets a lot deeper out there."

"Yes sir, I'll be careful. We'll gladly trade this boat for passage on a ship," said Wilson as he paddled away from the Scotsman. "We're going back north."

"Oh, you are, are you? If I had known that, I would have caught you for a reward," said the astonished Scotsman.

Shortly thereafter, Wood rowed to the opposite side of the river to enter a vacant cabin to cook their catfish, and over an open fire they roasted potatoes stolen from a field hand's boat.

"This is a nice cabin, Wood. Let's sleep here on the floor and leave when it gets dark," said Wilson to his traveling partner.

"That's fine with me," said Wood.

Apalachicola was only several miles from the apparently unoccupied cabin, and later after sunset, the men navigated past the town of Apalachicola, located fifteen miles north of the mouth of the Chattahoochee River, which empties into the Gulf of Mexico.

By now their arms were very tired and sore from constant rowing, but at least the men were fortunate to cook for themselves a nutritionally sound meal, in preparation for paddling out into the Gulf of Mexico in turbulent waters.

The hours passed quickly. Wood noticed a dense thicket on the right side of the river.

"Let's stop and sleep over there," said Wilson. "The tide is out anyway."

"I won't argue about that," said Wood. "It'll be easier to row out to sea, once the tide rolls back in."

"There's a good place to leave the boat. We'll cover it up so nobody steals it," said Wilson.

In another hour, the men entered the deeper

waters of the Gulf of Mexico, and somewhat later, their boat bumped into a live oyster bed.

"Hey, look at this. Oysters! Our breakfast has been brought to us by Almighty God our Provider," said Wilson.

"Eat up. Plenty of raw oysters. Almost too good to be true." The shoreline had disappeared, as these men were rowing in open waters.

"Look at all those dead trees out there in the sea," said Wood.

"Trees, my eye. You need glasses. Those are United States Navy blockade ships. Pick out a ship, Wood. We're going to row until we get aboard one of those freedom ships. Both men stood up in the boat and shouted until they were almost hoarse.

As the boat drew closer and closer to a selected Union ship, the commander, Lt. J. F. Crossman, looked through his binoculars and exclaimed, "What in God's name is this?" Then he handed the pair of binoculars to a shipmate.

"Yes, Commander, those are two men in a boat."

"I wonder why anyone would do such a crazy thing by rowing out in this deep water. Makes no sense," said Lt. Crossman to Robert Waterson, the ship's engineer, a tall, strapping 25-year-old sailor.

"Well, Commander, looks like we're going to have company," said Waterson.

Soon, Wilson and Wood ceased rowing, as their boat collided with the middle of the seagoing vessel.

"Hey, you down there. Identify yourselves,"

demanded the Commander of the Union gunboat. Wilson confidently answered the questions.

"We're from Sill's Brigade, Twentieth Ohio Volunteers. We are two of the twenty Andrews Raiders."

"Did you men capture a train?"

"Yes sir."

"What was the name of it?" asked Lt. Crossman.

"The 'General', sir."

"Who was your leader?"

"General Mitchel, sir."

"Where were you in jail?"

"The Atlanta Jail, sir."

"Grab the life raft and we'll hoist you up to the deck," said Lt. Crossman, ending the questioning.

"Whew! Thank God you guys were here," said Wood.

"You men have been treated far worse than animals. You all will get a first class bath, food, and a clothing issue, for starters," said the Commander taken aback.

The commanders of several blockading ships were curiously viewing this fourth pair of successful Atlanta jail escapees, who had beaten the odds by completing a 400-mile odyssey of danger, uncertainty, and indescribable physical and psychological agony.

Four sailors hoisted up Wilson, since Wood, who was in better health, electing to be the second man to be hauled up and onto the deck of the blockade vessel.

THE RUNAWAY TRAIN

The incredibly unwashed bodies, torn clothing, and moss covering their skin, unduly mortified Lt. Crossman and his enlisted crew. Wood was noticeably very weak from dehydration, malnourishment, and exhaustion.

"Gentlemen, let's sit down in the dining hall. I have told the chef to fix you some good food, and we're providing some brandy with your meal."

Having listened with great interest to the story of the horrible ordeal, Lt. Crossman vowed he would write his Congressman about the cruel, hateful, inhumane treatment of Union prisoners confined in Confederate jails, many of which were converted from warehouses or other types of buildings originally built for purposes other than the imprisonment of human beings.

Lt. Crossman said while munching on a piece of hardtack, "In a couple of days, I'm transferring you men to the 'Stars and Stripes'. You will go to Key West, Florida, the lowest point in North America. When you arrive in Key West, I want you to file a written report to the Quartermaster, before they return you to your outfit."

"Sir, we are very grateful for your help," said Wilson.

"Corporal Wilson, you and Corporal Wood have endured many hardships through your courage and steadfastness to undertake a very dangerous mission. As I see it, you are entitled to some kind of a commendation medal. Don't be surprised if the President awards you both accordingly," said Lt.

Crossman, with a solemn look.

Mounted to a sturdy, wide wooden railing on deck, was a telescope through which a crewman was looking at a reflected piece of glass that was communicating a signal to stand by for an important message to follow immediately. The message originated from Lt. Crossman's ship by means of two flags that a crewman was waving to designate the dots and dashes of Morse code.

"Look, a message from Lt. Crossman's ship," said the telescope user from a ship located one mile away. Another crewman came closer to listen to the transcribed message.

"Wow! Listen to this: the flags say, 'Two Union soldiers from Ohio on board after escape from Confederate jail in Atlanta. Incredible escape story. Send a ship to transfer soldiers to Key West ASAP.' The decoder said, "Take this message to the commander."

Within three minutes, the first ship receiving Lt. Crossman's message prepared to relay the message to the next ship anchored in Apalachicola Bay, Florida, and this procedure was repeated to 500 United States Navy ships that comprised the Federal Naval blockade extending to Key West, where the Morse code operator informed the Key West Base Commander of the returning Union ex-POW's from Atlanta. Such was the nifty communication network known in Union navy circles as the 'Morse code grapevine'. Wilson and Wood were unaware of such goings-on.

Beaming like a 150-watt bulb, Lt. Crossman said, "Goodbye, gentlemen. Remember, be sure to file that written report when you get to Key West." Soon, the "Stars and Stripes" Union gunboat carrying the escapees disappeared on the horizon.

Two weeks later, someone from the Key West News Scooper had learned of the Atlanta jailbreak and the odyssey of Wood and Wilson. A navy news media public relations representative attached to the administrative office at the Key West Naval Station, had leaked the information to his brother, a Key West News Scooper reporter.

CHAPTER 10
A PRISONER EXCHANGE

S everal days later, an angry Governor Joseph E. Brown spilled his coffee on his right leg, relaxing in his easy chair early one morning, while reading the leaked news in the "Atlanta Intelligencer".

"Damn it! Eight engine thieves escaped the Atlanta jail months ago. That's one thing, but the way it happened just galls the hell out of me. I'm going to order an investigation of that jail. I guarantee some heads are going to roll, Elizabeth," said Governor Brown.

"Joseph, when you hire wounded veterans and military cadets, you get the same unsatisfactory results that are no better than that kid who was supposed to be guarding the 'General'."

"You're absolutely right, Elizabeth," said Governor Brown.

"Two of the Yankee escapees were really slick. They pulled a fast one and went down the Chattahoochee, until they reached a Yankee blockade ship that took them under their wing. That makes me mad as hell," said Governor Brown.

"Calm down, honey. What's done is done. You can't change what happened," said his wife.

"I know. It's bad enough to have that jerk, Jeff Davis, in charge of the Confederacy. He doesn't have enough sense to pour urine out of a boot. Conscription does not work, and it has already eaten into my military manpower. I run this State, not Jeff Davis. By God, I'd like to place an advertisement to encourage desertions so I could recruit the deserters into the State Guard. We need bridge and railroad guards. I could care less about Davis's problems. I hope the Yankees capture the S.O.B. We're losing the war. He's the cause."

"Who knows? Maybe they will," said Elizabeth (it actually happened – in Irwinville, Georgia, on May 10, 1865).

* * *

Back in the Fulton County, Atlanta Jail, six remaining Andrews Raiders were still being held – however, moving day had arrived. For security reasons, perhaps prompted by the Governor's reaction to the jailbreak, the order to vacate the jail reached the Provost Marshal's desk within ten days.

Consequently, Corporal William Pittenger and others were transferred to Concert Hall, a Confederate barracks building two blocks away from the train depot. The building included two rooms with conventional windows of probable dimensions of three feet by five feet. A twenty-foot square room was assigned to the remnant of the Andrews Raiders – a far cry from the virtually unventilated, filthy, rat-infested Swims Jail in Chattanooga. Instead of burdensome, confining chains with padlocks, a guard was always on duty to closely watch the prisoners, while the corridor door remained open. Two windows fronted the building, and two other windows were perpendicular to a side street.

In addition to the six imprisoned Andrews Raiders, the Confederate barracks also included Union sympathizers known as "Union people of Atlanta". The barracks was equipped with a gas burner, which remained lit each night, and a large big-hearthed fireplace would supplement the gas heat with a generous supply of logs.

"We owe much thanks to God for allowing us to be in a decent prison. This confirms the fact that God has not left us," said Pittenger.

Private Jacob Parrott said, "At least we aren't still in that hell-hole in Chattanooga."

"Correct. Everything is better, but we're still in a military environment – under the wrong flag," said Pittenger.

"Pittenger, I see you're a self-appointed people-watcher", said Elihu H. Mason.

"Yes, I enjoy observing the stream of mankind passing by the window, so that the time goes by so much quicker," said Pittenger.

Parrott said, "Wood is getting low."

"That's not a big thing," said Pittenger.

The guard then spoke some of his rationed words. "You with the glasses. Go outside the door and bring back more wood."

Three minutes later, Pittenger returned with a full armload of dirty, half-rotten firewood, full of crawling doodlebugs. The bespectacled prisoner meticulously placed each piece of wood within the bright, pleasing, flickering fire.

Besides the six raiders, ten Tennesseans, and four Union POW's – all twenty were kept in one room. One inmate handed back to the guard a tray of uneaten meager rations – an action that angered the guard.

"All right smarty britches, you're coming with me. I have a plan for you," said the guard to a prisoner named John Doe Pierce, who had a bandaged head wound previously sustained on the battlefield. Pittenger and others watched helplessly as the vindictive guard grabbed Pierce by the left arm and led him into another room. The guard tied the inmate's hands on top of the knees, and placed a stick over the prisoner's arms and across, yet under the knees, a form of punishment known in military circles as "bucking". Pierce was left to endure the cold, drafty hallway for the duration of the night.

Another inmate named R. Sturdy Barker commented to a guard, "You Rebs may be one day taking a big fall for your high-and-mighty, holier-than-thou attitude. You guys will end up as field

351

hands to pay up the war debt. Don't mock us, because the tables will be turned when the North beats the South."

"Is that so, Yank? I'm going to teach you not to open your stupid Yankee mouth. I've also got a plan for you." Quickly, the guard handcuffed the inmate upon yanking him out of the room, as the door guard watched with pointed musket.

"Not half the plans we have for the South," said Barker.

"I'm gong to impress upon you who is in charge in this jail. When I'm through with you, you're going to be so sorry you ever opened your mouth," said the angry guard.

The jail guard proceeded to tie Barker's heals with one end of a long rope, which was strung up to a rafter in another room. In effect, inmate Barker was hanging upside down from the rafter for a few minutes; then the guard took the rope off the rafter and repeated the cruel, unusual punishment – but it did not end there. Twenty-four hours of starvation ensued for this victim – in the smallest dark chamber of Concert Hall.

Without due process of law, every inmate was incarcerated and was not allowed to have an attorney to defend them. Such was the unconstitutionality of wartime imprisonment for civilians guilty of aiding and abetting enemy prisoners. In one incident, Joe Smith, a Union sympathizer and Atlanta resident, slipped some money through a window to a prisoner who had fought the Confederates at the Battle of Shiloh. An observant outdoor guard seized and jailed the sympathizer in Concert Hall – also without benefit of legal counsel or a jury trial; however, the Confederate Government refused to acknowledge the United States Constitution, due to their political separation from the Union.

Pittenger must have recorded by shorthand much of the information he later used in two published books: "*DARING AND SUFFERING*" and "*IN PURSUIT OF THE GENERAL*". Of course, no one else would probably be trained to write and transcribe shorthand. Thus, Pittenger was, for all practical purposes, writing his observations of military and prison life in a secret code; and the Confederates did not detect what Pittenger was actually doing, with the exception of Major Jack Wells, C.S.A., the Barracks Commander, who asked, "What kind of hen-scratching is that?"

"Shorthand," said Pittenger.

The major omitted an important question: What was Pittenger writing? Oddly enough, Major Wells merely commented, "You seem to write a lot. I've been watching you, and you strike me as a literate man. I was wondering whether or not you could help me. I'm looking for a man who can do paperwork in my office."

"Why me, Major?"

"Pittenger, there is hardly a Southerner who can read or write. That's why I'm appointing you to be my chief clerk."

"Very well, Major. I'll do it for you – not for the Confederacy."

"Come along with me. I'll show you the office duties. I know you can do the work," said Major Wells with a smile on his face.

"So, what am I responsible for?" asked the literate, bespectacled prisoner.

"Pittenger, I'm going to show you how to fill out a Daily Report Form. There are different columns for the number of prisoners, how much rations are delivered to the inmates, and the supplies people requisition," said Major Wells.

"Sir, if you will provide the items I need, I will be able to do a proper job for you," said Pittenger.

"I will guarantee all the items you will need," said Major Wells.

As Major Wells approached the door guard, he said, "Guard, this man may pass to and from my office, but he is not to go anywhere else."

"Yes sir," replied the uniformed armed guard, who stood parallel to his musket at the position of "order arms", while his hand firmly grasped the barrel of the weapon, held vertically alongside and against his right leg.

A few minutes later, Major Wells returned with the paper, rulers, pencils, and of course, a desk that two other guards carried into the office, from a furniture storage room in a nearby building.

Several days passed, and it was evident on Pittenger's face he was enjoying his job, even though he was not receiving any compensation.

Suddenly, a loud, boisterous, drunken Confederate major was escorted into the jail.

"You're not putting me with those enlisted men in that room. I'm an officer. I demand to sit in your front office. I'm not dangerous. I'm not a traitor. As an officer in the Confederate army, I'm entitled to some respect. How about it, Major?"

Reluctantly, Major Wells said, "All right. Sit in my office. If you go anywhere else, you'll hang. Is that understood?"

A cursory body search revealed a cloth pouch containing five hundred dollars in gold coins. "We're confiscating this money," said Major Wells.

"You can't do that. You're stealing my money. I earned it. You never worked for it. What makes you think you're entitled to something that's not yours?" protested the Confederate officer, imitating the Southern drawl.

"Oh, all right. You can keep your money," said Major Wells in exasperation, not wishing to physically subdue a drunken Rebel officer. The Major had to leave Concert Hall to conduct a personal errand in town.

Committing an error in judgment, the Major left in charge a Sergeant Bobby White, a disabled veteran who had been severely wounded at the Battle of Bull Run. Sgt. White had been experiencing diarrhea throughout the day, and vacated his post to respond to the call of nature.

Seizing an opportunity for escape, the drunken officer stared at Pittenger and said, "You look very familiar. I know where I've seen you. I was visiting the Atlanta Jail when those idiots hung your fellow troops – and they were so brave. One thing for sure. The South will answer for it."

"Just what are you trying to say to me?" asked Pittenger, apparently immersed in his paperwork.

"I'm asking you for a pass." Then he whispered, "I'm a Northern spy. Help me escape," said the new detainee.

"First, answer some questions," demanded Pittenger.

"All right," said the detainee.

"What is the square root of four?" asked Pittenger.

"Two," said the Confederate officer.

"Good answer. Who was the conductor of the engine 'General' just before the Andrews Raid occurred?" asked Pittenger.

"Captain William A. Fuller," said the detainee.

"What kind of weapon was the cadet bearing at Camp McDonald?" asked Pittenger.

"A Joe Brown pike," replied the detainee.

"Correct," said Pittenger enthusiastically.

Pittenger continued questioning the detainee. "What is three cubed?"

"Twenty-seven."

Final question: Read this sentence to me."

"All written reports must be clear and legible."

"Excellent. I'm satisfied that you are from the North. You can read, you're good at mathematics, and you've been a very observant spy," said Pittenger.

"Sounds like I passed the test."

"With flying colors.....Grab the overcoat on the bed and leave now, since it's getting dark. It's a good disguise," said Pittenger.

"Thanks for your help," said the spy.

"Don't mention it. Just go," said Pittenger.

Two hours later, the spy did not return to the jail —successful escape. Pittenger was glad for him, but still somewhat envious that his previous escape attempts had been thwarted due to his bad eyesight.

When Major Wells returned to his office, Pittenger was routinely filling out supply requisition forms, as if nothing else had happened during the lapse of security coverage.

Entering the office, Major Wells exclaimed, "Great guns! Where did the prisoner go?"

Reacting nonchalantly, Pittenger looked up and said, "He must have gone to dinner."

Looking at the bed, Major Wells said, "Oh my God! My overcoat is gone. I must be having a nightmare....Oh, well, come easy go easy. It was just an overcoat."

Soon, the guard returned and Major Wells questioned him. "Sergeant, what happened to the prisoner?"

"Sir, he was not in this room when I came on duty," said the guard.

"Pittenger, that was an officer. Surely, you would remember him," insisted Major Wells.

"Oh, you're talking about the drunk," said Pittenger.

"Of course. Where did that S.O.B. go?" asked Major Wells.

"He put on his coat and said he was going to dinner," said Pittenger.

"Is that right? Sergeant, double time it over to the guard house. If that man gets away, I'll have every guard hanged – and I don't mean standing up." The search for the spy was an exercise in futility, as he made good his flight, well beyond the premises of Concert Hall.

"Yes sir," said the guard.

"Pittenger, was that S.O.B. wearing a coat?" asked Major Wells.

"I believe I remember seeing him pick up a coat," said Pittenger.

"Where did he pick up the coat?" asked Major Wells.

"He took it right off the bed," replied Pittenger.

Then the jailer reflected momentarily, cradling his head in his hands.

"You know, that was a pretty good practical joke," said Major Wells, while standing up from his chair.

Later during the day, a young man was peddling sweet potatoes near the front door of the Confederate barracks.

"Hey, Mr. Guard, may I go in and sell sweet potatoes to the prisoners?"

"All right, but no funny business, son."

"Yah suh, Mr. Guard. I always play straight," said the young sweet potato peddler.

"You keep it that way," said the guard.

Walking into Concert Hall, the young African-American vendor shouted, "Sweet potatoes – fifty cents apiece. Nice sweet potatoes – homegrown."

Confederate soldiers made bunk-side purchases of the agricultural product. Soon, the six Andrews Raiders stepped forward from their bunks and approached the sweet potato vender, a 15-year-old, five-foot-two-inch, 120-pound African-American boy with shoe-button brown eyes.

Two Union sympathizers strolled leisurely up to the door, and one of them said to the guard, "Nice day, isn't it?"

"Same ol' stuff, different day," said the guard, with a frown extending across his face.

"May we visit the barracks?" asked one of the Union sympathizers.

"You have five minutes only," said the guard, without changing his expression.

"Thank you," said one of the visitors.

Into the barracks the two civilians proceeded, discreetly easing themselves up to the six engine thieves, with whom money accompanied each handshake, which was a planned hand-to-hand transfer of Confederate paper money.

The benefactors were so adept with the handshake method of unobtrusively handing out money to the intended receivers, that the guard's eyes were not as quick as the visiting sleight-of-hand artists.

"Shh! said one of the sympathizers in a whisper,

as the raiders felt the Confederate notes "grease" their right palms. "God bless you," said a soft-spoken sympathizer, as he and his companion slowly walked to the security entrance doorway, quietly departing the barracks as the raiders were judiciously spending some of the pecuniary gifts for sweet potatoes, which the men roasted over the open flickering fire among its plentiful ashes.

When Sunday had finally come, Pittenger, who had been diligently studying religious books, had taken it upon himself to lead a Bible study for the other inmates of Concert Hall. However, the ever-present eyesore, the as-of-late obnoxious door guard, was grating against Pittenger's capacity for patience and longsuffering.

"Why waste your time reading the Bible? Don't you know you're going to hell because you people are engine thieves?" queried the guard.

"Guard, answer me this: on the cross at Calvary, Jesus Christ forgave the thief who was also nailed to a cross and said, 'This night you shall be in paradise.' You obviously know so very little about the Bible, and I invite you to listen to us discuss the Word. Where do you think you'll spend eternity?"

"Pittenger, you're a troublemaker," said the offended guard, who summoned the Major. "Major Wells, these prisoners are misbehaving. They're having a Bible study."

Walking swiftly toward the raiders' room, while puffing a cigar, Major Wells said, "What is the matter here?"

Pittenger replied, "Sir, we were simply having a Bible study, and that heathen guard is verbally harassing us, and we are not violating any rules. All we are doing is practicing religious freedom. Please tell your guard to cease from making all of his ignorant utterances."

"Is that all, Corporal Pittenger?" asked Major Wells pensively.

"Sir, Reverend McDonel owes me a reply to my request to bring me additional theology books to read," said Pittenger.

"You're request is reasonable. I will have a talk with the guard. You may continue your religious practices, as far as I'm concerned," said Major Wells. "I see nothing wrong with spiritual nourishment. I think we all could use some more religion," he said respectfully. As for the preacher, the Methodist Church customarily transfers its preachers after a short time. That's the way they are. Very few Methodist pastors stay more than two years at a church. The bishops make sure of that," said Major Wells.

"Sir, in that case, I need to catch Rev. McDonel before he leaves the neighborhood. Would you please send a guard to go with me to Reverend McDonel's house?"

"We can arrange that. I take it you have been acquainted with the clergyman for quite some time," said Major Wells.

"Sir, this may sound rather odd to you, but I have received the call to study for the ministry and to possibly be a preacher someday."

"All right. Your motive sounds justifiable. Soon, you will be accompanied with a guard, but don't try anything foolish, or he will shoot you and ask questions later – that is, if you're still alive."

"I understand, sir," said Pittenger.

Only one guard was posted on adjacent Atlanta streets, for which he was responsible to regularly patrol on foot, and it would have been so easy to overpower a musket-bearing guard, who had a tendency to walk so temptingly close to Pittenger's bunk. But something was holding the bespectacled, young, courageous ministerial student from acting upon the thought of an easy escape. By exploiting this situation, he would lose favor with Major Wells, who had implicitly trusted Pittenger and had rendered positive treatment to the other Andrews Raiders.

The young correspondent undoubtedly felt ill at ease on account of wearing dirty, tattered, disreputable clothing, through which he reeked of despicable, foul body odor, which Rev. McDonel overlooked. The minister was so pleased with the news of Pittenger's divine call to the ministry, that a positive feeling of fellowship, reverence, and genuine concern prevailed over Pittenger.

"Reverend, if I overcome this ungodly incarceration, I promise to go into full-time service as a minister of the Gospel, in my Lord's service as a humble and obedient servant," said Pittenger.

"I am moved by your obviously warm, sincere

pledge to serve the Lord," said the animated, excited preacher, who wanted to shout the good news from his roof top.

"I mean it, Rev. McDonel, I have felt God's calling – for quite some time – but I truly admit I've been running from God," said Pittenger contritely.

"Oh, so adversity accompanied you through the fire, as in the case of Shadrach, Meshach, and Abednego in the Book of Daniel," said Rev. McDonel.

"That sounds like an appropriate analogy," said Pittenger. "I'm giving you my copy of '*PILGRIM'S PROGRESS*' by John Bunyan. You will notice I wrote a vow to follow through with my commitment – it's on the flyleaf."

Obviously moved by this demonstration of very deep commitment, Rev. McDonel said, "Brother Pittenger, it is time to conclude our meeting with prayer. Almighty God, this man has endured much untold persecution at the hands of his adversary. However, he has held steadfastly to his unshakable faith in You, Lord God Almighty, King of the Universe. As Brother Pittenger yields his life to be in Your service, I ask You to be a lamp unto his feet and a light upon his path from this day forward. Amen."

Sensing the divine presence of God in the clergyman's home study room, the guard was visibly shaken by a planted evangelical seed, indirectly serving as a catalyst in remolding his life in its autumn years, since the average life span was about fifty years.

HENRY H. KURTZ

The young, aspiring unofficial seminary student shook the preacher's hand for the last time, but yet the two men wrote letters to one another during the following twenty-five-year period.

After a few more weeks had passed, the tedium of prison life seemed to linger like a sore that seemingly took forever to heal. It was near the end of November, 1862. A group of sharply dressed Confederate officers entered the barracks and the lead officer commanded, "Atten-shun." Everyone snapped to attention.

The captain of the contingent of officers declared in a calm, controlled, mannerly voice: "I'm here to make an announcement. We have been negotiating a prisoner exchange agreement with the Union army, and as a result of such talks, you will be exchanged in Richmond. We'll provide transportation to get there and back to Union lines."

This stunning event triggered fond memories of his association with all the executed compatriots, and Pittenger unequivocally perceived their deaths as nothing more than premeditated, cold-blooded murder. As for the fate of his surviving comrades, a sea of worry and uncertainty gripped his thoughts.

An article from the "Southern Confederacy" newspaper published in Atlanta, had chronicled the successful escape of John Reed Porter and John Wollam, who eventually ended up in friendly territory, Corinth, Mississippi, in a state of extreme fatigue and hunger. According to an unfounded news report, three Andrews Raiders had been killed while attempting to escape the old Atlanta jail. The lack of accurate, reliable information pertaining to his fellow soldiers, was enough to worry him.

"The lead officer also said, "It's 1200 hours. Be packed and ready by 0700 hours. Any questions?"

"No sir," said the audience in unison. Pittenger was so elated at the news of the upcoming release from captivity, he had much difficulty in controlling his hand to write legibly on his paperwork, such as requisition forms designating all the travel rations from Atlanta to Richmond. Reluctantly, Pittenger had to ask for another clerk to process the forms, during the remaining 31 hours of POW imprisonment.

Soon, Major Wells staggered into the barracks, slurring his words, and said, "Pittenger, I damn sure want you to have my felt hat. You're a top-notch clerk. You read and write well and that's why I'm giving you my hat."

"Thank you, Major Wells." Without delay, Pittenger concealed the soft felt military hat among his personal belongings stored on a wooden shelf, in case the major were to ask for the return of the gift upon transformation to his natural state. Naturally, Pittenger would wisely mention nothing to anyone about the hat. In the meantime, the road to Richmond beckoned.

The presence of ten musket-bearing guards marching twenty prisoners to the railroad depot, was indeed a reality check. The men kept saying to one another, "We're going. We're going," as they shivered in the dark on the cold morning of Wednesday, December 3, 1862. From another prisoner, Captain Frey, having previously escaped, had given to Pittenger a substantially thick overcoat. Although the six last-to-be incarcerated Andrews Raiders were grateful to be released from the barracks known as Concert Hall, they had appreciated the pleasant accommodations of heat, palatable, nutritious food, and the best treatment of any other previous detention facility, but yet the men were uncertain of the living conditions at their next quarters in Richmond, Virginia.

Later, at 3:00 a.m., the Dalton, Georgia railroad station came into view, as the engineer saw the conspicuous kerosene oil lanterns mounted on several wooden poles positioned on the perimeter of the station. The engine's carbide gas head lamp barely illuminated the tracks twenty feet ahead.

"Dalton. Change trains for Cleveland. Be ready to go in one hour," said the standing conductor whose eyes were bloodshot due to travel fatigue. As the prisoners left the train, a very icy, cold wind pierced them like a knife.

"This has to be the longest hour we've ever had to wait – in cold, moist shivering wind. It's kind of stupid to lock the station door. We could have been waiting inside drinking a cup of hot apple cider. These Southerners have missed a marketing opportunity," said Pittenger.

A guard chimed in, "Southerners love their sleep. Making money takes second place."

THE RUNAWAY TRAIN

Following the hour's wait in windy, freezing weather, everyone boarded the train for Cleveland, Georgia. As an hour passed, the train pulled in for a twenty-minute stop at Cleveland.

"Men, go behind those bushes if you must make a necessary trip, but you had best be back on this train before it takes off," said the head guard.

When the train crossed the state line into Tennessee, the guards had succumbed to drowsiness and fell asleep in their passenger seats, while lightly gripping their weapons. Throughout the evening, the clickety-clack of the wheels against the track lulled the Confederate prison guards into a deeper sleep, thus placing themselves at risk to be overpowered.

Suddenly, Sgt. White opened his eyes to address the prisoners. "You Yanks are free to escape, but it would be a bad idea. You've spent too much time in the woods. You've got it made on this train. Anyway, bad shoes, clothes, and snow are no good for traveling. Believe me."

Pittenger said, "That's a good point," but upon immediate reflection, he had some doubts about whether or not a prisoner exchange would happen at all. The voice of fear said they were like lambs being led to the slaughter. He recalled vividly that fateful Wednesday, June 18, 1862, when seven of his compatriots received only one hour's notice of their execution in Atlanta, leading to a justifiable element of doubt about his group's long-term survival.

Soon, the train passed through Knoxville,

Tennessee, and somewhat later, Pittenger saw Greenville, Tennessee, the home town of Captain Frey.

Wet, miserable, blustery weather greeted everyone the next day, Thursday, December 4, 1862. Although rations had been depleted, these men had grown accustomed to scarce food supplies. After traveling all day, the train arrived in Lynchburg, Virginia, for a 24-hour layover.

Inhospitable barracks conditions included a large unlit stove and drafty walls. Pittenger suffered so extensively from the bone-chilling, penetrating, moist, cold air, that he was unable to sleep; and to make a feeble effort to get warm, he paced the barracks all night.

Encountering another sleepless prisoner, a Confederate soldier, Pittenger struck up a conversation with the five-foot-nine-inch Southerner weighing 150 pounds, with blue eyes, and a scraggly, heavy beard.

"What are you in here for?" asked Pittenger.

"What's it to you, Yank?" said the embittered man.

"I was only making conversation," said Pittenger.

"My name is Lot Reeves."

"I'm William Pittenger. Good to meet you."

"That's debatable, but anyway, I'll tell you this much. I got thrown into this wretched place just for writing a letter to my worried parents, while I was on night guard duty," said Reeves.

"You know you did wrong," said Pittenger.

"Yeah, but my parents haven't heard from me in a long time," said Reeves.

"I see what you mean," said Pittenger sympathetically. "I hope my escaped buddies got word to my parents. In my situation, letter-writing was not allowed."

"Of course not, because you're a Yankee in my country," said Reeves.

"In other words, you don't live in the United States anymore," said Pittenger.

"Right. I live in the Confederate States of America. We've got our own president."

"I guess that makes all Southerners foreigners. Naturally, it follows that if we had taken out all Southerners, this war would have been over, and then there would have been no foreigners in the South," said Pittenger.

"You just don't get it, Yank," said Reeves angrily.

"Oh, I do get it. You Southerners seceded from the Union, and my job is to help restore the Union, because the United States of America is legally one nation – not two separate nations," said Pittenger.

"Your lack of compassion makes my blood boil," said Reeves.

"You Southerners made your bed, and you will have to face the consequences," said Pittenger. "As far as compassion is concerned, your prison official doesn't even know the meaning of the word 'compassion'."

"Get away from me, Yank," said the Confederate prisoner in a huff.

"Gladly," said Pittenger. "By the way, when the war's over, I want to look you up, so I can register you in one of our Ohio high schools."

"Good night, Yank," said Reeves.

"The offer still stands. Just stay alive," Pittenger said.

"Don't try being cute with me," said the Confederate prisoner. Pittenger walked away satisfied, having won the verbal jousting match.

The second day in Lynchburg was as miserably wet and cold as the preceding day; and fortunately, the prison officials sanctioned the issuance of heat from the huge stove in the middle of the room at twelve noon. Perhaps this was an eleventh-hour act of mercy to prevent severe illnesses or deaths.

An opportunity to escape the train after departure from Lynchburg, later during the afternoon of Saturday, December 6, 1862, presented itself as another temptation, as the train was halted to take on wood and water. But the apparently worsening wintry conditions would have led to death by freezing in the higher mountains in Virginia, and he reasoned well that escape was simply not a viable option. Whether or not anyone had considered it sinful to spurn an escape opportunity, the risk of failure was simply far too great. Pittenger decided to bide his time, believing that the Confederate captors were telling the truth about the upcoming prisoner exchange.

THE RUNAWAY TRAIN

About ten hours later, the train arrived at the train station in Richmond, Virginia, where most of the inhabitants were asleep during the wee hours of Sunday morning on December 7, 1862. Once again, the prisoners would have to endure the unfavorable chill and accompanying winds, until Sergeant Whitehead could locate the office of the Provost Marshal. Huddled together against the junction of two brick buildings, all twenty prisoners-to-be-exchanged derived a minimum of warmth from their mutually shared body heat.

After what seemed to be an unending wait, Sgt. Whitehead returned to lead the prisoners to the Provost Marshal's office. Having been awakened in his office, the Provost Marshal was especially in a very unsociable mood to speak to anyone, given his downcast serious, no-nonsense demeanor, to be put to work to process twenty incoming prisoners, at such an ungodly hour.

The prisoner exchange order papers were presented to the Provost Marshal, who readily took note of the following types of prisoners: four Union soldiers, ten dissident Tennesseans, and six engine thieves.

"Sergeant, I am placing these men under the custody of this post. I will have orders cut for your return to Atlanta later in the morning. I am providing an extra bed for your use," declared the Provost Marshal, a five-foot-five-inch lieutenant, a Mexican War Veteran. He was a white-haired man sporting luxuriant mutton chops sideburns and a battle scar permanently etched on his left cheek; he walked with a limp due to a bullet wound in the right leg. This burned-out, war-weary officer yearned for the comforts and conveniences of civilian life, but most importantly, he missed his wife and three grown enlisted sons and his only daughter, sixteen years of age.

The Provost Marshal demanded, "Door guard, send for a guide."

"Yes sir," said the corporal.

The sun shone brightly on the morning of Sunday, December 7, 1862, in Richmond, a town full of frustrated, angered, disillusioned citizens, who would inevitably reap the side effects of an eventual military defeat.

After a forced, tedious march to the banks of the James River, the twenty prisoners were halted near the façade of a rather intimidating brick building, encircled by a number of armed Confederate guards. This brick structure was known as Libby Prison, a former grocery store and ship chandlery, originally owned by Libby & Son before its conversion into an ill-suited prison, as the result of 61-year-old General John H. Winder's requisition order, authorizing the Confederate government's purchase of the private building, where candles were made and sold in addition to the retail sale of groceries.

Libby Prison was the headquarters of all the prisons in the Richmond area, and its primary function was the registration of all incoming prisoners and the discharge of out-going prisoners. General Winder was regarded by the prison population as a stern, rigid disciplinarian and a controller with regard to security matters. However, the Andrews Raiders were much better off here than in the Swims Jail.

The Andrews Raiders and the fourteen other prisoners walked up a steep flight of outside stairs leading to a large room of many more exchangees, consisting of mostly Union soldiers, who eagerly talked about their war stories in a congenial atmosphere of camaraderie. All the prisoners executed a right turn before entering the large room of starved, emaciated, rag-tag men wearing worn-out, filthy clothing, and none of them had bathed in months. Most of the men were probably infested with body lice.

Even though a small stove was the only source of heat, it was insufficient to properly provide the needed warmth in a room too large for the size of the stove, regardless of the intensity of its red-hot flames. Needless to say, the chill winds blowing into Libby prison were creating much misery, since the windows lacked shutters.

Every prisoner remained very close to the small heater, and one unidentified soldier said, "Guess what. There are some people up north making public demonstrations against the war, because they're out-and-out cowards and don't want to subject themselves to the risks of military service."

"Is that right?" asked Pittenger.

"Yep. It's true. I'd like to string up or put each one of them on the front line. I have no use for people like that. They're undermining the war effort," said the unidentified soldier standing by the stove, warming his body.

Presently, an officer came into the large room and said, "Attention. I'm going to call the names of the last fifteen new men."

All fifteen men were marched across the street to another prison known as Castle Thunder, an unfurnished former tobacco factory, that had the amenities of running water and primitive toilets. Before entering Castle Thunder proper, the prisoners had to walk through a guarded door, and had to remain for a period of time in the general office of the prison commissary, an evil-looking, hateful, black-bearded man named Chillis, who stared at the prisoners. "So, I'm told you men are Bridge Burners. In my book, the authorities should hang every enemy of the South."

Several days passed, and there was some talk about a planned prisoner escape, but an informant tattled on the planners and received as a reward, a parole from the prison commissary, the administrative headquarters of the Richmond prison system.

Pittenger then asked an Irish parolee to mail a thirty-cent letter to Pittenger's parents. Fortunately, the former Battle of Murfreesboro participant was successful in smuggling the letter out of Castle Thunder. The letter from William Pittenger to his father read as follows from the removed flyleaf of *PARADISE LOST*:

Dear Father: As a paroled prisoner, I'm faring well despite the circumstances. The worst is behind me. We are out of harm's way. Six of us are left. Confederates executed eight of us, and eight managed to escape in June.

It is depressing to hear of our frequent military defeats and heavy battle losses. Too bad Bingham lost the election. Tell me who is single, married, and drafted. Please send me a gold dollar in an unsealed envelope – no more than that, as it would be stolen. Rejoice and count your blessings for my continual survival and safe return home. Thirty cents is an outrageous postal rate for just one letter, and that accounts for no letters to my friends, but do tell them to write me.

Ever yours,
William Pittenger

In this prison, mysterious deaths occurred as well as death by smallpox vaccination – attributable to probable misformulation, contamination, or both causes leading to fatal consequences. Unvaccinated prisoners were also most likely to die of the dreaded disease. Cold, hunger, disease, and crime plagued this overcrowded inmate population.

In one incident, some Irish prisoners ran swiftly and deliberately, collided with other prisoners who were standing near the small heater, in a futile attempt to warm themselves. The victims of this crime were separated from the aggressive Irish prisoners and sent down to stay in the basement of Castle Thunder, where only eighty inmates were receiving much heat, from a gas stove in significantly smaller quarters.

One Union soldier, a Potomac Army scout, accosted William Pittenger one day while warming themselves in front of the heater.

"Pittenger, what are you in here for?" asked Charles Marsh, the Union scout.

"We stole an engine in Georgia."

"Oh, you mean the Andrews Raid at Big Shanty," said Marsh.

"Precisely," said Pittenger.

"Wait until you hear my story: I was supposed to burn a bridge, but the Rebs prevented me from doing that. They caught me trying to smuggle out classified documents to my outfit," said a tired, hungry, disheveled Charles Marsh, chewing one of many tobacco stems found lying around the former tobacco factory.

"When did this happen?" asked Pittenger.

"About two months ago. I owe my survival to quick thinking," said Marsh.

"How so?" asked Pittenger.

"When the Rebel sergeant got kind of drunk, I slipped over and grabbed the arrest papers, and soon afterwards he took me chained to a horse-drawn wagon and dropped me off here. Well, he was driving drunk and failed to see me, when I threw the arrest papers over a bridge into a small lake. So, when the drunken sergeant couldn't find the papers, the commissary had me locked up right away," said Marsh.

"Did they ever recover the papers?" asked Pittenger.

"Yes, and by that time, nobody remembered my face. So, a guard entered my room about a couple of days later. He called out my name, and I said 'Charles Marsh died last night', as I was pointing my finger at a dead man lying face up in the barracks," said Marsh.

"Then what happened?" asked Pittenger.

"The guard said, 'Isn't that a shame. I had reserved a noose for him. Lucky stiff'."

"Wow! What an interesting development," said Pittenger to this inmate, cleverly avoiding execution by taking the name of a dead man, who was either a victim of crime or a smallpox fatality.

Only a few feet away from the conversing pair, a prison guard was asking another Union inmate to enlist in the Southern army.

The prisoner replied, "Heck no, I won't go."

"How come?" asked Sgt. Whitehead, a thin, short man, probably five-feet-five-inches tall, weighing perhaps 160 pounds.

"I ain't doing any kind of work. Something's wrong if you can't give me a place to stay," replied the inmate.

"I'll deal with you later, Yank," fumed the angry sergeant.

Four other inmates refused to join the Southern army. The sergeant remarked, "Send them to the special room. They'll come to their senses."

Two guards grabbed the four Union inmates by their elbows, quickly escorting the dissident men to an unpleasant room known as "the cell".

Shortly thereafter, someone secretly conveyed a piece of a candle, a file fragment, and a very sharp section of stovepipe. These items enabled one inmate to cut an escape hole in the northern wall of "the cell", and flee on foot from the premises, amid the loud barking of a guard dog.

During the next day, a cloud cover held in the cold outdoor temperature. The addition of a strong wind, rain, and sleet were harming poorly-clad, very ill, weak inmates.

"I give up on these lazy inmates – no cooperation. They're a bunch of sissies," said Sgt. Whitehead, whose blue eyes dazzled and danced even on overcast days.

Captain Alexander listened politely and then said, "Don't do the slow death technique. If you intend to punish them, just shoot or hang them. I expect you to use good common sense. Otherwise, we'll be showing ourselves as downright fools to the whole world."

On the strength of Captain Alexander's order, Sgt. Whitehead took the four Union prisoners back inside the prison to quickly warm themselves – a bad mistake. They became even more ill the following morning. A few days later, three of the sick prisoners died of pneumonia.

One evening about three days afterwards, a Mr. Pierce arrived and called the barracks to order. Standing on a wooden box, the tall, lanky, blue-eyed man addressed the prisoners. "I hear tell some of you men have been reading the Bible, singing religious songs and all that stuff. I'm not into any of that, but I like to see it going on. As I see it, it can't hurt you one damn bit. However, I'm opening this up to a vote. I make a motion for the free exercise of religion in this prison. All in favor, say, 'Aye'. Opposed – No."

The men unanimously voted to continue preaching, singing, and conducting a Bible study.

"The 'Ayes' have it," Mr. Pierce announced with finality in his authoritative voice. The men were pleased to be allowed the freedom to conduct religious exercises, which helped to cushion the harsh realities of prison life – a situation of daily deaths from various causes, known and unknown.

Two days later, Sgt. Whitehead showed up in the barracks to make a momentous announcement to the inmates. "Do any Yankees wish to return to the United States? If you're going, form a line over to my right, and march to the office in an orderly, military manner."

Sgt. Whitehead paused to observe the effect of his communication to the Union inmates. Then he issued the commands: "Fall in! Forward, Maarch!"

Out of the building and into the courtyard, the prisoners-to-be-exchanged marched lively with a noticeable spring in their steps. Entering the office, the commissary, Sgt. Whitehead, stepped behind his desk and issued an advisory to the men.

"We demand one condition for your release and exchange. You must sign this written oath not to wage war against the Confederacy until officially exchanged."

Raising his right hand to ask a question, an inmate spoke. "I'm William Pittenger. Do you have my name on the exchange list?"

"Affirmative," said Sgt. Whitehead.

All of the inmates were overjoyed at the unexpected good news. Had sedatives been available, most likely the prisoners would have readily ingested the pharmaceuticals. Was this a real event or was this a joke or a prank? It was a fact that they were issued paperwork to document their prisoner exchange status. But they would not yet be emotionally calm, until their midnight devotion, when they would thank God for their new lease on life as soon-to-be-free men.

"Listen up. Go back to the barracks, eat your chow, and pack your belongings. The time has been changed. You will ship out at 0400 hours. Dismissed," said Sgt. Whitehead.

Very soon, the ship-out time of 0400 hours arrived, before the crack of dawn. After slightly more than three months of incarceration, all of the parolees passed through the gates of Castle Thunder as each of the names was called. The men were directed to halt on the hard cement pavement, before marching on with a prison guard at the rear of the formation, moving along a dark, muddy city street.

After their arrival at the Richmond train station, Pittenger bought the morning edition of the Richmond Dispatch and sat down in the train station to read a very enlightening article, stating the substantial savings to the Confederate government by implementing the prisoner exchange program, which was under the supervision of Major General Eathan Allen Hitchcock, U.S.A., and Colonel Robert Ould, C.S.A. Due to later disagreements and disputes over various issues, both armies agreed to end the prisoner exchange program in July of 1863. Fortunately for the remaining Andrews Raiders, their release occurred before the gate shut down. The prisoner exchange took place on Tuesday, March 18, 1863, at City Point, Virginia, shortly after 11:00 a.m., when a United States of America steamboat advanced toward the dock, as "Old Glory" was kept in patriotic motion with a steady breeze blowing along the river.

Shortly after boarding the truce boat, Pittenger was elated to drink his first tasty, good cup of coffee, since his army camp days near Murfreesboro, Tennessee, in April, 1862.

An unidentified prisoner approached Pittenger and asked, "How was the food?"

"Absolutely delicious," said Pittenger.

"So was mine. So long," said the unidentified prisoner.

As Pittenger walked to the middle of the deck, Robert Buffum, obviously upset about a certain matter, said, "Did you hear we're going to Annapolis instead of Washington?"

"Buffum, we must go to Washington," said Pittenger.

William Bensinger later spoke to Pittenger. "Did you know all the soldiers are being shipped to Annapolis and the civilians are going to Washington?"

Still resting in a comfortable deck chair, Pittenger responded, "Bull! We're going to Washington – nowhere else. I'm going to sort out these ridiculous rumors. Who ordered us to go to Annapolis?"

"Lt. Robert Gunstock," said Buffum.

"I'll locate him." Within five minutes after the brief conversation, Pittenger noticed several officers seated while eating a full-course meal in the ship's dining hall.

"Sir, please excuse the interruption. It concerns me that my group and I are being sent to Annapolis. There must be some mistake," said Pittenger.

"We are transporting all parolees to Annapolis, to be quartered in some very well-built, clean barracks," said Lt. Gunstock.

"Sir, I must point out that we're not P.O.W.'s – they called us engine thieves. They hanged eight of us ," said Pittenger.

"You must be referring to the Andrews Raid back in 1862," said Lt. Gunstock.

"Yes sir. Andrews and General Mitchel are dead, and I guess people probably think we're dead too." (Mitchel at age fifty-three of yellow fever in Beaufort, South Carolina.)

"What's your name?' asked Lt. Gunstock, a 29-year-old, 180-pound, brown-eyed, oval-faced, neatly-dressed, smoothly-shaven officer, who was a nonsmoker in glowing health, without respiratory or heart problems.

"My name is William Pittenger, sir."

"Tell me about the Andrews Raid – from start to finish," said an intrigued Lt. Gunstock.

For the next hour, over several cups of coffee and a delicious meal, Pittenger explained the purpose, plan, and the reasons for the failure of the mission, leading to very bitter consequences.

As Pittenger ended his explanation, while quaffing his last cup of coffee, Lt. Gunstock's pupils enlarged. "Obviously, you have a compelling, heartwarming human interest story," said Lt. Gunstock while beaming sympathetically. "Corporal Pittenger, you and your fellow soldiers are going to Washington! I will do everything within my power to render every means of assistance that is humanly possible."

"Thank you, sir," said Pittenger with obvious relief in his voice.

The six Andrews Raiders arrived in Washington on Thursday, March 19, 1863, to be sequestered for their protection against Confederate snipers. It was common knowledge that an overwhelmingly large number of Confederate sympathizers and spies were present in Washington, D.C., which seemed to have a strong Southern influence, even though it was located north of the Mason-Dixon line.

A Tennessean named Pierce complained bitterly. "What in blazes is happening? We're being locked down like we're still in a Confederate prison. I would be just as well off to escape and become a loyal Rebel, if this is the kind of treatment I'm getting here."

Bensinger retorted, "Then Jeff Davis would gladly lock you up again in Castle Thunder. I hasten to add that none of us stands a snowball's chance in Hell of escaping from this place."

William H. Reddick chimed in, "Let's face it, men, we all look like so-called 'rag-tag' country folks without any money. We have a price on our heads. Confederate bounty hunters want us out of the picture. Dead men tell no tales."

Suddenly, an orderly opened the door to inform the Andrews Raiders of some late-breaking news.

"I have orders from the commander. All Ohio men are permitted free access and full ship's privileges." The unexpected announcement upset the Tennesseans, including Mr. Pierce.

Pittenger observed Pierce's negative reaction and said, "I want to emphasize the difference between Confederate prisons and this lock-up. This is a much nicer place to be detained – much better

THE RUNAWAY TRAIN

here than in those rat-infested Confederate hell-holes. There's more good stuff to come."

In the next instant, a guard thrust open the door of the room. "Dinner is now ready, he said. "You men must have been so starved in the South. Payback will be in store for those Rebs."

A plethora of scrumptious, appetizing, appealing foods graced the long dining room table. It was a spectacular, sensational display of high-class cuisine found only in the most expensive restaurants. Plentiful soft bread, carefully-prepared boiled beef, among other items; and restaurant-grade, top-of-the-line coffee could be smelled all over the dining room.

"If this don't beat everything I've ever seen," said Pierce. "Jeff Davis could never hold a candle to Uncle Sam's hospitality – that's for sure."

Later, guards whisked away the six Andrews Raiders to the home of a Mrs. Fales, a wealthy Union sympathizer, who took the initiative to quarter these raiders in a pavilion located in her backyard. Also included in the pavilion were combat-wounded troops and other Union parolees. Mrs. Almira Fales, a former battlefield nurse with Clara Barton, the founder of the American Red Cross, went a step further to give Union Blues to replace their tattered, filthy, disreputable Confederate clothing. She hosted an open-house reception in which she served ice cream and cake. She later pressed into service her hired chauffeur, who drove the raiders via horse-drawn carriage to various select Washington, D.C. area tourist attractions. She was the wife of a United States Patent Office Examiner, Joseph T. Fales. The Patent Office doubled as a field hospital serving the needs of wounded Union soldiers involved in First Bull Run, Second Bull Run, Fredericksburg, and Antietam.

When the tourist group entered the Smithsonian Institution, a pleasant surprise awaited them.

Pittenger said, "That is President Abraham Lincoln."

Buffum said, "Yeah, right. Then I'm Robert E. Lee."

"Let's go and talk to him," insisted Pittenger.

As Pittenger went closer to the tall, bearded national leader, Pittenger asked, "What's the name of this animal?"

"You'll find its name written on the card. I can't even begin to pronounce it," said Lincoln. The two men continued to engage in conversation about the weather and local tourist attractions until they parted company.

"Don't you try to convince me that was Lincoln. Why would he talk to ordinary people like us?" asked Buffum.

"I tell you what. When we arrive at the White House, I'm going to let you be the judge," said Pittenger.

During their first Sunday in Washington, D.C., Mrs. Fales encouraged the six Ohio men to join her at a Baptist Church service, and the preacher soon asked one of the uniformed soldiers to tell the story of the Andrews Raid.

"I'm going to ask one of the soldiers to stand and give us an account of how God spared them from the enemy." Observing their reluctance to talk about the very unpleasant ordeal, the preacher said, "Well, maybe someone will speak to us later. Let's continue our worship by singing a John Wesley hymn. You might be surprised to learn that Wesley wrote 3,000 hymns."

After conducting a short service and making some church-related announcements, the preacher decided to omit the sermon, so that he could allot sufficient time for Pittenger to give his testimonial of the Andrews Raid.

Reluctantly, Pittenger stood up from his hard wooden pew, perhaps more to seek relief from its discomfort than to publicly speak to the congregation. He talked for twenty-five minutes as every church attendee listened with total concentration. At the conclusion of the account, he emphasized how God had favored him and his men, by delivering them from their imprisonment and sparing the group from execution.

Earlier in Washington, Pittenger had written to Judge-Advocate General Joseph Holt, to request back wages and money for meal expenses that would have normally been incurred. Later, the men would receive all monies, including retroactive salaries, upon rejoining their military units.

Each of the six raiders submitted a deposition

detailing the full extent of the Andrews Raid story. The United States government was in possession of the November, 1862 deposition of Alf Wilson and Mark Wood; and in the light of this literary bonanza of interesting information, the powers-that-be in Washington were thirsting for more sensational findings. Interestingly enough, Supreme Court Justice John Catron administered the oath, while a court stenographer recorded each word of their testimony.

Finally, on Tuesday, March 24, 1863, the raiders reported to Secretary of War Edwin McMasters Stanton, who presented to each one of the six Andrews Raiders the Medal of Honor, one hundred dollars from the Secret Service fund, and a refund to cover all the money and personal valuables that the Confederate government had seized from the men.

"Gentlemen, what are your plans for the future?" asked Stanton.

"We want to return to active duty," said Pittenger.

"Very well. You will receive commissions as first lieutenants in the regular Union army," said Stanton.

"Sir, we prefer to remain as volunteers until the end of the war," said Pittenger.

"In that case, your current unit will award the commissions," said Stanton.

Major General Eathan Allen Hitchcock, Commissioner of the Prisoner Exchange Program under Secretary of War Edwin Stanton, took the exchanged prisoners to the plain, simple office of President Lincoln.

"Good afternoon, gentlemen," said the President to the raiders. "Please tell me about your adventures I've heard so much about. I need you to give me more facts. I'd like to know how you handled so many calamities." Pittenger observed the President's office furniture to consist only of a long table and two chairs.

Pittenger said, "Mr. President, our Commander-in-Chief, we consider it an honor and a privilege to meet you. Regardless of newspaper reports, we are behind you one-hundred percent. United we stand."

"I like that motto. Maybe the government will adopt it someday. A bad press only encourages me to work harder and better. That goes with the territory," said President Lincoln.

"Did we not see and talk with you at the Smithsonian the other day? Why would you be allowed so much freedom to move around when your safety might be in jeopardy?" asked Pittenger.

"Can you visualize a guard walking behind me everywhere I go? I believe the news media have a natural tendency to report the news in a biased way," responded President Lincoln.

"Mr. President, what is your assessment of the war?" asked Buffum.

"If only we could have fortune to favor us, so that our brave men could soon stop fighting this long, ugly war and return home soon," said the

HENRY H. KURTZ

Sixteenth President of the United States.

"Goodbye, Mr. President. We must be on our way," said Pittenger.

"Gentlemen, I enjoyed your company. I'm very grateful you survived such an awful experience, and I hope your relatives will be alive and well to receive you at home," said Lincoln.

A REAL LIVE YANKEE
FORTY-TWO YEARS LATER......

Wilbur George Kurtz, Sr. immersed himself in a newspaper article about the famed Andrews Raid of 1862, while he was seated at the Telephone Exchange in Greencastle, Indiana, on Friday, June 3, 1904, only a few days after he was graduated from DePauw University in this college town. He was born in Oakland, Coles County, Illinois, on Tuesday, February 28, 1882.

Eagerly scanning the newspaper article, Wilber scratched his head in exasperation and frowned. This article differed markedly from a previous article depicting the famous railroad chase starting in Chattanooga and ending in Atlanta. He thirsted to seek the truth regarding the route of the stolen and the pursuing engines.

Wilbur said to a co-worker, "This newspaper article sharply differs from a previous account regarding the direction of the locomotive chase. It simply does not add up. You would think that professional writers could get their facts in order before writing their articles."

"You're talking good sense, Wilbur," said his co-worker, Heinrich Heinz, a five-foot-nine-inch, 29-year-old, 250-pound lover of Weiner Schnitzel sandwiches. He had blue eyes, a long nose, a clean-shaven face, and blond hair.

"Cover my calls, Heinrich. I'm going to see the boss," said Wilbur, getting up from his chair, after removing his headset.

"No problem, Wilbur," said Heinrich.

The proximal locations of Wilbur's job and the apparent benefits of living at the home of his parents, George H. Kurtz and Amanda H. Baum Kurtz, enabled him to pursue introductory art courses, since art was his chosen field of major interest, after satisfactory completion of the prerequisite courses, such as mathematics, science, English, history, and Latin. Much later in life, Wilbur would tell a grandson, Henry Harrison Kurtz, Jr., that as a DePauw University student, he despised mathematics and barely passed Latin. However, history especially fascinated Wilbur, and his command of English History was impressive.

Sauntering into the supervisor's office, Wilbur asked pointedly, "Mr. Jones, may I have three weeks' vacation?"

Bob Jones replied, "Of course. When do you want to take off?"

"I want to investigate the Andrews Raid story to find out, among many other things, where the chase actually started and ended. I've read conflicting stories, and I find that to be unacceptable journalism; and logically speaking, it could only occur in one direction. That's why I must get to the bottom of it."

"How will you conduct your investigation?" asked Mr. Jones.

"I'm going to the 'horse's mouth' to interview the old conductor of the stolen train, Captain William A. Fuller, in Atlanta.

"I read the same articles. I would certainly be interested in seeing your notes when you return to work. Have a good vacation. It starts tomorrow."

"Thank you, Mr. Jones," said Wilbur.

At seven o'clock the next morning, Wilbur boarded a passenger-and-mail train for Atlanta – but not without purchasing a daily newspaper. Instead of initiating small talk, he would focus his attention on a newspaper – in effect, burying his face behind the newsprint, as a faceless newspaper reader. Wilbur was basically a quiet, taciturn individual, not a gregarious outgoing person; nor did he easily make friends with other people. Yet Wilbur was the type of person who would grow on people, the longer they knew him. He had a sense of humor and enjoyed smoking cigars, while leisurely relaxing in his backyard brick studio building in Atlanta, as witnessed by his grandsons, during the 1950's and 1960's.

Five days later, Wilbur G. Kurtz arrived at the railroad station in Atlanta, after a long, grueling trip. It was Wednesday, June 8, 1904. He decided to act upon a hunch to ask an old railroad employee where to locate William A. Fuller.

"Excuse me, sir. I have a question," he said to a bearded W&A Railroad conductor preparing to go home.

"What's your question, mister?"

"I'm looking for William A. Fuller. Do you know where he lives?" asked Wilbur.

"Yes, as a matter of fact I do. Are you a friend of his?" asked the railroad employee.

"No, but I would like to ask him some questions about the Andrews Raid," said Wilbur Kurtz.

The old conductor responded, "What is your name?"

"Wilbur Kurtz."

"Where are you from?" asked the conductor.

"Greencastle, Indiana."

"You sure don't sound like a Southerner. That's all right. The Civil War is over. Times have changed," said the five-foot-six-inch, 180-pound, 66-year-old, bearded, bespectacled, square-jawed man. Due to arthritis in his knees, he walked much slower, but his eyesight and hearing remained sound.

"How do I get to his house?" asked Wilbur.

"Follow me to my carriage. I'll take you to Mr. Fuller's house. The Western & Atlantic Railroad had to let him go because he was a Democrat. They let me keep working because I voted for Rutherford B. Hayes. The Federal Army put Atlanta in the

Third Military District when the reign of terror began during Reconstruction in 1867. They fired all Democrats. Then came the vindictive radical Republicans who took over the Congress. However, God favored him, even though the sinister Congressional element acted to punish the South. He prospered as a retail merchant and as a prudent real estate investor. That man now owns most of downtown Atlanta. On paper he is very wealthy, but unlike a lot of rich people, he hasn't let it go to his head."

"Very interesting, mister, uh......," said Wilbur.

"Haney – Henry Haney. Come with me. Let's go to Mr. Fuller's house." After his promotion from fireman to conductor, Haney moved to Atlanta from Adairsville.

"I'm with you, Mr. Haney."

During the ten-minute ride, Haney took it upon himself to show Wilbur the town.

"There's the Mitchell Street Viaduct," said Haney.

"What's the purpose of that?" asked Wilbur.

"Several years ago, lots of people were getting killed while crossing the railroad yards. So, our city officials decided to build these overpasses to save lives," said Haney.

"Good decision, Mr. Haney," said Wilbur.

The horse snuffled and yawned as the men approached a swank hotel in old downtown Atlanta.

"Mr. Kurtz, that is the Kimball House – a very good hotel and also an excellent place to eat. For years, Mr. Fuller enjoyed the Kimball House as his favorite eating place, during his off duty hours or a long layover."

"Sounds like a good idea," said Wilbur.

"If Mr. Fuller is at home, I'll drop you off and be on my way home, Mr. Kurtz."

"Thank you for the ride, Mr. Haney, and also for the tour of your town. I like this town," said Wilbur.

"You're certainly welcome. I hope you get all the answers you were looking for," said Haney.

Wilbur knocked on William A. Fuller's front door at 327 Washington Street, a peaceful neighborhood of solidly-built two-story wooden houses, including Fuller's home, where he and his second wife of twenty-one years, Susan Alford Fuller, lived. However, she was out of town visiting relatives at this time.

Henry Haney waved while taking off in his carriage, as William A. Fuller appeared at his own front door.

"What is the purpose of your visit?" asked the venerable elderly man.

"Mr. Fuller, my name is Wilbur Kurtz. Henry Haney brought me here from the train station."

"Yes, I know Mr. Haney," said Fuller.

"Mr. Fuller, I understand you chased a stolen locomotive," said Wilbur.

"Oh, that was back in 1862 during the Civil War," said Fuller.

"Mr. Fuller, I traveled from Greencastle, Indiana, to interview you about the Andrews

Railroad Raid," said Wilbur.

"You've been reading unreliable accounts," said Fuller with a frown.

"True. Will you talk to me about what really happened?" asked Wilbur.

"Come in, Mr. Kurtz. I don't mind talking to you as long as you're not a newspaper writer. However, I hasten to add that the Atlanta papers have been kind to me."

"I'm a recent graduate from art school at DePauw University in Greencastle, Indiana," said Wilbur.

"Have a seat in the living room," said the 68-year-old, long gray-bearded, gray-haired William Allen Fuller, who had borne a heavy load of grief, from the loss of four children, and his first wife, Maria Lula Asher, to tuberculosis. He and his second wife, Susan Clementine Alford Fuller, lost a son due to an unknown cause of death. On the plus side of life, Fuller was worth about a half-million dollars in prudent real estate investments, as the owner of most of downtown Atlanta.

Captain Fuller could proudly look back at memorable accomplishments in Confederate Government Service: chasing a stolen train, and serving as Atlanta Chief of Police in restoring law and order in 1865. He had transferred the State's archives and records away from Atlanta to a secret location for safe keeping, and earlier, in May, 1863, Governor Brown had appointed Fuller to be Captain of the State Guard, responsible for overseeing the protection of bridges and railroads, in a position similar to the modern day Chief of Homeland Security.

As Wilbur George Kurtz remained seated in the living room of the Fuller home, the patriarch addressed his four grown daughters: "I want all of you to meet a 'real live Yankee'. He's sitting in the living room," said Fuller with a wink in his left eye, amid the gasps of his standing four daughters gathered around him.

As the Fuller daughters gracefully walked into their living room, Annie Laurie's sweet, innocent, cute face drew Wilbur's attention, as she had not ever seen such a strikingly distinguished, handsome, intelligent young man – Wilbur George Kurtz (1882-1967).

"This is Wilbur Kurtz from Greencastle, Indiana. He is here to interview me about the 'General'. He is a graduate of art school from DePauw University in Greencastle. Mr. Kurtz, this is Lelabelle, Nelle, Nina, and Annie Laurie."

"How do you do, ladies?" asked Wilbur, who couldn't keep his eyes off Annie Laurie, who started to become inwardly nervous, but she covered up well her initial uneasiness in meeting a Yankee.

Suddenly, the front door opened, and 28-year-old William A. Fuller, Jr. hastily entered the living room, showing curiosity on his face. He had arrived home to eat lunch.

"Son, meet Mr. Kurtz. He's come from Indiana

to ask me questions about the Andrews Raid. Mr. Kurtz, meet William A. Fuller, Jr.," said the senior Fuller.

"How do you do, Mr. Kurtz?"

"I'm glad to meet you, William," said Wilbur.

"Please call me Bill."

"Very well, Bill. You can call me Wilbur."

"Well, now that everybody has been introduced, I have a suggestion. Why don't we eat out this evening at the Kimball House?" asked Captain Fuller. "It's a beautiful, very nice yellow hotel with brown trimmings. It's a modern hotel, and you have never seen anything else like the mansard roof, decorative roof towers, central tower, and the protective iron framework wrapped around the first story."

"Sounds like one of the seven wonders of the world," said Wilbur.

"You could say that," said Fuller. "By the way, the wife is out of town visiting her parents in Griffin."

"Mr. Fuller, when did you first determine the true identity of the men who stole the locomotive?" asked Wilbur.

Fuller replied, "When I saw the first missing rail and cut telegraph wire, I knew that Confederate deserters would not do a thing like that. It had to be, and couldn't be anything else, but a 'Yankee trick'."

"Where did this incident happen?" asked Wilbur.

"At Moon's Station, going north from Big

Shanty where the twenty Yankees stole my train," replied Fuller, "and also the track maintenance men's tools."

"What were you doing when the Federals stole your train?" asked Wilbur.

"I was eating breakfast at the Lacy Hotel, jumped up from my table, and said, 'They're stealing my train.' Now, I did not trot – I ran down the tracks after my train. My engineer and superintendent also ran. I grew up on a farm in Henry County, Georgia. Farm labor conditioned me to chase my train," said Captain Fuller.

Wilbur continued the questions and filled in more pages in a notebook of penciled notes, and all that time at the Kimball House, the four daughters and William A. Fuller, Jr. were taking in the question-and-answer session, over a delicious meal served under very bright gas chandeliers hanging from the frescoed ceiling. Young African-American waiters were dressed in clean, well-pressed white uniforms, and wearing black shoes.

One waiter politely asked, "Mr. Fuller, do you folks want some Coca-Colas?" Readily, everyone nodded in the affirmative.

"Willy, get us seven Coca-Colas. Mr. Kurtz is from Indiana. This may be his first Coca-Cola bottled drink," said Captain Fuller.

Wilbur responded, "I've never heard of Coca-Cola. What is it?"

Fuller replied, "A man named C. S. Pemberton was experimenting at his soda fountain in Atlanta in

1885. He mixed carbonated water with syrup. He and his customers enjoyed the beverage samples so much, that Mr. Pemberton was selling them faster than he could prepare them at his soda fountain."

"How is the Coca-Cola Company doing?" asked Wilbur.

"It's actually called the Atlanta Coca-Cola Bottling Company, and they had a two-year-old building at 125 Edgewood Avenue. When City Clerk W. D. Greene issued them the business license in May of 1900, co-workers overheard him say that a 'bunch of idiots' were trying to sell some new drink that people would not be interested in buying. Well, I'll have you know – since the last half of 1900 to 1901, sales increased from 2,815 gallons to 8,961 gallons," said Fuller, beaming with pride.

Wilbur interjected, "That's almost tripled production. Since arriving here, I have observed the rapidity of the city's growth, and I suppose the company had to move to a bigger building to meet the growing demand for Coca-Cola."

"We received our first free public library in 1899, and Oakland Cemetery acquired a bathroom for its visitors. Also, the City of Atlanta completed the Mitchell Street Viaduct during that year. Mayor David Woodward told us all of that in a speech. Yes, Coca-Cola had to move," said Captain Fuller.

"What's the population of Atlanta?" asked Wilbur.

"It is 8,972. That includes sixty percent white

and forty percent black, according to 1900 figures," said Fuller.

"I've never seen so many black people. We don't have any or perhaps very few of them in Indiana," said Wilbur.

Annie Laurie asked, "Mr. Kurtz, what did you think of the car shed at the magnificent iron railroad depot?"

"It's no different from any other train depot. For example, Chicago completely burned in 1870. They had rebuilt everything including the train depot, which is about the same age and outmoded, overcrowded condition," explained Wilbur.

"Mr. Kurtz, I want to take you to visit the newly built Atlanta Coca-Cola Bottling Company on the east side of Ivy Street, between Decatur and Gilmer Streets. They made their latest move from Edgewood Avenue to their present location on Ivy Street," said Fuller.

"Mr. Fuller, I would like to see how they make Coca-Cola," said Wilbur.

"I'll see that we go there," said Fuller. "It's about time to collect their rent."

As everyone had cleaned his plate in the swank, exquisite dining room of the renowned Kimball House, Wilbur said, "Thank you, Mr. Fuller. This has been a very enjoyable meal with very good conversation."

"You're welcome," said Fuller, smiling broadly and eyeing Annie Laurie, as if to telepathically communicate to her his perception of a positive chemistry between her and the unexpected Northern visitor.

"Yes, it has been such a very interesting conversational topic," said Annie Laurie somewhat nervously. She had just turned twenty, without any previous male acquaintances or relationships. Similarly, Wilbur had been too preoccupied with his college career, consisting of a four-year stint at DePauw University, before furthering his ambition in art education at the Chicago Art Institute. She was his first object of admiration; both of them were pure in heart and mind.

Fuller said, "Well, shall we go?"

"Thank you, Father, for this meal and the fellowship," said Annie Laurie.

Lelabelle was the next to the youngest of the four daughters, at age twenty-two. She was immature, vain, and obviously jealous of the budding relationship sparked by love at first sight. Nina was four years older than Lelabelle, but could care less about having romantic relationships with men. For the rest of her life, Nina would be a spinster. Nina was an Atlanta Public School Teacher until World War I, when a school board policy change required all teachers to be degreed. She lived for many years at Wilbur Kurtz's home, then at an Atlanta boarding house, and eventually at a nursing home during her final two years of life. All the other Fuller daughters eventually married.

Nelle married under the perception that marital sexual relations were inherently wicked. Needless to say, the marriage was rocky, but ended only in her husband's death due to natural causes. Spending the remainder of her life as a widow, she lived alone in a large house on Tenth Street in Atlanta with her black poodle, "Muggins".

Fuller motioned to the desk clerk, Frank Warren, who was casually passing by the group's table. "Frank, here is advanced payment for one week for Mr. Kurtz at the Kimball House. Give him the deluxe suite and daily room service, including janitorial service."

"Mr. Fuller, you don't need to do that," said Wilbur.

"I insist. I want you to stay all week to get all your answers, including how I caught the train thieves. Without my willingness to begin the foot chase, the State of Georgia would never have seen that train anymore," said Fuller with deep conviction in his voice.

"Very well. I don't know how to thank you, Mr. Fuller," said Wilbur.

"It is nothing. The good Lord of Providence has showered me with abundance and countless blessings, despite the fact that the carpetbaggers caused me to get fired from the W&A Railroad, because I was a Democrat. Well, by God, I showed those scoundrels. Now I own most of downtown Atlanta through carefully timed real estate investments. But that was only after I excelled in the operation of my general retail store, where I sold everything from cough drops to rakes," said Fuller.

"Mr. Fuller, why didn't the State of Georgia award you a medal for your heroic pursuit of the 'General'?" asked Wilbur.

"Excellent question. Georgia didn't have any readily available gold to strike such a commemorative medal, but that's all right. I have at least the satisfaction of recovering that fine old locomotive for Governor Joseph E. Brown, then the Governor of Georgia."

"Tomorrow, I wish to continue questioning you about the Andrews Raid – especially the minute details from start to finish," said Wilbur.

"I shall be ready with all the true answers, Wilbur," said Fuller. Unknown to Wilbur, William A. Fuller, Jr. had surreptitiously left the Kimball House, hired a horse-drawn taxi, and picked up Wilbur's suitcase at the Fuller home on Washington Street, returning soon to the previous conversation, still in progress.

"Where is my luggage?" asked Wilbur.

"I went back to the house to get it. You will have more privacy and freedom at the Kimball House, and Father has covered all of your expenses, including your meals," said William A. Fuller, Jr.

"I don't know what to think of this treatment," said Wilbur, obviously taken aback. "Thank you, Bill," said Wilbur to William A. Fuller, Jr., who was attired in a business suit and tie after practicing corporate law for eight hours at 1115-1116, Empire Building in downtown Atlanta. He had begun the law practice in 1894, shortly after his graduation from John

Marshall Law School in Atlanta. He was financially able to eat regularly at the upscale Kimball House, a stellar tourist attraction, in a progressive, thriving city of Atlanta, that had meteorically risen like the mythical Phoenix bird from the ashes, created by the burning Union torch of General William Tecumseh Sherman. In 1904, Atlanta was experiencing growing pains in its elevation to be the future hub of the Southeastern United States, as it was in a similar vein, serving as the munitions and weaponry manufacturing center of the Confederacy during the Civil War.

Roger Foother, the son of an Atlanta pioneer in Marthasville in 1843, approached Wilbur Kurtz. Terminus and Marthasville were the two former names of the city until 1845, when Atlanta received its name as the feminine counterpart of the name "Atlantic".

"Mr. Kurtz, I'm Roger Foother. Welcome to Atlanta. I'm the General Manager. We're glad to have you here. I've been listening to you talk, and I'm impressed with your knowledge and education. You would be an asset to Atlanta, if you ever decide to make your home here. It sure beats that terrible weather up North."

"That's true," Wilbur said.

"Well, if I can be of any assistance to you, please feel free to call on me," said Foother, who paid a monthly mortgage on one of Captain Fuller's houses.

Later that evening, the Illinoisan went to bed with a hyperactive mind full of interesting true facts about the Andrews Raid; however, more unanswered questions remained: to obtain accurate information – at least in the pursuit of it – both the Northern and Southern perceptions and statements would have to undergo critical evaluation. The conclusions must be based upon objective findings, as Wilbur had come to realize, while ruminating in a seated position on his bedside, until he finally succumbed to fatigue and drifted off into a deep, restful sleep.

During the night, Wilbur kept tossing and turning, as a dramatic dream was gradually unfolding, and the final segment of his dream time ended at the wake-up noise of an unexpected knock on his hotel room door, at eight o'clock the next morning, on Thursday, June 9, 1904.

"Who is it?" asked Wilbur with some apprehension.

"It's me, William A. Fuller."

"Come in," said Wilbur, who had gotten up from his comfortable, high-quality mattress to unlock the heavy oak door.

"Young man, have you had breakfast yet?"

"No, Mr. Fuller."

"Let's go downstairs and have a good breakfast," said Captain Fuller.

Taking their seats at a glass-covered mahogany table, Willy Mawn brought them two large bowls of grits, a ceramic butter dish containing half of a stick of butter, and a sterling silver butterknife, in addition to the same type of knives, forks, and spoons.

Soon, Willy made a second trip to the kitchen to carry the coffee urn, sugar, and a small pitcher of carefully prepared tasty gourmet cream.

"Thank you, Willy," said Fuller.

Focusing his eyes on Captain Fuller, Wilbur said, "Last night I had an unusual dream."

"What kind of dream?" asked Fuller.

Wilbur said, "I dreamed I found and interviewed all the surviving Andrews Raiders."

"Is that a fact?" asked Fuller.

"Yes, Mr. Fuller."

"I believe you will do it. You have an advantage of being a Yankee, because they would more likely talk to you, since you were born in their part of the country," said Fuller with a grin.

The pair engaged in the second phase of interviewing, and Wilbur was elated due to the goldmine of information flowing so freely from Fuller's lips, over sliced bananas, whole cling peaches, scrambled eggs, sliced lamb with lamb gravy, including mint sauce for flavoring.

"Mr. Fuller, I feel compelled to act upon my dream, and leave Atlanta after the week is up, to locate the surviving raiders."

"That's a good plan, but you should stop over in LaFayette, Georgia. Since you are an artist, you need to get sketches of the old jails or jail sites in Atlanta, Madison, LaFayette, and Chattanooga. Technically, they are called the Fulton County, Atlanta Jail; the Morgan County, Madison, Georgia Jail; and the Walker County, LaFayette, Georgia

Jail; and the Swims Jail."

"Yes, I'll do that," said Wilbur," and then I might be able to interview the raiders up in Ohio. I think they all came from the same vicinity around Steubenville, Stryker County, Ohio."

Fuller said, "I'll pay your travel expenses."

"That's very generous. You shouldn't," said Wilbur, obviously moved by the aged train conductor's financial offer.

"I don't know how to tell you this, Wilbur, but I would like to suggest you settle in Atlanta, unless you want to spend the rest of your life among people whose veins are full of ice water. You're obviously an exception," said Fuller.

Wilbur laughed. "I will seriously consider your proposal, Mr. Fuller."

"I mean it, Wilbur. Whether I'm living or dead, I'll see to it you get a good start as an artist. I'm never going to spend all my money while I'm alive, and I sure can't take it with me to the grave and beyond," said Captain Fuller.

Momentarily, a young woman hopped off a horse-drawn buggy, parking in front of the Kimball House.

"Wilbur, a man of your high caliber can do great things for Atlanta. You should get the full story of the Andrews Raid – and put it in writing. I might not live to see your efforts come to fruition; my body has been telling me my life is almost over," said Captain Fuller.

"I see. I won't disappoint you, Mr. Fuller," said Wilbur Kurtz.

408

THE RUNAWAY TRAIN

The heavy double doors of the Kimball House flew open, as Annie Laurie rushed toward the breakfasting conversants. Upon entering the building, she did not look at the heavy granite caps over each large window. Perhaps she had too much on her mind. "Father, may I borrow Wilbur for a trip to Piedmont Park?" Two of my high school girlfriends will be in a badminton match. I want so very much to see it," she said.

"You may go, Annie Laurie, but I want you to drive carefully, especially if you encounter a horseless carriage coming toward you."

"Oh, those are motor-driven vehicles. Not to worry, father. I'll watch each intersection very carefully," said Annie Laurie.

"You do that, my dear daughter. I don't want you to be taken to the hospital," said Fuller.

"Yes, Father. Everything will be all right. Maybe Wilbur will drive," said Annie Laurie.

"Whoever drives must be careful. Go and enjoy the badminton match – both of you," said Fuller, who was by force of habit, very protective of his children, since he had five left over from a total of ten children.

One hour later, Wilbur and Annie Laurie arrived at Piedmont Park, but a sudden, unexpected downpour dampened their prospects of watching the planned athletic event.

"Annie Laurie, stay in the carriage with me. The rain should let up soon," said Wilbur.

"Oh, Wilbur, the game is rained out, but nothing is going to spoil our picnic lunch," she said.

"That was a thoughtful idea," said Wilbur tersely, while studying her behavior.

The covered horse-drawn carriage was small enough and appealingly cozy, but not big enough for any hanky-panky. However, that was not an issue for these two morally wholesome, decent, upright persons. Captain Fuller had no reason for concern, for he and his second wife, 46-year-old Susan Alford, ensured that their daughters were well-trained in morals, manners, and old-fashioned good, down-to-earth common sense. His son was impeccable in overall conduct.

Piedmont Park was a three-mile northward carriage drive from the Kimball House. A bolt of lightning crashed about one hundred feet from the picnic site, where a glassless, windowless, horse-driven, motor-less vehicle provided a black canvas ceiling for shelter against the elements. The City of Atlanta purchased Piedmont Park on Monday, June 20, 1904, the consummation day of the sale from the Piedmont Park Exposition Company.

Wilbur yelled, "Watch out! There's a hole in the road."

"Relax, we're fine," said Annie Laurie. "Let's eat our lunch. Put the picnic basket on my lap. It's too bad it started raining. I won't get to see your girlfriends play."

"It really doesn't matter, because I'm happy to be with you. I feel so much more alive when I am with you, as though we have known each other all our lives," said Annie Laurie, with a meaningful inflection in her soft, pleasant voice.

Wilbur was slow to speak and was very much smitten by her charm, poise, wonderful personality, a boundless vocabulary, a very keen wit, and of course, her good looks. To a certain extent, his poker face could keep her guessing.

"I must admit you are the finest, nicest, and most fun-loving girl I've ever met. The Northern girls are simply too sophisticated and stuck up to suit me. Beauty is only skin deep," said Wilbur. "Besides, you have a keen wit and a way with words."

"Why, Wilbur. You're so sweet to say such nice things. There is not a man in Atlanta that has the high order of creativity, intellect, and artistic talent that you unquestionably possess," said Annie Laurie.

"You have given me much food for thought, and I have only a week to spend with you, Annie Laurie. Realistically speaking, I must pursue an agenda to piece together and get to the bottom of the mysteries of the Andrews Raid. I have to ask your father more questions, and I must travel to Ohio to interview as many of the surviving Andrews Raiders as possible. In short, I have things to do, people to see, and places to go, and perhaps some letters to write to obtain needed information," said Wilbur.

"My word, you do have your work cut out. You have committed yourself to tackle a very big, challenging project, which you are undoubtedly capable of accomplishing. You are such a special person, Wilbur," she said.

"I believe very much you are a treasure of a person – one of the greatest secrets of the South," he said to her.

Annie Laurie laughed with pleasure. "Oh, my, let's don't overstate things. I merely am myself, and I'm not going to pretend to be someone I am not, nor ever could be. There is no one else in the world like either of us," said Annie Laurie.

"I suppose we're like two peas in a pod," said Wilbur with a lighthearted chuckle.

Suddenly, the sound of hoofbeats and wheels were distinctly heard, and became even louder, as a two-horse carriage was approaching a potential lover's lane scenario.

"Folks, I'm going to have to tell you to leave the park," said an Atlanta police officer. "I just got word from people leaving Buckhead. Peachtree Creek is getting higher and is expected to crest later this afternoon. You had best be going. Hey….you're one of Captain Fuller's daughters."

"Yes, officer, I'm his oldest daughter," said Annie Laurie with her winsome smile.

"I followed in my father's footsteps and become a cop. He told me stories about how Captain Fuller served as Chief of Police of Atlanta. He ran the City of Atlanta like a tight ship."

"I'm pleased to hear your compliments about my father. Thank you for warning us. We were having a picnic, but now I see that we must leave quickly," said Annie Laurie Fuller.

Yes, I strongly advise you to make haste before the roads get flooded."

"O.K., officer. We're leaving right now," said Wilbur.

"Good day, folks," said the police officer, who was patrolling the newly annexed area formerly known as North Atlanta.

Wilbur breathed a sigh of relief. Although he wanted very much to kiss Annie Laurie, he was mindful of the circumstances – being the only persons probably within five square miles except for the police officer.

"Annie Laurie, I'll take the reins. I know how to negotiate puddles and potholes on muddy roads," said Wilbur.

"Thank you. I'm not good at bad weather driving; and besides, that three-mile drive wore me out. I don't have the strength and stamina of a man," she said.

"Then, it's just as well that I drive. Sit back and take it easy, but hold on tight. I'm going to drive fast to beat this rain," said Wilbur. Cracking the whip, the picnickers took off with a jack-rabbit start.

"Oh, Wilbur, watch that rough spot in the road," said Annie Laurie.

"Everything is well in hand. We're going to have an uneventful return trip, or my name isn't Wilbur Kurtz."

An hour later, the driver stopped the carriage at 327 Washington Street, the home of Captain Fuller and family, during a very heavy downpour on a deserted neighborhood street.

Fuller rushed to the front door, with relief in his old shoe button eyes. He had spent the afternoon planning an itinerary for his tour with Wilbur for the next day.

"It's about time you got home, Annie Laurie. I was worried to death about you both," said Captain Fuller.

"A police officer urged us to leave the park, since there was a flood threat," said Annie Laurie.

"Thank God you two are all right. I saw a lightning bolt, and it made me uneasy," said Fuller. "When the rain stops, we will take Wilbur back to the Kimball House and eat dinner there together."

"This must be my week away from the dishwashing chore," said Annie Laurie with a giggle.

Looking out the living room window, Wilbur saw that Washington Street was extremely muddy, since no paved roads existed in 1904 in Atlanta.

Wilbur remarked, "Atlanta may be a one-horse town now, but I envision a much greater population and a versatile, solid economic backbone."

"And that's why I wanted you to live in Atlanta," said Fuller.

"Father! You mustn't try to dictate to him. He has his own life to live. He will ultimately make that decision himself," said Annie Laurie.

"She is correct. I did not mean to step out of line, but I want you to know that you will always be welcome at my house," said Fuller.

"Thank you, Mr. Fuller," said Wilbur with a sincere smile.

Two hours later, the rain, wind, thunder and lightning subsided, and the clouds parted smoothly to yield an azure sky with brilliant, pleasantly warm sunlight from above. Outside in the backyard, Captain Fuller's two roosters, Castor and Pollux, took in the sunshine as they chased the available hens. The neighbors were seeking relief from cabin fever, as a consequence of the thunderstorm.

"All right, Wilbur, Annie Laurie is going to drive you back to the Kimball House. I'm feeling a little puny today, so I'm staying at home. Castor and Pollux need to be fed so they'll have enough energy to crow and procreate," said Fuller.

"Oh, Father, you are a mess. I love you," said Annie Laurie, with her characteristic giggle that seemed to begin at her larynx and end up at her toes. Her giggles were especially contagious, a characteristic of an unquestionably merry, gleeful person, acting like a schoolgirl.

"Now, you two behave yourselves," said Fuller, with a friendly, toothy grin, sandwiched in by his old, neatly-trimmed gray beard.

"We are mature adults, Father," said Annie Laurie, as the two young adults were walking toward the front door of the Fuller home.

"See you later Father," she said in a polite, yet subdued tone of voice.

"Who is that woman staring at us?" asked

Wilbur looking out a front window.

"Oh, that's nosey Rosie Smith. She has nothing else better to do than be snoopy. She has probably seen enough of us to concoct a talebearer's diary of the neighborhood inhabitants," said Annie Laurie, as Wilbur listened.

Arriving a few minutes later at the Kimball House, she stopped at the sidewalk to discharge Wilbur at the curb. "See you tomorrow, Wilbur."

"Likewise," he responded.

At the hotel registration desk, Wilbur could not help overhearing a conversation between the desk clerk and a stranger.

"Your room number is ten," said Frank Warren, the 56-year-old bespectacled clerk.

"What is your name?" asked the clerk.

"My name is Daniel Dorsey. I'm from Ohio."

"Thank you, Mr. Dorsey," said the original clerk of the Kimball House.

"I have a question: Where is the Atlanta jail? I mean, the one used during the Civil War," inquired Dorsey.

"Oh, that one. It's just a short walk from here," said the puzzled clerk. "They tore it down in 1864."

Wilbur interrupted the conversation and said, "I'll be going there tomorrow. My name is Wilbur Kurtz."

"Unfortunately, I was one of fifteen Ohio soldiers locked up in that jail, for stealing a locomotive."

"Mr. Dorsey, eat breakfast with me tomorrow, before we go to the old jail."

THE RUNAWAY TRAIN

"See you in the morning, Mr. Kurtz. I'm turning in."

Next morning, Friday, June 10, 1904, Wilbur had an ulterior motive to breakfast with Dorsey – as a delaying tactic – for a very good reason: to present him the opportunity to meet Fuller, the man who led the chase that resulted in Dorsey's and his compatriots' incarceration.

Wilbur was walking around the Kimball House lobby to look for an Atlanta Journal newspaper, which he noticed to be on the desk clerk's counter. He purchased the newspaper, losing himself in another world while perusing each page.

A few minutes later, Captain Fuller entered the Kimball House to find a stranger seated and engaged in conversation with Wilbur.

"To whom do I owe this pleasure of introduction?" asked Fuller with curiosity.

"Mr. Fuller, this is Daniel Dorsey, one of the surviving Andrews Raiders."

"I am pleased to meet you, Mr. Dorsey. Welcome to Atlanta. You have perfect timing, sir. I will serve as your tour guide today at the old Atlanta Jail site," said Captain Fuller.

"What a coincidence," said Dorsey.

"First, let's enjoy our breakfast," said Fuller. The waiter was returning from the kitchen with plates of scrambled eggs, biscuits with gravy, bacon, and plenty of grits, including a silver urn full of hot coffee.

"You Southerners really know how and what to

eat," said Dorsey.

"Let's dig in and enjoy. Thank you waiter. Here's a dollar," said Fuller, showing no reaction to Dorsey's comment.

"Thank you, suh. Bless you, Mr. Fuller," said the surprised waiter before walking to the next customer's table, with a joyful spring in his step.

"Mr. Fuller, I've got to hand it to you. My men and I would never have figured you or anyone else – of all things – to start a foot chase and use three pursuing locomotives. That was unexpected," said Dorsey.

"Mr. Dorsey, with all due respect, I was responsible to Governor Brown for that train. You do what you have to do. All I can say is that we fought the Civil War as best we could, for the sake of our political and economic interests. We didn't want Washington telling us how to run the South," said Fuller.

"Well, we're now one nation again. This get-together is for seeking and sharing more information, but above all, it is a time for healing all bitterness and bad feelings," said Dorsey.

"Well said. Upward and onward," said Fuller, as he began chewing a strip of bacon.

"The more I reflect, it's becoming clear to me that the South's defeat was a blessing in disguise. My great-grandchildren will probably see Atlanta grow to be a large, very successful cultural Mecca," said Captain Fuller.

"Yes, Mr. Fuller. If the horseless carriage ever

catches on, your prediction will come true, and your town will prosper," said Dorsey, dressed well in a respectable brown suit, a gold tie, and very shiny black shoes that contrasted with his white shirt.

"Is everyone finished eating?" asked the old Georgia State Guard and former train conductor.

As each person nodded, all three men left the Kimball House to board a two-horse taxi carriage bound for the old Atlanta jail site. After a ten-minute ride through muddy streets, they reached the intended destination.

Wilbur was carrying in his hands a notebook full of loose-leaf notebook paper. This scenery was what he had been eagerly waiting to see and sketch with his pre-sharpened pencil. Finally, his golden opportunity presented itself to capture on paper the remnants of the old jail site, most of which became occupied by two yellow houses, thirty-eight feet and forty-two feet, in respective widths, from left to right.

"I hope you didn't think I was taking you on a wild goose chase," said Fuller with a mischievous grin.

Wilbur replied, "No, the purpose of this sketch is to construct the general layout of the area occupied by the jail, including the two yellow houses replacing the old jail itself, and to show the large front entrance, prison cells, the well, the courtyard, and the positions of the prison guards."

Across the street, a stranger stood staring curiously at the three men standing on the former

419

jail site. After several minutes, he walked across the street to seek an answer for the presence of the trio.

"Excuse, me, gentlemen. May I ask why are y'all here?" asked the stranger.

Fuller spoke first. "Hello, John, I want you to meet Wilbur Kurtz and Daniel Dorsey."

"How do you do?" I'm John McClellan."

"Mr. McClellan," said Wilbur, "did you witness the execution of any of the train thieves?"

"Oh, you mean that Civil War train in Big Shanty?"

"Precisely," said Wilbur.

"Sure. I was here when the military hanged seven train thieves in one day. I was also present at Juniper and Third Streets when they hanged Andrews," said McClellan, a stout, five-foot-six-inch, brown-eyed, 180-pound, white-haired 70-year-old man.

"What do you mean by the word 'here'?" On the jail grounds or somewhere else?" asked Wilbur, sounding like a cross-examining attorney.

"I meant to say the seven Union soldiers got hanged at Fraser and Fair Streets (near Oakland Cemetery)," said McClellan.

"Describe the hanging of Andrews," said Wilbur Kurtz.

"Mr. Kurtz, Andrews hit the ground and the hangman had to readjust the rope. Then Andrews died on the second hangman's try," said McClellan.

"I see," said Wilbur.

"The crowd was reverent and somber. Nobody

said anything or made any noise," said McClellan.

Wilbur continued questioning Dorsey and Fuller for the next few days at the Kimball House.

Annie Laurie drove alone to meet Wilbur on his last day at the Kimball House, on Wednesday, June 15, 1904.

"Annie Laurie, I've enjoyed very much spending time with you and talking Civil War history with your father. Have you come to take me to catch the train at Union Station?" asked Wilbur.

"Yes, Wilbur. But you must tell me something: When will I see you again?" asked Annie Laurie.

"Good question. I'm furthering my art studies at the Art Institute in Chicago. It may take a few years, but if I want to be a top-notch artist, I must be diligent. Do not worry. Between now and graduation – during a semester break – I will return to see you. Sorry I missed the opportunity of meeting your mother," said Wilbur.

"Oh, Wilbur, I will miss you very much. Mother is in Griffin where she's visiting her parents. You'll meet her some day," she said.

"Continue teaching school with Nina, Lela Belle, and Nelle, and I will write letters to you from time to time," said Wilbur. "I must soon give notice of quitting the Telephone Exchange, so I can work at a commercial art studio while attending art institute classes," said Wilbur. "I will have the opportunity to learn how to be a draughtsman and an engraver."

"I hope those high society people in Chicago

don't tarnish your good nature and positive outlook on life," said Annie Laurie.

"Don't you worry your pretty little head about such nonsense. I'm my own man, or my name isn't Wilbur George Kurtz."

"I want to see you again," she said, repeating her heartfelt request.

`Wilbur looked squarely into her eyes and planted a kiss on her sweet lips. They embraced for a full minute, oblivious of any curious onlookers in the fancy Kimball House, whose basement housed huge engines, gigantic furnaces, and large steam laundries. An efficient heating system kept the hotel comfortably warm during the cold Southern winter.

"Goodbye until next time," said Wilbur to the smiling young woman, obviously enthralled.

Almost each succeeding year, Wilbur Kurtz visited Annie Laurie. During the following five years, Captain Fuller (1836-1905) died after much physical suffering from a carbuncle on his neck, purportedly as a result of an infected foot, according to Mrs. Margaret Latimer Fuller, his daughter-in-law. Despite the presence of five attending physicians, and repeated applications of hot and cold cloth compresses to the boil, William Allen Fuller died at 3:25 a.m., Thursday, December 28,1905, from blood poisoning, on his death bed at 327 Washington Street, in Atlanta, Georgia. Gone was a celebrated railroad hero who was instrumental in delaying the federal military victories, that would later result in the advance of

THE RUNAWAY TRAIN

General William Tecumseh Sherman's army in its famous march to the sea in 1864, the burning of Atlanta, and the destruction of the Western & Atlantic Railroad, inside the city limits of Atlanta.

The estate of William A. Fuller generously provided for a two-story, six-bedroom brick home with concrete front steps and a separate backyard brick structure, to serve as Wilbur Kurtz's Art Studio and the storage of his Civil War History notebooks that he later bequeathed to the Atlanta History Center. The "Real Live Yankee" had established a genealogical tree consisting of five late offspring: Nell Louise, Wilbur G., Annie Laurie, Henry Harrison, and Eugene Allen – all born between 1911 and 1923. The two eldest Fullers: 96-year-old Peggy, and brother, 84-year-old Forrest are survivors at this writing.

If it were not for the theft of the "General", the author would not have been among the descendants.

CPSIA information can be obtained
at www.ICGtesting.com
Printed in the USA
BVHW071810030419
544505BV00001B/20/P